CW00521810

Thank you so much
for reading No 2!

Fuelling the Fire
by Roland Ladley

The second of the Sam Green novels

For my wonderful helpers: Mikki, Sally, Nicky, Annie W,
Annie B, and, of course, Claire.

Thank you for your encouragement and enthusiasm.

Morality *is doing what is right, regardless of what you are told.*
Religion *is doing what you are told, regardless of what is right.*

H. L.
Mencken

Prologue

Air-Traffic Control (ATC), Aeropuerto Internacional Ezeiza, Buenos Aires

3 June 2002

It may have been midwinter, but it was hot in the ATC room. Dario Giménez looked up over his main screen and around the office. There were fifteen controllers crammed in a space smaller than his lounge. Elbow room was in short supply, and their Latin temperament didn't help the atmosphere. He reckoned it was probably a lot calmer in a European equivalent. *And cooler.*

Each desk was equipped with two computer monitors. The bigger screen, which most of the controllers kept central, graphically displayed the aircraft in the sky. His and Fernandez's next door were primarily focused on routes heading northeast toward Europe. A smaller screen to his right glowed like a radioactive green and black bus timetable. Details of every flight in the air within three hundred kilometres were listed, each designated with a set of flight initials of two letters and three numbers. Other information included destination and arrival airports, departure and arrival times, airspeed, direction of travel, and height above sea level. If he wanted, he could have interrogated any of more than two hundred flights that were in the airspace above and around Buenos Aires.

Twelve of the flights on his green and black screen were underlined and highlighted in bold. They were *his* aircraft, the ones arriving and leaving from Ezeiza International that his supervisor had allocated to him for today. A few more in italics, but not bold, came and went when they were within five kilometres of his designated aircraft. Italics meant *caution.*

i

All of the pertinent information was displayed on his big screen as an electronic map. Against a dark-blue background, the red aircraft were his. The others were yellow. His job was to keep all the colours apart—well apart.

Dario couldn't stop his heart from leaping into his mouth when two planes got close. Anything within five hundred feet was classified as a "near miss" and would be subject to an external investigation. He mustn't panic, though. Being on top of each other on the electronic map might *look* like a disaster, but it would almost certainly mean that one aircraft was well above the other in altitude, even though in two dimensions it looked like a train wreck. For peace of mind, whenever two aircraft appeared to get close to each other, Dario always triple-checked elevations and bearings. He hadn't got it wrong so far.

He made a sign of the cross and exhaled deeply. Just thinking about it was enough to ask for divine intervention.

"Hello, EZE, this is BA244. We're now one hundred miles out from you. Any further instructions?" The air-band radio crackled in Dario's headset and jolted him. He was drifting off. He'd had a tough night. His young daughter, who was teething, had kept him and his wife awake. He'd eventually got some sleep but not enough to see him safely through a straight eight hours behind the ATC desk. The temperature in the room didn't help.

They really must get the air-conditioning sorted.

He did need to talk to his wife about the division of responsibility at night. The problem was, she was a theatre nurse, and he ensured the safety of five-hundred-seater aircraft. They both needed their sleep.

He had a quick glance at both his screens.

"Hello, BA244, I copy. No change to plan. Aim to adopt holding pattern, but it's likely that you will have a straight run in. Runway, Alpha, heading in from the north. Over."

"BA244. Copy. What's the weather like on the ground?"

Dario half stood and looked over three desks to the long glass window in front of him. "EZE, still clear here." He glanced across at the toolbar at the bottom of the green screen. "It's holding at twenty degrees. Over."

"BA244, copy. Speak soon. Out."

The crackling stopped. He prided himself on both his English and his radio procedure. Everything he said to pilots was recorded in case of an incident. Often his supervisor would listen in on conversations, or playback tape, to check that his staff were doing their job effectively. He'd always been complimented on the way he used the radio and his manner with his pilots. He tried his best.

Dario had a quick scan of the main monitor. He checked that his aircraft's vitals were as they should be by putting a finger on each and cross-checking with the green and black screen. He finished the round of all twelve within thirty seconds.

That's all OK, then.

He reached for a cup of cooling coffee that one of the off-going staff had made for him about twenty minutes ago. It was lukewarm, but strong. Good, he needed that. He checked his watch. Three and a half hours to go before the end of his shift. He'd talk to Maria tonight about who gets up for the baby. They would definitely talk about it. *Definitely.*

Dario leaned back on his chair with his hands behind his head. He yawned, closing his eyes as he did.

"Hello, EZE, this is KM959. We'll be out of radar range in fifteen minutes and then we'll switch to HF radio. Over." Dario looked up at the screen. It was the Dutch flight that had left Buenos Aires just under an hour ago, heading for Amsterdam. If he remembered correctly it was an Airbus A330, around 230 passengers. It flew daily to and from both capitals. The Dutch pilots were efficient and never gave him any problems. They spoke good English, were polite, and, thankfully, did as they were told—unlike some nationalities he could mention, including his own.

"EZE, copy. Give us one last call before you're out of range and I'll let LIS know you're on your way." Lisbon, Portugal, would be the next ATC to get a ping on its radar from the plane's transponder. But not for a good four or five hours.

Dario waited for a response, his mind already drifting as the tiredness began to take hold again. He shook his head, hoping to wake himself up. It worked a little.

Crackle. Crackle. "Roger . . ." Then the pilot's voice changed markedly as he spat out across the air, *"Bokkerful! YAA!"*

And then nothing. Silence.

Dario was awake now. Wide awake. He stared at the screen, not focusing. He tried to make sense of what he had just heard. It was Dutch, or gibberish. Or something else. The tone was sharp, fearful.

He immediately pressed the transmit button.

"Hello, KM959, this is EZE, over?" It was a question more than a statement, his voice rising uneasily at the end of the short sentence.

A loud, unwelcome emptiness was the response.

He tried again. "Hello, KM959, this is EZE, over!"

Still nothing.

He looked at his main screen. The red letters *KM959*, which when he checked a few seconds ago were bright, strong, and cheerful, were flashing. The plane's transponder was no longer communicating with the tower.

Dario tried again, but something deep inside him already knew that he would get no response from the Dutch Airbus.

"Hello, KM959, this is EZE, over?"

"Hello, KM959, this is EZE, over!" His voice was more fretful the second time round, his finger pressing far too hard on the transmit button.

Nothing.

Protocol in the tower now was to phone his supervisor. He stopped himself before reaching for the handset. The heat and dampness that he felt just minutes earlier had turned to cold. The sweat still ran down him, but now it left a sensation like getting out of a warm shower into a cold room. His heart was pounding and his mouth was dry.

"Fuck," he said under his breath. Dario always swore in English. It always sounded so much more purposeful.

He picked up the phone and pressed the button that would link him straight to his supervisor. This would be a call he'd always hoped he would never have to make.

Cock-Up

Chapter One

"Gotcha." Sam smiled, a smile that she reserved for moments of personal triumph. She looked again at the screen to her left and then back to the one in front of her. Both were forty-inch high-definition monitors having pixel resolutions that were lost on her. What she did know was that there were no cameras out there that could take a photo with a higher resolution than her screens could manage. In the last three years, digital photography, image enhancing, recognition software, and the screens to manipulate the whole caboodle had come on massively. She wouldn't admit it in public, but the whole technology thing excited her.

Just under five years ago, as a military analyst, she had spent most of her time in Camp Bastion, Afghanistan. She studied and compared digital photographs of men, vehicles, and locations—some taken from the air, some from reconnaissance patrols, and the odd one or two from spies and informants. At the time she felt that, while it was hardly *Mission Impossible*, they were truly in the digital age.

Now, today, here in the bowels of Vauxhall Cross—or, to those in the know, *Babylon*—they really could pick out car number plates from keyhole satellite images and recognise faces taken by a handheld camera over a kilometre away. It wasn't just the quality of the cameras; the software that automatically enhanced images was exceptional. Using her fingers on the touchscreen to enlarge or even rotate an image up to twenty degrees—with the software filling in any gaps—nine times out of ten times she could get a very clear picture of a face. The latest technology had made her job so much easier.

The software was making its own choices when it came to sharpening pixelated images and, doubtless, sometimes it cocked things up: a Roman nose instead of a Jewish one; a Ford rather than a Fiat. But she was trained to recognise *Doris's* foibles—her mum's first name and the pet name for the Dell tower that sat under her desk. She would caveat any match with the code word "ENHANCED" if she felt there was a chance that Doris was overcompensating for an original lack of clarity.

She rocked back on her chair and put her hands behind her head. She looked at the left screen. There, now enlarged to a twenty-centimetre square, was Captain Ivan Droganov. The picture had been illicitly taken at a recent Arms and Weapons show in Moscow. The image had an accompanying date at the bottom right of the screen: 15-Dec-14. He was wearing a military uniform and stood among a number of Russian officers on the Rostec stand—selling drones, probably to Syria and Yemen.

On the middle screen was a photo of a civilian, or what appeared to be one. Dressed in jeans, a grey hoodie, Asics sneakers, but shouldering an AK-47 assault rifle, the face was clearly that of the same Ivan Droganov. Sam leaned forward and, using a small swiping movement, turned the civilian Ivan's face from left to right and then back again. She glanced across at her left screen. She did the same thing.

"Yup," she said to no one in particular, "they're both Captain Ivan, for sure."

Sam hadn't been able to stop herself from thinking out loud. She didn't know whether it was therapeutic or not. All she knew was that at times of intense concentration, her thoughts often tumbled out of her mouth before she had a chance to stop them. While irritating to those around her, it was a release that she couldn't stop, and she hadn't really bothered trying. It seemed to help keep potential suitors away, which was a good thing. A love life was the last thing she needed right now.

She noted the date of the middle photo: 12-Sep-15. Then the location: Georgiyevka. Right on the border between government and rebel forces in Ukraine.

Sam swivelled her chair to the right and, looking at her third screen, opened up the secure database. She needed to log the two photos electronically, plus all of the accompanying information. And then she would drop an "Alert" e-mail to her boss, Jane, to let her know that she had made a match. Ivan was the third that week.

As she typed, her mind wandered. She'd only been operational with SIS for three months. Her training had taken four, and she had shadowed John, a fellow analyst, for a month before she had been given her own desk. She was now almost independent. There were five photo analysts in the team with responsibility for Europe, the Middle East, and Near Africa. It was where the action was; there was no doubt about that.

Between the five of them there was a continuously enlarging pool of photos and videos collected from every "open" source available: newsreel, papers and magazines, conflict tourists who posted photos on their blogs and on social media, and any other Internet source you could think of. Naturally, there were images taken by government-deployed and SIS-run sources and informants. They called these "closed" source material. Sam was surprised that more of their people weren't working in these major war zones. Military sources' input varied. Nearly all of the photos were posted by Special Forces (SF), and most of them were taken by the Special Reconnaissance Regiment (SRR). They also received a few photos from agencies of allied countries. All of these images were classified as "closed" source.

In Ukraine, their job was to identify serving Russian military officers and soldiers working among the pro-Russian rebels. It was, as was nearly always the case with image analysis, a painstaking job.

She was with a good team. Discovering that Jane was her boss was a surprising, but welcome, revelation when Sam was finally allocated a desk. She and Jane had gotten to know each other in Sierra Leone during the Ebola "incident." Jane's quick thinking had saved Sam from a grisly death in a burning building. They had remained in contact while Sam deliberated about joining SIS. Since Sam had accepted the post, she felt that Jane had kept a watchful eye on her—in a positive way, more mother hen than domineering schoolmistress.

What Sam loved about working for Jane was her clear direction. They didn't waste time picking any old Russian officer and searching the Ukraine database for matches. Jane had identified Captain Ivan Droganov yesterday. He was born and bred in Eastern Ukraine, an obvious choice for the Russians to dispatch to assist the rebels.

And Sam had found him. In Moscow, wearing a Russian Army uniform; in Ukraine, wearing a hoodie and fighting for the rebels.

Gotcha!

The Middle East work was the same, but different. Here the five of them were looking for Daesh—the new-to-the-West brand name for the so-called Islamic State. Or Al-Qaeda-trained operatives. Or other known Islamic extremists, who were making their way into the UK via the refugee deluge.

In the Cold War they would have been called "sleepers"—a bit before her time, but she remembered the expression from watching an early spy movie. The difference between the Middle East and the Russian/Ukraine work was that the former had a lesser number of leads; there were fewer original photos to compare the migrating mass with. Identifying the correct Middle Eastern or North African fundamentalist in Syria, Yemen, or Afghanistan wasn't as easy as glancing at the latest Moscow May Day parade and picking out a soldier.

The sure way was to get up close and personal to a Daesh or an Al-Qaeda training camp and photograph the trainees. But, she imagined, if the SAS had eyes on a confirmed terrorist training camp, surely the immediate action was to call in airstrikes or lob over a cruise missile. She wasn't sure if they were still launching cruise missiles from USS *Enormous*, but the image did flash in front of her eyes. However, that obviously didn't always happen, as they often received a number of mug shots taken in the desert with a long lens, for which the five analysts were very grateful.

They also got some good-quality images taken at close range. She assumed these were from informants or payrolled local police in cases where the individual had a known record. *Rather them than me.*

The bank of photos of high-value targets (HVTs) was close to a thousand. Her job was to see if she could track any of them, via the many conduits now open from the Middle East and North Africa, moving into the UK.

Until about ten weeks ago, this had been a question of comparing a couple hundred images with a couple hundred more. But since the summer and the tsunami of refugees pouring across the many European borders, it was no longer a target-rich environment. Add to this the need to put disguises on the original photos, as many of those coming out of training camps adopt physical aliases, and it was really now a case of finding a pin in a field of haystacks.

But still, Sam gave it her best shot.

Jane had been able to restrict the search to four HVTs for each analyst. As a result, Sam spent the morning focused on the Middle East, trying to match her four. And the afternoon on Ukraine, looking for Ivan, so to speak.

Just as Sam was about to press "Send" on her "Alert" e-mail, concerning good-old Ivan, Jane came into the room. Sam, closest to the door, looked up and smiled at her.

Before any pleasantries, Sam launched with her good news.

"I've got Ivan. This image was taken on September twenty-fifth at Georgiyevka." Sam pointed at the centre screen. "Clear as anything. And look here." Sam was pointing at her left monitor.

Jane peered over her shoulder and looked intently at both screens.

"Spot on, Sam. Impressive stuff. Really well done. We're getting close to building a Russian Army grouping among the rebels in this area. I'll go back and look at the wiring diagram and let you know what we're missing." She stood up, placing her hands on the small of her back as she stretched.

"How are you feeling?" Sam asked. Jane had picked up malaria in Sierra Leone, and it had taken some time to shift. As is the case with the disease, once you have it, it often resurfaces when you're at a low ebb. And recently they'd all been uber-busy, with long hours and short breaks.

"I'm fine, thanks, Sam. What about you? Are you sleeping?"

Sam turned back to the screens. She and Jane had had many a frank conversation about Sam's past and its impact on day-to-day life. She didn't sleep well, and when she did, the images of the "incident" in Afghanistan often crept into her dreams. What surprised her, but seemingly not her psychiatrist, was that she was rarely affected by the terror of the drugging and arson in Sierra Leone. Three years ago in Kenema, without Jane's and the Sierra Leonean Army's intervention, both she and her UN sidekick Henry would have been toast. *That must leave its mark, surely?*

But it was the other near-death experience, the earlier mortar attack in Camp Bastion, that wasn't prepared to leave her alone. Clearly, the thing she had still not come to terms with was her military past, particularly the Afghanistan tour. The impact of the death of the man she loved, combined with her insides hanging out of a hole that shouldn't have been there, were proving harder to shift.

"I'm fine too, thanks, Jane. I'm still not sleeping all the way through, and, as you know, I do have a tendency to fall asleep at my desk with my nose pressing the 'Space' button." Sam paused and sighed. "But it's getting better day by day." She looked back up at Jane and smiled.

Jane suppressed a laugh. "Well, your output is first rate, so the odd rogue e-mail consisting of lines of zeds, courtesy of your nose, is something I'm currently prepared to live with." Jane placed her hand gently on Sam's shoulder.

"Thanks, Jane. Means a lot . . ."

Jane smiled and moved to her left, stopping beside Frank. "How's it going, Frank?"

15° 23′ 45″ N, 44° 15′ 37″ E, Northern Yemen

Captain Tony James pressed the shutter button on the sand-coloured Leica S DSLR. There was no sound from the camera, the mechanical shutter beautifully silenced by Leica. He gently twisted the zoom lens, half pressed the shutter, checked the focus, and pressed again. He squinted at the LCD screen. It was shielded by a short plastic visor fitted at the SAS's technical centre in Pontrilas, so that pictures could be viewed in direct sunlight. The 37.5-megapixel sensor coped exceptionally with the distances they worked at. Using a small laser rangefinder, he knew he was twelve hundred metres from the target. It presented no problems for this camera.

The photo he had just taken was of an Arab-looking man dressed in a traditional floor-length white thawb. The top of his head and neck were covered in a red and white gingham keffiyeh, secured by a black rope around his scalp. On the streets of the Yemeni capital, Sana'a, the man would have looked like thousands of others and indistinguishable in the crowd. Here, now, on metaphorical celluloid, Tony could make out the man's facial details. He could pick him out from a thousand others.

He slid backward from the rocky outcrop so that he was out of the line of sight. Not that anyone would have picked him out at this distance. His observation post (OP) consisted of a desert-patterned waterproof poncho with a fifty-centimetre-square observation hole at one edge. He'd thrown it up on the night they'd arrived, two days ago. He'd erected one of these what felt like a thousand times before. He knew that, from any angle, the shape, silhouette, and colour of the OP blended in with the rock and the sand. Everything he wore and all his equipment was desert coloured. The greatest threat to being compromised was from the shadow thrown by the observation hole—they had a more colloquial term for it in the regiment—through which Tony had recently taken the photographs. Someone very clever at Pontrilas had developed a system consisting of a small bank of LED lights linked to a photovoltaic sensor that, depending on the outside ambient light, lit up the inside of the OP, nulling the shadow created by the "a-hole."

Tony scrolled through the photos. He counted thirty-two men at the makeshift camp. No women—no surprise there. In the past two days he had managed to snap all of them from at least three different angles. He had wirelessly transferred them to his Samsung tablet—also housed in a desert-coloured case—grouped the photos by individual, and annotated them with comments such as "weapons instructor"; "manager"; "chef"; "trainee." He reckoned the camp was being run by no more than ten individuals. The remaining men were being trained for combat with Daesh (or Al-Qaeda—currently the camp had no designation) in Iraq or Syria. Or they were destined for truck, bus, boat, or train transit to western Europe. And maybe, ultimately, into the UK.

The tablet was connected to an Iridium-style satellite phone—another Pontrilas special. He prepared the file package for upload to the cloud, using his two thumbs to swipe and tap as needed.

His earpiece burst into voice.

"Mike 20 Alpha, this is 21 Charlie."

Tony stopped what he was doing and found the pressel of his radio.

"Send." Radio procedure in the SRR was minimal.

"I've just had a ping from the northwest. The indication

is French."

Tony stopped himself from replying for a second. He closed his eyes; the sweat from the midmorning sun making them sting.

"Roger. Any visual?"

The soldier at the other end of the radio seemed to pause, as if he were using the break to look again.

"I might have something. Too early to say, but we've just been pinged again." A further pause. Tony assumed that Corporal Ted Groves was looking at his transponder.

"Definitely French. About five clicks away. Their machine has acknowledged us. Direction of travel is northwest, so away from the target. All's well. I'll keep an eye out."

"Roger, out." Tony closed the call.

What the hell are the French doing here? His troop had been given an Op Box of two hundred square kilometres. They were the only troop of the SRR on the ground in northern Yemen, and although he had been briefed that the French Special Operations Command was also in Yemen, he had been told that the SRR Op Boxes had been predetermined not to be anywhere near where the French were working.

Thank goodness for Terry the Transponder, Tony thought. Everything in the regiment had a nickname, and the "identification friend or foe" (IFF) was known as Terry. He wasn't sure of how it had been agreed to, but all US, French, and UK special forces carried an IFF transponder to prevent blue-on-blue whenever they were working in the same country.

He looked again at his tablet. He crooked his neck to get a view that didn't include his unshaven, ugly mug as a reflection, while also stopping his head from raising the roof of the OP and spoiling the silhouette. The photos were ready. He added the text: "Just been pinged by FR SF heading northwest. Thought you should know."

He tapped "Send" and the little wheel icon spun round a

few times in the top left of the tablet. It stopped as the centre of screen lit up: *Sent.*

He reached for a handful of raisins, which he kept in a plastic bag off to his right, took a swig of water from a sand-coloured water bottle, and crawled back up into the OP position.

He was just about to pick up his stabilised binos and focus back on the target area when he spotted a vehicle's rising sand cloud coming down the only track into the valley. He put his binos down and watched the scene unfold.

The vehicle was a black pickup, not uncommon in Yemen. After five minutes it pulled to a stop in the centre of the camp, with an ensuing billow of dust. The sound of gunfire continued to echo from the makeshift range up in the hillside to the left. There was no commotion; the truck was obviously expected. Two men got out of the truck, one from either side. At this distance, without binos, Tony couldn't make out any details, but he could see straight away that the men were not wearing flowing Arab dress. He reached for his binos.

He stared intently in the direction of the centre of the training camp. He blinked a couple of times.

Bloody hell.

He put his binos down and reached for his Leica.

He steadied the camera on its small tripod, and then, for about three minutes, he snapped and snapped, altering the focus of the lens manually as he did.

Eventually, after what appeared to be a round of greetings and casual chat, the two men, accompanied by three Arabs, walked into the central tent.

Tony took another four photos of the truck and then slid back down into the OP.

He scrolled through the images, chastising himself inwardly when a couple were out of focus.

Well, I'll be damned.

There was no doubt about it. The training team had just been joined by a couple of very interesting characters. One was a white man, he guessed five eleven, slim built, and dressed in a nonmilitary khaki shirt and trousers. The second was a black man. About the same height, but slightly thicker, more "medium build." He was dressed in lighter cotton trousers and a blue shirt. Both of the men openly wore holsters, and the black man carried a small holdall. *Both Western? Possibly American?*

An insignificant, but nonetheless interesting, point was that as soon as the men got out of the car, the black man reached into the flatbed and opened what looked like a cooler. He took out a silver can, pulled the ring, and took a swig.

He needed to get this back to RHQ as soon as possible.

A Nondescript Office, Fourth Floor of No. 17, Third Avenue, New York

Ned Donoghue took a bite out of his apple, some of the juice spraying onto the computer screen in front of him. He took a handkerchief out of his pocket and let out a frustrated sigh as the screen mistook his hankie-wiping for instructions and started to alter data, throwing up new tabs.

"Shit," he said out loud. He reached forward to the bottom left of the screen, turned it off, and then finished his cleaning, chomping his apple between wipes.

The other four screens, which almost circled him, updated away as stock markets from around the world went about their business of making and losing millions for traders in Frankfurt, Singapore, Hong Kong, Tokyo, London, Mumbai, and elsewhere.

He turned the central screen back on and, using his finger as a pointer, highlighted *PetroBelarus*, a fledgling oil company working in and around the Black Sea. Using Google, he electronically dug deeper, looking for news and comments, both official and that from everyday punters. Joe Ordinary sometimes had a better feel for where stock was heading. Nothing untoward came from the investigation, and he closed the tab down.

He swung his chair a half turn to his left and took in the screen he had set up showing the trading values and vitals of the "big six" public-owned oil and gas companies: BP, Chevron, Dutch Shell, ExxonMobil, Total, and ConocoPhillips. These six, known as the Supermajors, dominated the world's oil and gas supply, although they had recently been joined by two Chinese giants: CNPC and Sinopec. He had included these two on this screen, having first cleared his decision with Herbert, his paymaster.

Looking to his right, the second static screen—also set up by him—listed the major environmental and nuclear energy companies. This list was a lot longer than that of the eight oil giants. It included a number of state-owned companies, like the French nuclear giant Areva. The French company was currently struggling with orders and cash flow. He followed all of their vitals, keeping track of share price, comments, and future ambitions.

The two further "wing" screens had details of the emerging or fledgling companies, both oil and gas and environmental. In short, if he spun his chair around, he had, at his fingertips, the output and performance of all of the world's energy companies split into two: oil and gas; environmental and nuclear. And he had a permanent window open on the central screen showing CNN running its usual commentary on the world at large.

It had taken him about six weeks to get up to speed with the totality of all of the companies he needed to monitor. And an extra few days to set the screens up to display and follow the data he required. Now all Herbert asked him to do was write a daily e-mail report on how the "big eight"—the Supermajors and the two Chinese giants—were performing, in comparison to the others.

Herbert was particularly interested in start-up oil companies, which was why he had just drilled down into PetroBelarus. *Drilled down*—no pun intended! He had used that expression a number of times in his reports, seeing the funny side of it. Although, as far as he could tell, it hadn't tickled Herbert. The man seemingly lacked any humour.

A sigh brought him back down to earth.

Back to work.

He would need to include details (or lack thereof) of the start-up PetroBelarus in tonight's report.

Every so often Herbert would e-mail him with a tasker asking him, for example, to predict the eventual fallout of the BP *Deepwater Horizon* disaster or, more recently, the impact of the VW "cheat device" debacle on the future price of diesel. For these specific enquiries, he was normally given a couple of days, and the reports were to be "no longer than three pages."

He had met all of Herbert's demands, and every so often, he received an electronic "well done" and often a "thanks." What he never got was a visit. Or a phone call.

Indeed, he had never met Herbert, or anyone else he might be working for. It was all very strange, at times, uncomfortably so.

Ned had been recruited from the London Stock Exchange, where he had been working for Deutsche Bank, trading mostly oil stocks and their futures. One day, during a lull in trading, he'd received an e-mail from a chap named Herbert asking if he wanted to work in New York and "earn lots of money." The e-mail was as simple as that. At first he thought it was a joke—*is anyone called Herbert nowadays? And, what fool wouldn't want to work in New York and earn lots of money?*

He had interrogated the e-mail address and drawn a blank, which, with his knowledge of the Internet and coding, made him sit up and take notice. Not many people could hide behind their e-mail addresses with him at the keyboard.

Over the next week, once he had offered Herbert a personal e-mail address for correspondence, the digital exchange got more and more detailed. *And more and more real.* He knew he was onto something when $15,000 was deposited in his main bank account and a business-class flight ticket to New York pinged its way into his mailbox.

So now here he was.

Sitting pretty.

He didn't like to talk about his salary. Or his free accommodations: a beautiful, expansive flat on Fifth Avenue, which was as described in the e-mail Herbert had sent him. The office was also as agreed—it was out of the way, hidden among a number of small firms and apartments, but had all the technical firepower Ned needed. And his salary, paid monthly in advance, accumulated to $150,000 a year. Plus—*wait for it*—medical and six weeks of paid holiday. What was there not to like?

It was, as he had told his mum on the phone after he had arrived in New York, remarkable. He loved it. Although he did often wonder who Herbert really was *and* what he was doing with the analysis he was providing.

On the rare occasion that he paused long enough to ask himself who Herbert was, he interrupted that train of thought by congratulating himself on no longer having to work in the intense, sweaty bull pit of the trading floor. And on being promoted to New York and earning a hefty six-figure sum, plus some extraordinary benefits.

Herbert was his employer and a well-paying one. He wasn't asking Ned to do anything nefarious, just research and report. So he didn't wonder too deeply, mainly for fear that his current dream world would be shattered by a gate-crashing nightmare.

Not wondering worked just fine for him.

Chapter Two

Jane had got in early. There was a lot to do. The clear emergence of a Russian Army military structure collaborating in and among the Ukrainian rebels in Georgiyevka was something they all intuitively knew was happening, but, until now, they hadn't had the evidence to back it up. Her analysts, particularly Sam Green, had managed to identify a command structure headed by a serving major from the Ninth Motor Rifle Brigade based in Moscow. They now knew he was accompanied by at least seven other officers and upward of thirty non-commissioned officers and men. Sam had found one particular image of an off-duty Russian Army sergeant in Ukraine with an antitank weapon shouldered, ready to fire. It had taken Jane almost three minutes to follow Sam's image analysis on the screens. When she saw the match, it was as obvious as the nose on her face.

She's good, that girl.

Jane heard Moscow's argument that the Russian officers and soldiers in Ukraine were no longer serving in their own army; they had taken time off to go and defend their old homeland—sort of a busman's holiday. However, GCHQ signals intelligence (SIGINT) analysts from Cheltenham had intercepted uncoded mobile traffic that linked central staff in Moscow with Russian officers on the front line in Ukraine. And, although it was hard to believe that the Russians would be so casual, NATO SIGINT teams—both on the ground and in the air—had intercepted military radio signals between the rebel headquarters in Ukraine and Russian military teams within territorial Russia close to the border. The VHF radio signals were encoded, and GCHQ was struggling to decipher the content. But, with military communications winging their way across the border, there was little hiding the fact that the Russian Army had eastern Ukrainian soil all over their Kirza Army boots.

This information would never be disclosed publicly by the West—*well, not anytime soon.* But now that they had concrete proof of coordinated Russian military presence on the ground, the politicians and senior military staff could use this to help plan strategies. At the highest level, they could also bend the Russian leader's ear, when the time was right.

It was good work. But it wasn't finished yet.

Jane had taken off her jacket, put her small rucksack beside her desk, and fired up her computer. She tried to walk to work every day, but sometimes time pressures prevented that—she almost called it a "luxury." It was much more to do with keeping herself in shape than taking in the views. Since her promotion two years ago after the Ebola affair, her enhanced pay packet had allowed her to buy a small property in Manningtree, Essex, which she had let out. Her SIS lodging allowance enabled her to rent a bijouer-than-bijou studio apartment in Brixton. Her walking route, which was just over two miles, took her twenty-five minutes. By bus, she was a little quicker—and a whole lot drier—and by tube, she could get to the office within twelve minutes—if she had to.

Today was a walking day. It was getting light as she closed her front door. By 7.20 she was through both the Headquarters' biometric airlocks and had shown her pass to Barry, the main porter—who always seemed much friendlier than his reputation. Barry was, according to legend, an ex-sergeant from 22 SAS with numerous unmentionable accolades to his name. In the week prior to Remembrance, he wore a chest full of medals, including a bar to his Military Cross. And, most surprisingly, he also wore a George Medal, a civilian valour award of the highest level. No one had any idea what that was for. But it was impressive and frightening at the same time.

What also surprised Jane was that he never seemed to

take a day off. Barry was always at the front desk looking charmingly menacing whenever she entered Babylon.

She typed in her password and waited the few seconds it took for her computer to work its own way through a cryptographic labyrinth. As she paused, ready to access last night's e-mail traffic, she put her chin in her hand and drummed her fingers. If she were completely honest with herself, she hadn't maintained the tempo of her work just because she loved it. Nor solely because what she and her team were doing was of national importance. A part of her drive was that her boss, David Jennings, had four months left in the chair before retirement, and she sensed an opportunity. He was an exceptional man, one of the best in the building, and a fabulous boss who had taught her a great deal. His leaving would create a bow wave of movement within SIS midlevel staff. Although she knew she was too young and inexperienced to take on his role, there might be other opportunities to emerge from the imminent reshuffle. She wanted to be part of that.

Come on, look lively. Her fingers were poised above the keyboard.

Jane opened up her secure e-mail and glanced through the list of eight that were highlighted in bold.

"GCHQ—knew that was coming. Two from the team— they can wait. One flagged from the SRR—stuff in the cloud." Jane whispered her thoughts as she scrolled through the list.

Oh, hang on. She double-clicked on the e-mail from the SRR. SIS rarely received e-mails directly from the Special Reconnaissance Regiment, unless they had found something very unusual.

She opened it up:

Thought you should look at images SRR1245—1270 that we posted last night. The two non-Arab men look out of place and are new to us. Against protocol, we have tasked the troop on the ground to remain in situ for a further 24 hrs to see if they can get additional images.

Pse let us know if you recognise the two targets so we can make a decision as to how long they remain exposed at that location. We would like to extricate them asp.

Answer req by 10.00 Local.

Regards

Jane expanded a new tab that accessed the UK security forces' secure cloud. She opened the top drawer of her desk and took out her SIS passkey, which unnervingly looked the same as the one she used to access her Internet banking— although the SIS version was a lovely vermilion colour. She tapped in her four-digit password, pressed a yellow button, and was given a six-digit code. She then typed that into the computer, and, within a few seconds, the cloud was open.

Jane navigated her way through various layers of folders until she got to the one titled "Images, RSS, Oct 15." She opened it and saw immediately that there were about a hundred new shots that her team would need to negotiate.

She scrolled down until she found image SRR1245 and, with a tap on her screen, expanded it.

My God!

She took a deep breath as her eyes widened in disbelief. She held that breath and clicked for the next image in the sequence to appear. And the next. And the next.

She was breathing again now, but her heart rate was up, and her hands felt clammy. She continued to flick the images back and forth until the reality of it all sunk in.

Jane came to. She shook her head and glanced at her watch. It was 7.45. Would Sam Green be in? Possibly, possibly not. She highlighted the photos, and, using the authority invested in her position, she right-clicked and pressed "Hide." The photos disappeared.

For now.

She needed to see David straight away. What she had just seen was a hugely significant event in terms of what was happening on the ground in Yemen. But it also had much deeper, much more sinister ramifications for the whole operation. And particularly for members of her team.

She picked up the phone and pressed "*3."

"Hi, Claire, it's Jane. Is David in?" There was a pause at the other end of the line and then Claire came back to say that he was.

"Good. I need to see him now. Could you make that happen?"

The line went on hold for a second, and then Claire called Jane forward.

15° 23' 51" N, 44° 15' 01" E, Northern Yemen

Colour Sergeant Jock Mills brushed the sand from his nose with his left hand and turned away from the laptop screen, which was laid on the back seat of the twin-cab Toyota Hilux. He stood up straight and squinted his eyes against the sun. He stared out across Yemen's Barat Mountains in the direction of where his boss's team was currently in its OP position. He reached for the top left pocket of his light blue cotton shirt and pulled out his Ray-Ban Navigators, plonking them on his nose.

Around him the noise of the pneumatic drill was unavoidable, as was the low hum of the diesel generator that was providing for all of the camp's electrical needs. There were eight of them in the small camp, a mock survey team from the imaginary Rayfgo Engineering. They had driven to the end of the wadi in three white Toyota Hiluxes and a Mercedes ML SUV. He was getting used to the scenery. They had been at the camp, which was just off Route 11 and chosen to be within a two-day trek of the target, for four days. And now they had been tasked by RHQ to stay for a further twenty-four hours. This was to allow the reconnaissance team, which his boss had taken up-country, to gather some more images. The last time they had spoken, Tony's boss hadn't been pleased about staying longer. Every second in the OP was a second closer to being compromised. And this was by far the most exposed position they had ever worked in.

Jock had briefed his team about the delay. They had agreed to continue with the same daily routine, a sort of engineering *Groundhog Day* of drilling, cataloguing, and then drilling some more. It was all for effect. Only Trooper Nigel Field had any civil engineering background, having worked on a building site before he joined the army. Under instruction from the Royal Engineers, he had spent four weeks perfecting the process of extracting and examining ore from seams of rock. The rest of them were all dressed and equipped according to role, but they were picking it up on the job. By day three they were looking half-competent, but not anywhere near good enough to fool an expert.

"Hey, Jock. Vehicle cloud coming down the wadi." It was one of his team who, as well as putting dirt into a glass vial and adding coloured water, was also on point lookout.

Jock took off his sunglasses and reached into the front seat of the cab for his binos.

He nodded as he looked. They hadn't seen anyone since leaving Saudi and entering Yemen. They had crossed the thousand-mile-long, metal-fenced border with the help of some Saudi Special Forces, who had disabled the alarms. The only living things they had seen so far were a couple of camels. And a snake.

This is going to be interesting.

Looking through the binos, it seemed that the approaching vehicle was in Yemeni police livery. The police drove around in a variety of vehicles—mostly old Toyotas— painted light blue and white. By all accounts they were not well trained, but heavily armed—not the perfect combination. Jock would be able to confirm his suspicions when he could make out their uniforms. He'd be looking for a blue disruptive pattern with plenty of badges.

The building block of British Special Forces is a team of four. When deployed to the Middle East, one trooper would be a fluent Arabic speaker. The others were experts in either signals, medicine, or explosives. Jock's boys were no different. In addition, they were all proficient in the use of the weapons they had with them—currently hidden away from view but within reach. And all of them had been trained to be good in a tight spot. Jock was an explosives expert, as well as being the 3IC of the troop. He was particularly good in a tight spot.

The sun flashed off the approaching vehicle's windscreen—belching sand and dust its backdrop.

It was definitely an old Toyota Land Cruiser—the kind that looks like a World War Two US Army Willis Jeep. It was now about a kilometre away. He ducked into the back seat of the Hilux and reached for his satellite phone. He checked he had a signal and then speed-dialled Squadron HQ. It rang twice.

"Hi, Jock, wassup?"

"We've got company. Looks like Yemeni police, just one vehicle at the moment. I'll leave this on transmit so, hopefully, you can pick up what's going on. And, Steve . . ."

"Yeah, what?" Clear as a bell. Not even any satellite lag.

"If anything happens to me . . . you can have my trainers."

The SHQ operator sitting in Riyadh suppressed a laugh. And then he came straight back down to earth.

"Got it, Jock. Good luck. We'll let Tony know, so you don't have to."

Jock put the phone on the roof of the Hilux, and, after checking that the seven of his boys were all looking like busy but alert engineers, he stood and waited for the Yemeni police to arrive.

It took a further minute or so for the old light blue and

white Toyota to bounce its way to their location. They could only be coming to see them. Beyond where they were, the wadi closed in. What you might call the valley's main track ran out just before the dried riverbed off to his right. In that respect, they couldn't be in a worse place to escape from—by vehicle. There was only one way out on wheels, and that was back down the valley. Similarly, it was the only way in. Anyone who wanted to get to see them would be spotted well before they arrived.

That was the point.

"It's the perfect anti-mother-in-law spot," one of his team had said on arrival.

Indeed it was.

The old Land Cruiser eventually pulled up in a plume of dust. One of the policemen, sporting an AK-47 slung at his side and wearing a belt festooned with clip-on grenades, got out. He stood still as the dust settled, looking around, taking it all in. The drilling stopped. The scene reminded Jock of when he and his girlfriend had walked into a bar in deepest Wales—the place had gone silent and everybody turned to stare at them, nobody knowing who would make the first move. Then he imaged that someone in the depths of the pub, overcome with surprise, had missed the dart board.

As the policeman eyed up the camp, Jock did some quick calculations. Key to a successful extraction—if that was what was required—was knowing what state the police radio was in and whether any of the three men had mobile phones on them. Jock saw two long antennae attached to each of the wings of the Toyota—so that probably meant two radios. He listened, but he didn't hear any radio traffic. Each man would probably have a mobile. *Hmmm—lots of communications.*

With two of the policemen sitting nonchalantly in the vehicle and the other man still looking around, including a long gaze at the Rayfgo logo on the Hilux, Jock decided to break the impasse.

"Hi there. Do you speak English?" He walked a couple of

paces forward, his boots leaving size-eleven prints in the layer of soft light sand that covered the hard red floor of the wadi.

"Little. Arabic?" the man answered. He had casually brought his right hand around to the trigger guard of the AK-47. It was still hanging loosely by his side, but the intent to use it was clear. Jock, spotting the man's action, stopped, a small cloud of dust thrown up by his change of pace.

"No, not me. My engineer friend over there does." Jock looked up and beckoned to one of his lads who was typing away at a laptop. It also had the Rayfgo logo on its flip lid. "Patrick. Over here, please."

Trooper Patrick closed his laptop and half jogged over.

"Hello, sir. My name is Patrick." Arabic. He offered his hand. Jock picked up the "Hello." The rest was lost of him.

The conversation went on for about a minute. Jock decided that he needed to know what was going on. The policeman had begun to look agitated; his language had quickened.

Jock put his hand on the trooper's arm to get his attention.

Patrick turned to him as the policeman waved at his Land Cruiser and a second man got out. He was obviously of a lesser rank by the way he approached sharply, stood to attention, and then smartly bowed his head. The two policemen had a conversation that in any other language would have sounded like an argument. But, as Jock had learned after a number of tours of the Middle East, Arabs were like Italians: you never get anything done without scattergun words and plenty of gesticulations.

Patrick looked calm. "Not surprisingly, they know nothing of us. He's asking his pal to get on the radio and check."

"Tell him we have papers."

Jock turned and was about to move to the cab and get the papers when the policeman yelled.

"No move!"

Jock stopped dead. He intuitively felt seven other team members tense around him—even Steve in the small cooking tent, who, last time Jock looked, was preparing some soup for lunch; he had probably just let go of the ladle. Doubtless, those out of sight had their hands on a weapon. Or two.

"No move. No move." *A very jumpy policeman.* That's what you get in a country plagued by conflict and ruled by the gun.

He turned back around and, raising his hands in semisubmission, said, "Papers? Here." He pointed behind him, over his shoulder, in the direction of the cab.

"Wait."

From the old Toyota, Jock heard the two other policemen trying to contact someone, somewhere, on the radios. There were lots of high-pitched Arabic words and phrases followed by pauses, waiting for a response. Nothing. And then lots more Arabic followed by silent airways. They weren't getting through.

Jock softly gave instructions to Patrick. "Tell him who we are again. Tell him I have permission from the Interior Ministry in the cab. Tell him that he could use my Iridium if he wants to phone home."

Patrick had a further minute or so of conversation with the policeman whilst his two oppos tried desperately, but fruitlessly, to raise someone at the other end of the ether.

"Get papers!" Spittle accompanying the order.

Give a man a peaked hat.

Still with his hands raised, Jock carefully turned around, took a few steps to the cab, then reached for a see-through plastic folder that had a few papers in it.

"It's the second one in. Show it to him." Jock handed the folder to Patrick.

As Patrick and the policeman noisily reviewed the paperwork, Jock had a glance around. The Yemenis wouldn't know, but he picked out four of his team with hands on an automatic weapon. His eyes stopped briefly at the mess tent. A well-disguised, but not completely, 5.56-

mm barrel of a C8 Carbine poked out between a thin gap in canvas. It was trained at the policeman talking to Patrick. It would be over in seconds, if that's what needed to happen.

Throughout this, the hapless policemen in the Land Cruiser kept gabbling into the two radios, waiting for a response and getting nothing back in return.

The senior policeman made a few extra embellishing hand movements whilst talking loudly at Patrick, almost dropping the forged Interior Ministry letter at one point. And then he literally threw it all back at Jock.

"We go now. I check back at camp."

With a further burst of indecipherable, high-pitched words at the two other policemen in the Toyota, he got back into the truck and slammed the door. A few seconds later they were gone, pursued by a cloud of fine dust that rose in the still, hot air like smoke from an Australian barbecue working overtime on a bank holiday.

SIS Headquarters, Vauxhall, London

David was musing over the latest from Jane: Kurt Manning and Ralph Bell had turned up at a terrorist training camp in Yemen. *How did that happen?*

He paced up and down his office, staring without focus out across the Thames.

Both men had been at the centre of a conspiracy to release Ebola in a crowded London Underground station. After it was all over, he had been given categorical assurance from the CIA that Manning and Bell, classified as "rogue agents," were out of action. There were subsequent noises from CIA HQ at Langley that Ralph Bell was dead.

But pictures don't lie, even in this case, when they had been taken at a distance of over a thousand metres across the Yemeni desert.

He had agreed with Jane that "hiding" the images from her staff—more accurately, from Sam Green—was the right one. She would probably need to be told at some point. Indeed, Sam's forensic ability to interpret images and situations would doubtless be key in helping work out what was happening. But, just now, he needed to speak to Langley and find out just what was going on.

His phone rang. It was his PA, Claire.

"I have the deputy director, sir.'

"Thanks, Claire, put him through." He checked his watch. It was 11.30 here, 6.30 in the United States. Early doors for the East Coast, but that was their choice.

"Hi, Linden, it's David here. So good of you to take my call this early." David liked the CIA's new deputy. More importantly, he trusted him. Unlike his predecessor—who had since moved on and was now, according to what he had heard, a non exec of a huge Christian charity based somewhere in the Midwest. David still thought he'd had something to do with the whole Sam Green/Ebola incident. It frustrated him that they been unable to get to the bottom of his potential involvement before he left his post.

"Hi, David. Just got in. How can I help?" The accent was one of those mellow East Coast ones, laced with a touch of Irish.

"I'm about to send you three images taken by our SF in Yemen yesterday. It's a Daesh training camp. Well, we're pretty sure it's Daesh rather than Al-Qaeda, but we've yet to confirm which side this particular shooting match is batting for." David closed his eyes as he recognised his mixing of metaphors. He wondered if Linden was keeping count.

"The reason why I'm phoning now . . . hang on"—he paused for a second as he pressed the "Return" key—"I've just sent an e-mail with the photos. In the middle of the camp, bold as brass, are our two old friends Kurt Manning and Ralph Bell. Or should I say, *your* friends."

The line, which had a slight delay due to the distance that was further exacerbated by the encryption, paused for longer than the technology needed. David waited.

"You've got to be kidding? Wait while I get the e-mail."

David looked up from his own screen and across the room at the antique Vienna-styled wall clock that hung above the red leather sofa. It was too old to have a second hand, but as he waited, David was sure he saw the minute hand rush forward a tiny bit.

A countdown to retirement.

The thought warmed him. This time next year he would be tending his roses, dealing with blackfly and slugs as opposed to, well, the human varieties of the same. He didn't want to rush these last four months because there was a lot to do, including announcing his successor. But he couldn't look at the lovely clock without letting his mind wander just a touch. He hoped he had made enough of the right noises so that the organisation felt inclined to give him the wooden beauty as a retirement present. Might he need to hint harder?

"Gee whiz . . ."—*does anyone say that anymore?*—". . . it is them. I'll be pickled in hen's juice!" The deputy director blew out hard on the other end of the line. "How did they get there? And what are they doing?"

These were good questions, along with about fifty others that David could think of.

"We've still got a team on the ground hoping to take more photos and establish what they're up to. But I hope you could look to your own resources and help us establish what's what. I don't need to remind you that until just two and a half years ago, Kurt Manning was a Level 3 CIA operative with access to US/UK Eyes Only information, do I?" He didn't, he knew that. It was a cheap trick. But two ex-CIA men, possibly right-wing Christian fundamentalists, were alive and kicking. And currently very much alive and kicking in a terrorist training camp in Yemen. It didn't bear thinking about.

"Have you got available assets that could take this camp out? Strike now whilst you have eyes on?" The deputy director asked.

It was good to be talking to a DD who wanted to deal with these hoods, rather than deny their existence.

"No, sorry. Too far south at the moment. Have you?" David knew he could ask the Saudis, who would oblige. But he also knew that by the time they got Downing Street clearance, and then approached the Saudis, their team would be very vulnerable. As a workable alternative, he was confident that the SRR team could provide forward air control (FAC) with laser designation for a US airstrike. But he would need to check before committing.

"I'll get in touch with the Pentagon now. Your people could provide the FAC piece?"

"Should be able to, but it will take me an hour or so to check that. Shall we talk again, say, at seven thirty your time?"

"That's fine, David. Speak in about an hour."

The phone went dead. Which was timely, as he needed the loo.

He popped out the door and said to Claire, "Get Hereford on the line, please. And ask Jane to come back and see me. Oh, and a coffee. I'm off to the loo."

"Too much information," Claire said, reaching for the phone.

On a Wednesday, it was Sam's turn to cull the new daily "open" source images that had been deposited on the cloud—the ones that Mervin had thought worthy of their attention. Mervin was the SIS's temperamental image-processing computer that trawled all public networks, social media, and even e-mails, searching for images that might be of use for the SIS analysts. The five of them in the office did a day each. Her day was Wednesday.

Sam used her biggest screen and threw up twenty-four images at a time. She quickly trawled through all of them, selecting those of no relevance. With a single "Delete," she removed over 90 per cent. She kept around twenty that looked like they could be useful. Currently the richest vein of photos was from TV and newspaper shots at Calais, France, and on the Greek island of Lesbos. She paid particular attention to these.

Once finished, she decided to have a look at the images that had been placed in the cloud from their "closed" sources. Sam had the highest regard for the soldiers, spies, agents, and informants who took photos of likely HVTs in often extremely dangerous locations. She knew that she had a pretty deep well of personal courage—actually, it was more a complete disregard for her own safety, which wasn't quite the same thing. However, she wasn't convinced she'd be able to hold the camera steady whilst snapping away at some of these lunatics.

She opened a file:

"SRR/NYemen/15.23.45.N.44.15.37E/031015."

It would be the very latest from the SRR team in Yemen. Brave men operating at the very edges of the sane world.

Sam skimmed the photos. It was of cursory interest only, as her job was to pinpoint current movement on HVTs from the Middle East to the UK. None of those in the camp would be moving anytime soon—the images from Lesbos and Calais would be far more revealing. The SRR photos offered no recognisable faces and nothing that seemed untoward: a terrorist training camp in the desert preparing men from a number of nations to engage with and kill Westerners.

She stopped and pulled her head back so she could take in the whole screen. She studied the numbering of the photos and picked out an anomaly. Photos SRR1245 to 1270 were missing. That would be twenty-five photos not in the series. Nobody was allowed to remove images taken by "closed" sources from the cloud. And all photos had to be assigned a designated, ascending number from a predetermined list.

Photos just didn't go missing—where are they?

She searched for the images using the "Ctrl-F" feature, but nothing surfaced. *This is very odd.* Very odd indeed. She would talk to Jane when she next saw her.

Chapter Three

Having finished his daily apple, Ned decided that he'd had his fill of fibre and vitamin C. Now it was Jelly Baby time. He struggled to get them in New York. The closest they had was Jellie Bellies, which weren't the same thing at all—they were jellybeans with a hard coating. *No, they wouldn't do.* He needed teddy-bear-shaped jellies with a soft, sugared coating. The ones where you could bite off the heads, then the bodies, and finally finish with the legs. It was satisfying on both a confectionery and a sort of sado-animalistic level. It did not, of course, reflect his personality. *Not at all.* No, he just liked the taste of the sweets. And he had to eat them in a particular way.

He ate close to a pack a day. They were sent to New York by his mum, all the way from Cleethorpes. A Red Cross parcel of sorts. *Yum-yum.*

Overnight he had received the latest tasker from Herbert. He wanted a technical résumé of the new Tesla Home Battery, the one that stored excess solar energy from domestic solar panels and then regurgitated the power when the sun went to bed. And he wanted a prognosis of where this might be heading.

Tesla's boss, billionaire Elon Musk, was moving on from building all-electric cars and had surprised the whole world by announcing a gigafactory somewhere in Nevada that would build tens of thousands of these batteries to sell around the world. It was, considering Ned's responsibility, a new entrant into his power and energy portfolio. He could see why Herbert would be interested.

He'd spent about six hours gathering information from all different sources, including Tesla's website, which, as he'd expected, was more marketing hype than encyclopaedic fact. However, there were plenty of other commentaries: some positive, "sold out this year due to crazy demand"; some negative, "another rich kid's toy."

What amused Ned was that Tesla's main press conference was delayed for an hour due to power failure. A marketing whoopsie, as the whole thing had been powered by a bank of Elon Musk's batteries. *Bless them.*

Ned had established that a single Tesla Powerwall—to give it its proper name—which looked like a space-age flattened fridge stuck on a garage wall, held only about one of his own British pound's worth of electricity. So over a year, a householder could probably save about £300. And with the hardware coming in at well over £2,000, the payback would take a helluva long time.

Ned stopped surfing for a moment and jotted down a draft title for his paper for Herbert: "Tesla Powerwall—The Toyota Prius of Domestic Electricity. Looks good, costs a lot. And not the answer."

He congratulated himself on that and reached for another Jelly Baby. *A yellow one. Mmm.*

He was about to search for information on the solar irradiance—a big new word for him—in the UK, when the small screen showing CNN caught his eye. He turned up the sound.

There was a report about the anniversary of the 1979 US nuclear accident on the Pennsylvanian coast. The report expanded on the incident, which was assumed to have started with a fire just outside one of the reactors. This was further compounded by a failure of an operator to open a coolant-relief valve. The operator said at the time that the valve had been stuck. As a result, there was a partial meltdown of one of the cores and a release of radioactive gases and iodine. Nobody died.

Except the nuclear power industry.

Ned was waiting for the punchline from CNN. So far it was interesting but not illuminating.

The male reporter handed over to his female counterpart.

"Thirty-six years after the event, one man has come forward and claimed that he had been paid to fix the valve so it wouldn't open. *Apparently* . . ."—the woman emphasised the word with unreserved glee—". . . at seventy years young and suffering from leukaemia, he couldn't live with himself. So he has decided to speak now."

And the fire was also started on purpose? Ned thought it was the obvious supplementary. Arson, a stuck valve, and a nuclear power station. *The perfect storm.*

He lost the man's name in the noise, but what interested him from the CNN report—after all, power supply was now *his* business—was that, after the incident, the nuclear industry went into meltdown. *Another pun.* He loved it. Up until 1979, the reporter quoted, nuclear power plants were being constructed at around one a year. Post-1979 that number declined, with fifty-one planned reactors cancelled in the United States between 1980 and 1984. That was not an insignificant number.

This is big news. Somebody, somewhere, would have profited from this disaster.

Assuming the bloke who had come forward wasn't a crackpot, which—after just four months of temporary US citizenship—was a big assumption, he could sense the lawyers in Wall Street sharpening their Montblanc propelling pencils.

Ned reached for another Jelly Baby, but the bag was empty.

"Shit." There was nothing more depressing than an empty bag of his favourite sweets.

The depression was short-lived. He pulled open the top drawer of his desk and picked out a new bag.

"Come to Daddy."

Tony James had just begun to shake off the cold of the desert night. The sun had crept above the horizon, and he was focused back in on the terrorist camp, binos in one hand and his Leica S, with its zoom lens, just off to one side.

If you'd never been in the desert it was difficult to understand how cold the nights could be. The days were blisteringly, searingly hot. The nights had wide-open skies that sucked out the heat. The sand and rock lamely gave up their residual warmth to the voracious emptiness. Temperatures would often drop to below freezing. The differential between highs and lows could be debilitating.

His team of four, of which he was the observer and the others his wingmen, gathered together at dusk in the centre of the patrol base. His OP was high on a rocky outcrop, just off the pinnacle overlooking the valley below: twelve o'clock. During the day, his team members took the other three cardinal times: three, six, and nine; near enough was good enough. They had sighted themselves within three hundred metres of a central point, which was low down in a bowl, hidden from every direction. There, they had set up a makeshift camp under a couple of desert-patterned ponchos. Unmanned during the day, it was home at night: food, drink, their "maggots" (sleeping bags), battery charging via a small series of solar panels, team briefing and other essential equipment. They slept on rotation in threes, with the fourth on lookout with night-vision goggles.

During the day, all four of them were self-sufficient. In a crisis they could all go their separate ways and, via a set of predetermined RVs, end up back at the Hub with Colour Sergeant Jock Mills. Jock and his men were about seventy clicks to the south. In a significant crisis they had the wherewithal to make their way as a team of four back to the Saudi border, about two hundred clicks to the north. Should it be necessary, the other half of his troop was on standby in Saudi. They could be flown in by a pair of SF Merlin helicopters and effect a "hot" extraction. *Possibly.* He knew that what they were doing was on the very edge of international law, and probably on the wrong side of it. Launching the Merlins was a decision that would be taken at the very highest level. By which time they would probably all be out of ammunition and wearing orange jumpsuits.

Or dead.

He had the greatest confidence in his team of four—actually, his whole troop. This time around he had decided to take the Observation Team and leave Jock at the Hub with the insertion and backup group. His deputy, a very experienced ex-para sergeant major, was waiting with the final three teams by the Merlins in Saudi. If they had any sense, they were probably topping up their tans.

The camp below him was beginning to come to life. His stabilised binos picked out three men in Arab clothing, wandering about. He checked for the black pickup the two non-Arabs had turned up in yesterday. He scanned left and right, up and down. *Nothing.* Well, almost nothing. Just behind one of the larger tents there was evidence of a white bonnet of a vehicle. He was sure that had been there before the two Westerners had arrived. He'd need to check the images on his table.

If the black vehicle had gone, then maybe so had the two men. And they had disappeared between ten last night and six this morning.

I wonder where they are?

That would be a so-and-so. But at least it would mean that their work was done and they could extract. *Possibly soon? In daylight—back to the Hub?* He'd need to think that through carefully.

He slid off the ridge and fished out his tablet from his bergen. He wanted to check for the white pickup. He was sure he had photographed it before.

Then all hell broke loose.

Shots, high-velocity rounds, rang out to his left.

Crack! Crack! Crack! Thump! Thump! Thump! The gap

between the two sounds told Tony that they were fired about two hundred metres away. The crack of the round was overhead, the thump—the origins of the shot—to his right.

"21 Charlie, contact, wait out." A quick radio report. High-pitched; a gallop of words. From his nine o'clock. Ted Groves.

Multiple cracks and then a volley of thumps. This time seemingly from every direction. Nothing landing near him. As far as he could tell.

He tried to fathom where the rounds were coming from as he threw his camera and binos into the top of his bergen and reached for his SCAR-H rifle, releasing the safety catch as he did so. He turned expertly around under the cover of his poncho and gingerly stuck his head out of the entrance where his feet had been seconds before.

Crack! Thump! Crack! Thump!

"21 Charlie this is 20 Alpha—update, over!" Tony was on the radio. He needed to know what was happening with Ted. From where he was, he couldn't see anything.

"21 Alpha . . ."—heavy breathing from Trooper Sandy Jarman at six o'clock—"moving . . . up . . . toward . . . 21 Charlie now."

"'Roger." Tony paused momentarily.

Then back on the radio. "21 Bravo and Charlie?" A question.

What the bloody hell is happening with you pair? Nothing from either of them. The sand and rocks echoing silence.

Then more shots and a piercing cry off to his right. *Nine o'clock—Ted Groves again. He's been hit?*

The firefight started again in earnest. Tony was out of the OP and on his feet, but crouching. He knew Jock would have picked up the contact on the radio and would be thinking about how they could help. He had pressed the red distress (he hated that word) button on his satphone—immediately his deputy and SHQ would be aware that they had a situation. His phone would bleep a location signal until it ran out of batteries. He had a whole day's worth spare in his bergen—which he had purposely left under his poncho.

With enough ammunition to make a considerable difference at Rorke's Drift, he zigzagged his way toward 21 Charlie's location. Toward Ted Groves, where the cry had come from. Always alert, always looking.

He stopped dead, going down on one knee. Off to his left, some hundred metres away, he picked out 21 Alpha: Trooper Sandy manoeuvring his way carefully, but quickly, toward the last known location of 21 Charlie as he said he would.

He pressed the pressel on his radio.

"21 Alpha, I have you visual. Sitrep?"

Trooper Sandy stopped and looked in his direction. He put his spare hand up to his forehead. Tony thought he was probably shielding his eyes from the early sun.

And then the reality of what they were up against hit Captain Tony James like a fully stocked fridge.

A single high-velocity crack was the soundtrack to Trooper Sandy wheeling backward, arms and legs flailing uncontrollably as his body lifted and spun.

Thump!

The hollow sound filled Tony's ears, scrambled his thought processes, and made him shrink within himself, the gravity of what he had just seen dulling all of his senses. He was numb. Just for a second. What seemed like a long second.

His radio crackled into life.

"Hello, 20 Alpha, this is 21 Bravo." *Steve Bliss, three o'clock.* "I have you visual. Is that 21 Alpha down?"

The enveloping darkness that was so close to taking hold of him evaporated. He turned his head around, scanned left and right, and caught Trooper Steve Bliss's silhouette about fifty metres behind him.

Tony metaphorically shook himself. He realised he had involuntarily fallen to the ground and into a prone, almost foetal position. Self-protecting. *Shameful?*

He'd been in contact twice before, but he was never as

exposed as this. Always within the comfort of a much larger military grouping. He'd been awarded the Military Cross for taking out a group of Taliban in Helmand almost single-handedly, during a company-level attack on an enemy strongpoint. He had been alert, alive throughout that experience. And he had held his infantry platoon together during a second firefight a couple of weeks later, seeing off a Taliban assault whilst they were out patrolling. In both cases they were never far from the protection of armoured vehicles. If he needed air support, he could call for it in minutes. And there was always a doctor on hand should they have to deal with any casualties.

Here, just now, he was on his own. Away from the joined-upness of an infantry battalion, its close air support, its helicopters. *Its doctors.* A single SRR team miles away from nothing more than half a troop of help. And miles again from the safety of the Saudi border. 21 Alpha was down, possibly dead. He'd seen that with his own eyes. 21 Charlie had called the initial contact and then, that scream . . . *Where was 21 Charlie?*

He was on his haunches now. "Roger, 21 Bravo. Wait. 21 Charlie, Sitrep? Over." Nothing. He knew Ted was down as well. *After that scream.*

They had to get out of there. But he couldn't think about extraction without establishing what had happened to Alpha and Charlie. *Sandy and Ted.* He had to do something.

"21 Bravo—stay firm and provide cover. Keep watching your back."

Just then an odd flash of colour, possibly blue or black, flickered in the distance to his right and was caught in his peripheral vision. He shrugged it off and moved quickly behind a man-size rock to his left. He raised his weapon to his shoulder and looked through the times-five optical sight toward Sandy's location.

Trooper Sandy was lying on the ground in an uncomfortably twisted position. His weapon was in his hand, but there was no movement. He looked for entry or exit wounds. It was difficult to tell at this distance, but he thought he could pick out a dark patch where Sandy's body met the ground. Could be shadow—a quick check to where the sun was. Nope. It wasn't shadow.

He tried his radio again. "21 Alpha and Charlie. Sitrep?" *Nothing.*

He'd shut up now. Action was required, not words.

With care, he slid to the ground, gently pushed the barrel of his weapon around the bottom of the right side of the rock, and followed it with his eyes, looking directly above the sights, both eyes open. He nudged around a bit further. And a bit further still. He felt his heart pounding, bouncing between his ears.

He scanned right, looking across a short horizon, a landscape of rock and sand piercing a cloudless dark blue sky. On any other day, at any other time, it would be a heck of a view. *Nothing.* He stayed there for a few moments and looked again. *Still nothing. Was the right all clear?* He pulled back and then gently raised himself into a squat position. He left his weapon below the outline of the rock and, helmetless—he'd left that under his poncho—raised himself ever so slowly up over the left side of the rock, the side closest to Sandy. He had to get a view in the direction of 21 Charlie's—Ted's—original location. *Nothing.* He scanned left until he was met with Sandy's fallen body. And then back again.

Still nothing. It was as though the firefight had happened at a different time. In a different place. Now all was calm. *Was it over?* He would carefully make his way to Sandy and then to 21 Charlie. Find out what was happening.

"Chk . . . ," the click of his radio just before receiving a transmission. He pulled back. "20 Bravo. We have your predicament and location. Packing up here. Let me know what's happening when you can." No response was expected. Just a helpful, welcoming call from Jock. *Well done, Jock.*

He started again, in slow motion, exposing himself

almost a centimetre at a time.

Then he was up, crouching, moving slowly but purposefully toward Sandy. Left then right, right then left. From small rock to small rock, ducking behind cover where and when he could.

Ten metres, twenty metres. Soon he'd be able to see what state Sandy was in through his rifle sight. Check for vitals.

And then.

Crack! A single-syllable noise. The most deadly sound. Not as loud as, say, a grenade. But with so much more penetration.

Captain Tony James didn't hear the delayed thump as the round hit him. It got lost as the wind was forced out of his lungs as he hit the ground. He had no idea where or how badly he had been hit. All he knew was that from the moment the round struck him, his body was no longer his. It had become one with, and belonged to, the slug of metal that was travelling faster than the speed of sound. A projectile with as much momentum as a Ford Fiesta. He was a passenger at that point. An unwitting occupant. With no seatbelt.

He knew he was spinning, and he knew that he couldn't control the spin. He knew he was falling, and he had no idea how he would land. There was no pain. There was just floppiness, lack of control. He thought he had lost grip of his weapon. He hadn't had the time to put the strap over his shoulder when he had left the OP. He was impotent, like a bone thrown in the air for a dog to fetch.

And now he was static. There was dust in the air, and it got up his nose. Into his eyes. His mind was racing, trying to get a grip of what had just happened. Trying to do something that might save him from further attack. It was primeval, but ever so slightly controlled by his training and experience.

Crack, crack! Thump, thump! Not near him, but overhead.

21 Bravo. Steve Bliss. In contact? He didn't know if that was a good or a bad thing.

He moved his arms. Yup, he could do that.

He tried to bring one leg upward in order to crawl somewhere. *Fuck, no.* That hurt. Somewhere south. Somewhere below his pelvis.

There was more gunfire and then, "20 Alpha, are you OK?"

He lifted his head, looking for his weapon. It was a metre to his left. Covered in sand. *That might jam,* he thought. His training kicking in again.

He reached for his pressel. "I'm down. Leg wound, I think. Sandy is down . . ." He was fighting for breath now. He knew shock wasn't far off, and with it would come debilitation.

"Get out now! That's an order."

Crack, thump! Crack, thump!

Silence for a few seconds.

"21 Bravo. Roger. I'll get to Jock and we'll come and get you." Silence. And then a very regretful, "Out."

Tony tried to move his right leg again, but the pain overwhelmed him. He wanted to cry out. To scream like he had when, after a fall from his moped on his honeymoon, the Greek doctors had set the other leg. Without an anaesthetic. Bone against bone. Intolerable pain.

He felt that now. At first it had been a throb. Now it was pain as you'd expect if your leg had been ripped open by a bullet.

There was nothing he could do. Against the strength of a rising sun, the darkness started to close in. He knew his body was shutting down. A combination, he guessed, of a gaping wound and an accompanying outpouring of blood. The body was a remarkable machine. It knew when enough was enough. When it couldn't cope with what it was faced with. When the injury needed its attention more than the body's owner did. It was taking control. He was losing it.

As oblivion approached and light became dark, Tony knew there were only two possible outcomes of his current predicament. Death or, worse still, a period of time in an orange jumpsuit—followed by death. There weren't enough words to describe how much he loved his wife and their young girl. But, at this point, the first of those two options seemed infinitely more preferable.

He started to pray.

SIS Headquarters, Vauxhall, London

Sam was struggling to maintain her interest in the computer screens. On her left she had the latest newsreel shot by the US NBC news. It showed hundreds of migrants clambering out of overburdened fishing boats and rubber dinghies on the shores of Lesbos, Greece. There were so many refugees arriving at the moment that the five analysts were struggling to keep up with the footage. And they only saw what they saw. God knows how many of the poor folk didn't make it onto camera.

The weather was worsening in the eastern Mediterranean, and the journey from Turkey to Greece, across the often choppy waters of the Aegean Sea, was becoming more and more hazardous. The informed view was that thousands, maybe tens of thousands, were rushing to make the crossing whilst the weather held.

Sam and the team would have other opportunities—more images of some of the people they had missed. Not all, but a good number. SIS had facilities to take photos at the various choke points. They had surprisingly good access to a lot of cross-border CCTV images along the whole journey: Greece, Macedonia, Serbia, Hungary, Austria, Germany. Over the past month she had been able to follow a particular family from Kos all the way to Dortmund, Germany. What was heart-breaking was that Sam's family of five had morphed into a family of four somewhere in Serbia—a little girl of about two, lost along the way.

That family had no terrorist connection as far as she knew. They had just kept cropping up as she looked through the photos from various locations. The mum with her long, pale blue, lacy dress, grubby at the hem. Dad with the stock-in-trade short black beard, Nike jacket, and Giants baseball cap. And the kids dragging what few toys they had behind them.

Another wave of tiredness crept up on her. It was two thirty in the afternoon, and it already felt like a long day. She didn't like Thursdays. She had left her flat in Colliers Wood at about seven thirty that morning and made her way straight to her weekly psychiatrist's appointment a few blocks from the Headquarters. She usually took the tube: Northern then Victoria Line. It wasn't quite door to-door, but it was pretty close. She made up for the luxury of using the Underground to travel by dedicating her lunchtimes to exercise in the basement gym. She usually ran on one of the machines, normally between six and ten kilometres. She wasn't into upper body work, even though she knew it would be good to balance her phys.

In her defence, Sam had taken Jane's advice and joined her at weekly yoga classes after work on a Monday. It was an hour of all sorts of core body strengthening. And a good deal of chanting. She certainly felt much more relaxed following the yoga session than she ever did coming out of the psychiatrist's office.

This morning she had almost stormed out. Doctor Latimer was a monster. She didn't know where he'd learned his trade, but he had a real knack of finding the nerve. And then not letting go. What was doubly infuriating was that he was so nice with it.

"Can we talk about Chris?"

No, we bloody well can't talk about Chris. Chrissake. Why, oh why, did they all want to unearth things that she just wanted to keep buried? Chris was dead. That was that. If it hadn't been for the skilful hands of an army doctor who had managed to stick her insides back through the hole made by the mortar round, she would have been dead as well. It was four years ago now. History.

Come on, Latimer, let's get with the programme! There was so much more to talk about. Since Afghanistan she had been through the mill in Sierra Leone and almost copped it again there. It had been dangerous, exciting, fun. And it was raw; it was *almost* now. She could talk about that. For days.

Yes—let's talk about that.

But, no. It nearly always came back to Camp Bastion and that fateful day in November, four years ago. The blast, the noise, the dust.

The death.

She didn't want to come to terms with it. She'd had enough of it. Enough of it percolating through her dreams, keeping her awake at night, flashing like a strobe during her downtimes—wearing her patience. Making her irritable.

She had tried to move on. The Ebola affair, linking up with Henry Middleton in Liberia, and the pair of them travelling into Sierra Leone and tracking down the terrorist cell—*by mistake*, she kept reminding herself—had brought welcome relief to the lowest point in her life. And Henry was a sweetheart. They had faced death and come out the other side. Together.

She had tried to love him.

Before taking up the post in SIS, Sam had travelled to New York to stay with Henry for a week. By the end of her trip they both knew it wasn't right. For her, he was *too* nice, however bizarre that sounded—it certainly sounded bizarre to her. He was great to be with, but she couldn't connect— and she guessed that prevented him from doing the same. Maybe Chris's memory was still too strong. Or maybe she was just messed up. That was probably closer to the truth.

Even if she wanted to, she couldn't get out of the psychiatrist sessions. Not until Latimer had given David Jennings, Jane's boss, the all-clear. One of the caveats of her taking the analyst's job was that, weekly, she continued to see a shrink—and that David was given full access to the doctor's reports. She knew she was seen as a risk. And she knew that David had been brave to offer her a job on the

43

team. So it was job *plus* shrink, or no job at all.

Her wistfulness was interrupted. Frank was faffing about with the remote control to the TV that was on the wall behind them. It broadcast Sky News continuously. He was gaping up at the screen, his mouth slightly open. The volume now raised.

"Not again," he said to himself.

Sam swivelled around in her chair and leaned back so she didn't have to strain her neck to see the screen. *Which idiot put it that high up on the wall?*

She looked, took some of it in, and then her mind went blank. Totally. All she could do was watch the pictures and let the unrecognisable words enter into her head via her ears. In a few seconds of news broadcast she had turned from reasonably high-flying SIS analyst to a person-shaped machine capable of some functions, but not all of them. Reason currently wasn't on the list of functioning facets.

"It's shocking that we seem to have lost another passenger aircraft on a routine flight. The Fly Europe 737 was halfway between Rome and Munich when it came down in the Alps." The image was a jittery mobile phone clip taken from the centre of an alpine village, black smoke rising from the seat of fire on a nearby hillside. Wooden chocolate-box chalets put the size of the devastation into some sort of context. They were dwarfed by the smoke and flames.

"It's not clear if the plane hit any buildings, but, as you can see from the footage, there is habitation very close to the crash site."

Sam was now fully tuned out. Without taking her eyes off the screen, she reached into her pocket and dug out her mobile. She quickly glanced down, swiped her thumb to unlock her phone, and then searched her mail. She was looking for Uncle Pete's itinerary.

She really didn't need to look. She remembered everything. That was her training. She looked at something—she remembered it. Now she was checking for checking's sake. To confirm her only surviving relative's—

certainly the only one she spoke to—Peter Green's, travel itinerary. Checking that today he was catching a flight from Rome to Munich. He'd done the Trevi Fountain and the Colosseum. Now he wanted to see the Chitty Chitty Bang Bang castle at Neuschwanstein. He had e-mailed her yesterday. Rome to Frankfurt with Fly Europe. "Cheap and cheerful," he had reported in his e-mail.

She opened her mailbox.

There it was. Flight number, times, hotel details. Everything. It all matched with the ensuing madness on the screen.

Horrified to the point of numbness, she looked back up at the screen again. She heard, "no survivors" and "no indication yet of terrorist activity." And then it was all noise and the same short video footage being played over and over again. A blur to her. A repetitive nightmare.

She felt sick. The same sort of sickness she had felt when her mother died unexpectedly. Not throwing-up sick. Just really, really queasy.

And then the sickly feeling, which had started in the pit of her stomach, rose quickly upward. By the time it reached her head it had turned to anger. No, that wasn't strong enough. *It was rage.*

She didn't know what to do. She needed space. She needed to get out of the office. If she stayed where she was a second longer, she wouldn't be able to hold it together. Her eyes darted round the room, onto her desk. Everything was a weapon. A pen. A stapler. Her chair. Everything at this exact moment could be used to hurt somebody. Herself. Even Frank—*God no!*

She had to get out.

I have to get out!

Sam sprung up and ran from the office, diving to her right into the ladies' cloakroom.

Cubicles on the left. Sinks with mirrors on the right. She was panting. Rabid. Her eyes were out on stalks, her hands trembling.

Sam tried to stop herself. To be rational. To stare into one of the mirrors and talk herself through it. Her mum, her dad—and his slow decline and then death to dementia. And now Uncle Pete.

With that thought, she lost it. She turned to face the first cubicle. It was closed. "Under repair."

Fuck you! She thumped it with all her might. A proper boxer's punch. The door bounced, but it didn't give. *Shit—my hand hurts like hell!*

But it didn't hurt enough.

Smack! Smack! The door was still holding out manfully, but a fist-shaped indent was now evident.

Smack again! Noise and pain. Pain and noise.

Sam realised that tears were rolling down her face. She wiped them away with her still-clenched fist and tasted blood. She looked down. Her right hand was a red mess. She moved her fingers. *They were still working. Good.*

Take that!

Smack! She hit the door once more; this time the lock gave, and the door, thankful for any respite, bounced open to reveal the white porcelain pan.

Sam was shocked to find the door giving way. She took a step back. Snorted, snot dripping from her nose, mingling with the blood and tears. She looked down again at her hand. She moved her fingers. One didn't work. *That's not good.* She looked up again, focusing on the pan. Just now she was either going to kick it or throw up in it.

Her stomach made the decision for her. She bent down at the same time as she spewed. She fell into the cubicle. Some of the vomit made it into the pan. Much of it splattered everywhere. She was on her knees now. Heaving. The lining of her stomach fighting to make it through her oesophagus.

"Sam! Sam?" It was a voice of someone she recognised. It was difficult to tell with the thumping going on in her head, the sound reverberating around the pan.

Could it be Jane?

Sam turned and, through drenched eyes, made out Jane

standing just outside the cubicle.

The sight of a familiar face, a kind face, someone who had saved her life in Sierra Leone and now looked after her like a caring mother, was too much for Sam. She broke down, sobbing with a pathetic whine that dribbled from her throat. She raised both arms like a child who had found a parent after she'd been lost in a supermarket for an hour. Her right hand a splotchy red thing.

Jane reached down, her grey suit jacket touching the floor, mingling with the vomit. She was crying now—Sam had no idea why.

Jane met Sam's embrace, and then they were two people who became one mass of emotion.

"Sorry." It was all Sam could muster.

"Me too, Sam. Me too."

Sam had no idea why Jane was sorry. But she felt she truly was.

Chapter Four

Trooper Steve Bliss checked his handheld Garmin GPS. He had covered just over thirty kilometres in six hours. It was tough. Leaving aside the heat, which was debilitating, the terrain was rocky and never flat. He was either scrambling uphill or sliding down. He started almost at a sprint—parkour does northern Yemen. Pushing off boulders and jumping small rocks. Even with just a daysack—he had left his bergen behind—he knew he was carrying fifteen kilos. But he hadn't let that slow him down. Yet.

After a further exchange of gunfire in the direction of the enemy's position, he had made a quick radio call to Jock, his radio signal rebounding through two remote rebroadcast stations that they had inserted on the way in. He told Jock he was on his way. And that the enemy was good—he hadn't seen them. He'd just crouched behind cover as rocks and dust were thrown up by a hail of bullets. He'd managed to return fire, but only in the general direction. Jock told him that a team had already left, heading north in his direction. They had the GPS position of his beacon and would meet him somewhere en route. Then they'd have a discussion about what to do next. What to do about Tony, Sandy, and Ted.

He had slowed after about thirty minutes. As taught, he tried to put himself in the mind of the enemy. *What would they do?* If they came after him, and he assumed they would, how would they do that? He had been instructed on the terrorists' modus operandi (MO), but something nagged at him. The four of them had been taken completely by surprise. Result: three out of the team were down. And he was running for his life. That was something else.

Steve thought they would move quickly to a vantage

point and see if they could spot him—try to establish a direction of travel. So he had initially moved east for about four hundred metres, until he had put at least two small ridges between himself and the enemy. Then, just off the crest line, he had run in a southerly direction toward the Hub where Jock was, his weapon hanging loosely in his left hand, leaving his right arm free to steady himself against the slope and to push off boulders.

He had told himself that he wouldn't stop until he had been going flat out for six hours. Only then would he take stock. He didn't use the radio in case the enemy was listening. He'd almost turned off his beacon in case that was being monitored. Before insertion, they had been told that both the beacon and the radio were secure, that they couldn't be intercepted. But something felt different about this enemy. Perhaps it was the two non-Arabs whom Tony had spoken of last night, when he had briefed them on today's plan. A plan that didn't include three of them being shot and the fourth running away like a frightened rabbit from a fox.

He rested in the shade of an overhang, drenched with sweat and needing fluid. *Lots of it.* There were two litres of water in his daysack, much less than he would have lost since leaving the contact point. But he had to be disciplined. While sitting there, he did some simple maths, calculations he was incapable of doing as he jogged along. The Hub was seventy-five clicks to the south. He had travelled almost half the distance. The team Jock had dispatched would be following his beacon, making adjustments, and trying to intercept him. They would be travelling slower, carrying overnight kits, much more ammunition—*I must check how much I have left*—and provisions. It would be about two hours before they'd meet up.

The sun had moved since he had sat in the shade. Its heat burned through the toe of his boot, which was now out of shadow. He twisted his foot and pulled it into cover. A bag of nuts and raisins filled a hole, and he drank half a litre of water.

Tiredness stalked him, his whole body aching from the morning's exertion. He closed his eyes and tried to rehearse what he had been through—to try to give Jock something to go on when he got the chance. He went over the attack, the initial shots, the contact report from Ted. Then Sandy and Tony down, the further exchange, and finally the extraction. Steve was surprised to find that he wasn't at all emotional.

He'd felt nothing when he saw Tony fall. There was no overwhelming sense of grief, just lots of stuff going on in his head—all manner of information—which he had to process. He should feel something, some sense of loss—or even fear. Nothing came. *Maybe later?*

Steve opened his eyes. He had to get going. And he mustn't assume that they weren't following him. Although, unless they were on a mountain or trail bike, there were few people who could keep up with him on foot. He was among the fittest in a squadron of very fit lads.

Just one more minute.

As he stared out across the shallow wadi to the rocky face opposite, he listened for nondesert noises. Vehicles. Perhaps a helicopter? At one point, he thought Jock might call in the quick reaction force (QRF) in the Merlins, but he knew that they wouldn't fly forward without someone on the ground directing them. And the only person who could have done that would have been him. But not now. He was long gone. Might Jock perhaps ask for an air extraction? Or would the QRF fly into the terrorist camp and kick arse anyway? He was neither a strategist nor a tactical genius. At twenty-five and one of the youngest members of the squadron, he was still on his year's probation. So he didn't have the experience either; this was just his second deployment. But even he knew that without "eyes on," nobody flew into an enemy position blind.

That was if the camp was still even there. They'd probably have buggered off by now. He certainly would have.

"Come on, fella," he said to himself. He crouched, threw

his daysack on his back, and picked up his rifle. After a quick check of his compass and a scout to see if the ground looked any different, he ran out onto the hillside. Back into the blistering sun.

Jane led Sam into David's office. She thought Sam had cleaned up well. Apart from the bandage on her hand and her bloodshot, baggy eyes, she looked presentable. Jane had sent her straight home after the incident in the cloakroom, not even bothering to press Sam for reasons. She knew Sam well enough to give her space. After they had clung to each other for what seemed like an hour—it was nowhere near, but it was long enough for three women to come in, see that their presence was probably not helpful, and then go upstairs to use another loo—Sam had got up, brushed herself off, and asked Jane meekly, "What happens now?"

"If you're feeling slightly more contained, let's go to the medical centre to sort out your hand. Then you should probably go home. I'll give you a ring later, and we can talk this through. I'll speak with Doctor Latimer, but I'm hoping his advice is for you to come back to work tomorrow and settle back into some sort of routine." Jane paused for a second and then added, "You understand that I will need to tell David?"

Sam nodded whilst washing her face, flinching whenever she used her right hand. They walked down the corridor, and, with no explanation sought, the nurse had checked visually for breaks, cleaned up the cuts, bandaged her hand up to the wrist, and told Sam to pop along to A&E to have an X-ray. "To be on the safe side."

Jane accompanied Sam back to her desk and then to the front entrance. They still hadn't discussed why Sam had done what she had done. Jane knew that she would pick that up, either on the telephone later or in the margins elsewhere.

She was a spy, after all.

"So, Sam,"—David had ushered them in to sit on the sofa in his office—"Jane has told me about your uncle. I am so very sorry." He seemed to leave the sentence hanging, waiting for an answer.

Jane looked across at Sam. She was staring down at her hands, fiddling with an imaginary set of beads or something similar.

David coughed. "Are you fit enough for work, Sam? Do you need some time off?"

Sam looked up now, directly at David. She stopped moving her hands.

"Why were there twenty-five photos taken from the cloud the day before yesterday? This morning Jane said she had removed them and couldn't amplify on why that was the case. I'd like to know why." Complete clarity. No emotion.

David looked at Jane. She, sensing his surprise at where this was going, gently raised her eyebrows and leaned her head on one side. *Beats me . . .*

"Because, erm . . . look, it's complicated, and sometimes we don't share all our information with all of our staff. You know that." His voice raised perceptibly. David was affronted, confused—neither of which he could disguise in the tone of his reply.

No, you've got the wrong voice, David, thought Jane. *Sam's not stupid.* She knows something is up. Something that impacts on her, or one of the team of analysts.

Sam began to say something and Jane interrupted.

"I think, if you don't mind, David, we should get this all out in the open. Especially after last night's news from Yemen." In the four years Jane had worked for David, her confidence had grown. She knew she was in credit, and she often pressed David to change direction, not that he always did.

Just now, Sam was close to being irrecoverably broken after the death of her uncle. The news that Manning and Bell were alive and operating among Islamic terrorists would exacerbate her disposition. But Jane's view was to get all of this bad news out there *now*. Let Sam reconcile everything. *All of it.* And *then* work out if she were fit enough for work. With three members of the SRR either dead or in captivity somewhere in lawless Yemen, they needed their best analysts working on the case in London—while those on the ground sought out and sent home the clues. Sam was the best they had. If she were fit, they needed her.

David scratched at his bald patch, looked over his shoulder to the window, and then started. "Yesterday the SRR OP in northern Yemen was compromised. Only one man got out. The other three are either dead or being held. The soldier who got out, Trooper Steve Bliss, made contact with the insertion group, and they have all made it back over the Saudi border and are safe." He shuffled in his chair, leaning forward.

"Satellite images taken six hours ago has shown that there is nothing left of the training camp. You saw the original pictures?"

Clever of David to engage Sam, make sure she's on message.

But there was no answer, just an imperceptible nod.

"Sam! Answer me . . . please." The *please* was softer, but his initial retort demonstrated David's frustration. He could have sent Sam home indefinitely, pending a psychiatric and disciplinary report. Instead Jane saw that he was trying hard. Working to reengage one of the best analysts in the building. Anchor her down, to save her from herself.

He leaned back and held his hands up, an open stance.

"Sorry, sir. Sorry." A quick and heartfelt response from Sam. She was listening.

"Good . . . thanks." He was leaning forward again now. "Just before the compromise, the OP leader took photos of two new arrivals at the camp." He paused, waiting. Waiting for something. Jane didn't know what. "The men were Kurt Manning and Ralph Bell." He didn't stop for a reaction. "The MO of the attack on the OP was very un-terrorist. It showed all the signs of a professional hit. We think that the two either coordinated or carried out the attack."

He stopped now—letting all of it sink in. Jane looked at Sam. Her facial expression hadn't changed; she just stared straight ahead at David. She was either incredibly focused and calm or had tuned out completely.

The pause hung in the air. The outcome unknown. Jane was ready to hold Sam down if she tried to run out of the office. She was trained to do that—*although a little bit on the rusty side.*

Sam didn't flinch.

Nothing.

Then, almost at a gabble, "I'd like three days off please. I need to take with me one of those Nexus tablets that your field agents have. The ones that enable them to access secure information away from the office. Particularly for me: the cloud e-mails and those photographs, which I need you to 'Unhide.'" Sam stopped for a second, almost gathering breath. She stole a quick glance at Jane.

"I'd like to go now, or after any further briefings you have." Then Sam added, "Sir."

David smiled. It was a smile of bemused incredulity, rather than acceptance or acknowledgement that Sam's request was in any way acceptable.

Jane led, "Why, Sam?"

Sam turned sharply to Jane and gave a grimace of a smile.

"I can't thank you enough for being there for me yesterday. As we discussed on the phone, I have nothing left. Nobody other than my work colleagues who I can turn to." Jane saw Sam welling up, but womanfully holding it all together. She smiled at Sam—her best motherly smile.

Sam looked back at David. "I need to go to the crash site to see where my Uncle Peter died. I need to do that *now*. I hope you can understand. But I also need to work. I probably know Manning and Bell better than anyone, having been stalked and then taken by them in West Africa. I know the ground well, having studied thousands of photos of Yemen. And I have a good grip of both the Al-Qaeda and Daesh hierarchy in the Saudi peninsula." It was all matter of fact, almost rehearsed, but delivered at machine gun pace. She hadn't slowed down, her sentences melding into one. "And I can do both. Together." A pause. "Sir."

David breathed out. Jane could see his cogs turning. He stood up and walked to the window, his favourite place for thinking. She imagined that he was looking down over the White Water Horses sculpture just up from the building, emerging from the river as the tide slid out into the North Sea.

Without turning around, David replied, "What about yesterday? The breakdown. It is the elephant in the room." He turned, facing them both. "I can't just pretend that didn't happen."

That was tough. But fair.

Sam was looking back down at her knees. She had closed her eyes.

"Sir." *A good start,* Jane thought. "You need all the help you can get just now." Sam was now looking up again, glancing between both her and David. Her animation adding expression to her words. "Do an investigation, as you must. Get Doctor Latimer to review me again for suitability for employment. Sack me if you have to. But first let's find those two bastards, and, please"—she brought both her hands together—". . . give me a couple of days to get this thing right in my head."

David had walked to behind his desk and leaned with both hands on the top of his chair. There was another long pause. Nobody said anything. David looked at Sam, across to Jane, and then back to Sam. *God, this is all very dramatic.*

"There's a team brief in"—he looked up at the Vienna-style wall clock—" fifteen minutes. Analysts don't normally come to those, as you know; Jane represents you. But I'd like you to come." He looked across to Jane. "After get Sam a Nexus tablet and a secure phone. Make sure I have her number." He looked back to Sam. "You have seventy-two hours, which I'm prepared to extend by a further twenty-four if you need it. But in the meantime, it's fifty-fifty. Work and convalescence."

He stopped and turned off his incisive voice. Softer now. "I'm sorry to be so direct, Sam, but we need to be clear. If you break down again, I'm going to have to ask for your pass. Is that understood?"

Sam was on her feet, catching Jane off guard, who rose just after her.

"Understood, sir. I won't let you down."

Let's not count any chickens, Jane thought. *There's a lot of stuff going on in that head of yours, Sam. Not all of it helpful. I hope you can keep it together.*

Cafe Schinkelwache, Theatreplatz, Dresden, Germany

Wolfgang was convinced that the latest air crash fitted into the Lattice somewhere. He knew it would take him a good chunk of time, considerable effort, and probably some travel to sort it out. But the truth would be out there. He had read all of the newspaper articles that he could find online— certainly anything in English, French, and Spanish, the languages he spoke fluently. He had scoured the Internet for TV clips and video shorts. It was early days, but he was confident that this was all part of the pattern. It had to be.

He took a sip of his very decent coffee, served in a delicate china cup and matching saucer. He looked around the cafe, opulent in deep oak, etched mirrors, and rather odd but bright art, suspicious that someone might be paying attention to him. In his more aware moments, such as when his mobile rang and nobody was on the other end, he thought the Federal Intelligence Service (BfV) was on to him. None of his work—*well, almost none*—broke any law. He was just doing his own investigations, that's all. Looking for patterns. Trying to piece together a series of events that, if he were right, was the worst atrocity since his country executed the Holocaust. He thought "execute" and "Holocaust" knitted together really well.

He might only be twenty-eight, but Wolfgang had fitted a lot into his short, but privileged life. Like visiting Dachau, Bergen-Belsen, and Auschwitz, trips that sucked out any sense of decency you thought you might have. They unquestionably made him see the worst of humanity. It was all murder on an industrial scale, committed by men like himself. He didn't necessarily think it showed a predilection for Germans to follow orders, no matter how inhumane— although some of that was true. He had met enough central Europeans and some British whom he thought capable of being party to mass murder. But it was definitely men, not women, who had that one loose wire somewhere that enabled them to commit any crime if it was disguised as an order. *An edict from hell.*

He sipped some more coffee and opened up the cover on his iPad. He typed in his passcode and noticed immediately that it was connected to the cafe's WiFi. That was good and bad. Good that his machine was somewhat disguised by communicating through the cafe's router. But bad in that someone in the cafe might be watching him. Checking on what he was doing, making notes just as he was. He knew his iPad had none of the encryption his tower had back in his flat, so he was always doubly careful.

Of course he'd have to go to the crash site. He needed to feel the pain of those who had lost their lives. It wouldn't necessarily be as intense as Belsen, where the gardens were soundless—even now no birds could bring themselves to visit. Or as grotesque as Auschwitz, with some of the chicken sheds still standing. Sheds where thousands of pyjama-wearing inmates were housed—working to their death, or until they were just infirm enough to stagger to the gas chambers, where death was often a welcome visitor.

No, he felt sure that the crash site, incongruously nestled among the chalets of the Abondance Valley, would lack the depth of depravity of the Nazi death camps. But, as he had felt before, there would be a modern-day rawness, mixed with a media-fuelled explosion of grief, which would allow him to place this latest "accident" into context. A context he was convinced was as diabolical as the mass murder carried out three-quarters of a century ago.

If I am right about the Lattice.

Some people called him a crank. A rich kid with nothing better to do than while away his inheritance, chasing incomprehensible theories. Theories that cast shadows wider than international boundaries, that were darker than the deepest conspiracy. The few friends he had, following his three years at music college in the UK, had drifted away. They were now all playing in orchestras in Paris and Vienna or teaching their instruments to kids who often didn't want to learn.

He had come away from the Royal College of Music, or "College," as it was colloquially known, with a First and was immediately offered a postgrad slot—*if he brought his violin with him.* But his father had died during that fateful summer, and whilst one outcome was an inherited new title, a second was that his world fell apart. Count Wolfgang of Neuenburg had a ring to it. But the associated cost had been almost unbearable.

He loved his mother; that was true. She had dealt with her husband's death stoically, more prosaically, like the ageing countess she was. And Wolfgang drew some strength from that. But he adored his father. He was a man of great intellect, of huge talent—his violin playing was masterly against Wolfgang's—and of the widest compassion. Everyone who had ever met his father had loved him.

None more so than Wolfgang.

Anyway, *enough of that.* He was staring into space whilst he should have been researching. His finger hovered over the glass keyboard. *Would his father be proud?* Proud that he hadn't taken his music to the next level? Proud that he'd shaken off the shackles of privilege, hired a shabby bedsit in

Dresden, and devoted his young life to chasing metaphorical hurricanes across the prairies of humanity? OK, so his choice of metaphors wasn't necessarily anything to brag about, but that's what you get from a student of classical music—he was better with a musical score.

When he really thought about it, he reckoned Papa would be gently nodding approval as he looked down from his throne—he would definitely have one of those up there. Nodding kindly at his friendless son who was trying to piece together a bit of modern-day history that nobody else—as far as he knew—was anywhere close to reconciling.

Dover Docks, Dover, England

Sam scrolled through the images on the Nexus secure tablet that Jane had issued to her earlier in the day. It was WiFi enabled, and, after a lot of clicking and whirring, it had established a secure connection with the SIS portal, which gave Sam access to all of the photos on the cloud. Plus, all of the material shared among David Jennings's staff. She knew she was in a privileged position. None of the other four analysts from Jane's team had been at the meeting earlier in the day. And none had her level of access to all of the intelligence.

David had explained to his people at the briefing that Sam was one of two analysts—the other was Frank—who would now be exclusively assigned to Operation Glasshouse, the title given to the search for the three members of the SRR team taken by terrorists in northern Yemen. Their role was to unearth clues in previous and new images to establish where the soldiers might have been taken. The fact that Sam was crossing the Channel and mixing work with rehabilitation was not mentioned.

She stopped for a second and closed her eyes. As she did, the pain in her right hand congealed with the horror of reliving Uncle Pete's last few moments. Without restraint, she gently sobbed. She found crying so much easier nowadays.

He was just sixty-two. Recently made redundant from a local factory, Uncle Pete was spending some of that money on a holiday of a lifetime. He'd told Sam just before he left, somewhat prophetically, "I don't know if I'll be here tomorrow—I can't take it with me!"

She held her eyes closed and couldn't stop herself from nodding gently as tears ran down her cheeks and dripped onto her jeans.

The anger, *the fury*, was gone. Left was a pathetic mass of jumbled nerves and an enveloping sense of grief. It was all so unfair. A man who had worked tirelessly all his life, for not a great deal, had decided to spend a couple of grand on the holiday of his dreams, only to have everything snatched away from him. Just as he was probably at his most content—she could see him on the plane, talking excitedly with some hapless neighbour—death about to steal the very essence of his joy.

All because? Well? *Because of what?*

She wanted to call it an accident, but these things were never accidental. Someone, somewhere, had made a decision that had sent her uncle's aircraft crashing to the valley floor. She was not a vindictive person, nor was she ever particularly interested in establishing fault. It always seemed a futile exercise, when what everyone needed to do was clear up the mess and look forward.

Until now.

Now she wanted answers. Not answers to satisfy a vengeful curiosity. Answers so that she could put her uncle to sleep, both for his sake and for hers. She knew if she couldn't find out why, his death would join the events of Camp Bastion as gate crashers to her dreams. Both whilst asleep and sometimes in the starkness of the day. An ever-present reminder of the truly rubbish things that dogged her life.

She wiped her eyes clumsily with her bandaged right

hand, and with her left she swiped at a photo on her iPad, which exposed another. It was taken by Captain Tony James. She had found his name in the briefing material; he had a wife and a daughter—*I wonder if they know?* They had assumed that he was either dead or in captivity. The photos were good. Crisp and relevant. She was looking for vehicles and the camp accoutrements. Trying to match what she saw with previously shot images in other locations. Places to which the terrorists might return. A tear dropped on the screen, amplifying the pixels as if looking through a tiny fish-eye lens.

She dabbed it off with her bandaged hand.

This was what she was best at. The detail of photographs, looking for the absence of the normal—not necessarily looking for things that were out of place, more likely things that should be there, but weren't.

Sam had an outstanding memory, which continued to surprise her when there was so much fog obscuring everyday life. She could recall details from thousands of photographs and access them from the cloud, even if they had been deposited in the most unlikely places. She was particularly good at the nuances of an image. Small things: a badge here, a change of hairstyle there. Her military training had honed her skill, but her instructor at Chicksands had put her forensic ability, to dissect, compartmentalise, and then recall photos, down to a form of autism. "You're not normal, Green, you know that?" She guessed she could have reported him for some form of abuse, but he did have a nice bum, which suited his tight-fitting combat trousers. So she forgave him for his gentle daily insults, taking them as backhanded compliments instead. He was just a man, after all.

She spread the photo with her left thumb and index finger—her bandaged right hand as useful as a Plasticine teapot. The zoom picked out the front end of one of the white twin-cabs in the camp. She looked for dents and other marks. She swiped slowly left and found a green trailer. She dwelt on that for a bit. She did the same for the black Toyota

Hilux that Manning and Bell had turned up in. Moving right, she zoomed in further on the two Westerners and the two Arab-looking men they were talking to. Pretty clear. She hovered there for a second, making mental notes. She swiped back out again, until she had the whole photo. She studied it for a second, then moved on.

Her concentration was broken. A man with a high-viz jacket was knocking on the driver's window of her van. He pointed to the vehicle in front, which was moving in the direction of the ferry. Apologising with a nod, she closed her tablet, swivelled around in her chair, started Bertie—her four-year-old, bright yellow VW T5 camper and the only constant in her life—and, with a twist of the ignition key, followed the van ahead onto the ferry.

Chapter Five

No. 2, Block 12, Pillnitzer Strasse, Dresden, Germany

Wolfgang took his small black suitcase down from the top of the wardrobe. He had just booked a Lufthansa flight from Berlin to Geneva, leaving later in the afternoon, and a hire car to take him into the French Alps, up to the Abondance valley. He would bother with accommodation when he got there.

As a fairly serious environmentalist, he should probably be travelling by train or rental car—he didn't own a car—but, as the aircraft was flying anyway, he might as well jump on board. It was a poor excuse, and he knew that he needed to work harder on his green credentials. He found it difficult when his wealthy background hardly set him up for an eco-friendly lifestyle.

He packed meticulously, layering each of his neatly ironed clothes on top of each other so that nothing creased. His toiletries were next, carefully laid down in the checked Burberry waterproof bag that his mother had bought him last year. And then, finally, a pair of well-buffed brown English brogues, which he double-wrapped in the cloth he had recently cleaned them with. As footwear, they should be at the bottom of the suitcase, but they were his favourites, and, as everyone knows, suitcases have a knack of travelling in whichever orientation they damn well please after they disappear down the airport's grey conveyor belt.

He gave himself a once-over in the full-length mirror in his bedroom: tall, a bit gangly; a narrow-striped Pinks shirt; a deep red, long-sleeved cardigan with leather buttons; a pair of medium-green Ceruti chinos; and his Timberlands. Ordinarily he would have worn a pair of loafers, but they wouldn't do for wandering around the crash site.

Yes, he was particular with the way he dressed. He could

afford the finest clothes; at the Munich family home, he had wardrobes and drawers full of the very best from Milan to New York. Since he had taken up residence in Dresden, he had downsized to a single wardrobe and a chest of drawers. He still wanted to look his best, but he was also keen not to be too showy, not to stand out from the crowd. Dresden, certainly central Dresden, was old-fashionedly upmarket, so he had chosen his clothes appropriately. He could easily blend in with the local *menschen* in the restaurants, cafes, and even at the opera. After all, he had brought his white tie with him.

He had no idea where he had got his fascination for clothes from. His mother had always made a particular effort to dress him—maybe it was that he had never had a sister, and she felt the need to clothe him like she would a daughter. At one point, one of his College friends implied that he might be gay: "You spend far too much time choosing the right shoes. That can't be straight." But, as far as he knew, he wasn't gay, although he wasn't sure. He'd steered clear of all relationships. There had been a number of offers from both men and women, but none of them had stirred anything inside him.

With a touch of royal blood and the interbreeding that was associated with the realm, he thought maybe he was just a little odd. *Clothes—good; relationships—bad?* It had probably always been that way with the Neuenburgs. He should really ask one of his many cousins next time he met up with them.

He looked at his watch. He had thirty minutes before the taxi arrived to take him to Berlin's Schönefeld airport for the late-afternoon flight. He needed to set up his computer tower to do some work for him whilst he was away.

Wolfgang closed the suitcase, checked for his wallet, which, as well as cash and cards, held his photo ID. He reached for his passport from the bedside drawer. He put them all in the small over-the-shoulder "man bag," grabbed his suitcase, and placed both in the centre of his lounge, a room dominated by a single room-height sash window. Second in prominence and set against an adjoining wall was an old mahogany desk. On top of that was a thirty-two-inch LED screen connected to a home-assembled top-of-the-range computer tower.

Wolfgang started the machine, and within a few seconds the screen was up, displaying the desktop that he had designed. He was a concert-standard violinist—he still practised at least two hours a day when he wasn't travelling—and, if there were an equivalent grading in computer coding, he'd be concert standard at that as well. *Music, maths; maths, coding.* They were all interlinked. If you have an aptitude for one, you could do the other. He loved maths. Equations and trigonometry had the same beauty as an orchestral score. Coding, therefore, was something that came naturally to him.

He didn't start to piece the computer skills together until his music degree dissertation: "Programming a Symphony." For which he was awarded a graduation prize. He was sure his tutor didn't get it, but Wolfgang knew it was a good, if slightly clunky, piece of work. Write the violin melody and his programme would deliver complementary viola, cello and bass lines. It wasn't genius. But it was his.

He had learned how to code in C++ and was soon pretty adept with all Unix systems. As a bit of fun, he had hacked the College's computer system using a simple hashing algorithm that he had designed. Once inside, he rewrote some of the code to leave a "back door" for him to get in at any time he wanted. He never used the access to alter his grades—he didn't need to—nor to spy on anyone in the College. It was just inquisitiveness that made him do it.

Since leaving London, and only when he had a need, he used his newly acquired skills to open a few computers' doors for him. For example, he wanted to know the details of everyone who had been on Flight FY378. He could have waited for the details to be released to the press, *but he wanted them now.* He had pinged all of the mainframe ports of Fly Europe using a Rainbow Table—a highly powerful password-cracker running on the tower's graphics card. Within half an hour, he had access to all of the airway's data. He'd not yet had chance to look at the list. He would study it on the flight—the irony wasn't lost on him.

He drummed his fingers on the desk as he thought. Then, skilfully touch-typing, he wrote a couple of lines of Python script, another of the hacker's best friends. The code would set up the tower to ping a number of gateways around the world where he had spotted activity that might be of interest to him. He checked the lines of code, verified their destinations, and pressed "Enter." The tower would run in his absence and e-mail an alert to him if it found anything of interest. He turned off the screen.

Wolfgang brushed a fleck of dust from his cardigan as he stood up. He took his iPad and phone and slipped them into a nondescript neoprene case. One last look in the mirror and he would be ready to go.

He stopped himself, just for a second. He knew he was fussy, particular even. But he wasn't vain. He studied his face. It was hardly regal, maybe slightly Teutonic? He wasn't a good-looking man, but he had been taught to hold himself well, and he was always impeccably well mannered. He smiled a half smile and saw that his reflection did the same. Then it adopted its usual earnest, concerned look.

That's right, Count Wolfgang. When you smile, you may even be considered handsome. He dismissed the thought.

The "Count" bit would have to wait. As for smiling, he'd afford himself that luxury once he'd pieced the Lattice together in a plausible way. Currently, it was just "threads of unbelievable" sewn together by him to make a very unpalatable and threadbare quilt. *There you go again— rubbishy metaphors.*

In a moment of royal pomposity he'd given his incomplete work a title and afforded it a capital *L. Lattice. Yes, I like that.* So much better than *Matrix*, where all he could think of were hundreds of black-suited Mr. Andersons giving Keanu Reeves an unnecessarily hard time.

He looked at his watch. It was just past midday. *Come on, Wolfgang, move along.*

David waited for the members of the Operation Glasshouse team to make their way into his office and find a seat at his small conference table. He expected six of them: Jane—who ran the image analysts; Tim and Justin—who liaised with the Middle Eastern in-country team; Mike—his GCHQ rep; and Sue—who drew and shared information from Defence Intelligence (DI) and linked directly to the Special Forces (SF) when that conduit was open, as it was now. *Oh, and Claire.* His PA, who sat to one side and took a record of the decisions made at the meeting. It was a hastily pulled-together, bespoke team with a simple mandate: find the SRR three.

He looked up at the clock. It was five thirty, the lowering sun throwing autumn shadows across the room.

Time to kick off.

"OK everyone, quiet down. First, Jane, anything on the news—anywhere?"

"Nothing, David. Not a squeak. It's been"—she looked at her watch—"almost forty hours since the incident and nothing on the airways." She raised her shoulders in mock defeat.

"This is the biggest media event Daesh—hang on . . ." He had been looking directly at Jane, but now, with wide arms, he addressed the whole team. "Does anyone know if the attack is attributed to Daesh or Al-Qaeda? Anyone?"

The team collectively shook their heads.

"Mike—nothing from GCHQ?"

Mike looked at his tablet and then back at David. "Nothing from SIGINT we wouldn't expect from the region at this time."

"So, the first time we will know who carried out the attack is when they go live on Al Jazeera?—Jane?"

"That looks like it might be the case, David, yes. Sorry." She raised her shoulders again. *Everything was getting the better of her today.*

It all made him feel incredibly impatient. Those on the Joint Intelligence Committee (JIC) were advising the Cabinet Office Briefing Room (COBR) not to go public with the details of the attack until they knew more than what they knew now. Which wouldn't be difficult, as what they knew now was almost nothing.

It seemed like madness to him to wait for the terrorists to go live, then have the intelligence community comment, all "unknowing and apologetic." They would appear wholly inept. Better to beat the bastards to the front page. Admit that three of the very best soldiers, who had been working beyond the front line to safeguard the country, were now either dead or taken by an as yet unknown terrorist organisation. He had made his point at the last COBR meeting, but was beaten down. With only weeks left on the job, he almost felt up to a discreet leak to a broadsheet. But then again, he really did value his pension.

"OK. Around the room. Anything to add to your reports? Jane?"

"Working only from old photos and her knowledge of the area, Sam Green has identified three locations in Yemen and two in Saudi where we might want to start looking."

"Have you shared those with Tim and Justin?" David knew that his impatience was getting the better of his judgement at that point. Of course Jane would share her intelligence with the members of the team who could then direct agents in the country. He regretted it as soon as he said it.

"Yes, David, about an hour ago." Jane looked across at Tim and Justin. She hadn't flinched at his unnecessary question. *Bless her.*

"Yes, we have that." Tim led. "Two of the three Yemen

locations are urban, and we think we can get eyes on with some locals within the next forty-eight hours. Our Sana'a team has the instructions already. The third is trickier. It's a village location at Hajjah, in the midwest of Yemen and reasonably inaccessible."

David interrupted. "What's the rationale behind that choice, Jane?"

"Sam, and Frank and I agree, has this location as Ali Abdullah Sahef's headquarters. He's the deputy of Daesh in Yemen. It's a good choice to start looking, if we can get someone up there."

"And can we?" David put the question to the whole group.

Justin half raised his hand. "Not quickly, and not without risk to the agent/informer who might be tasked by our in-country team. I have posed the question, but I reckon we might be days away from anything concrete."

"What about satellite photography and signals intercept?"

Jane led. "I've arranged a call to my oppo in Langley for an hour's time. We'll get what we can. They, as I said in my report, have nothing on the attack, or where the three have been taken."

"Mike? GCHQ?"

Mike shuffled in his seat.

"I've passed the details of the Yemeni locations to the Doughnut, and they are currently tasking Cyprus to see if they can pick up anything. They have the Saudi locations as well." Mike kept his hands still; when finished speaking, he looked back down at his laptop.

"And, Sue, where are we with the Saudis?"

"DI is now liaising with the Defence Attaché in Riyadh. They reckon the Saudis should be able to get eyes on their two locations within thirty-six hours. It will probably be more of a blunt weapon, but it will be thorough. I've also spoken to our man in the embassy who will expedite things." SIS had to task Saudi forces through Defence Intelligence, although they had people on the top floor of the embassy who would always oil the wheels.

"Good." David looked down at his notes. "So, if I can summarise. We have three members of the SRR either dead or in captivity, held by either Al-Qaeda or Daesh. The three could be in Yemen or in Saudi. Or, by now, anywhere in the Middle East. And we are currently investigating five possible locations on the hunch of two junior analysts. We have nothing"—he looked up at all of them—"*nothing* new to add to the sum of all knowledge. And I reckon within twenty-four hours we are going to be the laughingstock of the world's intelligence communities because we will have no coherent response to a news clip showing our three lads in either crates or orange jumpsuits." He paused for effect.

"And, just to show you that I'm just as clueless as you are, I can tell you that officials at the CIA have nothing on the two Americans in the training camp: Bell and Manning. But, if I judged the tone of the telephone conversation correctly, they are very embarrassed by the pair of them. Especially as one of them was meant to be dead. Which he clearly isn't." He closed his tablet and gathered his papers. "It does mean that they are as keen to get to the bottom of this as we are. So that's at least one positive."

He paused again, looking round.

"Anything else to add?"

Nothing from the team.

"OK, let's meet again tomorrow morning at"—he looked across at Claire—"ten?" She nodded.

As they rose to leave, David motioned for Jane to stay behind.

He led her over to his desk.

"What do we think about Sam Green's work so far?"

Jane didn't reply straight away—she seemed to be lost in thought for a second.

"I think the five locations are inspired choices, myself. I'd forgotten about one of the urban Yemeni ones. Sam remembered it from a couple of photos taken of a Daesh truck driving into the compound in the capital Sana'a. She

70

was alerted by a particular image showing a man opening a pair of high wooden gates. She saw that the man carried an AK-47—whilst the rifle wasn't particularly unusual, it was fitted with a newish Russian sight."

Jane had put down her laptop on David's desk and was scrolling through a series of photos to find one to show David. "She'd seen the same weapon in the hands of possibly the same man—he was hooded so she couldn't be sure—in the background of a Daesh propaganda video released a few weeks later. The talking head on the video was Ali Abdullah Sahef. She made the connection between the rifle, the man, the location, and Sahef, then declared it a Daesh safe house."

"I see. Why haven't we targeted the safe house with more assets before now?"

"We tried, but our people were stretched on other tasks."

David nodded. "OK, good call by Sam. And is she holding up?" More aimed at gauging effectiveness rather than sympathy.

"Does she ever hold up—completely?" Jane's question was almost rhetorical.

"Good point."

David sighed. He reckoned it was just eleven weeks now, and then all this would be someone else's problem.

Abondance Village, Abondance Valley, French Alps

Sam had tucked Bertie away in the corner of a very large car park just a short distance from the centre of the town. She'd arrived as it was getting dark and was following her Internet directions to the French "Aire," a stopover exclusively assigned for "*les Camping Cars*." France has as much an affection for campers and motorhomes as the British despise them. As a result, almost every town in France has an Aire. Good news for people like Sam.

When Sam arrived she was met with a village-size circus

of media vans from what looked like every country known to man. The Aire was overflowing with TV crews, satellite dishes, and makeshift accommodation. Thankfully, the French gendarmerie had the sense to provide traffic police and, after questioning in poor English, and replying in unremarkable French, Sam had established herself as a relative and was shown to a spot out of the way of the media.

She'd left Bertie between two other larger motorhomes—*what are they doing here?*—and headed for the centre of the town. As she'd turned the corner, around one of many beautifully old, wooden chalets, she had to shield her eyes from a concentration of bright light illuminating a patch on the far side of the valley. She'd squinted her eyes and made out numerous powerful arc lights on tall towers, spotlighting a football-pitch-size blackened piece of earth about a kilometre away. Sticking out of the singed earth, she picked out segments of shiny metal and, in among the shards, little men in bright yellow jackets poking around.

The sight stopped Sam in her tracks. Mesmerised by it all, she felt her stomach start to churn as her mind ran over how she saw the last moments of Flight FY378. The last seconds of Uncle Pete's life. Retching, she had raised her hand to her mouth and dashed back around the corner of the chalet, throwing up in the shadows. That had been enough for last night.

This morning she felt slightly calmer. As she walked back through the media village to the main street, she tiptoed carefully over numerous thick black wires, as if she were attempting to escape a darkened snake pit. She avoided getting caught on camera, ducking out of the line of sight as a news crew reported its latest update to a station far away. As she weaved, she chomped at some biscuits she had brought with her—she had no appetite, but she knew she'd have to find something to eat later.

When it seemed that there were no more obstacles in her way, she looked down at what she was wearing: faded jeans, Dr. Martens, and an off-red Lowe Alpine fleece over a black

Status Quo T-shirt. She was hardly dressed funereally, but everything was clean. She'd even managed to wash her hair in Bertie's basin this morning. It was still a mess though—it was ever thus. In any case, Uncle Pete would be pleased that she'd bothered to come.

As she turned the dreaded corner, the blight on the landscape looked less stark, less unpleasant. In daylight she noticed that the site was cordoned off with blue and white police tape, which fluttered in the distance in harmony with a light wind, its movement catching her eye. She looked to her right and gave the main street a once-over, picking out a wooden-clad pizza joint in the near distance, just on the other side of a ski-hire shop. That would do for lunch—if her stomach were up to it. Nothing was appetising at the moment.

She was surprised at how unbusy the main street was. She'd expected it to be heaving with a mass of relatives, press, and, even this early on, "disaster tourists." Yes, it was busy, but not overly so.

Looking back to the crash site, Sam stopped and took stock. *Where now? And why?* It occurred to her that she had no plan. She knew that she had to come to see where Uncle Pete had died, but she had no idea what to do when she got here.

So, she had seen it. Could she go home now?

Not yet. There was something driving her on. Something that pushed her closer to the impact point. She knew she wouldn't discover any rationale here, no sense behind the disaster. Not now. Maybe later, when she got a chance to read any crash report that might be released to the public. At least then she'd be able to picture the scene in the context of the *why* behind the crash. In order to be able to do that, she wanted to get as close as she was allowed.

Absently, she attempted to cross the main street, but stopped herself just as an ambulance drove past, heading down the valley. No siren, but blue lights flashing. *Off to the morgue?*

On her second attempt, she crossed the road without being hit by a passing truck and made her way up a narrow, steep tarmac path that seemed to be leading to the blackened area of earth. She passed another gendarme, who was manning a barrier preventing vehicles from using the road. He didn't attempt to stop her. There were one or two official-looking people heading up and down the road wearing high-viz jackets and carrying safety helmets. And a number of nonofficials joining a small ant-line of people made their way to and from the crash site.

There was a commotion behind her. She turned and looked. It was a press team with camera and boom mike trying to get closer. The gendarme was holding firm. As all French police wore Kevlar vests and carried pistols, Sam knew who would win that battle. She allowed herself a little smile. Inwardly. Uncle Pete would be pleased that everyone was making such a fuss.

Just ahead was another small checkpoint, this time manned by the obligatory gendarme plus a man and a woman in nonsecurity uniform—grey suits with yellow shirts and blouses. Airline staff?

She stopped in line. There was a group of three ahead of her—a man, a woman, and a teenage girl. The girl turned to look at Sam. She seemed tired and red-eyed, no hint of a smile. Sam raised her hand a touch, an acknowledgement that she was a human being and capable of communication. The girl nodded in recognition and turned away. Her mum and dad were having an in-depth and slightly impassioned conversation with the airline staff, as they pored over a clipboard. Eventually, in what Sam thought was probably Italian, they agreed to something from the list. The female airline member of staff wore her most regretful face. She half curtseyed—*what is that about?*—as she pointed behind her, where Sam had noticed a piece of ground, fenced off with more police tape. It looked like a holding or viewing area. There were seven or eight people already there, and Sam thought there were possibly a couple more in a smart white tent, which was set off to one side.

Relatives' hospitality. Nice touch. Uncle Pete liked his pain au chocolat.

It was Sam's turn now. The gendarme stood back. She was greeted by the woman. Her face was immaculately made up, and she was impeccably dressed. And she was wearing an overly sincere face that immediately put Sam on edge.

"Bonjour. Vous êtes Français?"

"Non, madame. Anglais." Sam affected her best guttural French. She could get by with the language in a tight spot, but she needed to work harder. She should have thought about that when she was messing about in Miss Kelly's lessons.

"Ah, that's fine." No accent. Sam couldn't tell if the woman was French or English. Or any other nationality. *That's annoyingly clever.*

The woman now wore an obsequious smile. Her makeup didn't crack. Her teeth were too perfect. She managed to convey sympathy and efficiency all at the same time.

Smartarse.

"Are you a relative?"

No, I'm on holiday. Where's the nearest bar?

"Yes. I am the niece of Peter Green. He was on the flight."

"One second, please." The woman scrolled down the list with her finger, expertly turned the page, and ran down the list again. Sam looked at the man. He gave her a smile and imperceptibly nodded his head.

"Ah. There we are. Can I take your name, please, and a telephone number?"

Although irritated by the mannequin, Sam obliged.

"The relatives are all gathering over there to the left," she was pointing again. "Please help yourself to coffee, soft drinks, and some pastries." She paused. Sam thought the woman was studying her, waiting for an emotional response—on hand if she were to break down? That wasn't going to happen here. Not in front of Barbie the air hostess and her sidekick, Ken, the gay steward.

"Do you have any questions?"

Other than who's your dentist?

Sam dismissed the quip and thought for a moment.

"Do we know why the plane crashed?" It was a simple enough question.

"No, I'm sorry, we don't."

That is, your company might, but they've not told the airheads. Never mind.

Sam nodded and walked on through the checkpoint into the relatives' voyeuristic area. Despite her initial deliberations, she was already regretting making it this far and wished she'd stayed at the bottom and chatted to Uncle Pete from afar. He'd have understood. But, as there was free coffee and the chance to celebrate Uncle Pete's life with a croissant, she'd get on with it.

Sam had no idea why, against the backdrop of sickening pain, she was suddenly feeling so flippant. Shock? *Possibly.* If that were the case she'd need to keep checking her heart rate and look out for on-hand bodily warmth should she start to feel faint. *Oh God, there I go again. Get serious.* It was the grey-suited welcoming party that had kicked her off. She regretted her mood change, but it was better than falling to her knees and sobbing uncontrollably. Which was the likely alternative.

Sam's attention was drawn to one corner of the enclosure. A tall, slightly hunched man was surrounded by three much shorter men—at first glance they were from the Pacific Rim, likely Chinese or Korean. *Always the analyst.* The tall man was late twenties. *A handsome man.* Blond hair—rakish, but well cut. Angular features, someone straight out of Hitler's guide to the ideal Bavarian, and dressed in a low-key but classy combination of gentlemen's clothes. He was six three, maybe six-four, and slim built. *Franz the Austrian*—she had already named him—was in deep and animated conversation with the three shorter men. But he paused and looked across at Sam, stopped himself, and then resumed his conversation in lower tones.

Sam shot her glance away, embarrassed—which took some doing—having been caught staring. Curiosity got the better of her, and she glanced over again and met Franz's gaze. He returned an accusatory look, which unnerved her. Good-looking, confident—*and a bugger.* She wouldn't do that again.

Sam spent the next couple of minutes staring across at the wreckage. She tried to take it all in, but she couldn't. She was usually an expert at looking and registering. She could pick out a face in a crowd and get an artist to redraw it as if it were a photograph. But today, here with Uncle Pete, she knew that she wasn't getting any detail. She saw, but didn't register, the smashed fuselage, the burned seats, and other important bits of aircraft—she recognised the fins from an engine. With three or four people in hooded white plastic suits, she guessed there was the odd body part still being bagged. *Gross.*

Her fuzzy thoughts were interrupted as, out of the corner of her eye, Franz—she widened the nationality to well-heeled German or Danish—slipped out of the enclosure and started to make his way down to the checkpoint. He'd obviously seen enough.

So had she. She turned in the direction of the tent to grab a quick coffee. She needed a jolt before embarking on the rest of the day. But she was met by the three short men who, without meaning to, blocked her way. Sam moved to her left and they, trying to make room for her, collectively stepped right, inadvertently stopping her again. She grimaced a little and turned to her right and was just about to circumnavigate them when she found herself wanting to ask them a question. *Maybe I need some company right now.*

"Hello." She paused, allowing the men to register the fact that she had engaged them. As a threesome they stood still and stared at her, an intense but unthreatening stare. "Do you speak English?"

The three quickly stole glances at each other, and then the

eldest looking of the three said, "Yes, I do. Fluently. My colleagues also speak the language well, but mostly centred on a scientific vocabulary." At that point, he brought his hands together and bowed from the neck, just enough to show respect.

Sam found herself doing the same. She had no idea if that was the right thing to do, but it seemed polite. The other two men followed suit.

"Where are you from?"

"We are from Korea. South Korea. And you? You are either English or Australian?"

"English. Definitely English, although it's nice to be confused for someone with as relaxed an attitude as an Aussie."

"Are you a relative?" The senior Korean man was taking the initiative now.

Sam had already clocked what they were wearing. Smart, outdoor clothing. Sturdy, but not necessarily expensive. They smelled very clean, a soft deodorant scent wafted gently above the stench of burned grass, metal, and rubber. They all had pens in the pockets of their jackets, and one man carried a narrow, brown leather briefcase, big enough for two or three slim files. She thought that they were probably executives from an engineering firm, or maybe university professors. They had a kind demeanour, one that associated itself with trust and confidentiality. She felt she could tell them her closest secret and it wouldn't leave the valley.

"Yes. My uncle died on the flight." Sam held back a sharp rush of emotion. She so wanted to expose how she felt to these kindly gentlemen. She coughed to hide her embarrassment. "And you?"

"No. We are colleagues of a man, no, sorry, a great man, who passed away here. We have come to show our respects and hope that the gods allow some of his greatness to be bestowed on us whilst we are at his side."

"I'm sorry to hear that. I hope the gods answer your

wishes." They had Sam's attention now. She was curious, if for no other reason than that three colleagues would immediately fly thousands of miles in the hope that they might soak up some imaginary greatness that was seeping from the devastation. She caught herself. *Who am I to rubbish their beliefs?*

"Your colleague must have been very special. Do you mind if I ask why?"

The eldest man tipped his head to one side and smiled.

"We are from KSTAR, which stands for Korea Superconducting Tokamak Research." He spoke purposefully, with a slight Eastern accent. "I won't bore you with scientific detail, but at our laboratories in Daejeon we are close to achieving localised nuclear fusion using a very big magnet. Professor Lim was our lead researcher. Within him was the gift to complete small-scale nuclear fusion—limitless energy from the simplest of atoms."

Sam interrupted the gentleman.

"Hydrogen. You fuse atoms of hydrogen together and it releases a huge amount of spare, but very clean energy. The principle of the hydrogen bomb?"

"That is correct, Miss . . . ?"

"Green. Sam Green." She held out her hand. The man took it, and very quickly the other two men shook it warmly, nodding and smiling all at the same time. Sam returned their smiles a little awkwardly and bowed at them again. *Why not?*

"I am Professor Lee, and my colleagues are Professors Park and Kim. We all work on the project together, but always in support of Professor Lim. Recently we have had success with our latest round of experiments, but with the loss of Professor Lim, I'm afraid our project could be set back at least two years, maybe up to five. His death is devastating for KSTAR, but also for the world." Professor Lee maintained the look of complete dignity, but Sam could sense a real feeling of loss among these gentle men.

"I am very sorry to hear that. I really am. I do hope that

some of Professor Lim's greatness and understanding is granted to you from this visit. I really do." She bowed again. If the atmosphere weren't so grave, the whole exchange might be seen as comical. The three men bowed in reply.

"And, Miss Green, we sincerely hope that you find peace here with the loss of your uncle. I do not know you, other than to speak to you here in this dark place. But I know that you are a fine woman, with great integrity, compassion, and empathy. You will find your place in this world, and your uncle will be more proud of you than you could ever know." He paused and looked beyond Sam to the crash site. "It is so."

Sam closed her eyes and bowed her head again, this time to avoid the three men seeing the start of her tears. With her head still slightly bowed, she nodded and replied so quietly that Professor Lee had to lean forward to hear, "Thank you. Good-bye, and have a safe journey."

Looking up and catching the briefest of acknowledgements from the three professors, she turned and rather unceremoniously dived into the coffee tent.

A little later Sam was back down in the town, heading for the woodenly disguised pizza joint she had spotted earlier. On the way down she'd managed to pass the airline staff without shouting "airheads" out loud. She was proud of herself for that.

To her left in stationary traffic, Sam noticed the tall German—or Danish, or Austrian—man in a VW Golf hire car; the green Europcar sticker on the window was an easy giveaway. He was waiting to head down the hill. She didn't mean to stare, but there was something about him, something that infatuated and unnerved her all at the same time. It drew her eyes to him.

As she gawped, the man casually turned and looked directly at her. He didn't flinch. He just looked. Sam had stopped walking; the car was also stationery. The traffic was at a standstill. It was a sort of surreal standoff, their gazes caught in a time lock that seemed to last for ever. Sam knew she had an intense frown on her face. A sort of, "I'm looking at you, mate, because you interest me. And I don't know why." It couldn't be a good look. Especially as she was wearing her Quo T-shirt and hair that needed an appointment with a gardener.

After a couple of seconds, she thought Franz the Austrian's returning stare was arrogant, along the lines of, "Be careful, Sam Green. You don't know what you could be letting yourself in for." But she might have misjudged him by a country mile. *Could he be a darling?*

And then the traffic moved, and he was gone in an invisible cloud of pungent diesel. But not before Sam had clocked the car's registration number.

A Nondescript Office, Fourth Floor of No. 17, Third Avenue, New York

Ned scrunched up his face as he looked at his screen. The latest edict from Herbert needed his attention; the deadline for this one was shorter than usual. It was therefore a bit of a distraction to have to pursue a potential security infringement on his machine. There was a little red triangle at the bottom of the screen with a yellow exclamation mark at its centre. The icon told him that something wasn't right.

He reached for a Jelly Baby and ate it in his usual manner. He clicked on the security app, which opened up a dialogue box; its aim was to interrogate the system for breaches. He was just about to type in a command when, all of a sudden, CNN became very interesting. He turned up the sound and clicked the "Enlarge" icon on the corner of the inset screen.

The video was of two white men in orange boiler suits sitting in front of a black curtain. The curtain was decorated with an odd, black-and-white, comic-looking flag that Ned didn't recognise. There was a terrorist-type bloke behind them, his face covered. Ned saw he was carrying a gun. One of the men dressed in orange was talking at the camera. He was straight-backed, but his face was a mess—all black eyes and cuts. The other orange-suited man sitting next to him looked delirious, possibly unconscious. He had his head leaning on the shoulder of the upright man. Ned couldn't tell the state of his face because it was almost completely turned away from the camera.

The man spoke so quietly that CNN provided subtitles. He'd missed a couple of lines, but what he saw and read shocked him.

"Our keepers from the Islamic State have treated us fairly. As you can see, Corporal Groves to my right is not well." The subtitles froze for a second as the man coughed. His face grimaced as pain, somewhere in his body, accompanied the action. He continued to speak, the subtitles filling the audio gaps. *"The Islamic State is demanding that all countries, particularly the United States and Russia, cease bombing Syria immediately. They are giving the international community five days to stop this bloodshed, otherwise myself and Corporal Groves will be summarily executed."* He paused again, the subtitles hovering. *"I have been asked to apologise to the people of Yemen for our illegal invasion of their country. An invasion that led to the death of Trooper Sandy Jarman. And the legal internment by ISIL of Corporal Groves and myself."* He coughed again, closing his eyes to shield the pain from the viewers of the world. He then looked directly at the camera and almost imperceptibly mouthed a sentence that did not come with accompanying subtitles.

The screen flashed back to the CNN reporter.

"It seems that Captain Tony James added to the script he had been given by so-called ISIL. We believe his unscripted words were, 'I'm not sure that Ted will last much longer.' It is not clear why the released video, which was delivered to Al Jazeera just four hours ago, was allowed to keep the additional unspoken words. Unless the terrorists missed this brave call by the captured British officer."

Ned shivered demonstrably. He remembered the last time he'd watched a video like this. He couldn't for the life of him recall the date, but it was of the two airmen shot down by the Iraqis during one of the two Gulf wars. Both of the men looked like they'd spent ten rounds in the ring with Tyson Fury. At the time there was commentary that the airmen's injuries might have come from being ejected from the seats of their Tornado aircraft. *Nobody ever believed that, though, did they?*

Ned knew he was a coward to the core; he'd run away from a number of playground fights, rather than face the bullies who had confronted him. So he didn't scoff at the exploits of the British Army. As he looked at the ticker tape running across the bottom of the screen, he qualified his admiration to that of the UK's Special Reconnaissance Regiment—today he had the greatest admiration for them. In his more wistful moments he often imagined himself operating out of a sand-coloured, stripped-down Land Rover in the deepest desert somewhere. He'd look great wearing a blue-checked tea towel around his head and carrying more weapons and ammunition than Arnold Schwarzenegger could muster.

I'd have to get some Ray-Bans first, though.

The thought of being so close to danger made him shiver again. To find comfort, he reached for another Jelly Baby— *oh, good, a green one!* He then reminded himself he needed to check on the security breach.

Chapter Six

Aire, Abondance Village, French Alps

It was after dark. That is, it was way past sunset, but the media village emitted enough light to be seen from space. Sam had eaten a salad, washed up her few dishes, and was now relaxing on Bertie's bench seat with her SIS secure tablet open in front of her. Running low on battery, she was powering it from the VW's lighter socket. Energy efficiency was key when day-to-day living relied on a couple of vehicle batteries.

The inside of Bertie was small: the front passenger seat turned around, and with the rear bench seat, a small table, and a kitchen running along one side of the van, she had the smallest studio apartment in Christendom. But it worked for her. There was something womb-like about the compactness of these campervans that helped her to manage—*what should she call them?* Sensitivities.

She had watched the Daesh video seven or eight times, pausing it every few seconds to see if she could spot something that might give a hint as to where the two members of the SRR were being held.

The captain and the corporal gave no clues at all. The orange clothes were ordinary, their shoes and socks were unremarkable, and the beatings they had obviously endured were horrific. But there was nothing to tell where the video might have been shot. She did notice, and had already relayed the information to Jane, that she thought Captain James probably had a leg or hip injury. Although he was sitting, she could tell that the top of his right leg was slightly wider than the left and, on closer inspection, seemed to be wrapped or bandaged from the knee upward. Having read the briefing notes from Trooper Bliss, this tied in with his boss radioing that he thought he had been shot in the leg. The trooper couldn't attest to any other injuries. Sam's view was that, other than the facial beating—and that would tie in with him flinching when he coughed—he didn't appear to have any other injuries. Although, to be fair, having a bullet rip through your leg was bad enough. *As she knew.* In this case "Empathy" was her middle name.

Corporal Groves was another matter. Bliss had told them that Groves was the first to be hit and was out of view throughout the attack, "over a ridge." He hadn't even known if Ted Groves was alive.

Sam spent an age looking for Groves's likely injuries so that, should a Special Forces team effect a rescue, the accompanying doctor would know what he might be dealing with.

It wasn't easy. The man was clearly not well, and the captain had made the point at the end of the clip that Groves didn't have very long left. Sam had spotted bandaging under his shirt in his stomach region and, possibly, up around his shoulder; both arms were free—there seemed to be no injuries there. His legs looked like they were untouched, so it was probably an abdominal or chest wound. Add to this that the corporal was still alive, then the wounds were not fatal in themselves. Assuming he had been positioned in the chair for a bit before filming, there was no obvious leaking of blood. But he was clearly not well. *Possibly patched up and now had an infection.*

Sam had made notes and sketched a torso on her tablet, detailing where she thought the bandages might be. It would be up to the doctors to make decisions from that information.

Sam was now studying the terrorist who stood behind the two soldiers. She was particularly interested in his weapon. He was dressed in black: black trousers—*likely to be black denim;* a black cotton shirt, stained with sweat under both arms; and a black keffiyeh covering all of his face other than his eyes. She zoomed in on his eyes; nothing distinguishable came through. They could be the same eyes as those of Sahef's henchman from the previous photographs, but she couldn't say for certain. The man wore black gloves, so she wasn't able to study his fingers and nails.

The rifle was interesting. It was the latest version of the Kalashnikov AK-47—bizarrely named the AK-12. It was only recently brought into in service with the Russian Army—she thought December 2013—but available on the black market for a price. This weapon had a scratch on the barrel. The scratch was in exactly the same place as that on the weapon carried by the henchman at the Daesh safe house in downtown Sana'a—the Arab who had opened the double wooden gates. She was initially put off by the fact that this rifle didn't have the Vortex Strikefire II optical sight fitted, which was evident in both of the previous images. Otherwise it would have been a perfect match. As the sight was an obvious marker, maybe the man had been told to remove it for this video? To disguise the man, that would be a sensible thing to do. *Daesh might be militant murderers, but they weren't stupid.*

But it is the same weapon. Therefore—it was the same man. *Tick.*

This assumed that the same man kept the same weapon. Sam was sure that would be the case. In any army, that's what you did. You loved your rifle, cleaned it, oiled it, and zeroed it, so it shot things you were aiming at and not something else. And you often slept with it. Why? Because when the balloon went up, you were asking it to save your life and the lives of those around you. You never let it go. *It was yours.*

If she were right, then the man in the SRR video was the same man opening the door at the Daesh safe house in Sana'a and again in the propaganda video shot earlier in the year. And if that were so, then she could only recommend two of the three original Yemeni locations where the SRR might be being held hostage: the Daesh safe house in Sana'a or Sahef's headquarters at Hajjah, one of the remotest villages in Yemen. She had put all of that in her report.

Sam had also picked up one other interesting thing. The

Daesh flag in the video, a cartoonlike black sheet with a white blob at its centre that framed words in Arabic—*"There is no god, but God. Mohammed is the messenger of God"*—had a small rip on its bottom-right corner. She'd looked for other identifying marks and found none. Sam knew where all the clips and photos showing Daesh flags—or, as she remembered, "Black Banners"—were on the cloud, both in Yemen and Saudi. Sitting in Bertie, she found twenty-seven. Sam studied all of them to see if she could find a match. Some photos were grainy and hopeless, but for the majority she could see that the flags were different from the one in the SRR clip. The videos were more difficult because she had to pause the clip at exactly the right time, often reducing clarity. But she did her best. From what she could tell, none of them seemed to match the flag in the SRR video. *A flag she would definitely remember.*

Disappointed, Sam pushed the tablet to one side, picked up her secure phone to check if she had any e-mails, and was surprised, and delighted—it made her stomach lurch—that something was back from Interpol.

She was so excited that she almost opened the e-mail straight away. But, she needed a pee, and, with the same intensity, she desperately wanted a cup of tea. The e-mail would wait for a minute or two.

Sam opened Bertie's sliding door and hopped out into the ambient light of the media village. Just down the way, the thoughtful French had put up some Portaloos. They were hardly porcelain, but they were slightly better for her dignity than squatting over the tiny Porta Potti that she carried around in her van. *Needs must.*

Back in Bertie, feeling infinitely more comfortable, she put the kettle on one of the two gas rings and lit the burner.

Unable to restrain her excitement—actually it was now more nerves than excitement—she opened the single new e-mail. It had been remotely generated by an Interpol computer. It gave details of Franz the Austrian's hire car information.

Before she'd left for the Continent, Jane had afforded her three levels of remote security, which granted her access to the cloud and all its images. It also enabled her to read the secret reports distributed among the Op Glasshouse team. What Sam didn't know, until she checked, was that her clearance also allowed her to interrogate Interpol data.

It had taken her half an hour, but once she had it all sussed, she was able to find the portal for real-time hire car information from across Europe. Earlier in the afternoon she had quickly typed in the registration of the Europcar Golf and sent off the request.

The return e-mail gave the hirer's name as Wolfgang Neuenburg. *OK, so not Franz, but I was close.* Mr. Neuenburg lived in Berlin. Sam Googled the address, but it didn't exist. That closed that lead. Which was odd.

Who are you, Mr. Mysterious Neuenburg? And why are you hiding your address?

The Interpol e-mail did give his Visa card details. Sam used these details and interrogated the system further. It came straight back with an additional set of data—and a different address. One that did exist. Not in Berlin, but in Dresden.

So it wasn't so easy to cover your tracks, eh, Mr. Not Quite So Mysterious Neuenburg?

The kettle was boiling angrily. Sam switched off the gas and, from where she was sitting, poured the scalding hot water into a mug—which bore the caption "I'd rather be in my Camper." The fruit-infusion tea bag rose to the surface and bobbed about like a yellow plastic duck in a bath. She'd let it cool for a while.

Whilst she waited, she gently scratched her chin. Should she, or shouldn't she? *Bugger it, I will.*

Sam opened a new e-mail and, looking at a list she had accessed earlier—something else she had managed to unearth with her newfound security clearance—typed in the address of a senior clerk at the German equivalent of MI5, the BfV.

She wrote:

Dear Herr Gruber,

I am looking into an international drugs cartel based in the UK, with suppliers working out of Afghanistan. We are studying a number of leads, most of which we think are irrelevant. In order to remove a German national from our enquiries, I wonder, would you let us know if Dresden-based Wolfgang Neuenburg has a criminal record, or if there is any BfV interest in him?

Thank you for your time.

Sam Green. Analyst, SIS/MI6.

She might well be sacked for penning that e-mail. Whatever, she was expecting a negative outcome to a disciplinary enquiry regarding her beating the living daylights out of a toilet door, as well as her quack confirming her psychological unsuitability for continuing to work at SIS. *So, what have I got to lose?*

Sam sipped her tea and checked her watch. It was eleven thirty. Time for bed. She was about to close everything down when she was hit by a "doh!" moment. She pulled her tablet back toward her and opened Google. She typed in *Wolfgang Neuenburg.* The response was overwhelming.

Bugger. Bugger, bugger.

Her friend Wolfgang, now a potential SIS international drug baron, had pages and pages of entries, entries backed up by photos that she instantly recognised. There was only one Count Wolfgang of Neuenburg. *The Second.* German royalty with more Google pages than a UK soap star. And she had stared into his soul, here in the Abondance valley.

Sam had no idea what the infatuation was. She knew it had nothing to do with her current job—nor was it helping.

In any way. But, from the pit of her stomach, she knew she had to get more details on this guy. David had given her four days to convalesce. She'd taken one. Uncle Pete would want her to find out a little more about this Austrian Franz—who had turned out to be a German count. An enigmatic man who dressed well, but hid his address from the authorities. *Yes, she needed to know more.*

Sam changed into her nightdress, pulled down the rock 'n' roll bed, and laid out her maggot and a pillow. She'd spend no more than half an hour scrolling through the hundreds of entries for Count Wolfgang.

Tomorrow she'd drive to Dresden to continue her rehabilitation.

Joint Intelligence Committee (JIC), Whitehall, London

The JIC had finished deliberations about how to deal with the media fallout from the Daesh video. The Cabinet Office would lead and continue to issue statements along the lines of: *"We cannot discuss security matters that have the potential of putting the lives of the soldiers concerned at greater risk. We and our allies are doing all we can to ensure the safe return of Captain James and Corporal Groves, and the body of the late Trooper Jarman."*

They had also agreed there should be some leaking of early "fictitious" discussions at staff level, held between the UK, the United States, and Russia, about putting a hold on bombing Syrian territory. They'd get the Moscow embassy to release news of these imaginary discussions to a friendly member of the press that evening. The leak would quickly escalate and cross borders. To which the response from the UK would be "no comment." The hope was that Daesh chiefs would pick the details up on CNN or Al Jazeera and assume that the Brits were doing what they could to meet their demands. It might steal them an extra day or so. Even if it got under the skin of both the Americans and the Russians.

"So, do we know where the two soldiers are?" Jon Trent, a senior civil servant and chairman of the JIC, took the meeting forward.

David looked across at Lieutenant General Jack Downs, the director of Defence Intelligence (DI). He had agreed to lead on giving the JIC the Sitrep.

"We currently have five possible locations," he looked left to a screen that showed a map of the Saudi peninsula. "The two marked in blue are within the geographical borders of Saudi Arabia. The other three, marked in red, are in Yemen. Two of the red targets are in the capital Sana'a, and a third is up-country in the relatively inaccessible village named Hajjah. We've agreed these targets with MI6, sorry, SIS." To which David nodded, both agreeing the targets and acknowledging his firm's proper title: Secret Intelligence Service. Jack was pleasantly old school. He'd never learn.

"But we're not certain that any of these locations hold the soldiers?"

David stepped in.

"No, sir, we're not. Current satellite imaging discounts the two Saudi locations, pretty much. Target Red Three"—David was using his laser pointer to highlight the Daesh's deputy headquarters in Hajjah—"Has a white pickup in its compound. One of our analysts believes—*thank goodness for Sam Green; she'd turned that round from the satellite photographs in an hour, first thing this morning*—it is the same white pickup that was photographed at the Yemeni training camp by Captain James. There doesn't appear to be a great deal of activity going on in the compound." The screen threw up a satellite overhead of the Hajjah compound. David circled the buildings with his pointer. "But Daesh will know that we have satellites capable of watching them in near real time. They might be keeping a low profile there.'

"And is there any SIGINT coming from the compound?" The question was directed at Melvin Hoare, the senior GCHQ rep on the JIC.

"No sir, nothing unusual from any of the five locations.

Although, it is fair to say, we are at the edge of our capabilities this far south without deploying a team on the ground. US teams are helping, but they have their hands full on the Iraqi affair." Melvin looked down the table at David, who nodded.

"And what about the other two locations in Yemen?"

David led again. "We are discounting Target Red Four, although we do have a local agent keeping an eye on its front door—he reports no activity. Target Red Five is interesting." The map was back on the screen and David's laser pointer was marking the possible Daesh safe house in Sana'a.

"There is a link at this location to at least one member of Ali Abdullah Sahef's staff—Sahef is Daesh's deputy in Yemen. We believe the terrorist dressed in black in the SRR video clip has been seen here in the last three weeks. Again, we have a local keeping an eye on the place, but with nothing significant to report."

He looked across at Brigadier Alasdair Buckle, director of Special Forces. It would be his turn next. David wasn't expecting an easy ride.

The chairman led. "So, in summary, we have four locations of interest, two in Saudi and two in Yemen. The rural location seems the most likely, as we have tracked a vehicle from the original training camp to the compound. The second, in Sana'a, is of interest, but not significantly so." He stopped and looked up at the screen. "Alasdair, what do we do now?"

Brigadier Alasdair straightened up. David thought he looked grumpier than usual.

"The thing is, we have very little solid intelligence on which to launch a rescue. We have no significant SIGINT, and we don't have eyes on the Hajjah, the most likely hostage location. So no HUMINT. Launching without corroboration is, at best, a waste of time; at worst, if we have chosen the wrong location, it will be all over for the two SRR boys."

"Point taken, Alasdair. David, any chance of anything

else coming in the next twenty-four hours?"

David gently rocked his head from side to side and scrunched his face; it was all very imponderable. He and Alasdair had already rehearsed the arguments without agreement before the meeting. He took a deep breath.

"I take Alasdair's point. But, unless we're extraordinarily lucky in the next twenty-four hours, we are unlikely to get any further leads. We have eyes on Target Red Five in Sana'a, and we are making best efforts to get eyes on Red Three up-country. But if our man gets too close in Hajjah, the compound could be spooked. So we need to be careful."

He paused, just long enough for that to sink in. "The soldiers will be executed in less than four days; Corporal Groves may be dead from his injuries already. Time is not on our side. I am surprised and indebted to my staff that we have any targets at all this early on. Yemen, in its current state, is a hide-and-seek paradise. The soldiers could be in any one of a thousand undiscoverable locations."

David closed his eyes and rubbed his forehead. He needed to make a point. "SF will need at least twenty-four hours to prepare for an assault. If we agree to assault Target Red Three here, now, SF will not be ready until tomorrow night. That is less than two days before the planned execution of the soldiers. But Groves doesn't have two days, if he has any time at all."

He hoped his tiredness didn't show. "We need to act with what we have."

"Alasdair?" The chairman was looking for an SF counterresponse.

"We have a squadron on standby at RAF Akrotiri, in Cyprus. They have the images of the Hajjah compound and will have a reasonably effective, life-size model built before dusk this evening. Unless I stop them, they will be rehearsing a night assault tonight. And, with the SF Hercules transporter on the tarmac at Akrotiri, the squadron will be operationally ready for an assault tomorrow night. We would plan H-Hour for two thirty, local, the following morning."

David added, "And we hope to have a friendly national in Hajjah by tomorrow lunchtime. And, one of our people will be overlooking Target Red Five in Sana'a to coincide with the assault. Our person will gauge any reaction, should there be any."

"And the Saudis?"

General Jack half raised his hand to speak. Everyone looked at him.

"We have spoken to the DA in Riyadh. Apparently, the Saudi SF are chomping at the bit to have a go at the blue targets. We have liaison officers in place to assist, but, should you, sorry . . . should the PM give the go-ahead, the aim would be for all attacks to be simultaneous."

The chairman was about to speak again, but Jack hadn't finished.

"We need to be clear that the Saudis will do an extremely effective job. That is, they will raze both locations."

"Even if we don't think they're viable targets?" The chairman acknowledged the obvious humanitarian concern that everyone felt.

General Jack was clearly expecting the question. "The Saudis want to show us and the world what they can do. When our DA shared the targets, they apparently weren't surprised. I think they were after even the slightest bit of intelligence to have a go."

The chairman nodded.

"OK." He closed the flap on his tablet. "David, Jack, and Alasdair—I'm guessing you'll all be at COBR this afternoon?"

David and the other two nodded.

"Then that's what we'll tell the PM we should do. If any new intelligence comes up in the meantime, if there is just the slightest reason why we shouldn't go ahead with the assault, then let's share it as soon as possible."

The committee members all murmured acknowledgement and started to gather together their files, laptops, and tablets.

Sam pulled Bertie over, around the corner from Pillnitzer Strasse. She made sure that no one would park in front of her by stopping just short of a small junction—should she need to make a quick getaway. Using her Satnav, she planned a route out of Dresden, northwest toward Berlin. She had an escape route.

She waited for a while, aimlessly tapping her fingers on the steering wheel in time to a 1970s tune that was running about in her head.

What was she playing at? She had a real job. A *key* job that required her fullest attention. Yes, she had not missed a thing. Until some more images came in, there was little to add to the report she'd sent to the Op Glasshouse team this morning. The crucial find for her had been the white pickup, the one noted from the original series of photos of the terrorist training camp. She'd discovered the same pickup in the compound at Hajjah, whilst looking over the latest keyhole satellite photos provided by the United States.

In the terrorist camp she had only been able to see the front end of the cab, a tyre, some of the right wing, and a bumper. The rest was hidden behind a tent. It was a 1990s white Nissan D21 pickup. She had only got a side view from Captain James's camera angle, but she had identified the make of tyre and spotted a small dent on the wing. It was in remarkably good nick considering its age. The satellite image was taken from above, so she had no way of matching the tyres or the dent. But, and it was a huge but, both images had one feature that could only be original to the same vehicle. They both had a chrome wing mirror on the forward corner of the front right wing. She could see it in both images.

She checked on Nissan's own website, under the "Manufacturer's History" tab. It had confirmed that all D21s were fitted with plastic wing mirrors attached to the front doors—as you'd expect any relatively modern vehicle to have. The chrome mirror must have been retrofitted for some obscure reason. It made matching the pickup dead easy.

Having looked over all of the images that had come in overnight and found nothing else significant, she'd rushed through her findings to the team. It wasn't her job to make recommendations—she just reported what she saw.

While stopped for diesel at an autobahn *tankstelle* just short of Frankfurt, she'd checked her firm's phone for e-mails and opened a quick briefing note from David to the Op Glasshouse team. The note reported that the JIC was going to recommend to COBR that SF assault the Hajjah location tomorrow night. At the same time, they would gauge reaction from the Sana'a safe house, whilst Saudi Special Forces concurrently attacked the two targets within their borders. David had made the point that the team needed to keep pressing sources to see if they could verify Hajjah as the primary target.

It was all a little disquieting for her. On the back of *her* work, Hereford would be sending in a whole load of SF teams to rescue two members of the SRR held hostage by Daesh in a compound deep in the bowels of Yemen.

On the back of her work.

She didn't know how that made her feel. If it was a success, she'd take some comfort from what she had provided. If it were the wrong choice, or if the mission failed, then she knew she would take it badly. Very badly.

But I don't make the decisions—I just provide the intelligence. Sam pushed the thought to the back of her mind.

Whilst she had been looking over David's Sitrep at the petrol station, her phone pinged. It was a reply from the BfV. She opened it nervously:

Dear Fr Green,

Thank you for your e-mail. We can confirm that we have a file on Count Wolfgang of Neuenburg, although he does not have a criminal record. Our interests are in his Internet search history, which has been focused mostly on major international accidents over the past thirty years.

We are also aware that he has conducted some low-level, but quite sophisticated, hacking of nongovernmental firms across the world. As far as we can tell, he has not used his ability to hack into their systems for personal gain, seemingly just to get access to information.

We are due to pass our intelligence to the Federal Police, for them to deal with the count as they see fit.

Your country should be aware that Count Wolfgang is German royalty, the equivalent of perhaps a fifth-in-line to your Queen's throne. We suggest, therefore, that you deal with the count in a way befitting his status.

Please come back to us should you need any more information.

M Gruber

Sitting in Bertie, around the corner from the count's home, it wasn't the last paragraph that was making Sam prevaricate. It was more to do with her contradictory priorities. She needed to keep an eye on the cloud to see if more images came in—*if only there were some more pictures showing the Black Banner.* But, if she didn't keep herself occupied, she knew she wouldn't be able to stop herself from closing down and dwelling on the crash site and Uncle Pete's death. Chasing Count Neuenburg, for no other reason than he had looked at her in a funny way, filled the time quite nicely.

She'd been at the precipice before, post-Afghanistan. *The*

black dogs, as Churchill had called them. Despair, lethargy, anxiety, and, sometimes, irrational fear. She really didn't want to end up there again. Just thinking about it made her shoulders hunch.

Dammit! She hit the steering wheel with both hands. Her bandaged right hand throbbed.

Energised, she got out of Bertie and double-locked him with the key fob. She checked her watch. It was 7.30 p.m., starting to get dark. She looked up and down the street: substantial three- and four-storey houses, made out of big, heavy grey stone, topped with tall, acutely angled, blue-tiled roofs. She saw nothing untoward. Opposite her, an elderly lady was taking a dachshund for a walk, almost pulling the poor thing along behind her. She was no threat.

Block 12 of Pillnitzer Strasse was a couple of hundred metres around the corner.

Come on, Sam, let's do this.

It took her about three minutes to cover the distance; once there, she was met by a set of stone stairs leading up to an ornately framed pair of white gloss and stained-glass doors. To one side was a collection of bell pushes. She tentatively climbed the steps and ran her finger up the list until she found Number 2. She had a quick look up and down the street and picked out nothing. Her finger hovered over the bell button for a fraction of a second, and then she pressed it. It rang, somewhere in the distance.

Silence briefly followed—although she was a little spooked by a noisy car that drove past whilst she was waiting. Beside the set of bell pushes was a small speaker. She expected to hear acknowledgement from her ring. She leaned toward it. *"Ja?"* would do.

Nothing.

And then a buzz and a click as the front door remotely unlocked. But not a word from the speaker. *That's oddly disconcerting.*

She pushed the door open.

Number 2 was at the top of three flights of stairs. Number

1 on the left, 2 on the right. She made her way up quickly—
and quietly—to the top landing and stopped outside the door.

Green door, single Yale-type lock. Peephole. A big brass
2.

That was all to be expected.

What she didn't expect was the door to be slightly ajar.

There was no bell. Just a door-shaped slab of green
wood, jauntily positioned to beckon her into the flat. She
shouldn't go in. *I shouldn't go in.* Perhaps she should knock?

Yes, knock, you idiot.

Sam knocked. Once and then twice. No answer, just the
far-off siren of the *polizei* attending a crime. They'd be here
next if she broke into Number 2.

She knocked once more and, a fraction louder than her
speaking voice, called out, *"Guten Abend?"*

Silence was the resounding response.

The voices in her head had already assumed that she had
turned away from the flat and was making her way
downstairs. So they were surprised, as was Sam, when her
hand gently pushed open the door and her head looked in.

What she saw made her close her eyes. It was reminiscent
of three years ago in Kenema, Sierra Leone—*Mrs Tebie's
house.* The place had been trashed. There was stuff
everywhere: papers, books, pictures off the wall. In the
distance, in what she thought was the sitting room, a
bookshelf lay across the entrance, its contents no longer on
the shelves.

Get away, Sam, now!

She stepped over the threshold, whilst reaching down for
a small bronze statue that rather incongruously still remained
upright on the floor among a pile of papers. She picked it up
with her good hand. She couldn't stop herself from looking
at it. It was a green-coloured soldier, or similar, holding a
shield and thrusting a sword above his head. He wore a
pointy helmet. She shook her head briskly. *Get back on task.*
All that mattered was that it was heavy.

Sam made her way tentatively to the end room which,

with every step, came more into view. The corridor wasn't well lit, but the room ahead had its lights on. She stopped in the doorway, dead still. She looked for something, someone. Nothing.

While she held her breath, listening for anything untoward, she took in what had turned out to indeed be the sitting room. To her left was a single long window with the curtains hanging listlessly across it, having been almost pulled off their runner. In front of her, and on the other side of the bookcase obstacle course, a desk took up a big chunk of the room. The large computer screen had been holed in a couple of places by what Sam thought might have been a screwdriver. To one side was a computer tower. It seemed untouched. She looked wider still. An upturned sofa, a broken TV, rubbish everywhere, and two doors, one hard left—she thought it was open, and one to the right of the desk. It was closed.

Without any plan, she stepped carefully over the bookcase. In two more steps she was at the desk. It was a jumble of papers, some pens, and a printer, which had been smashed.

She leaned forward to pick up a book that looked like it might be a diary when, in an instant, something inside her set in motion a series of events that she would forever have difficulty describing.

Self-protection is an innate, Pavlovian reaction. And with Sam this had always manifested itself as: *strike first; then run.*

In the dull reflection of the dark grey computer screen, she made out movement behind her. Her reaction was as fast as it was spontaneous—although, on later reflection, she did feel that the events of the previous three days added venom to the way in which she hit out. Sam twisted quickly to her right, giving her left hand—which carried the mightily heavy statue—significant angular momentum. She instinctively kept her head low to avoid being struck by her likely attacker, so she had no idea where the bronze, with its pointy sword, would strike.

The sound of a fleshy thud was immediately followed by a yelp as the man toppled forward to protect his groin.

Sam knew it was a man; he smelt like one.

From her semicrouched position, with her head slightly bowed, she saw that he was wearing blue and white Nike sneakers—fake, she could tell from the lack of embroidery— grey socks and tatty blue jeans. It wasn't Count Wolfgang of Neuenburg. He would be much more nattily dressed from the knees down.

She didn't register anything else. Whilst her left hand was twisting the sword—and possibly the helmeted head— into the soft underparts of a man who she assumed was going to attack her, her legs were moving back toward the staircase, the rest of her struggling to keep up.

Her mind blanked and didn't allow her to think of much as she sprinted down the stairs and back to Bertie. She knew she'd left the diary on the desk—or on the floor. And the statue was implanted in the man's crotch. She now had to put space between her and Number 2. She needed to reflect on what had just happened. And, just as importantly, why she had thought it a clever thing to come this far in the first place.

Get in Bertie, get on the autobahn, and stop at the first tankstelle. Her first rational thought.

As she ran toward Bertie, she double-clicked the key fob. In the dark Dresden street, the VW's indicators flashed recognition that she was on her way.

A few seconds later she was in the cab. Fumbling a little with the keys, she turned Bertie over, who started immediately—as he had done every other time she'd asked him to. Sam flicked on the main beam.

Then she froze.

Standing in front of Bertie—about a metre from the bumpers, breathing deeply, but not out of shape—was Count Wolfgang of Neuenburg. *The Second.* She involuntarily checked his crotch for bronzes, but found just a pair of cherry red chinos. He'd changed since he'd left the crash site. *Nice trousers.*

He was staring at her. He wasn't menacing, but neither was he sporting a welcoming look.

She slipped Bertie into first gear.

Still he stared at her.

She revved the engine. But she was stuck. She couldn't reverse—there was a car behind her. And she couldn't drive forward without knocking over a member of German royalty.

Then, surprisingly, in the glare of Bertie's headlights, the count raised his hands. First to chest height, and then slightly above his head.

To confound her further, he tipped his head to one side and smiled. A "come on, mad woman who has followed me all the way to Dresden—we need to talk" smile.

With that smile, Sam's fear, anxiety, and days' worth of pent-up emotion just lost their edge. *A little.* Something, somewhere inside, told her to trust this man. She had no idea why. And, on this wildest of hunches, that's what she decided to do.

For now.

Chapter Seven

City Centre, Dresden, Germany

Wolfgang steadied his breathing. He had run as fast as he could to keep up with the inexplicable woman he had just watched in his apartment. *Mein Gott! Sie schnell war!* She had sprinted round the corner to a bright yellow VW transporter, jumped in, and quickly turned it over. Wolfgang had made it to the front of the vehicle as she switched on the lights. He just had time to lift his hands from his knees and recover his composure before he was in the full glare of the main beam.

Now, standing directly in front of the vehicle, exposed like an animal caught in its headlights, he was effectively blind.

The woman revved the vehicle, but it didn't move. He assumed that she couldn't reverse—there must be a vehicle behind her.

He had no idea what her facial expressions were—he couldn't see past the lights. He assumed that she was in some state of panic. He'd just witnessed her entering the flat, make her way expertly over bits of furniture, books, and papers and through into the lounge. When surprised by the burglar—*or whatever he was?*—she had struck him with the noteworthy bronze statue of his great-great-great-uncle, Ferdinand Neuenburg III. *Ouch!* It brought tears to his eyes thinking about it. Knowing his ancestor's predilection for men, Wolfgang imagined Ferdinand would be happy with his current resting place.

He had watched all of this on his iPad, which was remotely linked to eight hidden cameras in various locations in his flat. He knew there'd been a break-in as soon as the door was forced—his home-built security system had pinged his mobile. He was in a taxi heading from the airport at the time. Within thirty seconds he had full visual on his iPad, watching an oaf of a man, probably one hundred and ninety pounds, tall, black T-shirt, unremarkable denim jacket, tatty jeans, and the worst sneakers you could find on the Dresden *flohmarkt*, systematically going through each room.

The man's actions were all very odd. It appeared to Wolfgang as if he were looking for something. He seemed to inspect each room expertly, open lockers and drawers carefully, take things out and turn things gently upside down, inside out. Only then, once he'd checked each room in detail, did he trash the place. And he didn't mess about with the trashing.

The man with the bad shoes had tried to get into Wolfgang's computer by turning it on, but his machine had so many levels of security it was a hopeless task. He had taken off the back of the tower and removed the hard drive, then put it together again, as though it hadn't been touched. *Clever. But why?* He wasn't worried about losing the drive. Everything he worked on was immediately backed up onto his own baby "cloud" at the family home in Munich. He'd hired the fibre optic routing to ensure that it was all exclusive to him. And all of his work was encrypted with the latest 256-bit key cryptography. All that could be dug out of the drive would be recent shadows of some work he had undertaken. Nothing important.

With the hard drive placed in a brown rucksack the man had brought with him—along with one or two other of Wolfgang's more blingy possessions, and two thousand euros he kept in a pot on the mantelpiece—he'd taken a screwdriver to the very expensive LED monitor and was just about to do the same to the tower when the doorbell rang.

Wolfgang, who by now was crouched out of view behind the hedge of a garden opposite, had immediately stood up and looked across at the front door of the apartment block. He couldn't make out who the visitor was from where he was hiding, but it was a woman. She had a certain familiarity about her that he couldn't place.

He looked back at his iPad and was surprised that the man had gone to the flat's front door and pressed the "Enter" button on the intercom. More surprising still, he had opened the front door so it was just ajar, then retreated to the bedroom. Hiding?

What, up until now, had been a mildly annoying event, immediately became a "spectacular." It was like watching a female version of Clint Eastwood—his favourite—wander into a bar and kill all of the baddies without ruffling his poncho.

He had no idea who she was. The video quality was good, but the camera positions and the placing of the lights failed to give a good view of her face. But she had made his day. The good news was that the clip would have been rushed down the fibre optics to the cellars in Munich, where his Synology backup drives would hold it for posterity. He'd have to watch it all again later—*not necessarily just for entertainment value, you understand.*

And now, just like Mr. Eastwood, he was standing in front of the heroine's carriage, stopping her from galloping off into the hills. It was all very dramatic.

He held his ground. His breathing much easier now.

The engine revved again, the body of the bright yellow transporter rocking gently with the motion of the engine.

But nothing changed. They were still at a standoff.

Then the woman in the VW turned the main lights off, so only the sidelights were illuminated.

He could see her face now.

Scheiße! He rocked back ever so slightly. *It was her!* The woman from the crash site!

What? Why?

Wolfgang lifted his hands in mock defeat and involuntarily smiled at the ridiculousness of the situation. And that seemed to break the deadlock.

He didn't have time to process any more information as, while they both kept each other's stare, she was beckoning him forward, using a heavily bandaged hand to motion "get in the passenger's seat . . . *quickly*."

He paused, just for a split second. He looked into her eyes. She was too far away to make any real connection, but there was something about her that emanated trust. She had just damaged the man who had ransacked his apartment. Had done that expertly—and then run away. Not coolly enough that she had time to look round the flat, make a cup of tea and give the man one last kicking for his troubles. But still a very good show. Better than he could have done.

On reflection, she was good, but not that good.

Why was she here in the first place? From Abondance to Dresden. Why was she following him? So many imponderables.

Wolfgang looked down at his shoes as if thinking about the options. And then, with a slight shrug of his shoulders, swiftly but lightly made his way to the passenger door of the VW and got in.

This is going to be weird.

Somewhere on the Saudi Peninsula

The sound of the turning lock registered in Captain Tony James's brain. It grated somewhere deep. As did the screeching noise coming from the door's hinges. His mind fluttered, back and forth. Thoughts and images bounced around his mind, none taking the time to stay still long enough to coalesce. *No, that didn't describe it well at all.* More like they couldn't come to rest because the ground was too hot for them to step on. Burning hot. Yes, that was more like it. Thoughts and images floating about, unable to land for fear of scorching . . . *nice.*

Flashes of things.

His mother dressed in that summer dress she wore once, when she picked him up from boarding school. She smelt of Imperial Leather.

His beautiful daughter. Ahh, bless her. *No, no—stop that dog! Pleeeease. Somebody kick it off before it rips off her face! Stop it now!*

Then it was calm. The image was gone.

His MG sports car, British racing green with chromed wire wheels. His pride and joy. His wife. Naked. *And now a man, all he could see was his hairy back. She was being held down ... no, please no!*

Then Trooper Sandy. All bent and mangled, lying lifeless among the sand, his deep red blood blackening the earth. Surrounded by dogs or hyenas. *Stalking, getting closer.* Vultures flying overhead . . .

Splash!

He came to abruptly. Water was seeping through the hessian bag, a bag he had worn over his head for what seemed like a lifetime. The dampness took away some of the heat, heat that pervaded everywhere. It made him sweat in places he didn't know had the appropriate glands. He sniffed involuntarily. The smell was repugnant. He knew he was lying in his own urine and faeces. With his hands tied tightly behind his back, he couldn't even attempt to wipe the vomit and blood that had dribbled from his mouth, congealed since the last time they had beaten him.

There was a dim light shining through his hood. He was unable to describe his cell even if he had to—he'd always been bagged. But he had worked out that it opened onto the outside world.

It was light then—sometime during the day. Between six in the morning and six at night. But which day? God only knew. He had tried to keep count since the attack, but when you've been beaten into unconsciousness at least three times—or was it four?—it was difficult to rationally conceptualise anything.

The video had been shot the day after he and Ted had been taken. He'd been beaten once before the video shoot, but they had cleaned him up and dressed them both in the dreaded orange boiler suits in time for the cameras. After that they'd hooded him again and taken him away to beat him. The blows were hard, but mostly delivered by feet. He had lain on the ground, curled up to protect what little dignity he had left.

They had not used clubs or metal bars, but when a man kicks you as hard as he can, your ribs break, as does your nose. He daren't think about his testicles. If he ever got out, and he knew he never would, there was little chance that his Zoe would be joined by a baby brother. Not now.

Halfway through the beatings they had interrogated him. One of the questioners had a very strong southern American accent, which had caught him out to begin with. But now, such was the state of his mind, he wouldn't be surprised if Mickey Mouse had turned up to ask him who his commanding officer was.

That was the thing, though. The questions weren't in depth. They were simple, easy, nonthreatening questions.

As part of their training they had all been subject to low-level interrogation. The message was pretty clear: *If you are captured, your chances of survival are about 5 per cent. Your death, and the ceremony attached to it, is more important to the terrorist than information. Hold out for a while; then tell them everything you know. Give them a sense of victory. None of you know anything that might jeopardise the next mission. Trust me.*

However, he remembered that they had added: *if you have chance to destroy your equipment, then do so.* During the attack, he hadn't been able to break any of his kit. He assumed it was now in the hands of these thugs.

After the third beating—*was it the third one?*—where he knew they had broken at least a couple of ribs, as breathing hurt like hell, he had told them everything he knew.

There was nothing left to tell them.

A heavily Arabicised English accent interrupted his jagged thoughts.

"You smell like shit."

Back to the here and now. *Another beating? More inane questions?*

He thought it was probably two men who lifted him at that point. Immediately everything went into spasm. His right leg, which had a bloody big hole in it, ached like the worst toothache you could imagine. His chest, abdomen, and nether regions all cried out in sympathy.

Somebody grabbed his nose through the hessian and moved it violently from side to side. Tony couldn't stop himself from screaming as bone and cartilage scraped against each other.

"Like that, infidel?"

And then laughter from the men.

They dragged him outside, one on either arm—it was a short distance—then into another room. He didn't think he'd been in this room before, but he couldn't tell. One of the men undid Tony's hands from behind his back, and they manhandled him onto an almost flat surface, face up. It felt like a wooden table, slightly sloping downward, his head at the bottom. His heart was easily pushing blood downward and out of his newly rebroken nose.

They tied his hands by his sides with some sort of cloth so that he couldn't move them. Someone held his feet together. He was trussed on a table, face up like a piece of meat at a butcher's shop.

The men in the room—*how many were there now?*—spoke to each other in Arabic. He thought he heard running water, but he couldn't be sure.

Just then, for no particular reason, he thought of Ted. *I wonder how Ted is?* He had no idea if they were being kept together. He'd seen him at the video shoot, where one of the Arabs had said, "Your friend is almost dead." And laughed. He thought he'd heard moaning in the middle of the night when the world was at its quietest. One part of him wanted it to be a call from Ted, telling him that he was still alive. But he couldn't be sure.

Fuck! His head was slammed back to the table as his

hessian hood was pulled tightly round his face, his nose pressed at an angle that sent an excruciating pain to the appropriate receptors in his brain.

Then it started. He knew as soon as the water hit his face that death would be a much more preferable place than what he was about to endure.

The water kept coming. No matter how hard he tried, he couldn't turn his head. Water, filthy water at that, smothered his mouth and nose. He had to breathe. He *had* to breathe. But he couldn't stop the water from filling his mouth and nasal cavity. And then going down his throat. He swallowed. At some point—*I have to breathe*—he gagged, but the water kept coming. His body flinched and writhed. But the water was incessant.

He was drowning. Not in the way he thought drowning might take you. You know: *You're underwater; you're going to die. So you just breathe in water, like you drink it. And quickly oxygen fails to get into your bloodstream, and your mind shuts down.* Peacefully.

Not here. Not now.

Fuck! Make it stop! He coughed, swallowed water, gagged, cried, scrunched up his face, and then gagged some more. But still it came. More water. More drowning, but worse. Trying to get away to make it stop. Writhing. Gagging. Retching. And still more water.

Then it did stop. His hood was released.

He turned his head to one side. He coughed up water. Everything screamed out in pain. He coughed some more, retching as he did. He spat something out of his mouth. It could have been a piece of him. He didn't care.

More Arabic. It might have been Swahili—it was all beyond comprehension.

Then it started again.

He would have thought his brain would rationalise that there were only two possible outcomes to his predicament: he'd survive and cough up more water at the end of it all, or he'd die. To fight it was futile.

Unfortunately his mind had other priorities.

Fuck! I've got to make it stop! It was a natural survivalist reaction.

He wanted to be calm and let it all happen. But something inside him took over and fought and fought. Through the gagging, coughing, crying, gagging some more, and all of the many facets of pain that he felt, still his body tried to escape the torture.

Water. An essential ingredient for life. *You could have fooled me.*

And then it stopped.

Cough, cough, gag, retch, cough. He felt more pain than was humanly endurable.

His breathing was rapid and shallow. He knew he was sobbing. He wished he could stop sobbing. Without the hood he must look pathetic. He felt pathetic. *I feel pathetic.* He didn't know what was worse: the waterboarding, the associated pain, or the stripping of all dignity. He had failed on all counts. He was broken beyond repair. They had him now. They could take what they wanted.

"So, Captain James." That American accent again. "Tell me how you are assigned your missions."

Huh?

"Or shall we do that again?"

SIS Headquarters, Vauxhall, London

Jane checked the time on the bottom corner of her screen. It was 8.46. She had a couple of minutes before the next cabal with David and the Op Glasshouse team. She'd signed off her report to the team at eight o'clock this morning and would have little supplementary information to add to the briefing when they convened. She'd read everyone else's reports, and it appeared that there was no new intelligence.

The only positive thing was a confirmation from David that the embassy in Moscow had leaked that its junior staff members were in discussions with the United States and Russia about stopping the bombing in Syria. They knew it was out there because the State Department and the Russian Ministry of Foreign Affairs were both denying that the meetings were taking place. And David had received a curt call from his oppo in Langley asking for an explanation. It was a small but important result that might buy them some time.

As things stood, if nothing else came in today, the SAS would drop into Yemen this evening and assault Hajjah at . . . she did some maths, metaphorically using her fingers . . . eleven thirty tonight, UK time, two thirty in Yemen.

Tim's report, which she'd just closed, confirmed that they now had an SIS team staking out the Sana'a safe house, and they should be able to keep eyes on all day and overnight. However, they were apparently struggling to get somebody reliable up-country to provide overwatch on the compound in Hajjah. She understood the dilemma—she'd experienced it herself. Finding and tasking the right person took time. Sending the wrong individual in early was easy. But the last thing the SAS needed was a spooked compound, the result of an errant local caught with a pair of binos hanging around his neck.

The SAS might have to go in blind.

Jane thought initially that the SIS team would have been better employed in Hajjah, rather than keeping an eye on the safe house in Sana'a. But late yesterday evening Tim had made the point that, no matter how well you disguise yourself, two Westerners arriving in a far-off corner of Yemen would always be two Westerners arriving in a far-off corner of Yemen. No, it had to be a local.

Sam had sent through her report first thing. They had no new conventional images, and the latest keyhole satellite stuff seemed, to Jane, to show little change. Sam did note that the white twin-cab had moved a few metres. New tracks also seemed to indicate that, since the last overhead, it had been driven out of the compound at some point. And there had been a second vehicle visiting, but she could give no additional details.

On one of the recent photos, Sam had highlighted a well just outside the compound. The image showed a pipe of some sort leading from the well, over a wall, and into one of the buildings. Sam attached no importance to the find. Jane thought she may have noted it to fill a slow news day.

Jane wondered how Sam was. She hadn't found time to give her a call, or drop her an e-mail, since she'd left for the Alps. *She'd do something now.* With deft hands and a quick glance at the clock, she opened a new mail and started to type.

She stopped herself midsentence. She had absolutely no idea why she would pry, but just then, Jane decided to access Sam's account.

Jane had not had to look over Sam's e-mails since she'd started working in the building. Sam didn't know that Jane had the necessary clearance, but Jane and David had agreed that, until they were confident about Sam's suitability, Jane should have constant access to Sam's account and "keep an eye." But she hadn't. Sam had been working peerlessly, so why should she?

Until now. *Why now?* Jane couldn't explain it.

Sam's account opened after a couple of password submissions. Jane scrolled down the e-mail list, latest to last. And what she found surprised her. It *really* surprised her.

What the blazes are you up to, Sam?

Jane double-clicked on the reply from the BfV. And then looked over Sam's enquiry of Interpol regarding a hire car rented from Geneva.

She pushed a swirl of hair back over her right ear. And frowned. She glanced up at the location designation on Sam's screen, a security application that allowed all SIS operators to be tracked via their mobiles: Sam appeared to be on a motorway between Dresden and Berlin.

What?

She breathed out heavily through her nose. What

was Sam playing at?

Oops. Look at the time!

Jane turned off her monitor and gathered her things. She immediately decided not to bother David with this—not yet, anyway. He had too much on his plate. And Jane had to exert some of her own authority. Instead, she'd phone Sam as soon as she had the chance. She'd give her an opportunity to explain herself.

Tankstelle, Freienhufener Eck, Autobahn, Dresden to Berlin

"It doesn't make any sense to me, Wolfgang. Nothing you have told me so far makes any sense." Sam was trying hard not to raise her voice.

Last night when they had eventually started talking, and that wasn't until they were a good twenty clicks outside of Dresden, she'd quickly learned that Wolfgang's command of English was as good as, if not better than, hers. She knew she didn't need to raise her voice to aid translation, the typical British mind-set. Sitting opposite Count Wolfgang II of Neuenburg, the change of pitch in her voice was down to exasperation. Not an aid to translation.

"You're not giving me enough to add any plausibility to your argument. Help me out here!" She pushed herself back against the red false-leather seat with such force that it gave out a sigh. She looked out of the full-length glass window that provided the outside wall of the service station and practised picking out car makes and models as they plied up and down the motorway.

Blue BMW 3 Series. Silver Mercedes C Class.

As she looked, she raised her bandaged fist to her mouth and absently chewed on her exposed knuckles.

Sam could sense Wolfgang looking at her. He was a cool customer, that was for sure. Last night, without any explanation, he'd got into Bertie's passenger seat. With both of them staring ahead, Sam's hands tightly gripping the

114

steering wheel, she had driven away from Pillnitzer Strasse. It was a bizarre half an hour. Two complete strangers thrown together by a series of ridiculous events, with nothing to say to each other. *Madness.*

"You've hardly been honest yourself, Sam. I have told you what I know about Flight FY378 and given you the bare bones of a conspiracy theory that I'm investigating. And you? All I have is 'Uncle Pete.' Not a single believable explanation as to why you followed me to Dresden. Why you went up to my apartment." His English was faultless and, with an ever so slight German "clip," a little bit sexy.

Sexy? What was she thinking? Get real.

"I don't know who you work for—I'm sorry, but I'm not going to believe that you are a psychiatric nurse working for your health service. Especially after the way you dealt with that *dummkopf* in my apartment. I'm not going to say any more until you give me something believable." He paused. She continued to stare through the glass.

A blue Mazda 3, followed by a silver Ford Focus—four door. She felt his eyes on her, those enigmatic eyes. Eyes that displayed kindness and steel at the same time.

Breeding. That was it. It was the way he held himself. His clothes. His look. That unnerving confidence. She hated what he stood for: that upper-class, aristocratic self-satisfied air. Money, which bought time and power—and access. What infuriated her most was he displayed none of those traits—and all of them at the same time.

She dwelt on how they'd got to where they were now. They'd stopped at the *tankstelle* last night after their first exchanged words. She'd said something along the lines of "I'm tired and need to rest. I'm stopping here." He'd replied, "OK. As you wish." They'd both used the service's ablutions, and each of them queued up separately to buy some fast food. They ate in silence at one of the wooden tables in the restaurant.

"I'm going to get my head down. There's a bed in the van. You can sleep on the front seats." His reply had again been curt: "Sure. That'll be fine."

She'd apparently slept like a log and was woken as he closed Bertie's front door. It was light.

Amazingly, he looked just as neat, just as well put together first thing as he did when they'd nodded "goodnight" to each other the previous evening—no words. They'd been short on words. She watched him through the window, heading for the restaurant. He glided everywhere, serenely, as if riding on a Segway.

Sam had checked her watch. It was seven in the morning, German time.

"Shit!" She scrambled for her tablet, throwing her sleeping bag to one side—she'd slept in her clothes—and quickly logged on to the secure account. With the aid of her passkey and fingertip recognition, it took about twenty seconds to access the cloud.

The only new photos of Yemen were satellite images. Immediately absorbed in the detail, she spotted that the pickup had been for a run. It was the same vehicle, though. But there were also tracks from a second vehicle. She couldn't pick out any detail from the tyre prints.

On further inspection, she noticed that there was a hose leading from a nearby well into the compound, probably through one of the windows. It had not been there before. She collected all of that detail in her memory and put a brief report together for the team.

There were already one or two reports in from other members of staff. Having read them, it was clear that there was no new intelligence. She'd need to check again in a couple of hours.

Leaving Bertie in a bit of a mess, she'd picked up her valuables and made her way to the ladies room. Ten minutes of poor grooming later, she still looked unkempt. But her need for coffee was overwhelming. It was certainly more important than the five or six thousand hairs that were sticking out at strange angles, making her look like an undernourished Viking.

Oh well. It'll have to do.

And that's when they'd started to talk—back in the restaurant. Her with a white china cup and saucer of coffee, him with some mint tea. There was not much by way of words, just preliminaries. But neither of them seemed inclined to lead.

Sam's explanation had actually been very close to the truth, no matter how dishonest it seemed. She'd visited the crash site to pay her respects to Uncle Pete. She'd spotted Wolfgang and, mainly because he stared at her in an unnerving and penetrating way, had decided to follow him. She told him that she knew someone who worked for the police at home, and this person had, against all agreed protocol, found Wolfgang's address. The rest was pretty much as he'd seen on his iPad. Implausible it may be, but she was struggling to find another more believable version.

He explained that he had a great interest in plane crashes and other major accidents. His view was that Flight FY378 had been brought down on purpose, along with, over the years, a good number of other aircraft. He told her that he thought many other large-scale disasters—he didn't name any—were also preplanned. He'd gone to the Abondance valley to see if he could get some leads, to feel the place. He needed to soak up the emotion. It helped him with his research.

"Everything is connected. It's all connected." He'd kept repeating that.

In a moment of detail, he told Sam that he had felt vindicated when, last week, the American news reported that the 1979 US nuclear accident on the Pennsylvanian coast could well have been staged. Sam had scoffed at this, but Wolfgang had insisted that he had always thought that the accident was so unlikely that it had to be preplanned. And now a man had come forward and said that he had fixed a valve, so that the pressure in the reactor couldn't be released. Result? Nuclear meltdown.

"You see, everything is connected. These accidents aren't all accidents. Someone is pulling some strings."

When she'd asked for more examples, he'd remained silent.

She pressed him. "Well, come on. then. Tell me more."

Nothing. He shook his head. "Your turn first."

And that's where they were: absolutely nowhere.

She'd had enough.

Sam knew she needed to check her tablet for any direction from this morning's Op Glasshouse meeting. And then she should go home. She would ask Wolfgang where he wanted to be dropped. It was the polite thing to do. She had the time to take him to Berlin, and then she could drive due west, across northern Europe, to the ferry.

She was still staring out of the window. She was tired and overwrought. If she let herself think about it, her uncle's death was still massive. Even having visited the site, it was still stalking her, waiting for an opportunity to break her down. She felt the room closing in. The huge glass windows becoming opaque. She needed to get out.

"Why was my apartment wrecked by that man?" Wolfgang had let her stew for a bit.

The darkness lightened just a touch.

Sam thought and, while doing so, twisted her mouth to one side so her nose bent a bit. Her little pointy nose was one of her best features—her Mum had told her. She used that facial expression to aid concentration. She turned, looking back at Wolfgang.

"He was a thief." She was shaking her head. *How could he be so paranoid?* "You're a rich man and weren't at home. There's a lot of valuable stuff in your apartment. He may have been opportunistic. It happens all the time." And then she added under her breath, "It's not complicated." The last sentence wasn't necessary.

If her retort hurt Wolfgang, he didn't show it. Instead, he pressed on.

"No he wasn't. You haven't watched the video yet."

"Video? You have a copy?" He had her attention again now.

"Look . . ." Wolfgang leaned forward, opened his iPad, typed a few lines, and swiped here and there.

"Watch." He pressed the "Play" button and held the screen so they could both see it.

Sam couldn't believe it. The man—whom, after about thirty seconds, she reckoned she could pick out from a line-up of over a thousand—*was* looking for something. He searched meticulously, room to room, locker to locker. Only then did he trash the place. *To make it* look *like burglary.*

She watched with incredulity as he removed the hard drive from Wolfgang's computer and put it back together again as if it hadn't been tampered with. Of course, if he now smashes it . . . *yes, that's what he's going to do—so nobody would think the hard drive was missing.*

Hang on. This is my bit.

Sam's mouth dropped open as she watched herself move tentatively into the apartment, down the hall, and across the sitting room. And then she watched this stranger bring down a thief. For the last bit she visibly flinched and half turned away from the screen. Once it was over she looked back at Wolfgang. He was smiling openly at her.

"Neat work, Lara!"

It took Sam a second to get that Wolfgang was comparing her to Lara Croft. She half smiled at his rubbish joke. *Typical German.*

So it wasn't burglary. Wolfgang's apartment had been targeted. Someone was looking for something, something Wolfgang had. It was either tangible or, if they could read the disk, electronic.

"Was there much on the disk drive?"

"No. All of my information is wired into a backup facility in Munich. I don't save anything on the machine. There may be some ghost files that might be able to be recovered. But the security on the disk is the very best, so I'd be surprised if anything could be accessed." He had lost his smile and was

119

sitting back in his seat. He looked weary. It was his turn to look out of the window.

"I'm onto something. There is"—he waved his hands about—"*something* connecting a number of these major incidents and disasters. I know it. Your uncle's flight fits a pattern—the manifest was a combination of professional people and tourists. Kill all of them—hide the murder of one." His German accent was stronger when he was serious. He was looking back at her now.

"What?"

He leaned forward and dropped his voice.

"Mass killing, disguising murder. Who would guess?"

It hung in the air.

Sam thought for a second and then dismissed it. She had the look of amused disbelief again.

"No, no. That doesn't make any sense at all." But Sam's head was working through so many conflicting thoughts. Professional ones: *this is the worst conspiracy theory ever. Madness.* Personal ones: *What made Uncle Pete's plane crash? Could he have been murdered?*

She shook her head as if to empty it for further use.

"It's rubbish. It's . . ." She interrupted herself. "How do you account for the US nuclear meltdown? No one was killed when the accident happened."

Wolfgang took the final swig of his tea.

"I don't know. Yet. But it's all connected. I can feel it."

They were interrupted by Sam's secure phone vibrating silently on the table. It was moving slowly toward the edge. She stopped it before it fell on the floor.

It was Jane.

"Look, Wolfgang. You're as mad as a fish. A typical blooming aristocrat. I've got to take this." She was pointing at her phone. She pressed the green "Receive" button and raised it to her ear.

"Hang on . . ." She looked back at Wolfgang, covering the mouthpiece with her free hand. "Can I have a copy of that video? I know some people . . ."

Chapter Eight

SIS Headquarters, Vauxhall, London

Jane had left the Op Glasshouse meeting with the same level of frustration as everyone else. There was little new intelligence. The only tangible evidence they had was Sam Green's white truck, which could be placed at both the terrorist training camp and the compound in Hajjah. GCHQ had intercepted a mobile signal that had come from the compound. It was received by a handset that was located within a couple of hundred metres of the Daesh safe house in Sana'a. It had lasted seventy-four seconds, but there was nothing in the call that could corroborate the SRR soldiers being held at either location. All in all, it wasn't much. And time wasn't on their side.

At least there would be another satellite pass in a couple of hours, enabling Sam and Frank to look over a new set of images to see if there were any changes that might influence the decision making.

The SAS squadron was operationally ready at RAF Akrotiri. David had given his team only the broadest outline plan—even among the very highest echelons of the British Intelligence Services, everything still operated on a "need-to-know" basis. H-hour was confirmed as 2.30 a.m. local; that would be 11.30 p.m. in the UK. A small recce group would be parachuted in early from a Hercules air transporter; the assault group flown in by two SF Chinook helicopters within minutes of H-hour. They would all be collected by Chinook when the operation was over. She knew it would be much more complicated than that, but at least she could picture the scene.

Sam! I must phone her.

Jane dialled Sam's number and waited for her to pick up. Initially Sam was having a conversation with somebody, and then she said, "Hello." The melodic bleep in the background reminded both of them that the call was insecure.

"Who's that you're talking to?" Jane was confused.

Bleep. Bleep. Sam didn't reply straight away.

"Oh, it's someone I met at the crash site."

Bleep.

"How's it all going?"

"Fine. Thanks." Jane heard Sam let out a long breath. "I'm on my way home now. I should be back in the UK first thing tomorrow."

"Where are you?" Jane could have come out and asked, *"What the bloomin' hell are you doing near Berlin?"* However, she felt the need to test Sam.

Bleep, bleep. Was Sam searching for an appropriate answer? Bleep.

"Sam, are you still on?"

"Yes, Jane. I'm here." Bleep. A further pause. "Look, it's complicated, and I'd rather talk all this through with you when I get back to base. D'you mind?"

No lies so far. That made Jane feel a little better. Bleep. It was her turn to think for a second.

"Mmm, OK, Sam. Come and see me as soon as you get back." She held the phone to her ear and stared over her desk at the door to her office. She was looking for some inspiration.

No. She couldn't let Sam gallivant around Europe and abuse her security clearance by e-mailing international organisations without authorisation. Not without being pressed for an explanation. And Jane couldn't continue to tread on eggshells just because Sam was always on the edge of a breakdown.

"And you'd better come with a decent explanation as to why you've been e-mailing Interpol and the BfV. *And* why I'm talking to you within a stone's throw of Berlin. Which, if I remember rightly, is nowhere near the Alps." She inwardly flinched when she said it. At this distance, who knew what Sam Green would do now?

Bleep. Bleep. Bleep. Bleep. A sigh.

"I will. It's a short and unbelievable story. But all done in good faith. And, Jane?"

"Yes."

"Thanks for not jumping down my throat on this. What I did was wrong, but the outcome may be of use—certainly for me in beginning to come to terms with Uncle Pete's death."

"That's fine, Sam. We'll talk about it when you are back." Jane changed tack. "There should be some new images through in the next hour or so. As things stand, the operation is on for tonight. What do you think?"

Bleep. Bleep.

"I'm not convinced, Jane. But what else is there to do?" Bleep. "I'll have a look at the photos when they come in. Where will you be tonight?"

"In the office. David is heading across the river." Jane almost said, "to the JIC," but stopped herself from breaking security protocol in time. "I could phone you when we have something."

"That would be great, Jane. Thanks. See you tomorrow morning. And, hopefully, if things go well tonight, we'll be going to the pub to celebrate."

"After I've given you a bollocking for e-mailing the BfV?" Bleep. Bleep. Then in a softer tone, "Sure, that would be great. Drive carefully."

Jane hung up.

Sam Green. What are you on?

Jane reached for her landline and, using one of the secure lines, dialled the number of her oppo at the CIA in Langley. They might have something new on Manning and Bell.

Wolfgang waved good-bye to his new, if rather odd, friend Sam as she drove away in her bright yellow VW transporter. By the time she had dropped him at the main station in Berlin, they had started to get on reasonably well. That is, they were passing more than just the time of day with each other.

There was something about her that he couldn't fathom. She was sharp-witted, intelligent, obviously very fit—she'd beaten him over four hundred metres from the apartment to the van—and had lightning-quick reactions. He'd clumsily let his phone slip from his hand when they were walking together back to "Bertie," as she called her campervan. Before it had hit the ground, she had dropped her shoulder, reached down with her good hand, and caught it. He'd given up the moment he had fumbled.

Conversationally, it was slightly more tricky. Both of them were guarded, but he thought she was hiding much more than he was. At least he was honest about what he wasn't telling her. She'd ducked and weaved her way around his questions, often giving a monosyllabic "No" to something she wasn't going to answer.

She didn't work for the health service, that was for sure. Back at Bertie, after they had finished breakfast, he had casually looked across at her, sitting on the back seat. She was working with a very expensive and ruggedised tablet. He thought he saw her use her thumb to access the machine biometrically. And by her side she had a pinkish red passkey, which, a little earlier, she had used to obtain what he had assumed was an additional password. At that point, Sam had spotted him looking and she had turned her back to him, hiding what she was up to. No, she didn't work for the medical profession.

She couldn't be a spy, even though the equipment she used was stuff he would choose to keep state secrets secret. Certainly not a spy in the conventional James Bond sense.

There was something "missing" about her, which Wolfgang thought made her vulnerable, almost breakable. For him, she was too fragile to work for her country's intelligence services. Not that he was an expert.

He noticed her vulnerability most when she had been looking out of the restaurant window whilst they were at the *tankstelle*. She wore a hesitant, faraway look. Yes, she was attractive, in a basic, uncomplicated sort of way. She had a delicate nose, dark green eyes, and skin that smoothly covered midheight cheekbones and, every so often, gave way to an explosion of freckles. Her hair, which had been a mess at the crash site and even more so now, was thick, auburn, and unfathomably curly. Yes, she was *schön*. No, that wouldn't do. The English word *cute* was such a more descriptive word.

But it was her vulnerability mixed with her alarming efficiency that, when added to the casual way she looked and dressed, attracted Wolfgang. *Please—not in a physical sense.* Just in an "I want to look after you" sort of way. And that was the curious thing. He felt she needed looking after. Yet, she'd managed to fight her way out of his apartment against a man twice her size.

It was all very perplexing and, as he'd never felt like this before, a little bit alarming. She was unlike anyone else he'd ever met. After just a few hours in her presence, he wanted to get to know her better. But that was a hopeless thought— *wasn't it?*

He really should stay well clear of relationships.

Now she was gone. At least for the moment. She had to get back to work—whatever that was—with her high-end tablet and furtive ways. He needed to return to Munich to try to piece together what the last thirty-six hours had been about. His chance meeting with the Koreans had been interesting. Professor Lim was clearly a great loss to the world of emerging energy supplies—he'd need to investigate that avenue further. And, while he'd been away, his tower had accessed three accounts that required further study.

Along with Sam, to whom he had sent a copy of the break-in video, he should also study the clip and see what clues might be forthcoming. It would also give him a chance to see her in action again.

Most of all, he needed to practise his violin. He wasn't a man who suffered from any particular stress, but the events of the last couple of days had taken their toll. His way of relaxing was to play Bruch's quite glorious Violin Concerto. A number of times.

Bad Auetal, Tankstelle, Hanover, Germany

Sam pulled into the next *tankstelle* as soon as she could after her phone had pinged. The new images were in.

Those of the compound taken by the satellite showed little change. It was devoid of activity. Which was odd. *The absence of normal.* Was it more than a coincidence that every shot they had gotten of the place showed no signs of life? The previous set of images had the those coming from the well, and she had picked out that the white truck had moved. The new group seemed to show an additional set of tyre tracks in the compound's yard—the tread was different—she'd make note of that. But, so far, not a single shot of a human. Or even some cattle—*or a camel.* It wasn't as though the village was deserted; panning out, she could pick out a number of people wandering about close by. It didn't make sense.

There was nothing in the compound. It was as though they knew the satellite was overhead and, for the fifteen- or twenty-minute pass time, they had all scurried indoors.

Surely they couldn't know the timings of the satellite passes—could they?

With that thought, Sam couldn't get Kurt Manning's face out of her mind. When she had been at her most vulnerable in Kenema, in Sierra Leone, Manning had spoken to her. She couldn't recall it word for word, but it was something along the lines of, "So you're Sam Green. It's a shame we haven't been able to get to know each other better." He'd then drugged her—and Henry—and set the hostel alight to make their deaths look like an accident.

She shivered at the thought.

Now, here on the Saudi peninsula, Kurt Manning and Ralph Bell were helping to train Islamic militants. After Sierra Leone, the collective view was that these rogue CIA agents had orchestrated a plan to release Ebola within the confines of St. Paul's underground station. The plan had failed. But if it had been successful, the blame would have fallen to Daesh or Al-Qaeda. The outcome would have been a sharp rise of intolerance toward Muslims and the Islamic faith in UK and western Europe—*a dramatic rise.* The present, reasonably quick march to an all-out religious war between Islam and Christianity would pick up its pace.

Their appearance in Captain Tony James's photos indicated that they might be pursuing the same agenda. *But who was funding them?* Were they operating on their own? Critically for now, were they providing the details of the US military satellite passes to the Daesh militants in the Hajjah compound?

Possibly. It really didn't bear thinking about.

She sighed and closed the folder on the satellite photos. She opened a second set—marked "Terrestrial."

The SIS team in Sana'a had taken some good-quality and revealing images of the safe house in the Yemeni capital. There was a photo of one man entering through the big wooden gates. Sam didn't recognise him, but would certainly match him if his face ever turned up again. The photos of the house would give the military planners a good choice of entrances and exits, if they were ever needed. Other details of the busy street added further important intelligence. The safe house occupied a corner plot. On the main street side, it was terraced to another similarly constructed house. They were both made of sand-coloured blocks, with a flat castellated roof. The large arched opening, where Sam had seen the men entering and exiting, was secured with two big wooden doors. On either side of the front door were two windows, which were matched upstairs.

Down the side street, the house was about ten metres long, followed by a two-metre-high sand-block wall, which seemed to protect a large yard. The yard extended the plot by a further fifteen metres. The side wall of the house had another four windows—two up and two down—and you could enter the yard by way of a large, sliding metal gate. The gate looked new.

Sam couldn't make out any guards, but she did see two poorly hidden remote cameras, high up on the walls, looking up and down both the main and side street. Sam noted all of these details, plus many more, and added them to the report for the Op Glasshouse team.

If only they had the same detail for the Hajjah compound.

She knew from the briefing notes that the SAS was sending in a recce party before the main assault. This team would be able to get some images of the compound, but it would be at night and from only one or two vantage points. They couldn't afford to give the game away by moving about too much, or getting too close.

To provide the best support, Sam needed to be at her desk to view and manipulate the videos and photos. *I have to get going.* But, before she closed up and got driving again, she had a quick look at the "open" source images that the team hadn't culled from what had been deposited by Mervin overnight.

She quickly filtered anything that wasn't labelled Saudi or Yemen. That left thirteen photos. These were mostly from freelance journalists who had published images on their own or other websites. There were also two videos: one from KSA1, the Saudi equivalent of BBC1, and one from Al Jazeera. Both were short news clips of the latest fighting in 'Amran, northwest of the Yemeni capital, Sana'a.

The two video clips gave nothing away. Yemeni police

and army chasing up and down the streets, firing randomly at rebels.

She looked at the photos. She was just about to write them off when one caught her eye. It was dated 8-10-15. *That's yesterday.* It was taken by an American journalist, Kevin Pavey. She'd come across his work before. Most of his photos were war images, but Sam remembered that, a couple of years ago, he had taken some really atmospheric shots in Patagonia for *National Geographic*. He was a talented photographer and currently working in the Middle East. The last time she had seen one of his photos, it was from Karbala in Iraq: a young woman being summarily executed with a pistol. The perpetrators were unknown.

This photo had been lifted from his website; it was taken in 'Amran, in Yemen. The image was of two young boys cradling a baby girl in their arms. The backdrop was the ruins of a single-storey building with a sandy-green armoured personnel carrier (APC) camped unceremoniously behind one of the broken walls. From the angle of the photo, the APC appeared to be parked in the kids' living room.

The ridiculously young family looked lifeless, sapped of any energy—gaunt and afraid. Their clothes had probably once been brightly coloured, but any vibrancy had been washed out by the detergent of war. Blues and reds becoming greys and browns. Kevin had called the image "*Our house is now the police's garage.*" It was heartbreaking.

But Sam's interest was wider than the context of the shock of another Middle Eastern family torn apart by unrest. She had spotted something else.

The house, the family, and the APC were the story. To give them some perspective, Kevin had widened the view to include, in the far distance, a crossroads. It had also suffered from the ravages of the civil war: black-and-white striped traffic lights positioned at jaunty angles, no longer controlling anything. On closer inspection, crossing from left to right and not quite fully in focus, was a black pickup. She was confident it was a modern Toyota Hilux.

Sam's pulse rate quickened.

Quickly crosschecking Kevin Pavey's image against Tony James's original Yemeni photos, she was pretty sure it was the same vehicle that Manning and Bell had driven into the camp. Unfortunately, without the benefit of decent image processing, she couldn't make out the driver. But she was pretty certain it was the same vehicle.

What made it possibly a very special find was that there were a couple of signposts that not been destroyed by the fighting. One, in the direction of travel of the black Hilux, pointed toward Harad—thankfully, some signs were still written in both Arabic and English. Her geographical knowledge of Yemen wasn't perfect, but she thought she might be onto something.

She opened Google Maps and honed in on western Yemen. She *did* have something. If you were in 'Amran and wanted to get to Hajjah—where the Daesh compound was— you would take the N5, following the signposts to Harad.

Black Hilux following directions to Harad. *Therefore heading toward the compound in Hajjah.* Manning and Bell? Yesterday?

If she'd been on her machine in the office she could have used the software to sharpen the images. But she was in Hanover. *Bugger.*

With the photo still open on her tablet, she found the appropriate tab and pressed "Forward." An e-mail box opened up. Sam typed in Frank's address and cc'd Jane. She scribbled down her thoughts, suggesting to Frank that he do the work for her. She then pressed "Send."

She *so* needed to get back to the office.

David checked his watch for the umpteenth time. It was 21.40. H-Hour was in just under two hours. The senior JIC staff had decided to gather in the conference room for the duration of the operation. Their separate teams manned their desks back in their offices. If anything new came in, the seven of them could make a quick, collective decision. They'd been joined by the secretary of state for defence, Simon Bradshaw. He, unlike the PM, wasn't at a black-tie event in the city with some important bankers.

The conference room had all of the comms they needed. Joe Public probably thought that they could speak to the soldiers on the ground, watch their every move remotely via multiple satellites and roving cameras. The truth was that the best they could do was to follow team leaders on an electronic map and hear some of the radio traffic between key men on the ground and their headquarters in Saudi.

They could also pick up calls between the aircraft and the ground. The technology enabled them to listen to the Hercules transport plane that would drop in the eight-man recce party. David looked up at the electronic map; that had happened about ten minutes ago. They could also listen to the two SF Chinook helicopters, which would fly the main assault party into position, about two clicks from the compound. And return to pick them all up about twenty minutes after H-Hour.

That all assumed the comms and satellite links worked. Which they often didn't.

The map on the wall at the end of the long desk showed a returning Hercules and a blue spot with "30B" next to it: the designation of the recce party that had just parachuted in. To David, looking at the scale of the map, it appeared that they were a long way away from the target.

"Alasdair, isn't the recce party a bit further from the target than intended?"

The director of Special Forces was already on his feet and

up at the map. He was using his hands to judge the distances.

"About five clicks too far south, but out of danger. I've no idea why that's happened. Jumping is more of an art than a skill, especially if there's a strong wind, which there is tonight." He stopped for a second, staring at the map intently, calculating. "They'll still be at the target before the assault team and will get eyes on as well as marking the FUP." Alasdair had the confidence of a man who had commanded 22 SAS for two and a half years, as well as leading an SF troop and a squadron before that.

He was facing the team now.

David didn't get the jargon. He raised both his hands in a "what are you talking about?" way.

"Eh, sorry. FUP. Forming-up place. It's the location where the assault group will form up before they attack. The recce party will mark it with directional LEDs that are activated when the assault group is within five hundred metres. It allows them to attack without having to do their own reconnaissance. That's one of the reasons why the recce party goes in early: to get everyone to the right place."

That was clearer?

David hadn't joined the army's University Officer Training Corps whilst he was at Bristol. He'd been too busy rowing and drinking. Although he had managed to get to grips with a good deal of the military terminology over the past thirty years, there was still a lot that was mumbo-jumbo.

Alasdair walked across to the refreshment table and poured himself a cup of coffee.

"Fill-up, anyone?"

A murmur of "no thanks" percolated round the room.

The extra miles the recce party now had to tab heightened the tension in the room. On a positive note, for his part David was now more confident that the SRR soldiers were being held in the compound at Hajjah. Jane's team's work with the black pickup had helped. It seemed likely that either Kurt Manning or Ralph Bell, or both, had been heading up to Hajjah yesterday. Langley was clear that neither had current

CIA credentials. Manning, who had worked all his life as a CIA operative until three years ago, would still have residual information, such as US military satellite orbits and timings. That might explain why all of the overheads of the target showed no life at all. Insider knowledge of satellite trajectories would also allow vehicle movement into and out of the compound when the satellites weren't overhead. Manning and Bell could be in the compound now, their truck snuck in during a satellite blackout.

Yes, the intelligence pointed toward Hajjah.

David stood up and paced up and down. He went to one of the windows and looked down Whitehall toward the Cenotaph. It was a huge night. He'd only been on hand once before to witness an SAS raid to release British nationals. That had gone well, and two journalists held in northern Iraq had been pulled out unharmed. There had been no ceremony attached to it—indeed, all of the plaudits had been given to the Iraqi Army, which had provided two liaison officers for the assault. He'd also been party to plenty of botched rescues undertaken by other nations—along with some notable successes.

He had followed a good number of search-and-destroy operations by the British SF when there were no hostages involved. Those were less complex, slightly less sensitive.

Tonight was very different; it was complex and edgy. It lacked conclusive intelligence on the number of enemy, their weaponry, and their locations. That made it complicated when planning the attack—you didn't need to be a tactician to see that. And they didn't even know if Tony James and Ted Rogers were in the compound.

A wing and a prayer.

A mobile rang. The director of Defence Intelligence, Lieutenant General Jack Downs, picked it up from the table in front of him.

"Hi, Steve. Yep. What can I do for you?"

There was a long silence, interspersed with the odd high-pitched sound of the tiny speaker on Jack's phone. He was on his feet, walking to where David was by the outside wall, but he chose to look out of a different window.

"I see. I see. And is there any feedback?"

More quiet, punctuated by the squealing speaker.

"And the DA was clear that the assaults should have been simultaneous?"

Quiet. *Squeal.*

"OK. Thanks. We'll mull that over here now. I'll let you know if there is a change of plan."

Jack turned away from the window. The secretary of state and all six members of the JIC stared at him.

"The Saudis went in early. An hour ago. They've cleaned the place out. No casualties and no sign of the SRR."

David didn't know who should speak first, not that there was a lot to say other than, "What the hell were the Saudis playing at?"

It was the defence secretary who spoke first.

"What does this mean for the attack on Hajjah?"

David wanted to say something, but Alasdair beat him to it.

"Go ahead. Daesh will struggle to connect attacks in Saudi with locations in Yemen. We have troops in the air"—he pointed toward two blue dots moving south, about to cross the Saudi border—"And even if the news of an attack got to Sana'a and even Hajjah, we should still have an element of surprise."

"David?" Simon had turned to him.

"Let me get in touch with our team that is keeping an eye on the safe house in Sana'a. If there is any movement at that location, it might mean that the message has got around. And, Melvin—what about GCHQ?"

Melvin Hoare looked up. He had his mobile to his ear, his spare hand tapping away on the conference table. He pointed at his phone.

"I'm on to my team now. We'll know within ten minutes if there's been any increased signals traffic at either locations."

"Jon. You lead the JIC. What's your view?"

Jon Trent, the JIC's chairman, looked at each of his colleagues individually.

"Let's do it." He looked at the director of SF. "Alasdair, I'm guessing the recce party should be able to give some indication as to whether the compound has been spooked?"

Alasdair glanced across at the screen. The recce party's blue dot was closer to Hajjah than the last time they had looked, but still some distance away from the target.

"I'll get a message to them and tell them that time's of the essence. Rough estimate says they'll be in location no more than fifteen minutes before the assault group arrives." He paused. "And, before you ask, the last thing we want to do is to amend H-Hour."

The last words from the Alasdair hung in the tense air.

David let the atmosphere envelop him, his mind racing through all the possible permutations.

"What happens if the terrorists bug out? When's the next satellite pass?" David didn't think either was a stupid question.

"Then the boys will have a field day demolishing a worthless compound in deepest Yemen." Alasdair smiled. But David could see that his army friend's confidence had taken a hit.

Five Hundred Metres Short of the Daesh Compound, Hajjah, Yemen

Sergeant Mitch Riles looked through his Gen 2 thermal imaging sight that sat on a small tripod on the ridge in front of him. He was used to the inverted colours of the display. Hot was yellow; cold was dark blue. With no moonlight, he had the best seat in the house.

Just off the hill in front of him, the Daesh compound was a medium blue silhouette against a dark blue sky, the buildings still emitting a small bit of yellow heat from the earlier baking by the sun. The windows were a blackish blue, the glass reflecting any heat. Apart from that, it was pretty much one colour: navy blue. What surprised Mitch was that there were no hot spots. There was nothing warm-bodied in the compound that gave a spike of yellow heat. *You would have thought there might have been some guards.* Or a dog.

While his boss's team had laid out the FUP and marked it with guide lights, his team had quickly recce'd the compound from three sides. It had been a very short overview; they'd arrived late on task. The eight of them had dropped four clicks short of the planned DZ, mainly because the wind had changed direction and strengthened from the initial prediction. Making a full recovery whilst in the air wasn't possible, although with some skilful gliding, they had managed to reduce the error from six to four kilometres.

The good news was that the compound looked like the model they had knocked up out of wood and cardboard at Akrotiri the day before. His team had picked out some more details, like five windows and a couple of drainpipes. Of note, they had found two "pooh" holes, small openings at ground level on the outside of the building where excrement came out. Inside, there would be a basic wooden and brick toilet. It was a simple contraption: people did their business as usual inside and the pooh ended up on the street. Simple, but disgusting if you were walking nearby.

From his perspective, they had their uses. Like windows and doors, these were points of weakness where an attacker had to work less hard to breach a wall. From a hostage point of view, they were also perfect entry points. The enemy never held their hostages in the toilet. So you could blow a hole in the wall and be fairly certain that you wouldn't damage your cargo.

Mitch swivelled the focus on the sight. To his right he picked out seven—no, eight—hot spots. Moving right to left. It was the left-hand assault group. He looked in the distance beyond them and saw eight slightly smaller hot spots. The right-hand assault group.

The plan was straightforward: At exactly two thirty, left assault would breach the front gates, and right assault would breach the back wall—almost directly opposite the front gate—using one of the pooh holes Mitch's team had found. Once in, both teams would work anticlockwise, clearing room to room until they ended up at the other's original breach.

He checked his watch. It was 02:22. He looked again through his sight. Left assault hot spots were a few metres from the gate now; they'd be preparing the explosives soon. Right assault hot spots were twenty metres out.

It was as quiet as it was dark. The whole troop was on radio silence. All of their radios were encrypted, but a simple intercept receiver would easily pick up any transmissions and alert the enemy that something untoward was going on. Their radios would only be used in an emergency. *At the moment.* At two thirty it would all go live; you wouldn't be able to hear yourself for radio traffic.

Mitch checked again. Still no hot spots in the compound. That was good, in some respects. If you assumed the terrorists and hostages were safely tucked up in bed—the thick, sand block walls preventing infrared radiation from escaping the compound. *But no guards?* It didn't make a lot of sense.

02:29.

Here we go.

Bang! Bang! The breach explosions, set to exactly the right magnitude to blow a man-size hole, reverberated around the compound. Mitch pulled away from the thermal imaging sight, which was now a screen full of bright yellow as the heat from the explosions sent the sensors haywire. Instead, he watched the event unfold without aids. It was now a well-illuminated show.

Bang! A further explosion.

Shit. What the . . .? That wasn't planned!

A noise like a man in agony echoed from the compound. The airwaves burst into life.

"Contact. Claymore! Wait out!"

Mitch's mind reeled with the call. At lightning speed his brain scrambled through all the possible scenarios, but none made sense. Claymores were Vietnam-aged antipersonnel mines. Ambush was their speciality. Set at ankle height, the mine was designed on an outward curve and, when detonated, shot hundreds of ball-bearings and other pieces of shrapnel toward its victims in a wide arc. They could be devastating.

Did they still use them? And did the boss really just call a claymore?

We've been ambushed, but there's no firing. *Surely now, somebody should be firing.* Claymore first; then shoot. It was the perfect ambush technique.

Not this time. There was no firing—just an explosion.

"30 Alpha, two men down." Mitch recognised the voice of Captain Thomas. It had a sharp edge. "31 Alpha, carry on with the clearance. Watch for booby traps in every room."

"31 Alpha. Roger. Wait . . . *Room 1 clear*!"

The beams of high-powered torches led the procession from room to room on both sides of the compound.

"33 Alpha—Room 6 clear!"

And so it went on. Teams clearing rooms and reporting accordingly. There was no gunfire, no further explosions. Just beams of light, flashing around like a laser show at a pop concert. The light was accompanied by radio acknowledgments as the compound was cleared. The code word for the hostages, *cargo*, wasn't transmitted.

The SRR boys weren't there. It was an empty operation—the worst kind. All the effort and none of the reward.

Someone's fucked up.

Mitch's team was keeping an eye on neighbouring houses and streets. They used a different frequency to talk among themselves, confirming that, whilst some lights had come on in a couple of houses and a few of dogs were barking as if their tails were on fire, outside the compound, everything else remained relatively calm.

Finally, "30 Bravo—compound clear. No enemy and no cargo."

"30 Alpha. Roger. Find me now. I'm by the front gate with 32 Charlie. We have one walking wounded and one pax on a stretcher. 21A is with him, and he is stable."

Mitch kept his team in place. Their job now was to stay in overwatch while 30 Alpha and Bravo extricated to the HLS.

He reached for his pressel.

"30 Alpha and Bravo, this is 11 Alpha. All good from here. HLS is clear. We'll cover you as planned."

With that, Mitch, switching back to his thermal imager, watched the two teams leave the compound. It was dark again, the torches extinguished. He could see fourteen able-bodied hot spots accompanied, near the front of the group, by one dragging his leg and another lying on a stretcher. They were making their way to his left, in the direction of the HLS. They would be there in five or six minutes.

Once the others were secure at the HLS, and when he had confirmation that the two Chinooks were just minutes out, his and the boss's team would pull out. They would be the last onto the helicopters.

Pride of Dover, *English Channel*

Sam thought of nothing in particular. It had been a wacky forty-eight hours. Sitting on a blue bench, her back to the slanting windows of some deck way above the English Channel, she tried to sweep the fog from her mind. She wanted to piece it all together: the drive; the crash site with all its trials and fears; meeting the Koreans; her first unnerving cross with Wolfgang; the images from Yemen— so many of them, with so little to say; the mad dash across western Europe to Dresden; the apartment incident—*oh God, the video!*; Wolfgang again, standing in front of Bertie like the apparition he was; their discussions, which led to nothing of consequence; and now the trip home.

Was she any further forward? She had visited the crash site, but she found no closure. She and Wolfgang had exchanged e-mail addresses, and they'd both said they'd keep in touch. She would certainly try to find out who the man in the flat was. And, she guessed, Wolfgang would continue to pursue his ridiculous, poorly supported conspiracy theory that a good number of major international accidents had been preconceived by some higher power.

Did he really believe that Uncle Pete's plane had been brought down on purpose?

Murder hidden by mass murder. *Nonsense.*

It didn't hang together. No matter which way you looked at it.

The journey from Berlin to Calais had been an interminable one. After the stop near Hanover, where she'd had the excitement of reviewing the latest photos and making the connection with the black Hilux, there had been little to entertain her. She had been flaky, but not so much that she needed to stop.

Driving on the Belgian motorways, especially as the light faded, was akin to watching a French film noir without subtitles. It was dull as cold dishwater—incomprehensibly tedious. She understood why the Germans hadn't stopped for a picnic. Twice.

She had trundled along, the white lines thankfully providing Bertie with all the driving advice he needed, while Sam's thoughts had sloshed from side to side, not focusing on much. When she did dwell on where she was with her life, the grey mist crept in. As it always did. Mist that clouded rational thought and forced her to feel pathetically sorry for herself. It was the mist's fault, not hers.

Mum and Dad. And now Uncle Pete. Apart from her boss Jane, her next-door workmate Frank, a couple of old army pals, and, if she were pressed, probably Henry in New York, she had nobody to call a friend. Not like a best pal, one who

140

looked out for her no matter the time of day. She really felt that she had nobody.

Her mum had always been her best friend . . . *no, she couldn't think about her without crying.* She couldn't. So she didn't.

Wolfgang was an interesting diversion, and she struggled with defining his position in her sad life. She was military—well, ex-military. Everything had a part in the order of things. Nothing was allowed to drift about. If it stood still long enough, paint it white.

But Wolfgang defied defining. He was enigmatic and mysterious. And, she had to admit, attractive. Add to that, being honest, he was also rich. *Did that matter?* She would keep in touch. Maybe she would go out to Germany to see him during her next leave. If he wanted her to. *When was that due?* At least they had something in common to talk about.

Her phone rang. It was Jane. *God, an update on the Op.* She'd almost forgotten about it in her tiredness.

Bleep. "Hello, Jane. I'm on the ferry."

"I know, Sam, I have your location on my screen."

Great. She had to remember to turn the bloomin' thing off when she needed some space.

"The Op has gone ahead."

"And?" Pressing. Sam was in a rush now.

Bleep. "Noting the insecure line, I can tell you that the place was deserted. The boys were ambushed on the way in. A claymore. Two down, but both alive." Bleep. Bleep. "They have some photos and video, which should be on the cloud tomorrow morning—sorry, this morning." It was well past midnight.

Bleep. "So they knew we were coming?"

"That's the collective view here. The ambush tells that story."

They both said nothing for a few seconds. The line continued to bleep.

"The two other SRR lads will be dead now?"

141

"We think so. But let's talk about that when you're in." Bleep. "Oh, I don't know if it adds anything, but the Saudis went in early. Could have spooked the Op? Whichever way you look at it, it's been a helluva cock-up."

Bleep. Sam didn't respond. *Cock-up.* That's one way of describing it.

"Sam?"

"Sorry. Distracted. It's been a complicated forty-eight hours. I'll tell you all about it tomorrow. Let's hope the photos give us something. It would be nice to think we had the right target, even if it was empty last night."

"Yes, indeed. Drive carefully, Sam."

"Will do, Jane."

The line went dead.

How did they know? Did the Saudis spook Daesh? Was it Manning and Bell again? Have they still got connections that could have unearthed the Op details? Maybe there's another leak somewhere. Who else knew about the SF assault?

Sam was sure that the post-Op wash-up would pursue all of these lines of enquiry.

She stopped thinking, her mind blank. She was so tired. The driving, the excitement, the whole episode. And now this: the two SRR soldiers. Two of the army's very best almost certainly sentenced to death by the events of the past few hours. And two more injured. Chasing shadows.

Captain Tony James and Corporal Ted Groves. This one chance had been their only lifeline. And now it was gone.

God, it was all rubbish.

Sam was crying again. She sniffled and wiped her eyes. The ferry was full of eastern Europeans. She didn't have the energy to ask herself what she thought about their situation. At least they had passports and were free to roam. Unlike so many other families she'd been following on their miserable journey to liberty.

She *so* needed to get back to work.

Conspiracy

Chapter Nine

Parliament Square, London

David was tired. It had been a long night and a very early morning. The PM had wanted a face to face with him, Jon, Alasdair, and Jack, at six that morning at Number 10; a mini-JIC with the prime minister. His head hadn't hit the pillow much before 3:00 a.m., and that had been on his pull-you-down in the office. One of the luxuries of working for SIS: if you needed to sleep over, the firm could oblige.

The good news was that neither of the two members of the SAS injured in last night's rescue Op had succumbed to their wounds. Luck was the major factor, as the claymore appeared to have been set up in a rush; much of the mine's fragmentation had been fired at the floor. The first two soldiers into the compound were hit, and most of the shrapnel had struck them below knee. Anything above the knee had lost momentum, having bounced off the sand and gravel floor. Their body armour had protected their torsos from most of that blast.

It wasn't all good news for the soldiers, though. One would almost certainly lose a leg. The second would need major reconstructive surgery below the knee, but should be OK; he might even remain in the SAS.

As for Captain James and Corporal Groves, his analysts hadn't yet had a chance to look over the images from the assault in any detail. Only then would they know if the soldiers had been in the compound. *At some point.* If they had been, then why did Daesh pull everyone out? Could it have been that the early attack by the Saudis had spooked them? GCHQ had picked up some mobile traffic in the area, but couldn't pin it down to an exact location—not yet, anyway. Or maybe Manning and Bell had some insider knowledge and passed it on? The short answer was that they didn't know. And that's what they had told the PM.

"When are we likely to know what has happened to the two hostages?" the PM had asked.

"With our current level of intelligence, which is patchy, most likely when Daesh pass footage to Al Jazeera of their execution," David had responded honestly. It was an awful thing to say, but true. Now wasn't the time to be flowery.

The PM had mused for a few seconds. He looked surprisingly well for a man who had been entertained by bankers until the early hours.

"Do we go public with the failed rescue attempt?"

That was the million-dollar question. The JIC hadn't been able to come to a unanimous verdict on the answer. David's view was: not yet. They should prepare a statement that would respond to online or TV news footage of the soldiers' execution. Something that, whilst condemning the executions in the strongest possible terms, acknowledged that British soldiers had undertaken a dangerous rescue attempt, deep in Yemeni territory. By the time they had got to the location, the hostages had been moved on. *Blah, blah.*

Jon, the JIC's chair, didn't answer immediately. He was about to, his right hand slightly raised, but David thought his prevarication spoke volumes. The PM pressed again.

"Do we mention that we suffered casualties in last night's assault?"

That was an easier question to answer. Jon had no problem taking the lead, making up for his previous indecision.

"No, sir, we don't think so. Daesh, whilst they will know we went in, are unlikely to have any details of the operation. Any disclosure of casualties by us will only attract supplementaries from the press as to how they were injured. And how badly."

The PM nodded and then pressed on.

"Come on, fellas, why has the JIC not been able to come up with a unanimous view on releasing a line about the rescue attempt? I guess it's you, Alasdair—you don't want the Special Forces' role mentioned?"

Alasdair cleared his throat.

"That's correct, sir. And whilst I can understand why we may want to tell the public that we weren't exactly resting on our laurels, I do think it creates more questions than it answers. The most obvious: Why was our intelligence so poor?"

Alasdair wasn't being as pointed as he came across, but it was a question that they'd all been asking themselves. Alasdair, of course, hadn't wanted his men to go in in the first place. He could easily have been saying "I told you so." But he was much bigger than that.

"When will we know if the soldiers were being held in the compound?"

David answered. "We'll be much clearer by close of play tonight. My analysts are poring over the images brought back by the SF now."

"OK."

The PM collected his thoughts.

"Here's what I want to happen. If we get conclusive proof that the soldiers were being held at the compound, then we prepare a press release that says that we attempted to rescue them. This goes out after news of any execution. If we don't get proof, then we don't mention a rescue attempt." Whilst he was giving direction to the whole team, it was the Cabinet Secretary who was making notes. He was the one who would issue a briefing note detailing who was to do what when the meeting was over.

"And, Nigel," he now looked directly at the Foreign Secretary, who had been quiet up until that point, "If we do come clean about the rescue attempt, I want it out there that we believe that the Saudis spooked the operation by going in early. We can leak that from an embassy somewhere, possibly Washington. You choose. I want the world to know that, if it weren't for the blundering of the Special Forces of another country—you won't need to specify— Captain James and Corporal Groves would be with us now

146

enjoying a pink gin. Happy?"

Nigel nodded, a little sourly.

And at that point it was all over—6.22 a.m. according to David's watch.

Within a few minutes, David was out of the front door of No. 10, through the back gates of the Foreign and Commonwealth Office (FCO), across the FCO's courtyard, and out onto King Charles Street. For anyone prying from Whitehall, looking into Downing Street—especially the press—to all intents and purposes none of them had attended a before-breakfast meeting with the PM. Emerging from the building at slightly different times, they might have been in separate meetings at the FCO. It wasn't brilliantly deceptive, but it was one way of keeping the press guessing. They didn't want this going public.

As he strode down Whitehall toward Parliament Square, he reran the meeting in his head. The PM didn't mess about, that was for sure. Whilst David wasn't necessarily in tune with all of his government's policies, there was no doubt that the current prime minister was a decisive chap.

David headed away from Parliament Square, down Milbank to Lambeth Bridge. He'd made his mind up to walk over the Thames back to the office. It was longer than a tube ride, but it would help wake him up. It was overcast and breezy, and the trees had given up their fight to retain their leaves. But no rain. Not yet. Glancing west down the Thames, thickening grey clouds looked certain to empty themselves sometime later that day.

David's mind returned to the meeting. He knew, and this did make his life very complicated, that the PM and even the JIC didn't have all of the bricks to make a wall.

There were missing bricks.

Manning and Bell were somehow inextricably linked to all of this. Their presence at the training camp and their black pickup heading up to Hajjah the day before the rescue attempt added an uncomfortable dimension to the current situation. The JIC was aware of the two Americans, but not the complete history. Nor the very latest intel. David had painted them as mercenaries, hired by the extremists to sharpen their skills. He'd purposefully not publically rekindled their involvement in the Ebola crisis of three years ago. Nor played on their CIA history. He'd kept their reemergence in Yemen purposefully low-key.

They were the missing bricks. *My bricks.*

And he wasn't prepared to disclose them—yet.

Yesterday at lunchtime, he and Linden Rickenbacker, the DD and his oppo at the CIA, had made a pact.

"We've resurrected Op Greyshoe," Linden had told David on the phone.

"I didn't think it was ever closed."

Linden had replied, "You're right, but we've had our hands full with so many other things. And with no sign of Manning, we assumed that he had left West Africa and gone to live in South America, where he might have been able to find at least a couple of friends." That had made David laugh.

David, and his boss, were the only two UK staff aware of the code word "Greyshoe." Following the Sierra Leone incident, the CIA had set up an in-house enquiry that was on very close hold in the United States. He thought it was restricted to just the director, the DD, and maybe one other. The aim was to get to the bottom of Manning and Bell's involvement in the Ebola crisis. The Op was run by the then DD, Miles Johnson, whom David neither liked nor trusted.

He'd not been privy to the US team's written reports, but Johnson had given him occasional verbal updates as the Op progressed. In the end, after eighteen months of what David thought was unnecessary stalling, Johnson's final telephone call was best summed up as: Manning was a rogue agent, working on his own without any authority or direction; Bell was dead.

That was rubbish. And bearing in mind that it was the UK that had been the subject of Manning and Bell's attentions, David had protested. More still, he had got his boss to press the CIA's director. The outcome of his teddies being thrown out of the cot was that the CIA had agreed to keep the Op open in case further evidence came to light.

Such as now.

"So what are you going to do now? What do you mean by 'resurrected' the Op?"

"I've been given the authority to widen the disclosure here. I have assigned three agents, two of whom are Middle East experts, and the third has field experience among the Taliban and Al-Qaeda in Afghanistan. That makes five of us in the building who are now back on the case."

David thought Linden was expecting a round of applause. He didn't have the energy.

"And have you uncovered anything yet?'

"No. Well . . ." The Deputy Director paused. "Can you assure me that the only two Brit staff who know about Greyshoe are you and your chief?"

David didn't need to think through an answer.

"I can assure you, Linden, it's just the boss and me. Not, as we both agree, that there is much to tell."

The DD wasn't slowed by the dig.

"OK. Here goes. Yesterday morning one of the team managed to trace a payment of $500,000 from a CIA account to a bank account in Bogota." The phone went quiet just for a second. "The payment was made on the afternoon of the same day that your people took down the terrorist Wesley, the one carrying the atomised Ebola into that quaint metro station of yours."

St. Pauls. David didn't need reminding of the details.

"Paying off informers in Columbia for intel on drugs?" David offered an explanation.

"No. We had a lull in the operations at that point. We think there's a connection between the money and the end of the operation. What is significant is that only three of us in the building have the authority to sign cheques for over $100,000."

That narrowed it down a bit.

"But surely, if the payment were that easy to find by one of your team three years later, it would have been as plain as the nose on your face—or should I say your predecessor's face—when Op Greyshoe was set up?"

Linden let out a sigh on the other end.

"You would have thought."

Both of them were silent. David needed a little time to catch up with the enormity of what Linden might be suggesting: Johnson, the previous DD, was bent. Surely that was the only conclusion to half a million dollars going walkabouts to some South American account.

Linden was waiting for a response.

"Is it possible that Manning and Bell have been sleeping, keeping a low profile. And now, under the direction of Johnson—or somebody like him—they're back in the game?" It didn't bear thinking about.

"Possibly. As they say among our friends in the FBI, 'we're now following up on our leads.' Look, David, I need to be clear that the only person you brief from here is your boss." Linden's tone was emphatic. But the second time around, the reminder was very dull. David didn't let it show.

"Sure. You have my word. But you will keep me abreast with where all this is going?"

"Correct. And anything you get, you'll let us know?"

And that was that.

The missing bricks. Possibly. Probably?

David knew that keeping it on close hold was essential. If he'd mentioned Op Greyshoe to the JIC or, worse still, the PM in his current bullish state, who knows what the outcome would have been. The old man could well have directed that someone leak that the SAS Op had failed was because rogue CIA agents had alerted so-called IS that the boys were on their way.

And that wouldn't do.

If anyone were going to leak Op Greyshoe, it would be him. It was he and his staff who had skin in the game.

It was all go. A lot can happen in three days. Was it only three days ago that he had been watching the CNN video clip of the captured Brit soldiers? Only that long since he'd discovered the security breach on his machine?

Then, the breach had seemed like such a small thing, an inconsequential detail. Ned had interrogated his system and found nothing to put his finger on. He'd tagged on a single line to his daily report to Herbert and, almost immediately, the proverbial shit had hit the fan.

It gave him some satisfaction that Herbert read his stuff so quickly and in such depth. Within twenty minutes of him pressing the "Send" button, Herbert had come back with a long list of questions and instructions.

That was just three days ago.

In that time, a completely new suite of computers and monitors had been delivered to the office, and, according to Herbert, the company they had employed to provide the Internet routing and access had been sacked. Hey presto, a new firm had been engaged. It was strange—*the longer he stayed in the job, the more everything about the place seemed a bit odd*—that the routing had been replaced overnight. What was wrong with working during the day? Herbert had given Ned strict instructions to be out of the office by six thirty that night and not to return until he'd received a text to say it was OK to go back to work. He'd got that text at seven the following morning and had come in as usual. It was all very hush-hush.

The work had been done. The only discernible difference that he could see was that the old telecoms junction box had been replaced by a new one, which appeared to be tamper-proof. It was all dark grey and bright yellow stripes. "Do Not Touch" was all that was missing.

Herbert had then given him forty-eight hours to rejig his new systems and be back on task for today. Which he was.

The machines were the same make and models as the originals. So that was easy. It had taken him a day to set up the machines exactly as he wanted them. As he looked over them now, it was as if nothing had changed.

But something had.

The oil and gas—and the nuclear and renewable energy—stocks continued to rise and fall as before. Companies merged, some went bust, and new firms raised their heads high enough for Ned to spot them and include them in the matrix. There was no change there.

No, what had changed was the atmosphere in which he was now working. It felt just slightly uncomfortable.

One moment Ned was as happy as Larry. In the office, he worked just hard enough to earn his pay. Out of the office, he enjoyed the good life. OK, so his understanding of a good life was probably more online gaming, home-delivered pizzas, and a little too much Internet porn than how others might interpret the meaning. But it was still good—to him.

But his relationship with Herbert had changed. There was nothing tangible, just something in the ether. The tone of his instructions was less light-hearted, more direct. There were no frills with their exchanges. One or two times, as he read and replied to e-mail instructions about the rebuild, he felt that Herbert's manner had been—*how best to describe it? Menacing?*

Don't be stupid, Ned.

He had just finished rereading all of the e-mails from Herbert since the breach. And, yes, they were written differently from those before the security incident. *But menacing?* He looked over the last line of the latest missive: *"It is essential that this doesn't happen again, otherwise we may be forced to take more conclusive action."*

What the hell did Herbert mean by *conclusive action*? In any case, he wasn't responsible for the breach—was he? And what *was* the breach? He was a competent coder, but he couldn't find anything that looked like an effective intrusion. Did Herbert knew better?

Oh well. He could only do what he could do. The last thing he needed was to lose this job. He'd be more careful, although he had no idea what that meant.

SIS Headquarters, Vauxhall, London

Sam was leaning over Frank's shoulder. He was looking at his main screen, pointing at an upturned wooden table, next to which, leaned against the wall, was a long, wide-ish plank of wood. The plank had a rectangular block running along one end. It looked like a long and very gentle ramp. The plank had sturdy metal eyes on either side about halfway down. At its nonraised end there were signs of staining. The wood was pale, and under the stark lights of the soldiers' torches and flashguns, she couldn't give it a definite colour. The staining was a sort of dark brown.

The rest of Room One—they had labelled them from one to eight, starting on the right-hand side as you entered the compound—was empty, apart from a couple of chairs.

"What do you think the plank is for?" Frank asked.

Sam thought for a while. *No idea.*

"I don't know. It's the same room that, I think the day before yesterday, had the hose coming into it from the well outside. D'you remember? And look at the water staining on the middle of the floor, there." Sam touched Frank's screen and the picture zoomed in unnecessarily. Frank set it right.

"What do *you* think?" Sam questioned Frank.

He was scratching his nose whilst staring intently at the screen.

"I don't know. I can't find anything else of note among the rooms you gave me. This is the only one that shows something out of the ordinary."

"Well, we'll have a chance to look over each other's rooms in a second. I'm on my last one now."

Sam sat back at her desk and wiped the sleep from her eyes. If she didn't get her head down soon, her body would take control and do it for her.

She and Frank had split the rooms into odd and even numbers. Frank took the odd ones, Sam the evens. They'd agreed to spend an hour looking at their rooms and then swap. They were five minutes away from the switch.

Just now she hadn't been completely honest with Frank. Sam had looked at all of her rooms. And his. She couldn't stop herself. She'd come up with the same anomaly that Frank had with the long plank. She couldn't fathom it.

It all looked pretty hopeless.

The compound was clearly a Daesh base—otherwise, why booby-trap it? But there didn't seem to be anything noteworthy from the grainy videos shot by the SF soldiers as they had advanced from room to room. Nor was there anything that caught Sam from the seventeen stills that were taken by the one member of the assault team designated to record the events with a standard, but very competent, camera.

With the emergence of ultra-lightweight low-light videocams, all SF wore them on their helmets during an operation. The designation of a stills photographer among the team, who only took photos if the operational situation permitted, provided further essential evidence—especially at key times like this when the operation asked more questions than it answered.

Sam scrolled back through the photos.

Look for the absence of normal. She was always looking for what should be there, but wasn't. That's how you unlock an image's secrets.

Then something caught her eye.

All of the rooms, except Room Seven, had religious decorations or photos of prominent religious men or places hanging on the walls. It wasn't unusual for extremist or militant strongholds to festoon the inside of their buildings with religious imagery and iconography. Think of a Christian monastery. Most walls have crucifixes, or pictures or sculptures of Jesus, Mary, or saints, proudly displayed to remind you that you are in a house of God.

What was different about Room Seven was that one of its walls, the longest one, opposite the door that opened into the centre of the compound, was bare. It was empty. Just sand-coloured brick and block. And it was a big wall—crying out for decoration of some sort.

That didn't appear to be normal.

She had one photo and four video clips of Room Seven. She looked at all of them again in detail, but focused on the still. It was good quality.

The image must have been taken from one corner of the room. It showed all of the empty wall and part of a second wall, which had a window in it and, to one side of the window, a poorly framed photograph of Mecca.

Sam focused on the main, blank wall. Touching the screen and sweeping her fingers apart, she zoomed in. She examined the close-up of the wall, swiping gently left and right with her fingers, the enlarged brickwork following her movement. Left, right, up, down.

"There you go." Under her breath. "Now let's find the second one." She moved the image some more, using gentle movements.

"Gotcha!"

She left the detail where it was and rocked back, lifting her still bandaged hand to her mouth and chewing absently on the exposed knuckles.

On the screen to her left, she quickly opened the original Daesh video of the two SRR soldiers. She froze it after about ten seconds. Sam zoomed onto the flag, looking to its top left and right corners. *Thought so.* It was nailed into place; that's what it looked like. She couldn't be completely sure, as the image had started to pixelate when enlarged, but it was a very sound assumption.

Starting at one corner she counted bricks left to right—slightly out loud, "one, two, three . . ."—*this must be really annoying Frank.* She got to twelve at the second corner. She counted back again. *Yes, twelve.*

This might be something. She felt her pulse rate quicken and her mouth suddenly ran out of saliva.

Back on her big screen showing the still from the operation, bricks filled the monitor. She swept across to the right until she found a piece of mortar that had been dislodged. In its centre was a tiny black speck. A nail hole. She scrolled slowly left, counting out loud as she did. "Eight, nine, ten, eleven, twelve." *Perfect. Just perfect.*

To be sure, she zoomed out and checked the height of the nail holes. They were about the same height as the top of the Daesh flag in the video, although it was more difficult to tell. In the video the soldiers were taking up the screen.

But it was good enough. She was sure the exposed wall she was looking at on her main screen once displayed a Daesh flag—*the same flag in the original video clip.*

"Frank!"

"Hang on . . ." A muffled response.

"No, Frank. Come here, I've got something to show you. Now."

"No, Sam . . . you come here. Look at this." Sam realised that Frank's voice was a shadow of its usual self. It had the tone of a man who had just learned that his bank account had been raided by persons unknown.

Sam stood up and leaned over into Frank's booth.

"Look here."

His main screen still had Room One displayed, the upturned table and the low ramp/plank affair still visible. On Frank's second monitor he had a Google image open. It was a childlike drawing of how you might waterboard a prisoner. It seemed simple enough, especially when Google pictured it so clearly. You needed a table, a plank raised slightly at one end, and a hosepipe. *Oh, and a prisoner. And a torturer or two.* The plank was raised up on the table, and the prisoner's head was placed at the lowered end, covered with a cloth. His hands tied by his side. Next comes the water.

Sam felt her bottom lip wobble and her stomach tighten. She was determined not to cry, not to let her emotions get the better of her. Not here, in the same room, twice in the same week.

"Hello, folks. How are we getting on?"

It was David. Jane was just behind him.

Sam looked away and squeezed her eyes tightly shut and then opened them. She was relieved to feel that they were dry. There were no tears.

"I think we've got the evidence you need to say that the two SRR soldiers had been held captive in the compound and were certainly there until at least yesterday morning. And there's something more disturbing that Frank needs to show you."

Schloss Neuenburg, German/Czech Border

Wolfgang loved the circular room. Christened simply *"Runden Raum"* by his great grandmother, it had pride of place at the back of the family castle, with half of the room jutting out onto the main lawn. Apart from the height of the ceiling, the eight narrow full-length windows, and, at the wall's centre, a double door leading out onto the grounds, what clinched it for Wolfgang was the acoustics.

Music, and playing musical instruments, had been a family tradition for as long as anyone could remember. Many aristocratic families have life-size portraits of distant relatives adorning the walls of their stately homes. Most of the men are dressed in uniform, carrying swords aloft or shouldering rifles. Great men—and some women—fighting for the family cause and winning.

His ancestors were different. Apart from his great-great-great-uncle Ferdinand, whom history would cruelly tell never commanded an army but couldn't stop dressing as a soldier, nearly all of Wolfgang's relatives were portrayed—or, more recently, photographed—holding a violin, embracing a cello or double bass, or sitting at a piano.

That said, they weren't all shrinking violets. It was fair to say that the Neuenburgs played their part in defining central European history. But they were mostly peacemakers, rather than battle-winners. That might well be the secret as to how the family had been able to keep most of its wealth and much of its property and land. Schloss Neuenburg was one of five major family homes. Whilst neither the prettiest nor the most valuable of the family piles, its location in the dense *Bayerischer Wald* forest on the Czech/German border gave it a hidden-away feel. It presented Wolfgang and, he guessed, many of his predecessors, with a warm, secure feeling.

He dearly loved the schloss. After the trials of the last three days, its solitude was the perfect tonic to help him unwind without fear of intrusion.

With his eyes closed, his neck twisted, and his chin pressing down on the shoulder rest of the violin, Wolfgang let the music flow. Bruch's Violin Concerto No. 1 was three movements and twenty-three minutes of sheer ecstasy. It was written to showcase the violin, floating above the orchestra, singing and rising with pure romance. The themes were heartbreaking, and even without the backing of the orchestra, it was a beautiful, genius piece of music. It was both melodic and extremely technical.

None, and all, of these reasons explained why he loved to play it. It reminded him that he was as good a violinist as his instructors at College had told him. In this, the round room, the tone of his Höfner rang as true as in any major concert hall in the world. It was piercingly clear and, as such, a casual listener could pick out even the most well-disguised mistake. He had to play it brilliantly; there were no hiding places. That's how he liked it.

Unsurprisingly, his mother preferred their Munich home. It was more central, more playful. She was there now; he had left her there this morning. She was, he was pleased to see, in remarkably good health.

He had texted her as he left Berlin's Hauptbahnhof yesterday at lunchtime, letting her know he was on his way home. She had driven from their house to the station in

Munich to pick him up. The Munich house was on one of the avenues that backed onto the *Englischer Garten*. It was large, very grand on the outside, and elegantly opulent on the inside. Wolfgang forgot how many bedrooms it had—maybe twelve?

When she arrived at the station, he reminded his mother that Klaus, the butler, could have come to pick him up. "And, you know, they do have taxis and buses in Munich. Which I am capable of using."

She had ignored him and, as she always did, lavished him with words as they drove back to the house. It may have been three years since his father's death, but she still didn't seem to regard Wolfgang as a grown-up. She treated him just like she always had whenever he had come back from his English boarding school for the holidays. "How I have missed you, darling! Have you been eating properly? It doesn't look like you have. Are you managing to feed yourself? You look fabulous. Your clothes"—she reached across and felt his fine wool jacket—"they are fabulous, such *schöne kleider*. Such taste! You are a very handsome boy, Wolfgang. Have you got a girlfriend yet? I must hear you play your violin. I must! Within minutes! I will make some tea, and you go to your room and fetch your Höfner. What shall we play? I could sing!"

His mother did have a fine voice, although, as she had gotten older, it had slipped from soprano to mezzo-soprano. She only ever sang at family occasions, which frustrated Wolfgang. He was sure, if she had tried, she could have joined the Munich Symphony Orchestra's choir. His father was always admonishing her for not auditioning for a role in a local opera. Since his father's death, he had followed the same tack.

"Someone has to manage the house, Wolfgang."

That always made him laugh. They had four or five staff who ran the house in Munich meticulously. His mother was always busy—a charity event here, prison visits there, menu selections—but she never ran the house. Why should she?

Once ensconced in the house and satisfied that he had eaten at least half a cow, his mother had sung Handel's "Lusinghe Più Care" while he accompanied her on the piano. Then she had gone to dress for a dinner appointment with Herr Michael Schmidt.

"Not the lesser-known Schmidts of Lower Saxony!" He pulled her leg.

"No, Wolfgang, you tease. Michael is a film director, and he wishes to use the house on Chiemsee for his latest serialisation. I think it's a crime thriller, but it might be a musical. He's very handsome and *very* rich." She winked at him.

His mother always looked fabulous. A few years before her husband's death, she had been voted by some poll in the German upmarket magazine *Stern* as the best-looking countess in western Europe. And rightly so. But he knew that she had as much interest in Herr Schmidt's looks and money as Wolfgang did in working as a farm labourer at the local *bauernhof*. But she did love to party. *And why not?*

Once she'd disappeared upstairs to change, he went down to the cellar and checked his Synology servers. The twin four-terabyte hard drives matched each other. If one went down, the other was always ready to receive or supply information. The power supply was regulated and backed up with the latest Sonnenbatterie home battery should there be a power cut. But this was Munich. *There would never be a power cut.*

He logged onto the machines and checked the outcome of his latest enquiries. Whilst he had been at the crash site, he had asked his tower in Dresden to interrogate—and hopefully gain access to—five sources. One was in Dortmund, Germany; one in London; one in Jerusalem; and two in the United States: the first in New York and a second in Los Angeles. He'd chosen these mainframes because the firms behind them, or in the case of New York, a single client, had shown a trend toward investigating and monitoring global power and/or transport businesses. These hacks were all part of trying to put some flesh on the bones of the Lattice.

As he scrolled down through the results from his sophisticated, but reasonably shallow, hacking, he was pleased to see that he could probably delve deeper into the London and Jerusalem mainframes without too much trouble. He discounted the Dortmund source—getting in was too easy. The Los Angeles enquiry had come up with nothing, so he would need to look again at that. But it was the New York ping that interested him the most.

His attempt to hack into the New York client had not only been rebutted, but the client, or a subset or subsidiary of the client, had subsequently attempted to gain access to his machine. *He had been attacked.* From what he could see, so far they hadn't been able to gain access to his own servers.

It was the first time that he'd been attacked. He'd have expected that from the FBI or BfV, where they had a wealth of staff permanently assigned to look for, and deal with, hackers. Or maybe even Mercedes or Siemens, where industrial secrets needed to be kept secret. But not from an almost unknown source that he'd come across by accident. What were they hiding? And why were they so incensed by his clever, but very casual, hack that they needed to retaliate? It was odd. And a little bit alarming. He'd need to tread carefully here. With that thought lodged firmly in his mind, he'd gone back upstairs to pack his things.

Wolfgang had finally broken the apron strings in Munich late yesterday afternoon and had driven the two hours up to the schloss in a hire car. In the mild autumn sunshine it had been an easy drive, although with the later enveloping darkness, the temperatures had dropped. He'd slept and eaten well, and now, after Tomas had cooked him a fine breakfast of eggs and fresh bread, he was enjoying the best acoustics in all of Germany.

He played the last three bars of Bruch and let the final note ring out for much longer than Bruch, he was sure, had intended. He gently dropped his violin to his side and looked out through the doors on to the lawn. It was a mesmerising view. All manner of greens piercing a cloudless, light blue sky.

In that moment of tranquillity, his new, odd, quick-witted, and unsmiling friend came to mind. *Sam Green.* There was something about her that meant she was never far from his consciousness. *Special?* Maybe. *Different?* Certainly. Perhaps he should get to know her better?

It was true to say that a combination of Bruch, and now Green, had made him feel so much more relaxed than just an hour earlier.

Tomas would call him for lunch soon. Doubtless it would be pork of some kind, albeit beautifully cooked. Tomas would eat with him. He was ten years older than Wolfgang and, whilst technically staff, was an old friend. So why not share great food and palatable wine with those who worked for you? Otherwise he'd be eating alone. And, at the moment, he didn't want that.

Then he would get out his laptop, connect to the servers in Munich, and try and establish what the people in New York were up to. If it turned out to be a governmental organisation, he would leave well alone. But that seemed unlikely. So he might just have to press harder.

Westminster Bridge, London

It was a great relief to learn that Jane's team had established that the SRR soldiers had been in the compound. He felt that the new intelligence had vindicated the choice of target. On the negative side, and much more disturbing, was the news that one of soldiers—probably Tony James—had been waterboarded. David, who was away with the fairies as he meandered in and out of the rush-hour crowd heading over to Waterloo, wasn't surprised. Not that either of the soldiers would have much to give up.

He'd experienced waterboarding. Not firsthand, of course. But he had seen it in use. He'd spent fifteen years in

162

the field, mostly in eastern Europe at the height of the Cold War. But he had also been posted to Jordan for a tour, where his remit had required him to travel into Iraq, Israel, and Syria—the latter before the current breakdown. Then, all three countries had a good smattering of SIS people. Now their presence in Syria was limited to just a handful of very dedicated and specialised agents, working among the rebels in the north of the country.

In some ways he envied them. His missions from the distant past were never directly involved in war zones, although his time in Iraq, following the coalition invasion, had been hairy at times. For the most part, he had been running local agents and informers, intelligence gathering, and other "not quite above the line" activities: looking at emerging threats and, even then, investigating burgeoning terrorist cells. But never with an accompanying hail of bullets and bombs.

Today, you couldn't dispatch an SIS agent anywhere in the Middle East without throwing away the health and safety handbook. It was dangerous. But for the individual, it was very fulfilling.

Many, many years back, all intelligence agencies used whatever methods and tactics they needed to gather information to protect their national interests. Waterboarding was ugly. But it was cheap, effective, and left no marks— externally. Thankfully, things had moved on considerably since then. Certainly within SIS. Truth drugs, such as sodium thiopental, were still frowned upon. But they were sometimes effective. Often, just offering amnesty and a wodge of cash did the trick. Not everyone was Daniel Craig.

David was on Westminster Bridge now. He weaved past a small group of Pacific Rim tourists who were walking, pointing, and taking photos with their iPads all at the same time. He didn't mind. He wasn't in a great rush. The COBR meeting wasn't for another thirty minutes.

"Sorry!" he said, as he bumped into a commuter, a pinstripe-suited missile on a collision course with the 5.45

from Waterloo to Godalming. Thankfully he had a place in town that he used during the week—and on weekends, when it was busy. His thoughts drifted to his rose garden in Suffolk, his bench on the patio, and a glass of decent Cabernet Sauvignon.

He weaved again, missing a jogger—*that was close*—but couldn't stop himself from bumping into a second one, just behind the first. A collision was inevitable.

"Ow! Oi!"

The so-and-so had caught him on his calf muscle, as though the jogger's trainer had a spike in it. That hurt. *Ow!*

Momentum carried him forward, and, with his mind still in wandering mode, he thought of the last time he was spiked. It must have been—*hang on, difficulty concentrating*—forty years ago when he was running the eight hundred metres for his house at school. *Oh dear, a bit woozy now.* Charlie Broadbent had crossed in front of him with about two hundred to go and caught him with a spike . . . *I need to stop and get a grip. What's happening to me?*

David staggered to his right and grabbed at a rail on the wall of the bridge. He struggled to stay upright. People walked past him, ever so slightly out of focus. Everything and everyone was moving, left to right, right to left, up and down. A blur of movement. Colours were lost. It was all black, white, and greys.

"Are you all right, mate?"

An unfamiliar voice. David turned, his head moving but his brain remaining still. That sudden movement made him feel very unwell. He tried to focus on the man who was talking to him, but all he could see was a smudge of lips, accompanied by unrecognisable sounds.

He knew when his legs gave way because the man's face became his crotch. He found that amusing for some boyish reason. *He really should grow up.*

Then he didn't feel anything at all.

Chapter Ten

SIS Headquarters, Vauxhall, London

Jane had the whole Op Glasshouse team seated around the table. She'd chosen for them to meet in a small conference room, just down from her office. There was no way she would have used David's room. That wouldn't have been right.

There was a gentle murmur among the small team. They all knew about David. And they would all have seen the missive from the chief about her taking responsibility for the Op until further notice. That might have caught one or two of them by surprise. It certainly had her.

She'd been called personally by Clive, that is, Sir Clive Morton, the chief of the Secret Intelligence Service, late last evening. She had almost dropped the phone.

"Hello, Jane, it's Clive here."

Jane's brain spun as she tried to work out who it was. Whirr, click, whirr. For a while now it had all been "just call me Clive," SIS keeping up to date with the latest management trends. Gone were the days of standing up when the chief came into the room and folks subserviently calling the man "Sir." The new approach had made things easier, more manageable. But she wasn't sure she could ever cope with "Clive."

Jane had only been to his office once before, three years ago, directly after the Ebola affair. That time it had been a "well done" for her, and he had handed Jane a written commendation for her work in West Africa. It was a nice touch; so nice she'd had it framed, and it now hung, pride of place, in her loo. So, it was an understatement to say that she was surprised to get a call directly from the chief asking her to come down to his office "immediately." She couldn't think of a single reason why he'd want to commend her for anything she'd done recently.

What on earth is up?

She was swiftly ushered into the chief's office by his PA. On seeing her, he put his pen down, walked around his desk, and led her to some comfy seats in the corner of his office. He was wearing a serious face. After the very briefest of preliminaries he'd told her of David's condition. He kept his explanations precise and factual. In short: David had collapsed walking to that afternoon's COBR meeting about Op Glasshouse; he was in Saint Thomas's hospital; the doctors had placed him in an induced coma; they knew little else.

"Was it a heart attack?" Jane had asked, although her mind was chasing so many other conflicting thoughts and questions: *God! Poor David; does his wife know? I thought he'd kept himself reasonably fit? Who takes on his responsibilities now? What will be my role?*

It shamed her that the last thought entered her head when David was obviously so unwell. It shamed her further to hear herself think of the situation as an opportunity. But nobody was bigger than SIS, and, with David out of action, the business of spying still needed oversight and direction. It couldn't happen in a vacuum.

"Nobody's sure. They don't think so. But at the moment they really don't know." He had stopped in thought and then added, "So we're clear, just in case you were considering it, there's no point going to the hospital at the moment. They're not allowing visitors. As far as I can tell, David's in an isolation unit."

Jane wasn't a medical student, but she knew that meant they were worried about contamination, or maybe even contagion.

What has he got?

"And his wife?"

"I phoned her. She's metaphorically at his bedside. I'm going to pop along in an hour to see her. It's all very shocking."

"Yes, sir. It is. Poor David."

Poor David.

"Look, Jane, I'm assuming that David will be out of action for a while. I'd like you to continue to hold your portfolio, but also take on the leadership of Op Glasshouse and any operation that might stem from it. I've informed the JIC and will be speaking to the CIA later. You have David's authority on both counts, which will mean attending all meetings, including COBR if it needs Glasshouse input." He was staring intently at Jane. "You can do this?"

Jane wasn't sure if the last comment by the chief was a question or a statement. She took it as a question.

"Of course, sir."

"Good. Claire, David's PA, will look after you, although she will need sensitive handling. As you know, she's been with David forever. And I have a daily cabal at five o'clock. I don't expect any prebriefing, unless you think that's needed. Come along tomorrow afternoon. And, of course, my door is always open." He smiled.

Jane knew he meant it. Sir Clive Morton had a reputation for being a first-rate leader: tough, fair, and human. She guessed you didn't become the head of SIS without learning a thing or two about leadership and management.

And that was the end of the meeting. He went back to his desk, and she left the office unsure of how heavy the weight of this new responsibility would be.

She would start to find out about now. Jane looked across and around the conference table at the assembled team. This wasn't going to be easy. Jane was junior to at least two of the staff here. She hoped she knew them well enough for them to get on with where they all found themselves. *I'll know soon enough.*

"OK, team. Order please."

The murmuring stopped, and everyone turned to face her. Jane was standing. The others sitting were Tim and Justin—Middle East contacts; Mike–GCHQ, Sue—Defence Intelligence; Sam—analyst; and Claire, David's PA, whom she had asked to sit at her right-hand side. Jane took some comfort from that.

"First an update on David, not that there's much to give." Out of habit, she looked down at her watch. "As of seven o'clock this morning, David was still in an induced coma and remains in isolation. The doctors have ruled out most natural conditions, such as a heart attack, a stroke, or an aneurism. They"—she stopped midsentence—"they think David might have been attacked. Spiked, poisoned, who knows what."

For such a small group of people, the spontaneous incredulity levels rose perceptibly. Jane could see by their expressions that what she had just told them had hit them hard.

"Look, calm down." *Oops, that was a bit too patronising.* She was still standing and pressed her hands downward as if to dampen the atmosphere. It did the trick. They were looking her way again.

"I know. It seems incredibly unlikely that anything like this could happen in London. But, as we know, we've seen the likes of it before. But not an attack on one of ours." She steadied herself. "Ordinarily this information would be on close hold, and, of course, nothing will be disclosed to the press by anyone, or any of us. The reason I have been given authority to tell you that David may have been spiked, is that we"—she paused, collecting herself—"we are all being asked to take special precautions when we are outside the building."

Tim spoke without being asked.

"What do you mean? Are we targets? Should we be looking over our shoulders all the time?"

Jane sensed a degree of fear in the tone of Tim's delivery. Jane had heard that he'd last been in the field a couple of decades ago and had been withdrawn for "personal reasons." He was, however, very dedicated and particularly good at manipulating field agents and getting the best from them. That was his job. And he did it well.

"No, Tim." She needed to qualify that statement—to take out some of the intrigue. "I don't think so. But I've been asked to tell all of you to take more care than you would normally, that's all. And I think that's a sensible suggestion under the circumstances."

Jane looked across at Sam. She was the only one who had shown little emotion, nor spoken to anyone. Her very junior position would make her disinclined to ask questions, but her impassiveness was either a sign of remarkable composure or a disinterest in the current situation.

So she surprised Jane by putting up her hand.

"Yes, Sam?"

"Do we know how Mrs. Jennings is?"

Bless her.

"The chief saw her last night. She's holding up well, apparently. Thanks." She looked away from Sam, back to the whole team, "Any other questions on David's situation?"

Nothing.

"OK, Glasshouse. I guess we've all read each other's reports. There is nothing on the wires about the fate of James and Groves. As you saw from my report, which I gleaned from the notes of yesterday afternoon's JIC meeting, the FCO will lead with the press should the two soldiers be executed. And, now we know that both men were very likely to have been holed up in the compound—well done, Sam and Frank." She looked directly at Sam and nodded. "Any press release will include a statement that the military did try to effect a rescue but missed the pair by a whisker."

She pointed toward Tim.

"Tim, anything on the ground from Yemen that wasn't in your report?"

Tim still seemed agitated; he shuffled around in his chair as he spoke.

"No, Jane. The safe house has seen a little movement. A couple of men entering and exiting the property. And you have the photos of that—but nothing significant. All of our other contacts have hit a brick wall."

"Mike?"

Mike was playing with a pencil. He stopped and looked across at Jane. "Nothing to add from GCHQ. There is still admin-type traffic coming into and out of the safe house in Sana'a. Other than that, it's all pretty quiet with regard to Glasshouse. Sorry."

"Thanks Mike. OK, let's do what we do. My guess is the next event will be the execution of the two men and its disclosure. At that point we might be able to piece some more intelligence together and maybe give DI and the SF something to target. Although, by now, the horses will certainly have bolted." She hated the metaphor as soon as she said it.

"Please keep Glasshouse near the top of your list, and keep pressing your contacts. You never know—we might just get lucky. Thanks, everyone."

She knew that they had almost no chance of getting lucky, unless Daesh decided to drive the SRR soldiers directly into a friendly police station and give themselves up. Even if new intelligence were forthcoming, the JIC would be loath to relaunch SF without certainty of success. The two SRR soldiers were as good as damned. *If they weren't dead already.*

The thought that the fate of the two soldiers depended almost exclusively on the intelligence *her* team gathered made Jane force out a sigh—rather more loudly than she would have wanted. It was now *her* job to direct the appropriate intelligence gathering. It was a big task.

Do I really want this sort of responsibility? She was already beginning to understand why David always looked so tired.

As Sam walked out of the conference room, Jane gave her a friendly wave. She'd need to speak to her at some point about the abuse of her authority while she was away, but that could wait for a bit. Possibly until Op Glasshouse was closed.

She checked her watch again. She had a call lined up with

the CIA's DD in twenty minutes. He had asked to speak to her. She guessed it was about David and the current Op. Did he have some positive info on Manning and Bell? There was always hope.

As she gathered up her things, she noticed that Claire was still sitting beside her.

Without looking up, Claire said, "Well done."

Jane smiled, relief gently washing over her when she realised that she wasn't doing this completely on her own.

"Thank you. Thanks very much, Claire." Jane placed her hand on Claire's shoulder.

"Can I give you some advice?"

Perplexed, Jane replied, "Yes, sure."

"Sit down next time. Only stand when you need to be emphatic."

Jane thought about it and nodded.

"Thanks. Yes, thanks. Good advice."

Claire smiled at her; gathered her tablet, pen, and notepad; and, as she left the room, finished with, "I'll go and put the kettle on."

Schloss Neuenburg, Germany

Wolfgang pulled back from his laptop and stretched. He had been so engrossed in his work that he'd forgotten about more fundamental questions, like what to do about the apartment in Dresden. There was nothing there that he couldn't live without, and the bills were paid by direct debit, so he could leave the place as it was indefinitely. He supposed he could go back at some point and collect what few valuables there were, or he could pay somebody to do that for him. He'd have to see.

Although many would find it strange, he wasn't going to involve the police. He'd looked over the video a couple of times, and he had to agree with Sam's final words on the matter. This wasn't a normal break-in. Someone was either trying to find something that they thought Wolfgang was hiding, or they were hoping to scare him. Maybe both? The last thing he needed at the moment was the *polizei* all over him like a rash.

He had the luxury of not having to think about the apartment for a while—he could just let it stew. He wasn't a procrastinator by design, but some things were best left to find their own way.

His research was intriguing. Last night he had set up a delayed ping to eight potential ports on the now defunct New York server. It had certainly been closed down—an enquiry earlier in the evening had come up with a time out. But, sometimes people think they've closed down web addresses and portals, but every so often they miss things, or leave a trace. Electronics have a habit of doing that—a bit like the historical architecture. The Romans build a city. It gets ransacked by the Gauls; they build on top of it—as it was obviously a good place to live. The Gauls move on, and some other empire takes over; so it goes on. Now, in the twenty-first century, a new block of flats is about to be built where the Romans once used to bathe. And guess what? As the pile drivers move in to create the foundations of the new high-rise monstrosity, they unearth the residue of ancient Roman habitation thought lost for ever.

Servers, websites, e-mail addresses, and all computers have a tendency to leave a trace, a shadow. *And if you know where to look . . .*

Using his craftiest Rainbow coding, he had set his machine to ping, open, and then grab anything it could find at the web and IP addresses related to the original search. The programme had been timed to start at six thirty that morning, German time, making it just past one o'clock in the morning in New York. He'd hoped that by then everyone in New York would be out of their offices. All he had to do was surprise the servers.

And it had worked. Well, sort of. The ping-and-grab strategy had accessed just one port and had lasted microseconds before it was closed down. As a result, he now had three e-mail addresses associated with the original IP address, a whole group of e-mails—a number of them only titles and the first couple of lines—and six associated documents. In such a short time, he was lucky to have what he had.

The good news was that he might be able to trace and hack the e-mail addresses. The bad news was that the rest all looked innocuous: reports on power companies; research into oil and gas start-ups. It seemed pretty tame. He'd need to look over the whole lot again.

He rolled his head from side to side, stretching. Looking left through his bedroom window, he could see the morning's mist still clinging to the trees, dark pointy evergreens dominating over wistful pale grey. To his right was a minor portrait of his grandfather, who had a kind smile but had sharp, penetrating eyes. Wolfgang imagined *Grossvater* Hans gently nodding his head, urging him on.

The burden of lineage.

He turned back to his screen. As he reflected on what he had, scrolling through e-mail titles, one thing did stand out— something that was a mirror of his own research. There was an e-mail entitled *"The 1979 Pennsylvania nuclear meltdown: accident or arson?"* He'd very recently watched a CNN report on the same incident, and, after investigation, had decided that it needed to be included in the Lattice. It was a gut reaction that came from nowhere. It didn't meet his "somebody was murdered" criterion, but evidence was now emerging that the meltdown was not an accident and might have been planned.

Nobody *had* died—he heard Sam's recent accusation regarding the incident ringing in his ears. But they could have—or should have?

Or, was the incident not about killing people per se, but designed to undermine nuclear energy as a whole? That thought had just come to him.

Have I been missing something?

173

Maybe this wasn't about killing people. Maybe it was about money. Power? Influence?

Maybe it was about killing an industry. Did the airliner crashes kill prominent industrialists?

Why were the New York people investigating the same incident as he was, whilst also looking at firms and companies that generate power? And why were they so sensitive to his hacking that they'd launched an attack on his servers?

What nerve had he touched?

He needed to look over the results again. Maybe now was the time to call for a second opinion. Another pair of eyes.

Why did he feel that he trusted Sam Green enough to ask for her help?

Underground Carriage, Northern Line, Approaching Colliers Wood, London

It had been a shitty day, not made any better by being stared at by a spotty youth who sat directly opposite her. The carriage clickety-clacked through the darkness, all manner of humans surrounding her. Thankfully none were in her personal space. It was well beyond commuting time, but she knew she wasn't alone in having just left work. There were plenty of men in suits, top buttons undone and ties at half-mast. Leather briefcases nowadays usurped by small rucksacks with big labels. Women wearing smart blouses, warm woollen skirts, and matching jackets jostled for room. There was a nurse—she could be going to work or coming home. And a couple of late-night shoppers, Sainsbury's bags brimming with overpackaged processed meat and not enough veg.

The lout opposite chewed and stared. Sam stared back. Others would be nervous about a visual engagement with "the youth of today," but he didn't bother her. Her council estate background, combined with ten years in the army, enabled Sam to see that the spotty youth was only twelve weeks of army training away from becoming a half-decent human being. And he was an operational tour away, in some far-off war zone, from being her best mate.

Still, he chewed and stared. Sam got bored, breathed out heavily, and tried hard not to think of poor old David lying unconscious in his hospital bed. When she left the office, she had stuck her head around Jane's door and asked for an update.

"Nothing to add, I'm afraid. Are you off home?"

"Yes. You should too."

Jane smiled. "Just a bit more to do. And, Sam . . ."

"Yes?"

"We will need to talk about the e-mails at some point."

"Of course, Jane, I understand."

And she was off. Down the stairs, a quick wave to Barry at the front desk, who nonchalantly waved back. Then through the airlock and out in the direction of the tube.

That afternoon, she and Frank had worked hard with the latest images that had become available on the cloud. Along with those from GCHQ, who might pick up some rogue signal traffic, the pair of them were the most likely to uncover something useful from the raw intelligence that was available. What they needed was a stroke of luck. Sam secretly held out for a photo of a Daesh flag that matched that in the original video. Or, maybe a chance sighting of one of the men from the training camp from Captain James's original shots—or even one of the vehicles. She remembered all the details as if she were looking at them now. She just needed to find a match.

There was nothing today, though. There were plenty of new images to process as part of their ongoing work of trying to match militants moving eastward through the refugee conduits across Europe. But nothing that seemed to help the two SRR soldiers.

By 6.45, well beyond their regulated working hours, she and Frank had agreed that they were in danger of going picture blind and might miss something. Even the best analysts lose focus—both literally and metaphorically—if they spend too long at a monitor. It was time to go home and restart the whole business tomorrow morning.

Her station was approaching. The carriage was now only a quarter full. Spotty youth was still staring at her. And chewing. *Idiot.*

It was time to move. Sam stood, picking up her daysack and shouldering it. The youth did the same. In such a small space between the facing bench seats of the carriage, they almost touched each other. He was about the same height as Sam, probably seventeen or eighteen. Chunky. Ugly. And he was so close she could smell him. *Cheap lager.*

Catching her by surprise, he grabbed her arm above her elbow. Not so it hurt, but enough to seemingly take control.

"D'you wanna a shag?" His chin was on her shoulder, his mouth close to her ear. The words were quiet, a little slurred. Nobody else would have heard.

Just then it seemed like the carriage was empty, although there were probably about ten other passengers around and about. But Sam knew she was on her own. Very few people would help if this lout decided to have a go. She didn't blame her fellow passengers. He might be carrying a knife. *Best not to get involved.*

Instinctively, Sam pulled back a fraction and turned to him so their faces were no more than an inch apart, nose to nose. He was still holding her arm, but that action seemed to unnerve him. He loosened his grip. A little.

"With you? Do me a favour—I'd rather stick knitting needles in my eyes." She spat it out.

The lad coughed a laugh, finding Sam's retort amusing.

What he didn't find so funny was the force with which Sam's forehead came down on his nose. He yelped, let go of Sam's arm, and brought both hands to his face, blood already seeping from his nostrils.

"You broke my nose, you bitch! You broke my fucking nose!" His words were deadened by his hands, which were held close to his face.

Sam didn't hear any further protestations, as she was out of the carriage and running swiftly up the stairs. *Attack and run.* It always worked for her.

She ran and ran, only stopping just short of the corner of her street. She checked behind her—nothing. The idiot hadn't followed her. She took three or four deep breaths, and, feeling much more positive about life all of a sudden—*how did that work?*—she walked the short distance to her flat.

It took her about an hour to shower, change, and knock up her stock-in-trade spaghetti and something red, accompanied by a green leaf salad, covered in the best homemade dressing this side of Lyon. As she munched away at her food, she opened her secure tablet and accessed her e-mails. There was a new one from Jane. It had a red flag to one side, signifying its importance. The title was: *"SRR soldiers."*

Sam opened it up.

The rush that accompanied teaching the spotty youth a lesson he might not forget for a while—*had she been too tough on him?*—was instantly washed away by a tsunami of despair. The e-mail read:

Al Jazeera have received footage of Captain Tony James and Corporal Ted Groves's execution. The two soldiers were ritualistically beheaded. Al J is not showing the video but is repeating the original clip with James speaking to the camera, then showing a single still of the two soldiers prior to their deaths. The accompanying Daesh diatribe is expectedly along the lines of "God is Great" and "Death to all infidels." There doesn't appear to be anything in the statement that affords us any clues. But we can look at that tomorrow.

The complete video was released on Daesh's Yemeni website, which DI is currently trying to close down. Google and similar are not allowing their search engines to find the video. We have a copy. I have decided not to upload it on the cloud until first thing tomorrow. Frankly, having seen it, I think we could all do with a night off. And looking at it now is not going to add much.

We will meet tomorrow morning as per usual. Unless I hear otherwise, I will close Op Glasshouse down and use tomorrow's session to review the Op and make a list of lessons learned.

Thanks.

Jane

Sam closed her eyes and leaned her head back against a cushion that rested on top of the sofa bed she was sitting on. Along with a small dining table and four chairs, a TV, and an occasional table, that was her sitting room. Add a bedroom overcome by the size of the double bed Sam had squeezed in, a small kitchen, and a similar-size bathroom, and that was her flat. It wasn't much, but it was home.

So, it was over? A team of four highly trained SRR lads had been ambushed, shot, captured, killed, tortured, humiliated, and now executed by Daesh. The militants were obviously getting better at what they did and how they did it. *But that good?*

She saw the context as this: those on the SRR team were experts at seeing without being seen; they blended in, their training was rigorous and detailed, and they could defend themselves expertly when needed. She'd met a couple of the lads in Camp Bastion a while back, and they had swapped war stories. Hers were incredibly dull by comparison.

Trooper Bliss's testimony from the attack indicated that

everything Tony James and his team had done, they had done well. And yet, they had been beaten in the desert by an unknown force, and they paid with their lives.

Sam knew it was true that Islamic militants were getting better equipped, but they didn't have the weaponry, or the day-and-night sights, that the SRR had. Their training was basic. How to shoot straight. How to clean a weapon. How to detonate explosives. Sam had seen recent footage from training camps that showed them working as teams, one pair giving covering fire while a second moved to get close to their targets. But it was all basic infantry training. With basic infantry weapons. Not a match against the SRR.

How could the imbalance of expertise be so easily flipped? Was it that Tony James's team had just been unlucky? That they had come across a crack group of militants? Or were they beaten by somebody else?

Manning and Bell.

She knew she'd rehearsed the arguments before, as had the whole Glasshouse team. But, just now, she needed to toss something around to keep her brain occupied. To keep her mind off the catalogue of disasters that had plagued her recently: Uncle Pete; the death and capture of the SRR soldiers; the failed SF Op and the two casualties; David. And now the executions.

Why was it that Disaster insisted on crashing into her life on a regular basis? What had she ever done to him?

She needed a drink.

Sam put her tablet to one side and, with her plate in one hand, she staggered over to the kitchen. *God she was stiff.* Probably the aftermath of the adrenaline surge from the spotty-youth incident.

She felt lifeless. Devoid of anything. A bundle of dead nerves. And now, overpoweringly tired. She yawned, remembering at the last moment to put her hand in front of her mouth; *"Come on, pet, we don't all want to see your tonsils." Mum! Where are you when I need you?*

She was too tired to cry.

Sam placed the plate to the side of the sink—she would clean the small group of dishes before she went to bed—and reached into a cupboard for a wine glass.

Which bottle? Sam was no expert, other than she liked what she liked. In her book, wine was like art. People paid too much money for stuff that the so-called experts said was good, when all you needed to do was use your own judgement. Or, in her case, trust Tesco to get it right. Their *Finest* collection was more than good enough for her ignorant palate.

Ping. From the sitting room. She'd received another e-mail.

If form were anything to go by, someone else was dead.

She shook her head at her lack of respect for Captain James and Corporal Groves. Sometimes the inbred army response to a crisis was to deploy humour. Which, after the Apache gunship, was its most effective weapon. She was good at that.

She poured herself a large glass of Argentinian Malbec and, after checking the time—it was nine thirty—she sat back down on the sofa bed, put her glass down, and reached for her work tablet.

The new e-mail was from Wolfgang to her private Gmail address.

Ehh, wow!

It had a two-word title: *"Help! Please?"*

Her stomach gave a little flutter, and, she hated to admit it, further south she felt something too. *How many different emotions can you squeeze into such a short space of time?* Her life was crazy.

She opened up the mail.

Hi, Sam, Wolfgang here.

Yes, I know, you idiot.

I need a second opinion on something I've been looking at. To be honest, it's too embroiled—is that the right English word?—to go through in an e-mail, but it is concerning my mad theory about the worldwide conspiracy that we spoke about.

Could we meet up? Please?

I'm happy to travel. Or, if you come over here, I think we can spoil you.

Let me know.

Best.

Wolfgang

He left his number on the bottom of the e-mail.

Bloomin' hell!

Bloomin' hell! Why not? Yeah, absolutely, why not? This would be the perfect tonic to help lift an otherwise rubbish time.

She could already picture him getting off the Eurostar at St. Pancras, wearing his brightly coloured chinos, brown brogues, checked Viyella shirt, and cashmere cardigan. *Or, how about:* she drives—or flies!—to the family home in the Black Forest; she had no idea where he lived. What about a huge Germanic hunting lodge with open fires, stag-head-adorned walls, and beer served in glasses the size of the *Titanic*? She couldn't get giant feather duvets, mellow pine-covered walls, and accordion music out of her head. *Perfect.* Or, how would they say it over there? *Wunderbar!*

She preferred the second option. But was she entitled to

leave? She'd need to ask Jane. First thing.

Sam thought about replying straight away. But that would smack of desperation, and, whilst she was the least qualified to judge on dating rituals, she intuitively thought that was the wrong approach. She'd either reply before she went to bed or first thing in the morning.

How exciting! Thanks, Wolfgang.

She meant it. *Whatever your intentions, you have just brightened a very dark day. Thanks very much.* So what now? TV?

Or . . . how about looking over the break-in video of Wolfgang's flat and, using her illegal security access, try to find out who the intruder was? *Yes, she would do that.*

Chapter Eleven

Jane was mulling things over as she walked the final half mile to work. She had her own Glasshouse wash-up this morning, and the JIC was meeting again at 2:00 p.m. This would be her first-ever JIC. An all-male, *very* exclusive club, where the best and the brightest come together to discuss intelligence gathering concerning national-level security threats. Doubtless they would allow her a honeymoon period, to mess things up and then finally get things right. But she was twenty-five years David's junior, so she couldn't imagine they'd attach too much credence to any advice she would offer. Although, as the mouthpiece of SIS on the committee, they would have to listen to what the intelligence was saying.

And she knew something they didn't. Yesterday at lunchtime, after they had exhausted how David was and any likely prognosis, the CIA's DD had briefed her on Op Greyshoe. This was new to her. The deputy director had said that, even since his last conversation with David a couple of days ago, things had moved on. Whilst still on extremely close hold—"You Limeys understand that Greyshoe is as tight as a drum here, and we expect the same in the UK?"—it had widened into a multiple-agency operation.

"A senior pal of mine with the FBI and another at the IRS are looking into Miles Johnson's business. They're doing it very carefully so no one is spooked."

So the old DD was under investigation internally and for tax purposes? That's good news, Jane thought. But, whilst he might be pulling the strings, it was Kurt Manning and Ralph Bell that she'd like to get her hands on.

"Where do we think this is going, sir?" *Look at me, asking the deputy director of the CIA supplementaries.*

"We have no idea. We've got the one lead, a half-mill payment to an account in Bogota three years ago on the same day the Ebola incident was closed. We reckon that was signed off on by Johnson. Nothing else. But something doesn't seem right." The DD paused. "You were the girl on the ground in Sierra Leone?"

"That's right, sir, yes. And I was Kurt Manning's opposite number in the UK while he was at Langley. You might argue that I knew him well."

"What do you think's going on?"

Get this right, girl. Good practice for this afternoon's JIC.

"Kurt Manning held very strong Christian beliefs. I would argue that they influenced the way he did his business and the decisions he made." Jane held off just for a second.

"And?"

"This is conjecture, and as a trained analyst I'm not used to making wild prognoses. But, my view is that the Ebola affair was an ultra-right-wing Christian-sponsored operation, designed to instil fear into Londoners and foreign tourists alike—whilst apportioning the blame on Islamic extremists, such as the so-called Islamic State." Before the DD could say anything else, she continued, "Do you mind if I add one further hypothesis?"

"No, go on." Not a hint of impatience from the DD.

"This was—is—bigger than Manning and Bell and the one failed terrorist attack. I believe it's all part of a well-funded, well-organised Orthodox Christian–based conspiracy to undermine pluralism in the Western world. To polarise all of us. Are you a Christian? Or are you a Muslim?"

It wasn't a question directed at the DD, although Jane did wonder what his religious views were. *And how much I might be poking at them.*

He let out a snort on the other end of the line.

That wasn't a good reaction.

"If you don't mind me patronising you just a little, that

sounds like an opinion my nineteen-year-old daughter would offer. The world is more complex than that. Right versus left; good versus evil—that's all too James Bond. No, sorry, Jane. Johnson, Manning, and Bell were trying to mop up after a Liberian jungle disease clinic had got a bit out of hand. What we're trying to do here is establish why, now, the two ex-agents are still at large. And why Johnson signed off on that payment three years ago. Two disconnected events. No more, no less. That's my view. There's no international conspiracy here."

The DD had a relaxed tone—all motherhood and apple pie. She didn't feel chastised, but she did feel a little patronised, as he had warned. It wasn't a great feeling.

She took a short breath, determined to try to influence him further.

"I take your point, sir, but from where we're sitting"—*was it fair to paint the whole of SIS with her views?*—"Manning and Bell are inextricably linked to the death of four British soldiers on the Arabian Peninsula. We have photos of them in an Islamic extremist training camp. So, they've either both gone *Homeland* on us, or they're helping make Daesh more effective so Westerners will hate and fear them more. Pluralism will be the loser."

Did she just say all of that to the deputy director of the CIA? She wasn't sure she would have had that conversation with David, let alone his oppo in the United States. But, she felt strongly about this, and the DD did seem to offer the opportunity for discussion.

And, as she clearly remembered him, Kurt Manning was so far right on the Christian spectrum that it wouldn't have been a surprise to find a white cape and pointy hood in his wardrobe. For his job, his hatred for Islam was on the wrong side of helpful. Add to that, he had been in the thick of the Ebola affair. Something was going on.

There was a connection. She was sure of it.

"That's an interesting viewpoint, Jane, although you have no conclusive proof that Manning and Bell were instrumental in the deaths of your four unfortunate soldiers. But, you are right about views held by organisations such as the KKK. They're still viable over here, and there are plenty of others like them. And, yes, I'm sure if they could find a way to force us all into their camp, they would. But, no extremist reaches into the centre of the CIA and makes these sorts of things happen. We would know. As I'm sure you would over there." His tone was now conciliatory, flattering. Like he was talking to an equal.

She let that hang for a second.

"I don't mean to have the last word, sir, but we don't all need to be in the Klan's camp. We just need to sit by and do nothing while their view of religion, possibly supported by future hard-line governments, goes to war against the other side. You have to admit that post 9/11 we were close to that. And we're heading that way now."

The phone went quiet for a second. Jane had no idea if she had crossed a line or if she had moved the argument forward. But she'd rather get sacked for speaking her mind than remain employed for keeping shtum.

"Another good point, but you'd need some very hard evidence to persuade me that you're right, Jane. The terrorists are doing fine without support from some fascist fruitcakes over here. In the meantime, make sure you don't let strongly held opinions affect your own decision making. It is key that we all keep an open mind, so that we don't miss the things we don't want to see."

That's fair.

The DD finished with, "And can I remind you that this is on the very closest of holds?"

"Sure, sir. Yes. Just the chief and me. Good to talk to you."

"You too, Jane. Keep thinking outside of the box. And pop into my office next time you're over here. Promise?"

"That's a promise, sir."

And that was that. She'd held her end up with the CIA.

Faced with tricky situations, bullish was the only thing

she knew. It had worked for her more often than not. Now it was time for the JIC. That might require more tact. She had always found that Americans opened themselves to questions and comment. Senior Brits were slightly more reserved and often more prickly.

As she walked past the entrance to Vauxhall, where she ordinarily would have exited if she were taking the tube, Jane picked up a copy of *Metro*. The front page was ablaze with the deaths of the two SRR soldiers. The title "Execution: SAS fail to rescue army's best" saying it all.

She walked and read some more at the same time. On page four there was a short article that led with "British banker found hanged in the Big Apple." She scanned the words and picked out *London banker*; *likely suicide*; and *plush Fifth Avenue apartment*. She'd forgotten the name of the poor chap even before she'd turned the page.

SIS Headquarters, Vauxhall, London

The video clip of the execution was as bad as Sam could have imagined: Two men, dressed in orange coveralls, their faces beaten almost to the point of being unrecognisable, hands tied behind their backs and their heads resting, faces to the camera, on stone plinths—one each. The weapon was a scimitar of some sort, the executioner dressed all in black, with only his eyes showing. The background was scrubland with a nondescript, low hill in the distance. It could have been anywhere in the Middle East. The execution was carried out in the middle of the day, the sun at its highest; there was almost no shadow. Time of death, therefore: yesterday lunchtime.

Sam checked the weather for the Saudi peninsula. There was no cloud cover anywhere yesterday. So that didn't help; it could have happened in Yemen, Saudi—Iraq, even.

She scoured the footage for something in the background, among the stones and the rocks. Something that might be identifiable, either from previous images or something she would see in the future. It appeared that Daesh had been very thorough about their choice of location. Bland. Forgettable.

The executioner was probably six foot tall for an Arab, and broad. His black thawb was unremarkable, as was his keffiyeh. He wore black gloves and sandals, although his feet were difficult to see among the sand and rock. There was nothing there to help her.

The scimitar was new to Sam. She'd not seen it before. The handle was dull-gold coloured with a guard, which was slightly ornate. She zoomed in and tried to picture the detail. It was difficult because the pixels were too large even after the image-sharpening software had kicked in. She looked for marks on the curving, dull-silver blade. There was nothing as helpful as a maker's mark, but the blade was chipped in a couple of places—probably where it had smashed against stone, or sliced through bone. She made a note of where the chips were by circling the dents with an electronic pen. She'd check the three other Daesh executions that they had on the cloud—none were of British nationals—to see if the same weapon had been used before. She thought it unlikely.

Finally, and not without her stomach tightening and the feeling of rising rage making Sam clench her fists, she spent a good while looking at the two hostages' ordeal. They were positioned ready for their deaths before the video started. Their faces were looking into the camera with their bodies side-on to the viewer. They both looked completely lifeless, escape beaten out of them—if they were alive at all. Even though they faced the camera, it was difficult to make out the soldiers' features.

Having said that, she recognised Corporal Ted Groves after just a little investigation; he was executed first. Groves was the less beaten of the two. How she pictured his face from the original video—then it was partially obscured, resting on Tony James's shoulder—matched the new clip. His lifeless body appeared very similar to the way she remembered it. Without further inspection, she put Ted

Groves to one side.

Captain Tony James was a completely different story. His face was almost unrecognisable, disguised by very heavy beating. There was literally nothing on the latest video that she could easily compare with how she recalled the previous one. It was a mess.

Poor bastard.

Sam decided to open the original clip and, at an opportune moment, paused the screen so she had the two men, James and Groves, in the best possible focus.

Sam looked at James's face in the new video and then in the previous clip; she eventually saw some similarity, but it wasn't an instant recognition. She pulled her head back as far as her chair would allow and looked again, needing only the slightest flick of the eye to move between the two screens. Then she leaned forward and stared hard at both faces, left then right, one after the other. Yes, it was the same man. *Probably.*

Was *probably* good enough? *Why am I even questioning it?*

If it wasn't Tony James, then who was it?

She was chewing her knuckles again. *Come on, this doesn't make any sense. It's Tony James.*

If it's not James . . .

Trooper Sandy Jarman? The fourth soldier. The one who Trooper Steve Bliss had seen shot. Nobody had any idea where his body was. It had not been on public display. The assumption was that so-called IS had just tossed it away; they had Groves and James, who were alive; why would they need a third body?

She had to rule him out.

Did she? Did she really? Sam scrunched her face up, which she knew wasn't a good look. *This was mad.* But she had to do it. She knew she had to.

Using a simple paint programme, she drew straight lines down the lower legs of James and Groves on both video shots: previous and now. On the original video, the thighs were pretty much out of shot, so Sam could only compare lower legs. She was very careful to start at exactly the same place on both knees and finish at exactly the same place on both ankles. She then measured all four, putting them into the ratio—James:Groves. On the original shot the numbers were 41:36—Groves was shorter. On the new video, the ratio was 25:24—no discernible difference, but the perspective was slightly askew. You could lose some length in the angles.

She checked again. Her first set of readings was correct.

Sam then compared their lifeless arms, albeit the left arm for Groves and the right arm for James, as that's what she could see in the latest shots. She used the same ratio technique comparing the original shot video and the execution. Groves's arm was shorter than James's on the first shot. On the second, they were comparable.

Arms and legs. She had come to the same conclusion. Either James had shrunk between the first video clip and the second, or one of the men wasn't who he was supposed to be. Or, her calculations were wrong. The latter option was possible, especially with the perspective issues on the images.

"Frank!"

He stood up and peered over the small partition into Sam's space.

"Yes? You rang?"

"Do we have any images of Trooper Sandy Jarman? You know, the fourth soldier? I don't remember seeing any."

Frank laughed. "If you don't remember seeing any, then we don't have one. Why would we need one?"

Sam thought about sharing her current work with Frank, but wanted to be sure first.

"No worries. Thanks."

"OK. If you need me, I'm just next door." He made a gesture, pointing to his desk, before he sat down again.

Sam opened up her e-mail account and typed in the address of her contact in Defence Intelligence. She really needed some photos of Sandy Jarman. And the height and weight of all three men. And she needed them *now*.

Sam pressed "Send."

She looked back at the recent video clip. The more she looked at it, the more she thought that whilst one of the men was definitely Ted Groves, she wouldn't bet a month's wages that the second was Tony James.

Which asked so many questions.

JIC, Whitehall, London

"Thanks everyone. The only outstanding question is, why was Op Glasshouse compromised?"

That was Jon Trent the chairman. Jane had studied the list of attendees and their photos before she had arrived. He was a career civil servant, his previous post was Second Permanent Under-Secretary in the MoD. Intelligence wasn't necessarily his area of expertise, but he had a wealth of contacts and huge experience in the upper echelons of the civil service and the MoD. His job wasn't to delve into the details—he corralled and balanced opinion, sorted disputes, and then made decisions. From what Jane had seen so far, he looked to be very good at it.

"Thoughts? Anyone?"

"Jane. These two Westerners? David attached some import, but not a great deal, to their existence. What's your view?"

That was Brigadier Buckle, DSO, CBE, MC, director of Special Forces and all-around *action man*. Jane had read about him; he was the most interesting of the bunch. He was awarded the Distinguished Service Order for leading his SF squadron during a torrid, but highly successful, tour of Afghanistan at the height of the fighting in Helmand. He was the youngest recipient of the DSO since the Second World War.

Jane gathered her thoughts.

Here goes.

"Our view is that the pair are almost certainly 'guns for hire.' Both have history, and, whilst, on the face of it, it does seem difficult to believe, Daesh were probably paying for their services. They may have been central to the initial capture of the SRR soldiers, say, helping with tactics and maybe even directing the assault. It is unclear whether the pair stayed at the camp overnight. So they might not have been on the ground for the capture." She had to be a bit careful in case she contradicted anything David may have told them.

She continued fluently.

"With the intelligence we have, we think it's extremely unlikely that they warned Ali Abdullah Sahef about the SF rescue attempt. As I understand it, the Op Boxes were drawn wide enough for neither the Americans nor the French to really have any idea where we intended to operate. So any leak is unlikely to have come from our allies. So, how would Manning or Bell know? It would mean that they had gotten the information from a source close to here." She opened her hands to signify that she meant the JIC members, or their teams.

She let that hang.

Nobody seemed to want to press for more.

"What do you mean 'have history'?" This time, from Jon Trent.

"We came across them three years ago in West Africa: the Ebola incident. They were kicking around Liberia and Sierra Leone. They had links with the CIA,"—*no tales out of school there*—"and, although it's never been proven, they were probably involved with the secret US biological clinic in Tubmanburg."

"So what are they doing in Yemen now?" Jon Trent pressed.

That's a good question, Mr. Chairman.

"As I said, they are guns for hire. Daesh need advice on everything, from tactics to weaponry. If the price is right, then we guess these two are willing to sacrifice their souls."

This is going OK, I think?

"So, SIS's view is that the Saudis probably spooked the compound?" A follow-up from Alasdair Buckle.

"I think so. Please correct me if I'm wrong, Melvin." Jane leaned forward and looked down the table to Melvin Hoare, the director of GCHQ. "But we've now confirmed that there was SMS traffic at about the time of the Saudi assault on targets Blue 1 and Blue 2. And we now believe one of the recipients of the SMS was in, or close to, the IS safe house in Sana'a."

Melvin nodded at Jane.

"That's correct. We can't say for certain that the SMS was received by a mobile actually in the safe house, but we can be accurate to, say, fifty metres. That's as good as we can get."

"But not the compound in Hajjah? The text was sent to the Sana'a safe house, not the compound? It was the compound that was spooked." Jon Trent pressing again.

Jane stepped in.

"Looking at the keyhole satellite images, we can confirm that both locations have landlines. The safe house could have phoned the compound—like we used to before we all had mobiles." Jane unnecessarily lifted her own off the table to make a point.

"Are we saying we don't have the landlines bugged?" Brigadier Alasdair was showing signs of impatience.

Melvin took back control. "We didn't have the time or resources to make that happen. Although"—he looked casually at his watch—"we should have a tap on the safe house by close of play this evening."

Jane helped. "SIS couldn't get a reliable man on the ground to get eyes on the compound in Hajjah in time for the assault. So the chances of placing a reliable tap were nil."

The room went quiet. Jane thought they'd answered the chairman's question. They'd taken a risk on assaulting the right location—the SRR soldiers had been in the compound at some point. SIS had done a good job there. They just missed the window by a few hours. The likely reason was Daesh got spooked. Probably by the early Saudi attack. But they might never know. These things happen. End of.

"OK. Anything else?" Jon Trent again.

Everybody, including Jane, shook their heads.

"Let's call it a day."

As they all got up to leave, Brigadier Alasdair came over to where Jane was standing.

"Well done today. It isn't easy coming into this forum even when, like me, you've been around the block a couple of times. But, for a young newbie, it must be daunting. I thought you held yourself together really well. David will be pleased when he finds out."

Poor David. Jane hadn't thought about him all day.

She cleared her thoughts. Work to be done.

"Thanks, Brigadier. Maybe I'm older than I look." She smiled at the senior officer and feigned a slight wink.

He raised one eyebrow and snorted a laugh.

"Touché."

On reflection, Jane thought it was good of him to come over and say something. But would he have done the same if she had been a man? She hoped so.

SIS Headquarters, Vauxhall, London

Sam knocked on Jane's door. She'd let her get back from the JIC, but only long enough for her to get to her desk. She was still dressed for the inclement weather. It wasn't quite winter, but it certainly wasn't an Indian summer.

"Come in, Sam." Jane could see who it was. Most of the partition walls in the building were glass, as was Jane's door.

Jane was unpacking her rucksack and sorting things out on her desk. She'd managed to take off her coat, but still wore a striped scarf.

Which university? Something Sam didn't know. She'd find out.

"Hi Jane. How was the JIC?"

Jane stopped what she was doing, looked up at Sam, and smiled.

"Good. The female Christian returns unharmed from the Colosseum, where all the lions are alpha males. Sorry, that was a poor analogy. I survived."

"Great." Sam wanted to press on. She bobbed a little from foot to foot, not concealing her impatience well.

"Have you officially closed Glasshouse?"

"Yes. That was the point of the JIC, Sam. You knew that—a post-Op debrief."

"Don't." Sam had managed to keep herself still long enough so that she didn't appear like an excited child.

Jane stopped unpacking her rucksack mid-file.

"What?" There was confusion in Jane's voice. No, it was more like frustration than confusion.

"Don't. Not yet. Come with me. I've got something to show you." Sam directed Jane with a flick of her head. She didn't wait for her boss to acknowledge her instruction and set off down the corridor. She assumed Jane would tag along.

Sam was back at her desk in no time; Jane took a few seconds longer. It had obviously been a long day. She came in, still wearing the scarf. It hung from her neck like an oversized woollen tie.

"OK, Sam, what is it?" It was definitely frustration now—not confusion.

"Trust me. Look, I've prepared a short presentation." She nodded to her main screen, her hands hovering over her keyboard.

Jane sighed. Sam didn't care; she ploughed on.

She and Jane, with Frank peering over the partition—he'd wholeheartedly agreed with Sam's prognosis about an hour earlier—looked over a series of slides that Sam had put together earlier in the afternoon. In essence, they told the

195

story of different-size limbs. Working with a number of images, some measured lines, and her ratio system, Sam showed that Captain Tony James was taller than the second man executed in the Daesh video. Using the information she'd got from Hereford earlier in the day, Sam also demonstrated that the second man was likely to be Jarman—the soldier killed at the start of the firefight. And whose dead body everyone had ignored, as they had been too busy searching for two live people.

Other than the fact that Jarman was shorter than James, what had given Sam real confidence was that, having accessed an up-to-date photo of Sandy Jarman, the badly beaten second executed man looked much more likely to be Jarman than James.

"And, look, as I build the stills from the execution of the second man."

Sam clicked away, moving the image forward shot by shot. It would have been heartbreaking if you were watching it for the first time. But now, with the possibility that James might still be alive, the three of them were far too engrossed with the detail to be sickened by the event.

Jane stared open-mouthed at the screen, trying to fathom what Sam was showing them with the latest slides.

"Yes, Sam. I see that. What's your point?'

"No blood."

"Sorry?"

"Look. In the first execution"—Sam replayed the images—"even though we know Corporal Groves is close to death, when his head leaves the body, there is an escape of blood. Here."

As gruesome as it was, there was definitely some blood.

Sam clicked back to the exact point where the head of the second man left his body.

"Here, look." She was pointing with her finger. "There's no blood. The second man has been dead for some time. Now, that could still be Captain Tony James. But, he would have had to have died as a result of his injuries, or have been murdered pretty soon after the initial video. That's unlikely, don't you think? However, we all believe that Jarman was probably dead on the day of the assault. It's Jarman, not James."

Sam had been leaning forward, manipulating the screen for the duration of the presentation. Now, she pushed back on her chair, looking up at Jane.

"Tony James is alive. Or certainly not executed here."

She felt some real satisfaction at having pieced this together. First, for identifying the anomaly of the size of the limbs. But, much more importantly, she had discovered it was likely that one of the SRR soldiers might still be alive.

Jane stood completely still. She displayed no emotion at all. It was as if she had been struck by some mystery force field that held her motionless. She closed her eyes for a split second—that seemed to break the strength of the thing that was holding her.

"Frank, what do you think?"

"Sam's right, Jane. The man in the shot isn't James. It's somebody else and likely to be Sandy Jarman."

Jane raised her hand to her forehead. She slowly rubbed it.

Sam watched. Time passed.

"Wow. Right. OK. Fabulous work, Sam." She looked at her watch. Sam knew it was about five thirty. "I'll get the team together, but first I'd better go and have a chat with the chief. Sam, send me the presentation, and, if I get summoned, be prepared to brief him with me. OK?"

"Sure thing, Jane. Eh, before you go"—Sam gently touched Jane's arm, enough to stop her from moving—"I need to ask you something. Something private."

Jane hesitated.

Sam was on her feet now. She'd just stopped Jane, but was now ushering her out of the analysts' office. Jane took Sam's lead and walked ahead, absently commenting, "Come to my office."

In Jane's office, Sam paused and waited in front of her

desk while Jane eventually managed to remove her scarf. It lay messily on her desk. Her hair looked ruffled. Her eyes tired. Sam wasn't sure why the briefing had hit her boss so hard. She knew that Jane had left the office very late the previous night, and she was in early this morning. And the JIC was a big task for anyone—it's the last thing Sam would have wanted to do.

She guessed that it all took its toll. And the Tony James discovery, whilst good news across the board, would mean a whole new stack of work for Jane. She was already studying a new file that she'd taken off the top of her in-tray, a pile that looked like it might be about to topple over.

Jane spoke as she read the paper in her hand.

"That's really good work, Sam. I don't think anyone else would have paid that much attention to the two men. I would have assumed that it was James and Groves. Actually, I would have struggled to watch the video at all for a second time." She stopped reading.

"What can I do for you?" Jane looked directly at Sam as she hung her scarf over the back of her chair. Progress.

"I need some time off, please."

"No, sorry." Jane didn't even think about her reply. It was instantaneous.

Jane was back doing stuff on her desk now. Not making eye contact with Sam.

Then she stopped and looked up. She seemed to have gathered herself.

"Without David, we're stretched. I'm stretched. Your new intelligence is crucial, and we will need all of our resources to try to understand why Daesh are keeping James alive. And, just as importantly, to establish where he is being held."

"I understand that. And I will continue to work remotely to the same capacity as I am now . . ."

Jane interrupted her. Her steel was back.

"You know that's not the case! The tablet and the phone only give you so much granularity. I would argue that you wouldn't have made this find on a Nexus? True?"

Sam closed her eyes. Jane was right. As much as it hurt, she couldn't take time off now. *She couldn't.*

But she could work to rule, maybe? Wolfgang could come over—*where will he stay? My place?*—and she could help him in the evenings. *What day is it? Wednesday.* Unless Jane called a lockdown, she could travel after work Friday night and be back in on Monday. She had plenty of money saved, so catching a plane wouldn't be a problem. *Yes, that would work.*

Sam had obviously taken too long to reply, so Jane carried on.

"Look, Sam, I'm sorry. I have to get this news to the chief and then put a briefing note to the JIC. I do need to move along. But, why do you want time now? Is it still your Uncle Peter?"

Sam was alert now, her focus back. Jane was right. It was a selfish request.

She softened her approach. "Sort of. Look, it's all fine. I'll do what I need to do in the evenings and this weekend. I'll assume you won't call a lockdown, and I can travel then if I need to. Don't worry about it."

Jane was about to let Sam go, but then she added, "Is it to do with the person you met while you were in the Alps?" Jane smiled, a touch cheekily.

Sam, who was about to turn and walk out, stopped herself. She smiled at Jane. It was good to have her back.

"It might be. I'd better get back to the office so I can forward that presentation. By the way, can I call him Clive?"

"What?"

"The chief—you know, 'Call me Clive.'"

Jane laughed out loud.

"Call him what you want, but if you value your job, I'd stick with 'Sir.'"

"OK then."

No. 17a Roundgreen Lane, Colliers Green, London

Sam was thankful that she had managed to get home from work without having to break someone else's nose. She half expected the spotty youth to be waiting for her with a couple of friends, but thankfully he was nowhere to be seen. She only had one forehead and didn't like to use it that often.

The day had ended in a rush, with a sharp call to brief "Clive." Jane had let her lead on the briefing. He'd seen it straight away, even before Sam got to the end of the presentation. He swore—quietly—at the outcome.

"Bugger."

The chief stood up, walked to the window of his office, and looked down the Thames. She was familiar with the move. She'd only been in David's office twice before and, both times, he'd gone through the same routine when he needed to think. Look out of the window, gather one's thoughts. Sam's mind drifted to how she imagined him in his hospital bed, and a lump grew in her throat. Tears were never far away at the moment.

"Well done, Sam. Excellent work. The big questions are, why have they kept James alive, why fake his execution, and where are they keeping him? Jane?"

"I don't know, sir. Could be all manner of things. Future bargaining counter. Doing a Damian Lewis on him and trying to convert him to Islam—although I think that is very farfetched. If they've broken him, and we have evidence of waterboarding, then maybe he'd be a source of useful advice on our MOs and lower-level tactics."

"Sam?"

What, me?

"Jane's third point, plus the first, in that order. He's broken—I think there's no doubt about that. As a result, they can ask him anything they want, and he will give them a sensible answer. And, sometime in the future, he might just be a useful trade."

"I think that's a fair assessment from both of you. Have

you briefed the JIC yet, Jane?"

"I was writing the note when we got a slot to see you, sir."

"OK. All good. We now need to find this soldier. Please let me know if you need any more resources. And, both of you"—the chief waited for an answer, but clearly wasn't expecting one—"call me Clive. Please."

Sam had almost wet herself at that point. But she managed to get out of his office without sniggering. And then it felt great to walk down the corridor with Jane, laughing out loud at the chief's last comment like two naughty schoolgirls. When things were tough, you needed to pull together. Humour was an effective glue.

It had, without doubt, been a good day.

Now, what she needed to do—other than eat and possibly have another half glass of that very slurpable Malbec—was to e-mail Wolfgang.

She had sent him a holding reply late last night and was delighted that, within a few minutes, he had come back with: *OK. Let me know what your boss says. I can be at Heathrow within eight hours.*

With the pasta boiling away—*how long does it take? Eight or twelve minutes?*—she opened her Gmail account and typed away:

Hi Wolfgang,

   Can't get time off just yet, although the weekend is free at the moment—work may come crashing in. Happy that you come here when you want, or I could catch a flight on Friday after work? Would need to be back here late Sunday night.

   I have a couch. Or I understand they've got room at the Dorchester.

   Where do you live? And, as it feels such a long

201

time ago and such a fleeting meeting, are you for real?

Looking forward to it. Anything to break the mundanity of life here.

Sam

Should she put some kisses at the end, like everyone does nowadays—but not really mean it? *No, sod it.* It's too early for anything like that. I'd probably frighten him off.

Sam pressed "Send."

She ate, washed up, and was about to watch something banal on TV when she remembered that she had started looking through Interpol mug shots for the man who had ransacked Wolfgang's apartment.

She opened up the Nexus and logged in. What she had managed to do last night—with some limited manipulation afforded by her access to SIS securenet—was to play with the video and get a reasonably good mug shot of the man. She now had a photo that looked like something taken in a police cell.

The Interpol database had thousands and thousands of photos. And, whilst she was never short of patience, what she didn't have was the time or the energy to search through all of them. She reduced the number of images by narrowing the fields for her search. After some trial and error—she was still learning the intricacies of the application—she managed to restrict the search to males, thirty to fifty years old, German. Search results: six hundred and fifty.

What time is it? It's ten fifteen—must go to bed soon.

Ping.

An e-mail to her Gmail account.

It was from Wolfgang.

Dear Sam,

I am alive and as you remember me. "Nice chinos," I think you said. I have booked a flight out of Munich— where we have a house—for 3 p.m. tomorrow. I can be in central London at six thirty, all being well. Or we can meet at Heathrow. Your choice.

I'm not keen on the Dorchester; the rooms are slightly on the small side. Happy to use your couch, although—seriously—I can book into a hotel if you wish.

Let me know your address.

Looking forward to it.

Wolfgang xxx

That was such a good feeling. She had no idea what the man was really like, or whether or not she could trust him. But it felt great to be doing something other than work.

So, "Clive" had gone well. Now Wolfgang—*I wonder if he likes to be called Wolfie?*—was going to make a guest appearance. And, as we know, good things come in threes— *come on Interpol, don't let me down.*

Inevitably, it wasn't as simple as that.

Sam painstakingly looked over page after page of mug shots and, at one point, fell asleep with the Nexus almost slipping off her lap.

She woke suddenly. She looked across at the plastic clock sitting on the plain-wood mantelshelf above the electric fire. She'd lost fifteen minutes.

Onward!

And then, there he was. Three-quarters of the way down page ninety-seven. *Was it him?* She sat up, adjusting the pillow behind her back. She reached for, and finished, the half glass of wine she had poured a couple of hours previously. Then, she tapped on the image—it enlarged before her eyes.

It was him. OK, so he had more hair in the Interpol shot and a weaselly moustache. But she was confident. It *was* him. *Herr Heinrich Bischoff.* Forty-nine years old. Domicile: Leipzig, Germany.

Leipzig wasn't far from Dresden. That made sense.

She was onto something. But, she also knew she was dog-tired. And her place needed a tiny bit of sprucing up before Wolfgang's arrival tomorrow. She screen-captured the image and then closed her machine.

This would all have to wait.

Chapter Twelve

Somewhere on the Saudi Peninsula

The guard came into his cell with a plateful of meat, some bread, and a very green orange. He placed it carefully on the floor and nodded. He then went over to an old Philips cassette player, opened it, turned the tape around, and pressed "Play."

He gestured with his AK-47, and, in thickly disguised English, admonished Tony.

"No touch!"

Tony nodded. It was all he had the energy for.

The guard left the cell and locked the thick wooden door behind him. Clunk, clunk.

The subtle whirr of the spooling cassette was quickly hidden by the fairly melodic voice of someone who sounded like David Niven—a *proper* English accent. It had taken Tony half an hour to establish that he was listening to the Koran. Next to the cassette player were twelve tapes—about fourteen hours of religious words. All of which were in a language he understood. He thought he was already listening to it for a second time, maybe even a third. It was hard to tell; his mind hadn't been his own for a while. He heard some of the words and even managed to assimilate a phrase or two. But much of it he tuned out. No, that assumed that he had control over what his brain currently registered. He didn't. Some of it got through—whatever his brain wanted him to hear.

What he heard made perfect sense to him. As had his Bible classes when he was at school. All of it seemed well meaning and something that any rational person might subscribe to. There was nothing wrong with religion. It was the people who preached it who were the problem.

Tony shuffled across to the plate, his legs shackled in

medieval irons, fixed to the wall by a long chain. His hands were free.

Leaving aside what was going on in his head, his body seemed to have settled down, if you consider "racked with surges of pain" as settling down. He had been visited by a doctor yesterday. At least, he assumed he was a doctor. He was an Arab, carrying one of those black bulbous briefcases that held all manner of medical implements and pills. It was interesting that he wasn't wearing a thawb, but loose-fitting trousers and an open-necked shirt. He sweated a lot and looked a little uncomfortable with what he was being asked to do. He was probably there under sufferance, which made Tony feel that at least the guy might be trying to fix him, rather than hurt him. That was a novelty.

The leg stung like hell, but the swelling that had been there since the beginning had started to go down. In a more lucid moment, and there hadn't been many, he had checked the wound and thought that he had a hole on both sides of his leg: a small entry wound on one side and a massive gash of an exit wound on the other. The doctor had made him scream by daubing the wound with what was probably alcohol. The pain had calmed down once he had bandaged it. He still couldn't stand up easily. Not without being helped.

His ribs were sore, as was the whole of his head. He remembered spitting out a bit of a tooth at one point and chewing was akin to sticking a Stanley knife in his cheeks— but he managed. His nose throbbed, but that was just cartilage. It would be fine.

But it was his stomach that hurt the most. He knew he'd taken a good number of kicks to his middle, but he didn't think that was the problem. He couldn't keep anything down—or more accurately, inside. He reckoned he probably had dysentery, or something similar. His stomach contracted with extraordinary cramps that made him curl up in a ball and weep. Recently, crying had come easily.

At least now he had a bucket where he could relieve himself, and they had provided a couple of cloths to wipe himself. There was a second bucket with clean water in it, and next to it some soap. Earlier on, his guard, again gesticulating with his rifle, had said, "Clean! Clean!" Nothing was done around here without an exclamation mark.

But it wasn't the injuries or the disease that hurt him most—although both made him cry out, at times uncontrollably. Since Ted and Sandy, something else hurt more. He hadn't been able to stop weeping since Ted and Sandy. He was surprised he had any fluid left, what with it coming out of both ends and then seeping from his eyes.

Before Ted and Sandy, he had got through the beatings and the torture. They were transient events, spikes of horrendousness on a plateau of pain. He had screamed, cursed, and cried as they kicked him; he had begged and blubbered when they had waterboarded him. He had told them everything. He'd even told them things he didn't know, but thought might please them. He actually made things up. It was unimaginable what your brain would do to stop the pain. He couldn't run away, so his mind did what it could do to try to end the cycle of violence. He hated himself for it. But he couldn't stop, even though he tried.

But that, somehow, was all manageable. There were gaps in the horror where all he had to deal with was the throbbing pain and the deep self-loathing.

Now, having seen them execute Ted and Sandy, sever their heads with a blunt sword, he was faced with a new enemy. Something stronger and more debilitating than beatings, more devastating than the torture.

He'd assumed that Sandy was dead. He'd seen him go down, but not made it to him during the attack before he took a bullet to his leg. And, as Sandy was not on the video he and Ted shot days ago, he thought that he was gone. Dumped somewhere—surely they wouldn't have bothered to bury him?

But they hadn't dumped him. They had saved him to be ceremoniously executed alongside Ted. And Tony had been made to watch the proceedings from one side.

Guest of honour.

He had been continuously hooded up until that point. He had been dragged along and sat on a chair in the midday sun. He still had no idea where he was, or where he'd come from.

How *did* he get here from the first place he'd been kept? Where they had waterboarded him? He thought he'd been thrown in the back of a pickup in the middle of the night. Flesh; a filthy, thin thawb that you might call clothes; a corrugated metal floor—all squashed together. As they drove along, the bouncing was as painful as anything he had endured so far. He banged and lurched against other things in the truck that he couldn't fathom. On reflection, the things might have been Ted and Sandy.

When they got to where they were now, for him, his disposition had got better. They'd stuck him in a room with a single door and a barred but opened window. An Arab, whom he now thought of as his guard, brought him food, water, a toilet bucket, and something to wash himself with. And the Koran recited by David Niven. He had managed to stand once to look out of the window, but only stole a fleeting glance of rock and sand before his legs had given way.

And then he was guest of honour at the execution of Ted and Sandy.

Sitting on a chair and still hooded, he heard a commotion. Once that had died down, and after what he now thought was a rehearsal of the words to accompany the execution, his hood had been removed.

Bright, penetrating sunlight.

He couldn't stop blinking. For about a minute. But it took less than that for the horror of what was in front of him to come into focus.

He couldn't recall the next five minutes, not in a coherent way. Not now. The video camera on the tripod. The small cheering audience. The Arabian tea on a table in front of him. His hands had been freed and an Arab to one side had said to him, "Tea. Drink!"

He had.

The interminable words prior to the double flash of the sword. Two bodies; two heads. No longer joined together.

To him, then, there followed a noisy silence. Words became a sea of background hum that didn't register. And his mouth wouldn't utter a thing. He tried to shout "Stop!" as the blade was held aloft for the first time. But nothing came out. It was as if his tongue had been replaced with a piece of leather that he could no longer control. As the blade came down for a second time he couldn't hear anything either, just a dreadful, unrelenting background hum.

He was mute. Deaf and dumb.

That was then. It was nearly two days later. At least he could count. He could sense time, and his hearing was back. The Koran was coming over loud and clear. But he still couldn't speak.

The doctor had talked to him in poor English, asking for his symptoms. He hadn't been able to respond. He'd tried to tell him about his stomach, but could only mouth what he was feeling. Down there. He had pointed. Maybe words would come back, but then he'd have to describe out loud the horror of Ted and Sandy. The worst thing. Worse than the pain and the torture. Worse than the beatings.

It was the unmitigated horror of watching two of his friends being executed whilst he drank tea that tormented him. No, he couldn't think about it. And he certainly couldn't talk about it.

He had made it across his cell floor as far as the plate with the meat and bread. He noticed that there were also a couple of tablets. They were the same colour as the ones the doctor had prescribed yesterday. He'd take those. Pills to make him better. Better than Ted and Sandy.

As he lifted them to his mouth he realised that he was crying.

Just like a child. Like the child he had become.

Consultant Freddie Pilming called them to order.

"Settle down, please. Where are we with Jennings?"

He had four doctors and the ward sister in his office. Two of the doctors were registrars, who monitored the ICU patients on a twelve-hour shift. The third was the senior anaesthetist, whose job it was to keep a check on all of the patients' vitals and had ultimate responsibility for keeping them alive. The fourth was a visiting toxicologist, who, he hoped, had some news on what had actually caused David Jennings's liturgy of symptoms.

The anaesthetist spoke first.

"We've got the kidney failure under control with dialysis. He has partial liver failure, a result of the toxic shock, and yesterday he had three minor heart attacks, all of which we managed. I'm now waiting for pneumonia, which, with the state of his lungs, is next on the list."

"He's still on a ventilator?"

"Yes. Note, this morning we stuck in a trachi-tube. Oxygen saturation levels are at 80 per cent, which is fine for now. But we will try to get those down if his lungs stay fit. Which I doubt."

"And the liver?"

"Holding out at the moment. The drugs are what's causing the partial failure. It would be good to get something prescribed that actually dealt with the cause of all of this, rather than dealing with the symptoms. We're running out of choices of suitable antibiotics."

"OK. Some of you may not know Doctor Badger, our visiting toxicologist. I'm hoping he has some news from the lab. Jimmie—what have you got?"

"Thanks, Freddie. First, I think I'd like to talk to you alone about this. If I may? Maybe Stephen"—he gestured to the senior anaesthetist—"could stay. But other than that, just the three of us. Please."

Freddie raised his eyebrows and put his arm out in the

210

direction of the door. The ward sister and the two registrars shuffled out.

"Close the door!" Freddie yelled. The ward sister turned and pulled the door closed.

Born in a bloody barn.

He settled himself. Patience wasn't a virtue of his, but when you're in the business of saving lives that are on the very edge of living, he didn't think it was a virtue he should worry about.

"What's this about, Jimmie?"

"I've had to take Home Office advice on the findings of the toxicology report. That's one reason it's taken a little longer to sort this out, although getting to the bottom of the cause was unlike anything I've come across before. There were so many false trails. We only had the light-bulb moment yesterday afternoon." The toxicologist waited as if preparing for a statement of some magnitude.

"And?"

"David Jennings was injected with a combination of *Clostridium botulinum* and ricin." He paused. Freddie rocked back in his chair. "About eight to ten milligrams of each, although I can't be sure."

The toxicologist reached into his black leather folder and got out a pink file. Freddie noticed the word "Secret" printed in scarlet letters on the top and bottom of the file.

"It was really difficult to separate the two to begin with. It was made more complicated by the fact that, as soon as I realised we might be dealing with a biological agent, I had to clear the building. That wasn't for contamination purposes, although that was a consideration. It's the usual procedure in the case of a designated list of biological agents. *Clostridium botulinum* and ricin are at the top of that list."

"Blow me down." Freddie was still rocking in his chair. As he did so, he breathed out strongly.

Jimmie continued.

"The Security Services are aware, and I have been given very strict instructions as to whom I can tell. I'm afraid you've both got to sign the Official Secrets Act. Today. I have copies with me prepared earlier by MI5." He pointed to the pink file. "Once they have your details, someone, apparently, will come around and brief you."

"Sure, sure." Freddie's impatience had hit the surface again. *To hell with all the security bullshit.* "What about treatment?"

"There is none. There is no reliable antidote for either. I have a concoction of drugs, none of which will be a surprise to either of you, or your staff. We just need to keep him steady and see if his body can fight this."

"What do we put on top of his notes?" the anaesthetist asked.

"You choose. But not *Clostridium botulinum.* And not ricin."

Terminal 1, Heathrow Airport, London

Wolfgang wasn't a discerning passenger. He thought people made much too much fuss about where they sat and what they ate.

At over six feet tall, he struggled with some coaches where the solid seat back in front of him crushed his knees. And he often bit his tongue on an aircraft when the passenger in the row ahead reclined the seat so that his legs became entangled with the safety instructions and in-flight magazines. What he'd never got a grip of was how the food tray still managed to remain horizontal whatever the angle of the chair. The person who had invented that was a clever chap.

The BA flight had taken an hour and three-quarters. The staff had looked after him really well—even in cattle class, and, thankfully, he had sat next to a man who was neither fat nor fidgety. It had been a stress-free couple of hours.

He didn't have that much to think about, other than to wistfully imagine what on earth he was doing travelling to the UK to see Sam Green, a woman he had met briefly on a mountainside. It was clinically bizarre—the whole episode. And he was compounding all this oddness by flying to London to meet up with someone he hardly knew, to talk about something that was well off the rational scale. Life could not get much more unfathomable.

Wolfgang had taken his laptop on board and played around with his Lattice database. He'd looked again at the passenger manifests of a number of the air crashes, trying to make connections between those who had died and why someone might want to kill them.

His view was that nearly everyone wanted someone dead at some point in their lives, even if it were only a result of a fleeting surge of rage. He reckoned that every flight had at least three adulterers among the passengers, as well as one person who might have stolen from this or her company or embezzled money from some other hapless soul. Someone would probably want all of those dead. But they probably wouldn't bring down the whole aircraft just to make that happen.

He was looking for a reason to kill a single passenger on each of the flights he had chosen. Those passengers would all be linked by a collective motive, a motive so fundamental, so critical—*and so secret*—that the only way to maintain control was to hide the deaths of those chosen among the bodies of hundreds more.

It had all started with a teenage fascination with aircraft—how they managed to get airborne, stay up in the sky, and land at the right place without breaking apart. It was true that his main passion was music. But his teenage hobby had been aerodynamics. Lift, created by the separation of airflow over a wing. Stability and control in the air. Lightweight materials. Fly-by-wire.

And, as a typical teenage boy, he couldn't stop himself from exploring the macabre side of flight: near misses; crashes; disasters.

People thought air travel was safe. That all depended how

you interpreted "safe." Around one hundred and twenty thousand passengers and crew had been killed in air accidents since the Second World War. Historically, 2001 was the worst year, with over four thousand deaths, although that did include 195 passengers and hijackers on the three US internal flights that created their own piece of history: 9/11. In comparison, 2013 killed the least number of people, with just 265 deaths. But that's still a lot of people when you recall the old adage that "air travel is safer than driving a car." The worst single air crash was a Japan Airlines 747 that went down in 1985, with the loss of 520 souls, although the Tenerife crash between two jumbos on the apron had a higher casualty figure—but that included two planes. Whichever way you looked at it, it was a lot of dead people.

It was clear to him that flying was always accompanied by an element of mortal danger, an irony not lost on him as he walked through the terminal toward the baggage return.

His interest in air disasters became more forensic when he was thinking about committing the "perfect crime." He liked to tell himself that the notion of hiding the murder of someone by killing the individual with a whole load of other people came to him when he was trying to think of a foolproof way to eliminate Josh Baxter. This was a thug of a boy in his fifth form class, who picked on anyone who was smaller than he was. Baxter's list didn't include Wolfgang, who, even as a sixteen-year-old, was nearing six foot. In addition, his Teutonic thick skin and casual acceptance of pain meant he didn't take any rubbish from the likes of Baxter. The boy knew this and, as with any bully, only fought battles where success was not only guaranteed, but didn't hurt. He gave Wolfgang a wide steer.

Wolfgang also had the Neuenburgs' pacifistic approach to life: never pick a fight, and bring people together where you can. So whilst he wouldn't be bullied by Baxter, neither did he wish to use his own violence to stop Baxter from bullying others. It wasn't in his nature.

However, what if Baxter just disappeared? *Now that was*

a completely different thing.

Wolfgang had considered widening the perfect crime to include trains, coaches, and buses, or major fires in big buildings. In a more grown-up moment and away from the fantasy of eliminating Baxter, he felt that the people targeted for murder would be high achievers in their field: great intellects, senior politicians, or substantial businessmen. They wouldn't travel by coach; they would fly. And, even if they did get on a bus, one couldn't guarantee to kill everyone in a coach crash. It didn't happen that way. The beauty about planes was that when they fell out of the sky from forty thousand feet, the chances of survival were pretty slim.

Wolfgang first looked in depth at a crash in 2002 when, still thinking of Baxter and the perfect crime, he read about the KLM plane that was lost over the Atlantic. It was all over the news. The aircraft was an Airbus A330 carrying 217 passengers from Buenos Aires to Amsterdam. It dropped out of the sky an hour into its flight. At that point, the Atlantic Ocean is pretty deep; whilst they eventually discovered some wreckage, the black boxes were never found. The transcript of the last radio exchange between the cockpit and the air-traffic control was short. The pilot swore in Dutch, and then the airways went quiet. Even now, some thirteen years later, no one knew for sure why the aircraft crashed into the sea.

Out of the 217 passengers on the KLM flight, five made it onto Wolfgang's fledgling list of "noteworthies." He remembered the names as if he had written them down yesterday: Victor Hammenbeck—CEO of Hammenbeck Industries, makers of beef-processing plants; Bishop Miguel Mendoza—the bishop of La Plata; Doctor Frenz Haggitude—senior vascular consultant at Ziekenhuis Hospital in The Hague; Professor Simone Candoza—senior partner and research chief at Modetta Solar Industries; and Major General Hans DeGuie—chief of staff of the Dutch Marine Corps. They were all *very* senior individuals, at the top of their game. Doctor Haggitude had just perfected human elephant-trunking for aortic aneurysms. Professor

Candoza was close to industrialising a solar furnace, where huge mirrors reflected sunlight onto a solar array the size of Wolfgang's suitcase—which he'd just spotted on the carousel. The array was photovoltaic, and the electrical energy harnessed in the process was five times that of normal solar panels laid out on the same acreage of land. It was genius.

Wolfgang was about to rehearse the talents of the other three when his phone pinged. He opened up his mail. The new message had the title "*Read this please.*" There was no body to the e-mail, just an Adobe pdf attachment. He knew pdfs were inherently free from viruses, so he opened it.

What he saw made him miss his suitcase. It rattled past him and back down toward the hole in the wall.

The attachment was a single piece of paper carrying a message. The message was made up of letters cut from newspaper cuttings, straight out of *The Blackmailer's Handbook*. The letters were large, and his phone's screen wasn't big enough to show all of it. He had to scroll down.

It read:

Stop. Right now. Or you, or somebody close to you, will get hurt. We know where your family live. Check the local news to see that we don't mess around.

That was it. *Stop. Or someone will get hurt.*

Wolfgang felt the blood drain from his cheeks. He closed his eyes and had to think about closing his mouth when he realised it was hanging open.

Which local news? Munich? Dresden? Where?

If they could get his e-mail address, they could find any of his family's residences.

Mother!

No. Wait. It says, "Or you, or somebody close to you." The *or* was important. So maybe no one's been hurt. Yet.

He swiftly closed his mail, opened up the *Dresden*

Fernsehen website, and scanned the latest news.

And there it was: "Fire in Pillnitzer Strasse destroys top floor of apartment block. Police report that no one is hurt."

Scheiße! The bastards have burned down my flat! And probably Herr Doppner's next door! He didn't deserve that. Poor, poor man.

Wolfgang was pacing now, his free hand on his forehead. His other squeezing his phone as if to strangle it.

What gate of Hell have I opened?

Sam had thought about making a sign. Maybe with "Wolfgang" on it. Or, how about, "Count Neuenburg II"? Then she thought better of it. Anyhow, she didn't need a sign. There'd be only one person coming off the Munich plane looking like a model for a bespoke tailor.

And there he was. Sure enough, Wolfgang as she remembered him. A multi-green checked woollen jacket— best worn on a day out at Sandringham. A light blue all-cotton shirt with a stiff collar, pinstriped mustard yellow cords, and a pair of sandy-coloured brothel creepers. Behind him, like an obedient black Labrador, he pulled a medium-size brown suitcase on a long leash.

But he was also wearing something else. Something Sam had not seen before. A mournful face, one that didn't look like it could be cheered up anytime soon.

Sam raised her hand when he was a few metres out.

"Hi, Wolfgang."

He smiled, but it was forced. He leaned over and kissed her on both cheeks.

"Hello, Sam," was his muffled response as his cheek touched hers.

"You OK?"

He took in a deep breath and exhaled loudly, looking left to right as if nervous that he might be being watched.

"I need a drink. Please. Can we go somewhere noisy? Busy?"

Sam frowned, nodding at the same time.

"Sure. You don't want to go to my place and drop your bag first?"

Nothing came back. He stared over her shoulder.

"Sorry?" He didn't even look at her. At that point he was absent from the terminal building. Sam felt that she was on her own. It was not a good feeling. She was immediately frustrated. What had she let herself in for? This man was a different man from the one she remembered. He was distant, distracted.

How long was he staying? How long would she have to put up with this?

She needed to take control.

"Follow me," she said.

At a pace quicker than Wolfgang expected, they headed through the concourse and onto the taxi rank. She hailed the first one available, the driver taking Wolfgang's suitcase and putting it in the boot.

"Colliers Green, please. The Rose and Crown." It was her local. There was a darts match on a Thursday night. It would be busy and nosier than Wolfgang probably wanted. But just now she felt a little vindictive. It would serve him right if it were too noisy for him.

They both sat in silence as West London sped past the taxi's windows. She wasn't going to say anything else. Not until he had made some effort to talk. She wasn't sulking; she was just a bit tired. That's all. What would it have been like if she had flown to Germany? At least here she had some control. *Damn.*

Wolfgang was looking away from Sam, seemingly mesmerised by the London skyline at dusk. He had his chin in his hand, his elbow resting against the bottom of the taxi window. He held that position for ten or fifteen minutes, staring into the distance.

Then, just as they hit the city centre, he reached into his pocket and dug out his phone. He played with it and opened a document.

He passed it to Sam without a word.

She read it. Then read it again. Her mind spinning.

She was already looking for clues as to who may have sent the e-mail, having instantly forgiven Wolfgang for being distant.

"Do you recognise the address?"

He looked at her and his face softened, relief in his expression—a small smile. She had to admit that when he smiled, even a little, her legs went a bit wobbly.

Get a grip, girl.

"No. You can see it's a Hotmail address, one probably made up on the hoof. I may be able to find out where it was sent from, within reason."

"But it will be a public library, or Internet cafe. Untraceable," Sam added.

His face now wore a frown as if to say, *how do you understand all of these things?*

She ignored his look. "What about the document? You're good with the web. Does it leave any trace, a hook?"

He was smiling now. More relief, as though he was no longer alone in the world.

"Thanks, Sam."

"For what?"

"For being the person I thought you'd be."

It was her turn to look out of the window now, a touch embarrassed by his affection. Her brain spun, trying to bring everything into focus. If Wolfgang *were* on to something with his madcap conspiracy theory, and this message seemed to tell them that he was, then maybe Uncle Pete had been murdered. All because somebody wanted someone else on the plane dead.

That's rubbish. It didn't matter how you unpicked it, it still didn't seem to make any sense.

"They torched my apartment."

"What?"

"Just before I came through customs, I checked the local TV station. The top floor of the apartment block has been arsoned."

"Anyone hurt?"

"They don't think so, but my neighbour, Herr Doppner, his place suffered from the fire as well. He didn't deserve that."

They were both looking at each other now as the taxi driver navigated the late rush-hour traffic. Thankfully, most of it was going the other way.

Both of them remained quiet, reflecting on the newly shared news.

"I found the man in your apartment."

It was Wolfgang's turn to show incredulity. "What?"

Sam motioned ahead with her hand, pointing at the taxi driver. Then she raised her finger to her mouth, indicating silence.

"Let's wait until we get to the pub. Then we can discuss this further. We might have something."

"Sure. Good thinking."

For the rest of the journey they both sat in silence. Sam didn't feel the need to say anything, and, it seemed, neither did Wolfgang. It wasn't an uncomfortable silence; it just seemed right.

When they got to their destination, Sam paid for the taxi and led Wolfgang into the pub. They took a small table in the corner of the lounge bar, away from the noise of the darts match. She sat, while Wolfgang returned from the bar with a bottle of house Merlot and two glasses.

As he was sitting down, Sam said, "You need to think about your family in all this. These people, whoever they are, are serious. If they don't get to you, might they have a go at your mother?" Wolfgang had mentioned the death of his father and his surviving mother the first time they had met.

"I'll speak to my mother. She has good relations with the local *polizei*, and they will look after her. She knows nothing of my work, but I can make something up, and she will take some precautions." He took a sip of his wine. "Who's the man?"

Sam took out her Nexus, which she opened in "nonwork" mode. It was easy to disguise, and it looked just like a normal tablet, other than its ruggedised shell.

"Here he is." The tablet displayed the non-Interpol version of the image of Herr Heinrich Bischoff that she'd put together. "He's forty-nine, lives in Leipzig." She handed the Nexus to Wolfgang, who studied it intently.

"I've been able to do a little more research on him. He's ex-Stasi, although he was a very junior agent when the Wall came down. He has a minor criminal record, most of which is for public disturbances at right-wing rallies. But, wait for it, he was cleared of arson in November last year."

Wolfgang stopped staring at the tablet and looked at Sam, a frown on his forehead.

"What did he set alight?" There was no *allegedly* from Wolfgang. He had his mind made up about Herr Bischoff.

"A sports centre"—Sam paused for effect—"that was housing refugees from eastern Europe and Afghanistan. Nobody died, but that was due to the quick thinking of a janitor who raised the alarm."

"Bastard." Wolfgang made the statement through gritted teeth.

He tilted his head to one side. "I don't suppose you can tell me how you know all this?"

Sam looked across the pub to the bar. The landlady had just come down the stairs and was serving a customer. She waved at Sam, who waved back. The landlady stared a bit longer than was necessary. Then she winked. Sam grimaced back.

No, there was no way she could tell Wolfgang how she had accessed an Interpol database of national criminals considered to be an international threat. Nor could she tell him that she had interrogated their systems and dug up Bischoff's police and court records.

What she hadn't been able to do—mostly because she had spent nearly all of the day going over new and old images from the southern Middle East, trying desperately to find something that might lead them to where Tony James was being held—was look at the scores of video clips SIS had of far-right demos in Germany. She wanted to try to paint the man onto a canvas, which was wider and more descriptive than just a mug shot.

"I know someone who knows someone. Let's leave it at that." She took a sip of her wine. "To complete my research, my friend did establish that Herr Bischoff has links with the Church of the White Cross. It's a thinly disguised Christian/fascist group that advocates white supremacy and takes much of its doctrine from the Masoretic Bible."

Wolfgang looked confused.

"It's a Hebrew version of the Old Testament and thought to be the oldest known version of the Bible. I had to look the last bit up," she added with a smile.

"So, is it Bischoff or the Church of the White Cross who is after me?"

Sam didn't answer immediately. She took a final sip of her wine. It felt late, and she hadn't eaten yet. She looked at her watch. It was 9:00 p.m.

"Have you had anything to eat? I've made up a chilli, if you'd like some."

Wolfgang was all smiles again now. *Not that look again. He's got to stop that.*

"My favourite," he replied charmingly.

Grrr.

"Let's go back to my place. It's a short walk from here." Sam was pointing unnecessarily in the direction of her flat. "You can do some more research while I get food on the table."

"What about the wine?" Wolfgang placed his hand on the unfinished bottle.

"Take it with us."

With that, Sam led, giving the landlady a final wave. She winked back again, mischievously.

Oh, don't.

As they got outside, Sam turned to Wolfgang. "Turn the

data off on your phone. And if your iPad is data enabled, do the same."

Wolfgang stood still for a second and, before following Sam's instructions, asked, "Why?"

"If your phone is on data and they know your number, they will be able to triangulate your position." *Oops, probably shouldn't use such technical language.*

Wolfgang didn't ask any questions about how she was quite so savvy. He just turned off both devices.

Once in the flat, he was very complimentary about this and that. She had tidied it before she'd left for work that morning, although it was always immaculate—too long in a barrack block for the discipline to wane. While she busied herself in the kitchen, he walked round the sitting room, making kind, but banal, comments like, "This is a nice vase."

Sam ignored them.

"Tell me about your conspiracy." She raised her voice to be heard in the sitting room. She was putting some more cumin in the chilli, whilst helping herself to the glass of the Merlot Wolfgang had poured for her.

So he started. It was a long story, which included some amusing anecdotes about a boy called Josh Baxter. By the time he'd finished bringing Sam right up to date, they were halfway through the chilli, with Wolfgang helping himself to some more salad.

"Nice dressing."

"Thanks. It's my mum's speciality. How many crashes do you consider to be significant?"

"OK. You ready?"

Sam took another mouthful of food. Wolfgang was sitting opposite her at a dining room table just big enough for the two plates, salad bowls, and their wine. He'd mellowed over the past couple of hours, and she was fascinated by every action—the way he pushed his pasta onto his spoon with a fork; the way he wiped his mouth with his napkin after every mouthful. He sipped his wine just as you'd expect someone who lived in a castle might—she was no further forward in discovering exactly where he lived, but she *hoped* it was a castle—and his manners were impeccable, but not overly fussy. He helped her to food, served her wine, and only started eating when she was ready. He was, there was no doubting it, a perfect gentleman.

As Wolfgang opened his iPad, he beat her to any admonishment by commenting, "It's OK, it's not connected to the Internet." He swiped and prodded the screen and then started.

"First, 1975, Air Maroc 707 out from Casablanca—one hundred and eighty-eight dead; same year, Olympic Airways NAMC YS-11A out of Athens—fifty dead; 1979, American Airways McDonnell Douglas DC-10, an internal flight from Chicago—two hundred and seventy-one dead; 1982, Pan Am 727 internal flight out of Dallas—one hundred and forty-five dead . . ."

Sam interrupted him. "Hang on, Wolfgang, this might take some time. Save you reading out all the detail, can I look at the document?"

"Sure." He handed her his iPad. She studied it for a moment.

"There are thirteen aircraft on here, dating back to 1975. Although this doesn't include Uncle Pete's, I notice. How many passengers are we talking about?" She did a quick sum. "Two thousand three hundred?"

"Actually, two thousand four hundred and seven, to be precise. And I'm sorry, but I haven't yet found the energy to include the latest crash, although I do think it will be the fourteenth."

"And how many individuals are you interested in?"

"Well, if you look at the other tabs on the spreadsheets, you'll see that I have all the manifests. Go on from there, and I have associated age"—he was pointing across the table and touching the bottom of the screen—"nationality, gender, occupation, and some other fields against all of the passengers."

"Religion?" She looked up from the tablet.

"Yes, where I have been able to find out."

"And what's the diagnosis? Can you find thirteen or fourteen connected victims?" Sam could have smiled at that point, mocking him. But with his latest news, who was she to say he was wasting his time?

Wolfgang cleared his plate and took a sip of his wine. He placed his napkin, ruffled, on the table beside his plate.

"No. Sorry." He shrugged his shoulders. "I have tried to cross-reference many individuals against all number of fields, but I can't, yet, find a common thread."

"So, not religion?"

"No. Not that I can see."

"Although . . ." He paused.

"Go on," Sam pressed.

"Look. Some of the stuff I've being doing hasn't quite been above the law. Low-level hacking and similar. Very recently I was attacked—that is, my machine was breached—by a server I had targeted. The person who did it was interested in nuclear power. Actually, power companies per se. You remember that I mentioned the Pennsylvania meltdown event in 1979, the one that may not have been an accident? Well, they were looking at that as well. So, I thought maybe this is about energy. The control of energy. Worldwide reserves and things like that." He was excited now. Like a child. His enthusiasm was infectious. *And attractive.* "I did a very quick enquiry on my database, and there is someone on nine of the flights who has an energy-related background. I need to look again at the remaining flights and see if I can find anyone else."

"And the Koreans!" It was Sam's turn now. "They were professors from KSTAR, the experimental nuclear fission centre in Daejeon. You met them."

"Yes, of course. That would be ten! I need to look at this. Now!"

"Hang on, Wolfgang."

Sam put her hands out to signify "stop."

"I have to work in the morning. And the dishes need to be

225

done. We have time tomorrow. You could sightsee and do some research—but not here in the flat. If anyone is watching your data, you know—and we could compare notes by e-mail during the day and make a plan for tomorrow night. And the weekend."

Wolfgang was already on his feet, collecting the dishes. He was almost in the kitchen when he said, "Let's go to Leipzig."

"What?" Sam was on her feet now, but not because there was washing-up to do, although she would help. She couldn't talk about this sitting down.

"Let's go and find out more about Herr Bischoff. And if we fly into Munich, we can overnight at my castle."

Sam dropped the plate she was carrying. Thankfully it was only a few inches above the table and, apart from making a clattering sound, didn't break.

"Everything OK in there?" Wolfgang was making his own noises in the kitchen.

"Did you say *castle*?"

"I think I did." Wolfgang was making more noise now, as if trying to hide from the question.

"Is it a big castle?" Having got a grip of her plate, Sam was now chasing after him into the kitchen. It didn't take long.

"It's more of a schloss than a castle. But aren't all castles big?" It was a nonchalant remark, yet the impact was anything but.

Sam put the dishes to Wolfgang's right. He had already turned the hot tap on and was reaching for the washing-up liquid.

"OK then. Yes, let's do that. Yes. That would be great."

Blimey.

Chapter Thirteen

SIS Headquarters, Vauxhall, London

Jane was running on empty. She had left the office after midnight and was back at work by six thirty.

Yesterday was about two key meetings. The first was the JIC. The focus there was the direction of intelligence gathering to try to find Captain Tony James. The mood was buoyant, but other than "do what you do," nothing substantive came out of the meeting, save a small reallocation of money between departments. The chief's "five o'clock" was a prolonged affair, focusing on the news that David had been spiked with a *Clostridium botulinum*/ricin cocktail.

It was an unparalleled attack on British soil. But who was behind it? Was David working on something that had made him a target? Was it a revenge attack? They had identified the main organisations that had the wherewithal to plan and carry out an attack. But the emergence of so many terrorist groups, loosely affiliated with religious militants—including a number of independent two- and three-man cells—made narrowing down the field almost impossible. And the breakup of the Soviet Union, even though it was some time ago, still provided opportunities for residual experience, talent, and resources to be bought and used. It was all highly complex.

The chief had asked Jane to stay behind. After metaphorically checking her pulse, they had discussed Greyshoe.

"Doesn't it strike you as more than just a coincidence that David was attacked within a day of the reopening of Greyshoe?"

The link hadn't been lost on Jane, especially as she was now code-word-cleared and, as such, a potential target.

"If they can run ex-CIA agents as far afield as the Middle East, then whoever, or whatever, it is must be capable of almost anything," Jane had replied. She was still convinced that Greyshoe was a worldwide conspiracy. Probably led by the West's far right, to further polarise opinion and force an all-out religious war between Christianity and Islam.

"Maybe. I guess you're on the East-versus-West conspiracy theory. I'm more along the lines of paying back David for thwarting the Ebola incident. If Linden Rickenbacker is putting the pressure on his predecessor, then Johnson might just be warning everyone to leave well alone. But, I have to say, it all seems pretty unlikely."

He had been tidying his desk and was now reaching for his coat. It was late.

"Press your team on who might be capable of producing the poison. Stick to Europe only, as we discussed at the meeting. See if they can come up with anything. Who is it, Tim . . .? Sorry, I can't remember the chap's surname. He's an old Iron Curtain man. See what he has. And, Jane . . ."

"Yes, sir?"

"Be careful; someone is after us." He was staring straight at her, his coat in his hand. "And get some sleep. In that order. You're no good to me if you can't function."

It was all well and good, the chief sending her home, but she had a mound of files greater than the number of weeks she had left in the year. And now she had to put something out so that her team would be thinking about the poison issue in preparation for tomorrow morning's meeting.

That was yesterday. Now, still under pressure and still feeling tired, she was arriving a couple of minutes late for said meeting.

"Sorry I'm late."

There was a steaming cup of coffee in front of where she normally sat. Claire was ready to take notes and half pulled out Jane's chair so she could sit down easily.

"Thanks, Claire. And for the coffee." A soft retort,

228

almost under her breath.

Jane looked up at the group. It now included a new team member: Mo Alfari, an Iranian-born analyst who specialised in the emergence and spread of so-called IS or "Daesh." The chief had seconded him onto the team as soon as it was clear that Tony James might be alive.

"I hope you've all had chance to say hello to Mo, although I guess most of you have met him around and about. And you've seen my note about David's attack?"

Everyone around the room nodded.

"So, two things. First, Mo. Anything to add on Glasshouse?"

"Thanks, Jane. There's a lot happening among Daesh's hierarchy on the Saudi peninsula at the moment. There has been a rift in Yemen between the so-called leader, Abu el Afari, and Ali Abdullah Sahef, the deputy. The latter has claimed responsibility for the capture and murder of the SRR soldiers. In Saudi, Daesh's leader, Omar Ahmad, is reportedly unwell, either from natural causes or after a US drone attack on his headquarters in Al Jawf a couple of weeks ago. My understanding is that Sahef is looking to consolidate Daesh leadership in both Saudi and Yemen." Mo paused for breath.

"And where does that put Tony James?" Jane asked.

"He's a prize. Sahef has scored countless brownie points with the hostage affair. Now he has his own tame British soldier, whom he can showboat."

"You mean like a tiger on a leash?" Sue asked, in a disgusted tone.

"That's exactly what I mean. But this is good news for us."

"Why?" Jane pressed.

"Because you can't showboat quietly. What's the point? Sooner or later we're going to find out where James is because Sahef can't keep quiet about it."

Sam, who, as always, had remained quiet throughout the meeting, put up her hand.

"Sam?" Jane gave her the opportunity to say something.

"Is there any chance that they might be trying to convert him? Could we, potentially, lose him?"

Mo continued, "It's possible. But I reckon in a very low-key way. Make him attend prayers. That sort of thing. There's always a possibility that he might just become affected by the Stockholm syndrome and convert without being pressed. Who knows what state his mind's in."

Sam nodded a "thanks".

"Anything else?"

Nothing came back from Jane's question, just a flat hand from Mo.

"OK. Tim. What about the attack on David? Does this sort of approach ring any bells from your days on the other side of the Iron Curtain?"

Tim puffed himself up a bit.

"The KGB, the East German Stasi, the Hungarian AVH, and the Polish SB have all used ricin to murder opponents when the target needed to be eliminated without being brought in for questioning. Or where they've wanted the hit to be undertaken at a distance. Put air between them and the murder." Tim used his hands to demonstrate a gap. "Ricin is reasonably easy to manufacture and contain, but it will kill you if you ingest, or get injected with, just two milligrams. To be clear, a normal paracetamol tablet is five hundred milligrams."

"And remind us where it comes from?"

"It's made from seeds of the castor oil plant. Simple as that. My understanding is that Porton Down might have developed an antidote, but it's never been tested on a human." Tim was enjoying himself.

"And *Clostridium botulinum*?"

"It's botulism. A bacteria found in some foods, but never normally in its most deadly form. It doesn't last long outside of a donor and cannot survive at temperatures greater than one hundred degrees. In a reasonable dose, it's the most dangerous toxin in the world."

Tim paused for a second, looking around the table. "Combining the two has the advantage of keeping the lethality of *Clostridium botulinum*, whilst mixing in the fairly swift effect that ricin has on the body. As a compound, it is also very difficult to separate and very confusing to a toxicologist. I'm not surprised it's taken the quacks this long to establish a cause. However, and this is key, I was in the Berlin Embassy for six years, and I have only heard of the combined compound being used twice before. Both cases were in the early eighties. And both were used to murder political opponents in East Germany—at the hands of the Stasi."

Sam let out an involuntary snort on hearing the word *Stasi* for a second time in under a minute.

"Sam? You OK?"

"Sure, Jane. Thanks. Just got something caught." She tapped her throat with her hand.

"So, Tim. Can you dig deeper and see what you can find out about how the compound might have made its way to Westminster Bridge? All the usual: delivery method; transit; setup; likely protagonists; backing et cetera. We're calling this Operation Umbrella. It's hardly original, but at least it paints a picture."

"Sure. Will do, Jane. Thanks."

Jane ran around the houses at that point. Sam had something on the tasking of new satellite images, which Jane agreed with some negotiation among the group, but there was little else. After that, she quickly brought the meeting to a close.

She was the first out of the room. Time was precious. She really needed to do what David used to do. Find a moment and a couple of blank sheets of paper, step back, and try to visualise both operations: Glasshouse and, now, Umbrella.

She knew she was far too deep in the details. She needed to lift herself out of the tactical and start to work at an operational level. She would do that now and blow the consequences to her burgeoning in-tray.

Wolfgang did love the College, and it was good to be back inside the old red-and-white building, its facade very similar to that of the Catholic Westminster Cathedral. Here, of course, the god was music. Absolute reverence was paid to it in that regard. It made him smile to think that Sir Andrew Lloyd Webber and Mika were both alumni of the College. That was the beauty of the place. Music was music, whatever the genre. Classical to pop.

He still had his entry swipe card. Just before he'd left four years ago, on one of his many forays onto the College's mainframe, he'd allocated the card "all area access" and given it a "no runout" date. Getting in had been easy. Thankfully, nobody recognised him—yet. For him, today, it wasn't a security concern. It was that he had too much work to do and didn't have time for pleasantries. Not now.

Sam had left the apartment well before him. She had managed to get from her bedroom to the bathroom wearing just a simple nightdress, without being bothered that he was snoring away on her couch. To be accurate, he did have one eye on her as she came back out, still in her nightie. She wasn't Claudia Schiffer, but she really did look after herself. Bright, resourceful, *and* fit? He was glad she was on his side.

Maybe when this is all over? Would he ask? And might she refuse?

They had agreed that if she found time today, Sam would do some more investigation into Herr Bischoff. Importantly, she would aim to leave the office at 5.00 p.m. on the dot. She had taken her overnight gear, so she could travel straight to whichever airport Wolfgang had chosen for them to fly from.

He would lock up the apartment and turn his telephone on every hour for five minutes, so they could communicate. He'd decide on the weekend's itinerary and book the necessary flights. She had given him strict instruction that she needed to be back in the apartment no later than midnight on Sunday. She was always very clear, but not necessarily in a bossy way. Just very military. Something that no longer surprised him, as the one thing he had uncovered last night was that Sam Green was an ex-sergeant in the British Army's Intelligence Corps.

Impressive. If slightly scary.

He had a mental list of things he needed to get done at the College: book flights and car hire; try to establish an exact location in New York for the three e-mail addresses his electronic "open and grab" had managed to secure from the other night; and reinterrogate the Lattice, to establish if there were other individuals on the manifests who might have been involved in energy industries.

But at the top of his list was his mother. He'd already phoned her. The cover story was that he'd read somewhere of a new wave of kidnapping and extortion, targeting the rich in southern Germany and Austria.

"Have you heard about it, mother?'

"No, dear. Do you think I should be concerned?'

"Yes, of course! And please speak to Inspector Danzig. You gift enough money to the *polizei*'s annual fundraising. He would be delighted to pay a little bit more attention to the countess, I'm sure." Wolfgang played to his mother's gentle vanity.

"Do you really think so?"

"Yes. And please text me when you have spoken to him. Do it today, Mother. Please?"

"Yes, of course, Wolfgang. If you insist."

"And brief Klaus to be extra vigilant around the house, especially when locking up at night."

His mother sighed, a wistful, motherly sigh. "Of course, Wolfgang. Of course."

He was delighted when he put his phone on at eleven to find that she had already texted him back to say that she'd spoken to the inspector.

Wolfgang wasn't sure how credible the threat was, or how much him digging deeper would endanger himself and those he loved. It all seemed so unreal. In a matter of days, the situation had transformed itself from interesting hobby to life-threatening spy thriller.

He was confident that his father wouldn't have stood idly by. *So neither will I.*

He was on one of the College library's computers, thankful that they hadn't moved the furniture around since he had left. As a result, he was able to sit at the only monitor that was hidden behind bookshelves and a poster screen. If anyone interrupted him, he'd be able to clear the monitor before someone could be nosy.

Using the College machine, he accessed his servers in Munich and got to work.

SIS Headquarters, Vauxhall, London

First thing—and she had been at work very early—Sam had looked through all of the "open" and "closed" source images from Saudi and Yemen, but she found nothing of consequence. She had come to realise that the net they had thrown wasn't wide or deep enough to guarantee finding Captain Tony James. OK, they had eyes on the Sana'a safe house. GCHQ, with support from the Americans, had gotten much of Yemen covered for mobile traffic. They had also physically tapped the safe house in Sana'a. And their agents and informers in Yemen were sniffing around, looking and waiting for titbits of intel.

The problem was they didn't have anyone within Ali Abdullah Sahef's inner circle. Reports from Tim and Justin suggested that they were trying, but they hadn't been able to get their hands on an informer. Tim was pressing the team in Yemen, but Daesh were very good at allegiances. Apparently they regularly murdered members of their team to keep everyone on their toes.

It wasn't worth snitching on Sahef.

Mo Alfari's point, that sooner or later Sahef's boasting about "owning" Captain James would pop up as an opportunity, was all well and good. But it was hardly proactive. So, Sam had attended this morning's Glasshouse meeting with a new request: to spread the keyhole imaging wider, to include seven hamlets she had identified in Yemen.

"Where did these come from, Sam?" Jane had asked. The rest of the Glasshouse team members were looking at Sam as though she had spoken out of turn.

"There is no direct intelligence linking any of these with Sahef," Sam replied confidently.

Tim let out a derisory snort.

Sam pressed on. "But there is some logic. I assumed that Daesh deserted the Hajjah compound at one thirty, just after the Saudi SF attacked their targets. It gets light at six thirty, and I guessed that Sahef wouldn't want to be driving in daylight with the SRR hostages on board. Based on an average speed of twenty clicks an hour—the maximum anyone could possibly drive on these Yemini roads and tracks—and heading south, or southeast, toward Sana'a, these seven come into range. As I've said, it's logic, not intelligence, based."

"But there could be seven more?"

"Actually there are at least twenty-nine more. I used Google Earth. I narrowed it down to just seven by ensuring there were hills close by, but not mountains—to match the execution video shoot. I then discounted anything as large as a village, where Sahef's influence might not be able to spread as wide as the whole population. Hence, the shortlist of these seven hamlets within ninety clicks of Hajjah, where the topography looks like the execution video. I can produce a slideshow brief if that would help."

"No, no, Sam. That won't be necessary." Jane looked down at her tablet. She seemed to type something. She lifted her head back up again and looked directly at the analyst. "You understand, Sam, that if we target these with the level of satellite imaging you'd need, it will eat into the one hundred and fifty thousand pounds that's just been allocated to widen the informant network in Sana'a. We're talking of maybe reducing that total by as much as forty thousand pounds."

"How much *useful* intel have we had over the past three months from Daesh informants in Yemen?" Sam was on a mission. She knew the answer was none. Even the intel on the original SRR-overwatched terrorist training camp had come from US sources.

Jane looked across at Tim and Justin.

"Justin? It's a fair question."

Justin looked uncomfortable. He glanced at Tim, who was absently tapping his pen on the notebook in front of him.

"Sam's right. Our agents are running seven informers in Sana'a and one in Taiz. They're spread between links to Al-Qaeda, the local rebels, and one in government. The team is finding it impossible to recruit a Daesh man at the moment. Truth is, we may not be able to spend the new money. Although we'd be loath to give it away."

Jane thought for a moment.

"OK, Sam, you're on. And, Mike, can you speak to the Doughnut to see if they could target these hamlets for SIGINT? And I'll liaise with the Americans, reference the imaging. We should, all being well, get our first satellite shots by"—Jane closed her eyes in thought, her head nodding as if counting the hours—"tomorrow morning. But it could take two or three days to get all of it."

Sam knew she had chanced her arm, but she was tired of waiting for images that, in the case of Tony James, might actually make a difference.

After the Glasshouse meeting, Sam had got straight on with looking at the new "open" source images that Marvin had put on the cloud. She was about halfway through her work when her e-mail box lit up. It was a message from Wolfgang.

She checked her watch: 11.10. So he'd managed to get off the couch, then? She couldn't help but smile to herself. It had been a very relaxed, but hardly romantic, evening. She was happy with that. It was just great to be doing something outside work—even if it was just like work—with someone different. Someone kind, intelligent, and amusing. Although, she thought, "amusing" should be caveated with "in a German sort of way."

She smiled again when she thought about how she'd showered and then walked back to her room wearing just her skimpy nightdress. She knew she was in good shape and was pleased that she'd spotted Wolfgang discreetly following her with his eyes, even though he pretended to be asleep.

So the current score was: *British spy—one; German count—zero.*

She opened up the e-mail.

Hi Sam,

Spoken to Mother. She will look to be more vigilant; she has contacted the police.

We're booked on BA 136 leaving LHR for MUN at 19.20. Will be in Munich at 20.00. I have booked a hire car. It will take us about an hour and a half to drive to the schloss.

Have also managed to establish the location of one of the three e-mail addresses in NY. I can only get to within one apartment block—I won't disclose details here. However, click on this web address http://cnn.com/1206.345.45.1. It's all very interesting.

Am now looking over the Lattice to widen the search for energy moguls among the list. I should be closer to that when we meet later.

Have you got any timings?

Wolfgang xxx

Sam clicked on the link and was taken straight to a recently archived CNN clip: a reporter was standing outside of a New York apartment block. She pressed "Play." The clip concerned the apparent suicide of a British man. He'd hung himself from the ceiling of a reasonable-size office, an office that the presenter was pointing to over her shoulder. Sam guessed the block was the same one associated with the e-mail account that Wolfgang had hacked, otherwise why would he have sent it to her. The reporter went on to say that what was odd about the whole affair was that the office was devoid of all furniture and equipment. There was nothing at all in the room other than a single chair. It had been apparently been knocked over to enable the man to hang himself. The police's initial thoughts tended to suicide, but they couldn't comment until after the postmortem and inquest.

Could it be that this was all linked? The threatening note, the arson of Wolfgang's apartment, and now the apparent suicide of a British man in slightly macabre circumstances in New York? *Oh, and David's attack.* The comment this morning by Tim, that the only organisation he knew with links to a *Clostridium botulinum*/ricin concoction was the Stasi—the same organisation Herr Bischoff originally worked for.

There were too many similar threads for all of them to be coincidences. *Surely?*

She replied to Wolfgang along the lines of "interesting video clip" and told him she would meet him in Terminal 1 at six fifteen. *All being well.*

She had run out of Yemeni images to look at, but she was expecting some more just after lunch. She should have moved on to Ukraine—there was still work to do there. Jane had a key report to put together for the chief by the middle of next week. And they needed to identify a couple more Russian soldiers among the rebels' ranks to fully expose Russian Army involvement in Eastern Ukraine. But that could wait. Just for a bit.

She accessed an area of the cloud that she didn't normally need to look at: right-wing disturbances: Germany.

In the folder there were a hundred and seventy-five

images and sixteen video clips. SIS had little interest in this murky area of German politics but kept some useful information just in case.

Sam looked at her watch. It was 12.05. Twenty-five minutes and then off to the gym for a session.

Here goes.

She started with the video clips that were taken around the time that Bischoff was cautioned. They were hopeless. Poorly shot. She discounted them for now. She looked at the photos. She was able to flip through at about one every five seconds, stopping here and there to mark a photo. After five minutes she had reduced the images to just five that she thought might be relevant.

She was looking for a medium-built man with Bischoff's face, lurking somewhere in the crowd. The problem was that all those who looked menacing had their noses and mouths covered with a scarf or were wearing hoodies that threw shadows over their foreheads and eyes.

But, in her chosen five images, Sam found him. She thought. The second image provided the initial "spot." It was the rubbish blue-and-white Nike sneakers that she'd caught sight of in Wolfgang's flat that grabbed her attention. She looked up at his chin and his mouth. Yes, it was the same man as the Interpol mug shots. *Gotcha!* Here he was wearing a grey hoodie, sporting a Bayern Munich football team logo on its breast. Now that Sam had him, she was able to refine what she was looking for.

She discounted two of the five photos. But the other three were positives. In the first two photos Bischoff wore the same clothes: the sneakers, the blue jeans, and the grey hoodie. In one of those he wore distinctive brown gloves.

In the third, he wore the same jeans—and she could see more of his face, so she knew it was him. But he wore a red hoodie, which also had a Bayern Munich logo on its front. He had different shoes on this time—dark army-style boots—*could be German Army para boots.* He was throwing a brick or a rock in the shot, his shortened sleeve exposing a

239

watch. It was a silver-grey TAG Heuer. She zoomed in. She could clearly make out the red-and-green maker's mark. It could be fake, but that didn't matter.

She sent all three photos to herself so that she could show them to Wolfgang later without having to access the secure cloud.

She checked her watch again. It was 12.25.

Sam unzoomed the last image, leaning back in the chair and taking in the whole scene. The photo was of a demonstration in a small town called Hoyerswerda. Reading the attached notes, it appeared that the group had come together under no particular banner, probably called to arms by a transient Facebook page. They were protesting against an influx of Syrian and Afghan refugees who had been afforded accommodation in the local church. The protest was ugly; a number of police had been hurt and three protesters arrested. But not Herr Bischoff this time.

It was all pitiful. The whole thing. Xenophobia on the front line. Racism at its worst. The image on her monitor disgusted and unnerved her. She involuntarily shivered.

Then Sam stopped thinking. Her mind went completely blank. Except for one thought: *no, it can't be?* She felt her heart beating loudly between her ears, trying to escape. Her mouth went dry.

She physically shook herself. And then focused back in on the image.

Gently, as if she were defusing a bomb, she used her left hand to get a close-up of a man at the back of the crowd. A man she had previously ignored because he wasn't in the thick of the riot. She zoomed in until it started to pixelate. Quickly, she pressed an icon at the bottom of the screen and Doris's image-sharpening processor spun into life.

There he was. Bold as brass.

She knew she was right. The black man she was looking at had a can of Diet Pepsi in one hand—the same drink he'd reached for when he'd got out of the black Terrano in the training camp in Yemen. And he had a mobile phone attached to his ear in the other.

Ralph Bell; my other friend from Sierra Leone. *My God.*
You're like a bad penny. Turning up all over the place.

What on earth was he doing in Germany eighteen months
ago?

Flight BA136, Heathrow Airport, London

It had been a rush to get to the airport and meet up with
Wolfgang. As soon as she met him, he couldn't stop talking
at her about the dead man in the flat and his new list of
"energy worthies" among the crash victims. What Sam
actually wanted was to settle on the plane for two hours of
nothing much.

The aircraft taxied down the runway. At least now she
was sitting down.

"Well, what do you think, Sam?"

"Sorry, Wolfgang, about what?" She was almost ready to
focus, but not quite. Her mind still had momentum, moving
with the flow of passengers, herded from place to place by
the meanderings of Terminal 1.

She was no good at airports. That was because somebody
else was responsible for her; all that "go here," "stand there,"
and "put your bags through this." She much preferred to be
in charge, especially of her own destiny. If she never had to
check in again, it would be too soon.

"You know, the man hanged in the apartment?"

Wolfgang was fidgety. All excited.

She looked at him, a resigned, half smile signifying that
he was too over-the-top for her at the moment. It seemed to
make him shut up. For a moment.

"Thanks, Wolfgang." She gently touched his knee,
stepping onto, but not over that boy/girl line. "It's been quite
a day. And I have some stuff for you, but let me finish this
first." She pointed at the complimentary pretzels and a glass
of red wine. "And then we can start."

He smiled at her, pushed his head back onto the seat rest, and closed his eyes. Almost immediately he opened the one closest to Sam to check that she was still looking at him. She was.

"Five minutes," Sam added sternly.

He closed the errant eye, nodded, and relaxed, breathing out loudly through his nose.

Sam's biggest problem at the moment was Ralph Bell. She knew her discovery was huge, and it was key in some way that she didn't yet understand. But what to do? She could have exposed the whole Wolfgang thing to Jane this afternoon, which, even now, still seemed so off-the-wall that she didn't want to have that conversation. Short of that, there didn't seem to be any way of casually letting Jane know she'd found a picture of Bell at an antimigration riot in Germany eighteen months ago.

Straight after the discovery, she had decided to exercise in the gym. During her six-kilometre run, she had come to the conclusion that she'd leave Ralph Bell until after the weekend. Something might come up with Wolfgang that would allow her to have a conversation with Jane that didn't start with "I met this German count in the Alps. He's a plane-spotter . . ."

But, had she made the right decision? Doubtless, the CIA would want to know immediately of any new intel on Ralph Bell. And Jane would be furious if she found out that Sam was withholding key intelligence.

And what about Bischoff, the Stasi link and David? She'd finished her run before she had any time to explore that link in any detail.

She'd expose nothing for the moment. Decision made— for now. And that was that.

Trying to push the Ralph Bell image to one side, she'd spent the rest of the afternoon on Ukraine, where she had found one more Russian. Which was a positive. She had typed up the report and winged it off to Jane. Unusually, she had left work promptly at five, telling Frank that she would be spending the weekend in Germany, "staying in a castle." To which he had replied, "And I've got a hot date with Angelina, who's on the rebound after Brad decided to leave her for another man."

London's best transport system had still made a forty-minute tube journey to Heathrow into one that lasted an hour and a half. Sam had rushed through the terminal to meet up with Wolfgang just before the gate closed. He had met her with a smile. *Which had been nice.* Now her mind drifted as the glass of red wine took effect.

The aircraft bumped a bit in some turbulence. It broke what little train of thought she was having.

She was ready now. She spoke without looking at Wolfgang, who, she could sense, still had his eyes closed.

"I could recognise Herr Bischoff at a thousand metres now. I know his whole wardrobe and what make of watch he wears. I also know where he lives." Further digging into the Interpol database had handed over the last piece of information.

Wolfgang kept his eyes closed.

"And *I* have ten individuals, nine men and one woman, who were at the cutting edge of new methods of energy generation, before their lives were cut short by a sudden drop in air pressure." He opened his eyes quickly and turned his head to her. "Sorry, Sam, that was insensitive, what with your Uncle Peter."

Sam smiled. *I seem to do that a lot when Wolfgang is around.*

"And what about the Brit in New York?"

He half turned in his chair, his face alive. His hands were scrunched together, white showing where the skin was tight over his knuckles.

"I can't be sure because the e-mail tracking only goes as far as a central junction box, which can supply up to eight individual lines. But, I reckon that the man who tried to hack my machine earlier this week killed himself. Can you believe that?"

Sam stared away from Wolfgang, looking down the aisle. Thinking.

"Or, he was murdered." It was a casual statement from Sam. But its enormity wasn't lost on her.

She turned to face him and took a deep breath.

"We have to be clear, Wolfgang, that this is not a game. Don't ask me how I know, but I can tell you that people like this, like the ones who sent you the message, are ruthless. Deadly. I don't mean to repeat myself, but it's not a game. Trust me."

She touched his leg again.

Schloss Neuenburg, German/Czech Border

Sam was up early, had a quick shower in a wet room the size of Lower Saxony, and dressed in a pair of jeans, a pink cotton shirt, and a turquoise Lowe Alpine fleece—another T.K. Maxx special. She took out a paisley silk scarf that she'd been given for Christmas. It wasn't really her, but she'd brought it with her in deference to the fact that she was staying in a castle. *Oh, what the hell.* She put it on.

She packed the rest of her things away in her carry-on bag and headed down the stairs toward where she thought she remembered the kitchen was. At one point she wasn't quite sure she was using the right staircase. However, a full-length portrait of an elderly man with Wolfgang's eyes, standing alongside a stringed instrument bigger than a cello—*is it called a double bass?*—reminded her that she'd seen him yesterday on the way up to bed.

"Morning, Sam."

Her thoughts were broken by Wolfgang coming into the kitchen. She was standing by one of the pine worktops, staring at a very elaborate espresso machine that had too many buttons to decipher. She felt clueless.

"Did you sleep well?"

"Eh, yes, thanks. The bed is bigger than the queen-size

one I have in the flat. I didn't realise they made them that big. I'll have to get a new one."

"We Germans like our sleep, Sam. Hence the bed and the feather duvets. All designed to help you recover from a hard day at the brewery."

She laughed and continued. "I'd offer you some coffee, but the espresso machine here has more dials than a hydroelectric power station. I'd be frightened of opening the sluice gates and drowning a small valley nearby."

It was his turn to laugh now.

"I think, first, we should go for a walk on the grounds. We agreed to leave for Leipzig at nine?" It was a question. Wolfgang waited for Sam to nod, which she did. "Tomas will knock up some breakfast for us while we're out."

"Is that really necessary, Wolfgang? I'm capable of getting the cereal out of the cupboards. I can even boil an egg."

"Not like Tomas, you can't." He softened his tone. "It's his job, Sam. If we do it for him, he'd have to find another castle in which to boil his eggs. That is, of course, a metaphor for all the fabulous things he does round the house." He looked at her across the huge pine table that tried, without success, to fill the middle of the enormous kitchen floor.

"OK. If you say so."

"Are you ready to go outside now?" Wolfgang was reaching for his boots, which were in a separate cupboard by a door; it appeared to lead to the garden.

"Yes. Think so."

Sam hadn't seen the outside of the schloss in daylight. It had been dark when they arrived, although tell-tale lights indicated that it was big—and turreted. Out on the expansive lawn, she turned back to take a look. Sure enough, she found a Balmoralesque castle, but in red sandstone rather than grey granite. There were towers, wings, turrets, and tall, green roofs, the tiles pleasantly stained by the elements. The lawn was about half a football field in size and looked like it curved around to the front of the castle. But there were no far-reaching views. Everything stopped at the dark green pine forest, which clung to the edge of the lawn and gently rose up into the low clouds.

They were in a bowl, of sorts, which was secluded and breezeless. It felt achingly quiet. Sam stood still and listened. All she could hear were Wolfgang's feet, quietly pressing against the lush grass of the lawn as he ambled toward the wood.

Still nothing. Not a sound. Except, just then, a single screech of a buzzard, probably waiting for the cloud base to lift so it could go hunting.

It was idyllic and like nothing she had ever encountered. A castle in the depths of the forest. *Where are the witches and gingerbread houses?*

She jogged along a few yards and caught up with Wolfgang, who seemed to be lost in the silence.

"I love it here." He looked down at her. He was maybe five inches taller than she was. He smiled again. "It is my favourite place."

They both walked casually on, lost in the tranquillity.

Then Wolfgang continued. "When my father died, I spent three months here trying to fathom the unfathomable. Hoping to reconcile why God had decided it was his turn. I didn't get anywhere. It was all a sea of emotion. Nothing in my head stood still long enough for it to be understood. That was, until Tomas joined me one day on the lawn. I was just over there on that bench." He pointed to his left. "It was unusual for him to sit next to me without being asked, but he did." Wolfgang stood still at that point, his head raked slightly upward as if he were still looking for answers.

"Do you know what he said?"

Sam knew it was a rhetorical question and didn't answer.

"He said, 'Your father didn't die so you could sit here all day and think about what is wrong with the world. He died so you could go out there and fix it. That's what Neuenburgs do.'"

Sam waited for something else. Nothing came. She touched his elbow.

"And you are. You're doing something. He would be proud."

Wolfgang looked at her, his eyes ever so slightly moist.

"Come on. There's a short walk in the woods that takes us down to a hidden stream. Let me show it to you, and then we must eat some of Tomas's very best boiled eggs."

They set off across the lawn to a piece of the edge of the forest that was darker than the rest. When they got close, Sam realised it was a path winding its way through the wood, its base soft with a thick coat of old, brown pine needles. They walked in silence for ten minutes, both in their own worlds. The forest and path weren't as dark as they first seemed. There were shafts of light illuminating the floor, thick, lush grass growing where the forest and the brown, ageing bracken had succumbed. Just ahead there was more of an alleyway of light, snaking left to right. Sam assumed it was the hidden stream. She was at peace. Work, Uncle Pete, David in his hospital bed, Jane, Tony James, Bischoff, even her past life—they were all as far from her mind as they could be.

And then that peace was shattered.

Crunch.

She heard the sound behind them. Twenty or thirty metres away. It was so out of place that her nerves twanged. Wolfgang didn't seem to register a change; he just kept walking slowly by her side. But, for Sam, everything was now on edge. Her hearing tuned to all frequencies; her pupils set at exactly the size to let in the right amount of light.

Click.

It was almost imperceptible. It could have been anything. But to Sam it sounded like metal on metal. A key in a lock. A latch lifted on a gate. The safety catch of a rifle being set to "Fire."

And then everything all happened at once.

"Get down!" she screamed.

Crack!

She pushed Wolfgang away from her, whilst dropping to her knees, turning at the same time.

Thump. The sound of the explosion reached them from the rifle's chamber. There was rustling in the woods behind them. Sam looked across at Wolfgang. He was on the ground, holding his upper arm, blood seeping between his fingers.

"I'm OK." It was a whisper. Not the voice of a frightened man. Just loud enough for Sam to hear.

She was below bracken height. She looked back at Wolfgang. They were both below bracken height. The rustling from the woods behind them was getting closer. Sam kept Wolfgang's attention. Using just one hand, she pointed to him and then in the direction of the stream. She did it again, this time more forcibly.

Wolfgang looked confused, but then the penny dropped. Wincing with pain, he nodded, turned, and started to crawl on two knees and one working hand toward the stream. Sam looked round for a weapon. Nothing. She looked back at Wolfgang. All she could see was his backside moving off into the distance. He'd be at the stream in no time. The good news was that he was making some noise. A target for the shooter to follow. She might go unnoticed.

To her right was the nearest tree. Sliding on her stomach, she got to it and knelt up, listening. The crunching had stopped now. It had been replaced by steady but purposeful steps. The shooter had made it to the path and was heading their way. She put her back against the tree and impatiently felt on the ground for anything heavy. Nothing to her right. *Come on!*

Wait . . .

To her left she found a rock, about the size of half a house brick. She picked it up and transferred it from hand to hand—she still couldn't use her right one without some pain, but needs must. In no time she had a curved bit of stone nestling in her palm, with a sharp piece of rock sticking out.

It wasn't perfect, but it would do.

Step. Step. Step. In quick succession, getting louder.

She couldn't see Wolfgang. He must have made it to the stream.

And then the shooter was there. Half a step, and then one step, and then two steps in front of her. Sam leaped at him, her right hand above her head, launching her new favourite weapon at the back of the man's head. He heard her. Bending and turning to face her, the rifle came round, following the turn.

Smack!

She hit him on his left shoulder with a force that hurt her hand like hell and made the rock bounce away into the bracken. The man dropped the rifle and cried out, his knees giving way. His right hand reached for the wound over his shoulder, trying to protect it from further assault.

Sam was on her haunches panting. Adrenalin was coursing through her veins, trying to escape through her ears.

The man, hunched on the ground, clearly hurting, looked across at her. Immediately he seemed to realise that his assailant was a woman. His pained face became rage, his cowering now set to unleash his own attack.

Sam looked for the rifle, but couldn't see it. Her initial reaction was to run. *Strike and run.* It had always worked for her. If she ran now she could get away. She'd be quicker than this guy. But what about Wolfgang? She couldn't leave him.

That split second was gone. Now it would be too late. He was facing her, a short leap from making his own contact. She steeled herself, about to launch preemptively by throwing herself at him.

Thud! The man's facial expression changed from rage to confusion. And then the light went out inside him and he collapsed to the ground.

Sam was shaking. Lost in a sequence of events she no longer understood. Man ready to launch. Man down. She was coiled like a spring. Wound up, but not released.

She focused just beyond the assailant. And then it all became clear. Standing over him was Wolfgang, the barrel of the rifle in his hands, its butt now resting on the ground. He looked contained, but his breathing was erratic.

"Who *are* you?" he said, his face a picture of complete disbelief.

Sam slowly raised herself to full height, her shoulders rising and falling in harmony with her own rapid breath. Just then she had run out of words. She knew nothing would come for a short while. Until the adrenalin had run its course.

He could have stood and asked the question a thousand times, but he sensed that it wouldn't elicit a response. Instead, he walked forward, and, dropping the rifle to the ground, took her in his arms. It was a protective action, almost fatherly.

"Do you know him?" It was a bit of a snuffle from Sam.

Still holding her, he turned to look at the man.

"No."

Sam gently pushed herself away. It was her turn to look at the ground. She didn't recognise him either, but there was a strange, distant familiarity about the man that she couldn't place. It was a weird sensation—she'd always been so good with faces. She blinked and looked him over. The man's chest was rising and falling slowly. He was still alive. She couldn't have cared less.

She was already feeling better. More in control.

"We need to get whatever ID this man has and take photographs. I have my phone on me. And then . . ." Sam stopped to think, the mist in her mind clearing.

"Yes, Sam?"

"Get Tomas to report this to the police, and we should get out of here."

"Sam, I don't know if you remember, but I've been shot." He had his hand back on his wound, stopping the blood flow. He indicated where the wound was by nodding in its direction.

Sam looked at Wolfgang's face and then dropped her gaze to his arm. She moved forward and took his hand away. It was a deep graze, having ripped through a bit of muscle. It was nasty, but nothing that a few stitches and a couple of weeks wouldn't sort. His jumper and shirt were badly torn. She ripped them further, exposing the wound. He flinched. She ignored his minor protestations and took out a clean hanky from her pocket, gently closing it over the wound. Holding it in place with one hand, she deftly took off her silk scarf and wrapped it round the wound, tying it tight enough to stem the bleeding. Wolfgang closed his eyes as she tightened the knot. She stepped back and admired her work.

"You're right. Sorry. Let's do everything I said, but we'll clean and wrap the wound up again before we go." She paused. Wolfgang was looking at her with mild amusement. She looked at the man who had just clubbed their assailant with a rifle and who had potentially saved her life. She had to get him to understand what doors he had opened.

"This man just tried to kill us, or certainly you. Where there's one, there's another. I can tell you now that nowhere is safe. Nowhere. We need to keep moving."

"I should go to the hospital, and we should go to the police!" It wasn't an emphatic statement, but the tone was strong.

"No, Wolfgang. Just now you don't know who to trust. Except me. And some people that I know. I'll tell you everything when we're on the move." She picked up the rifle by its barrel with a thumb and a finger, being careful not to cover it in fingerprints. She didn't know the make, but it was a hunting rifle with a scope. Probably 7.62 mm with a small magazine. Possibly six rounds max. *I wonder if he has more rounds in his pockets?*

"Can you shoot?" Sam was twisting the weapon, giving it the once over.

Wolfgang had that bewildered look on his face again.

"I'm a German count. We own more land than Switzerland. Of course I can shoot."

"Good. We need a second weapon. Maybe a couple. Do you have any in the schloss?"

Wolfgang didn't reply.

Not for a second or two. It seemed to Sam that exactly at that point the gravity of the situation hit him. He stammered a response, but was unable to form any words. He was unintelligible.

Then he steadied himself and took a deep breath. A pause . . .

"We have a small armoury full of hunting rifles. You can take out whatever you want, Sergeant Green."

"Good. Let's get out of here."

Chapter Fourteen

It didn't take Wolfgang long to convince Sam that they should carry the unconscious man back to the schloss. She was all for making a dash for it. Putting distance between them and the scene. He persuaded her that leaving the man in the woods might give him the chance to escape when he woke up.

"Better in police hands?" Wolfgang suggested.

Sam nodded, and Wolfgang, with Sam's help, picked the man up and put him on his shoulders in a fireman's carry. He was determined not to flinch.

They walked quickly down the path and out onto the lawn. The distance between the lawn's edge and the schloss felt further than he remembered. He didn't like to show it, but his arm hurt like hell. A throbbing, gnawing pain. They walked across the precious lawn, beautifully kept by Ludwig the gardener. No matter the weather, it always framed the schloss in its rightful place. Majestic but becalmed. Grand yet homely. His bolt-hole away from the stresses and strains of the world. Where he could be himself. Until that idyll had been smashed apart by the man he was carrying. *The bastard.* He purposefully bounced him so his shoulder blade dug into the man's crotch. It was an unusually spiteful act for him.

What has gotten into me? Where's the peacemaker now?

Tomas was out of the kitchen door before they were halfway across the lawn.

"Was ist heir los?" Tomas cried out.

In German, Wolfgang explained that the man, whom he had just unceremoniously dropped to the floor, had tried to kill them. He pointed to the wound.

Tomas immediately launched into "nurse" mode, starting

to undo the knot in Sam's scarf. Wolfgang was enjoying the attention when Tomas was quickly interrupted.

"Hang on." Sam stepped forward. "Tell Tomas I'll dress your wound. His time would probably be better spent trussing the man up." Sam was on a mission.

"Don't worry, Sam. Tomas speaks very good English. Got that, Tomas?"

"Yes, sir." The voice came from a distance. Tomas was already on his way somewhere, probably to the cellar, to get some rope.

"Let's go in and clean you up," Sam said calmly. She smiled and led him inside.

Her words had that wonderful mixture of order and compassion. He still didn't really know what she did—or who she actually was. But, she would have made a fabulous nurse.

It took Sam ten minutes to boil some water and, on Wolfgang's instructions, find the first-aid box. In that time he'd popped upstairs and dug out a new shirt and jacket. He carried both down and put the originals in the kitchen bin. He was bare chested and felt a little exposed.

Sam didn't bat an eyelid. She sat him down and, with a mixture of hot water and antiseptic, started to clean the wound with cotton wool.

Scheiße. That hurt! He bit his lip. "So who *are* you?" Sam had promised him a revelation. She stopped dabbing for a moment and then started to concentrate again.

"I work for my government. I'm an intelligence analyst, looking at photo and video clips. I am very much at the bottom of the ladder, but my boss has connections with people at the more higher levels."

"So you're a sort of spy? You certainly behave like one." He let that hang, waiting for a response. There wasn't one, just more dabbing. "The man in my apartment and now the guy over there." Wolfgang pointed— thankfully their assailant was still out cold, tied tightly with thick rope. "Come on, Sam, you're more than just an analyst."

Sam dabbed harder than was necessary, and Wolfgang flinched.

"Ow! That's sore."

"Don't be a baby."

He looked at her hands working on his arm. One hand was holding the wound together, a second working on Steri-strips to seal it. Her tongue poked out the corner of her mouth as she concentrated. *A cute look.*

"I had ten years of service in the army. As a woman, you have to punch above your weight, and I learned a thing or two. Bring that and the government analyst together and you have today's Sam Green."

Wolfgang nodded. He still wasn't sure.

"Thanks for saving my life, by the way."

Sam stopped and frowned at him.

"When did I do that? You were the one who knocked the idiot out cold with a rifle."

"When you pushed me to one side. If you hadn't, this hole might have been in a more interesting place. One where hot water and a bandage might not have been enough to stem the flow of blood."

Sam was working again, gently but purposefully. She had started bandaging, carefully rolling the crepe around his arm.

"How do you know he was shooting at you?" Her concentration didn't slip.

What could he say to that?

Ping. It was Sam's phone.

"*Shit.* It'll be this morning's images." The words came out through a tight jaw. She secured the bandage with a safety pin, which, for about a minute, she had kept between her teeth.

"Look, Wolfgang. I have to go over some work. It's nothing to do with what's been happening here. Promise. It's something else that I really can't talk about. So I'm going to sit and look at the stuff. In the meantime, I reckon we need to be out of here in an hour."

As she sat at the huge pine table, Tomas put a cup of coffee in front of her and placed some fresh bread in the centre of the table. He followed that with a wicker basket lined with a blue gingham cloth. Nestled among its folds were six boiled eggs.

"Thanks, Tomas," Sam said.

"And what should I do while you work?"

Sam had already opened her tablet and was working. She looked up.

"We need another car. The hire car must have been clocked last night, leaving the airport. How else could they have found us? They may have intercepted our email exchange earlier in the day. Do you have another car?" Wolfgang was just about to say something when Sam stopped him. "It needs to be bland—discreet—easily lost in a crowd."

Wolfgang smiled.

"So my father's bright red 1984 Ferrari Testarossa might be a bit too conspicuous?"

Sam didn't look up from her work, but raised her eyebrows.

"Probably. Although I am impressed." He saw that she was flipping through images, staring intently.

"How many cars belonged to your father?" Sam was still looking down.

Wolfgang sat down opposite her and helped himself to bread. He took a sip of coffee.

"Here? There are ten in an air-conditioned garage across from the schloss."

That got her attention. Sam looked up.

"Ten!"

"And there are eighteen more spread among our other houses. Cars were his big thing."

Sam was working again, swiping and zooming. She hunched a little to get closer to the screen.

"Surprise me, then." She reached for a boiled egg and, in some way that Wolfgang couldn't fathom, managed to take the top off the egg without looking up. She had some talent, this girl.

"Nothing," Sam said to herself under the breath. "Oh well, there'll be plenty more over the next couple of days." She was still talking to herself. Wolfgang saw her type something and firmly poke at the screen. She was probably sending an e-mail. She closed the tablet's cover with a slap.

Sam reached for some more bread and checked her watch. He had been watching her every move. Delicate, whilst purposeful. Feminine, yet decisive.

Sam looked across at Wolfgang. He was still staring at her.

"What?"

"Nothing." He couldn't stop himself from smiling, even though his throbbing arm begged for a different emotion. "You were going to tell me more?"

"No, not yet. When we're on the move."

"Where are we going?"

"We have nothing on this guy," Sam pointed in the direction of the expertly trussed body, "Other than his phone, which is locked. Can you do something with that?"

Wolfgang finished off his breakfast and took a final sip of coffee.

"I could use the machines here. I have all the connectors . . ."

"No." Sam was emphatic. She softened her voice. "We need to get going. My tablet can work remotely, and I can access some pretty high-level stuff. But I think we should do all of that somewhere out of the way."

"By out of the way, you mean somewhere central, public. You can't get much more out of the way than this." Wolfgang used both arms to signify where they were. *God, that hurts.*

"Correct. And I'd like to go to Leipzig and have a look at Herr Bischoff's address. I did tell you that I got that yesterday, right? We should go and get a feel of the place."

Wolfgang was on his feet.

"Let's go to Leipzig's central library. We can use their machines."

"How long would it take us to get there?" Sam was obviously doing the maths.

"In my choice of car . . . about a couple of hours." He was disappointed that his comment didn't draw an immediate response from Sam. Like—*go on, Wolfgang, tell us about the car!*

"Good. We can talk theories on the way. What's Tomas going to do?"

Wolfgang looked across to where Tomas was standing. He appeared to be making sandwiches.

"Tomas!"

"Sir?" He had a roll of German sausage in one hand and a very sharp knife in the other. He was so glad Tomas was on his side.

"Send Gertrude home and ask her not to come in until I tell you. Please phone the police as we discussed. Tell them this man shot at me and I have a gash in my arm." He was thinking on his feet. "Explain to them that I've gone to hospital and that I'll be back later to make a statement."

"Yes, sir."

"And then lock up and go home."

Tomas stopped chopping for a second. The knife hovered above the sausage.

"No, sir." It was a quiet, but absolute, response.

"What?"

"I will stay here and look after the schloss. I don't think it has ever been left unattended in its history, and I have no intention of doing that now. Sorry, sir."

Wolfgang nodded. *Well done, Tomas.*

"Who's Gertrude?" Sam asked.

"She's the maid. She keeps very much to herself when guests are in the house. She's almost certainly in the schloss now, cleaning something to within an inch of its life."

"Oh, OK." Sam turned to Tomas. "We'll leave the gun behind, Tomas."

"Why?" It was an immediate response from Wolfgang. *Didn't they want the weapon with them?*

"Have you touched the trigger or the trigger guard?"

Wolfgang very quickly ran over recent events in his mind.

"No."

"Good. Then the police should match the prints from the man to the gun."

Wolfgang looked across at their assailant, who was still out for the count. *Was he wearing gloves?*

"I checked," Sam said. "He's not wearing any gloves."

Bully for you. Is there no detail that gets past this woman?

Sam was checking her watch again. "We do need weapons, though. Can we go to the armoury?"

"Sure." He was confident that his father's set of rifles would impress Sam as much as his choice of car.

SIS Headquarters, Vauxhall, London

Jane had worked more Saturday mornings in the past three years than she could remember. Today was different though. It was her first since she'd taken on David's responsibilities, and, unlike previous Saturdays, she didn't see herself getting away by lunchtime.

Her main focus was the COBR report on the Russian Army involvement in Eastern Ukraine. The chief needed to sign it off midweek. She also wanted to spend a bit of time looking over her digital mind-maps that she'd produced for Operations Glasshouse and Umbrella. She wanted to share them with her team before she left the office. It was possible that one or two of them might look at them over the weekend.

Sam had already e-mailed her. They had satellite images of two of the seven locations Sam had targeted. The Americans had done a good job. The images were in sharp focus—she reckoned you could get ten-centimetre resolution with what they had. The e-mail said that there was nothing in the images that had caught her attention, although she would look over them again later.

Cheekily, Jane had checked Sam's location, pinged from her phone.

Bayerischer Wald in Germany. Very romantic. *Well done.*

Jane had a soft spot for Sam. It wasn't just the Ebola thing, although that had created a pretty strong bond. It was the way that Sam didn't appear to have a rheostat. It was either everything—or nothing. She had thrown herself wholeheartedly into her job, and although Sam probably wasn't keeping score, Jane knew that the intelligence she gathered was as much as that of the other four analysts put together. She was a human dynamo. And, and this was key, Jane trusted her completely. That's why she didn't bat an eyelid when she noted that her best analyst was waltzing through central Europe on her weekend off.

Jane's phone rang. It was a ++01 number on her secure line. The CIA.

"Jane Baker."

"It's Linden, Jane. How's it going?" Jane stiffened herself slightly. It was the DD. She unconsciously checked her hair.

"Good, thanks, sir. How can I help?"

"First, how's David? Any progress?"

Jane reached for a note that Barry, the doorman, had stuck on her desk first thing. He'd picked up a call from the hospital. Barry didn't do e-mails unless he absolutely had to. "You can't kill someone with an e-mail, but you can with a piece of paper—trust me." It was his stock response when asked.

"He's still in a critical condition. The good news is that everything has stabilised. He's on dialysis, but his liver is holding up. He's still attached to a ventilator, but, and I'm not sure what this means, oxygen levels are down to fifty per cent. Which seems to be a good thing." Jane waited for a response.

"That sounds positive to me, Jane. The lower the oxygen levels, the less they're having to help his lungs. Good."

"And what about Greyshoe?" Jane took them both forward.

"That's why I phoned. I'll back this up with an e-mail later, but, in summary, we have gone forward two steps and back one. The IRS has come up with nothing. It seems Johnson's affairs are in order. He's a non-exec for a security firm in Washington. It's called Libertas. We know of the company. It provides security advice and boots on the ground to governments and NGOs in the Middle East and Asia. It's full of ex-military and the odd CIA and FBI has-been."

Jane tried to butt in, but the DD stopped her.

"It's easy to make the jump from Libertas to Manning and Bell. And I guess you were going to do that. My team here has dug deep, including a number of files we already have on the company. Everything we have uncovered appears to be legit. It's a professional and well-respected American company."

The deputy director paused for a second. Jane waited for him to continue.

"The FBI questioned Johnson in his office about the five hundred thousand dollars. He was charming about it and said he couldn't recall anything of the sort. He added that we might want to try the other two signatories, which was below the belt, if you ask me. The FBI has issued a subpoena to Johnson's lawyer, to get him to verify his statement under oath. So that's going to take a little longer."

He seemed to pause for breath.

"Anything else?"

"Just one thing. The Bureau has been very gently investigating an ultra-conservative church down in Abilene for the past year or so. Their ministry didn't appear to be up to anything nefarious, until recently. Four weeks ago there was a spate of firebombings at mosques in California and across the border in Vancouver, Canada." Jane thought he added the country just in case her geography was a bit rusty. "Seven Americans and one Canadian died in the subsequent fires. The Californian State Police thought they had apprehended one of the arsonists a couple of days later, but some very heavy lawyers were parachuted in, and the man was released. No charge."

Jane was fascinated by the story, even more so because the outcome had to be linked to Johnson. Otherwise, why would the DD be telling her all this?

"The church in question is called the Church of the White Cross."

Never heard of it.

"Sorry, sir. I've never heard of it."

"It follows an ancient lore, one drawn up at the very beginning of religion. It uses Hebrew scripts. I've got my people looking into it, but, in short, it's anti-everything, and pro-stoning of women who get out of bed the wrong side. Sackcloths are essential evening wear."

"The Church of the White Cross?"

"Correct. Its emblem is a white crucifix on a black background. In the middle of the cross is a black thistle. Apparently, followers have the logo tattooed between their shoulder blades."

"Wow. Sounds pretty hardcore."

"Yup, sure is. The FBI's preliminary investigations point to the church being extraordinarily wealthy. They're not sure yet, and they're treading very lightly, but we could be talking billions of dollars."

Jane didn't know what to say, so she said nothing.

"And do you know what?"

Ehh, no.

"No, sir."

"Miles Johnson is one of only six known pastors of the church. The FBI also believes he is the secretary of their accounts. Accounts that, again, this is only preliminary at the moment, appear to distribute money to both Europe and the Middle East. In large quantities."

Jane felt her heart picking up a bit. She wanted to say something. To make the obvious connection between the extreme right and funding Islamic fundamentalism, but she thought better of it. It was too obvious.

The DD concluded.

"In my book this doesn't add anything to your East-versus-West theory. Yet. The so-called Islamic State, or Daesh, doesn't need fanatical right-wing Christian groups to make the general public fear and loathe it. They already do. Christian or not. But I do take your point about provoking general Islamophobia. So we do need to take this seriously. Which we are. End of message."

"Thank you, sir."

"And, Jane, I don't need to remind you that this is on close hold?"

"No, sir, you don't."

You only need to tell me once.

Schloss Neuenburg, German/Czech Border

"Wolfgang."

He was loading the two Browning LongTrac hunting rifles into their cases and wrapping them in a check blanket.

"Is there a second route out of here?" Sam asked.

"Not on tarmac, no. Why do you ask?"

"Someone might have eyes on the main way out. It would be better to go out of a back gate. Can your choice of car manage that?"

He smiled, although it was accompanied by a wince as he lifted the rifles onto his good shoulder.

"Follow me," he said. Wolfgang led Sam into the high-ceilinged entrance hall, where Tomas was waiting.

They didn't have much with them: the rifles; a hundred rounds of ammunition; an overnight bag each; and a cool bag, stuffed full of goodies that Tomas had made up. There was a strong smell of garlic sausage coming out of the cool bag. Just after breakfast, Sam wasn't sure if that was a good or a bad thing.

"Cheerio, Tomas," Sam said. She felt the need to give him a hug, which he accepted graciously.

Wolfgang and Tomas started to shake hands, and then they embraced as well.

"Look after the place. And yourself, Tomas. I will put an e-mail together today and share my work with you. If anything should happen, then you can go to the *polizei* with all the stuff I send you, and then they can sort it all out."

Tomas nodded.

Wolfgang led on across the gravelled front drive to a chalet-style building set back into the trees. He pressed a fob, and much of the frontage slid apart, in a manner that wouldn't be out of place on a *Thunderbirds* film set. The gap revealed an immaculate whitewashed garage; ten cars were parked precisely the same distance apart, side by side.

Sam was only a partial car buff, her knowledge mostly forged from vehicle recognition training she had undertaken as part of her job. What was laid out in front of her was a series of classic cars that would be prized by any motor museum. She spotted the red Testarossa immediately. Next to it was an early 1980s metallic blue Porsche 911 SC Targa, the one with the ridiculous rear spoiler that looks like a bolted-on picnic table. To its left was a dark-blue Aston Martin V8 Vantage, all muscly and "look at me." She was just about to reel off the remaining marques to herself when Wolfgang stopped short.

"Which one?" he asked.

Sam continued her overview of the cars and knew straight away the one she'd choose for their next journey.

"That one." She pointed in a direction that could have meant any of three cars.

"You don't mean the 1967 Beetle convertible?"

"No, you idiot. The gold one. Next to it."

"My choice exactly. Well done, Sam Green. You have passed that particular test. What can you tell me about it?"

"I'm at my limit here, Wolfgang." She thought for a second. "Came into production in the mid-1980s. World Rally Champion car for who knows how many years. Blew the competition away with its four-wheel drive. I love it in gold, its best colour, and I'm hoping it's got the Audi logo running down the door sills."

"Yes, it has. The mighty Quattro. Two hundred brake horsepower. A hundred-and-fifty-mile-an-hour car. The four-wheel drive should help us stick to the road and negotiate the paths to the back gate. It's my favourite car of my father's complete set."

"Let's go then, Tommi Mäkinen."

They were loaded and off in no time, Wolfgang driving through the forest as if the car were an extension of him, even though he had only one and a half working arms. Sam didn't stop flinching until they were out of the trees and onto tarmac. Then things settled down. A little.

"Do you need directions to Leipzig?"

"No, I'm fine, thanks. We're going through the Czech Republic, but only cutting the corner." Wolfgang expertly shifted through the gears, the five-cylinder turbocharged engine making noises like an angry bear.

"Can you drive and think at the same time?"

"If you want me to crash."

"Well, let's not do that. If you slow down a bit, I could go over what we have and you could add what you think's important."

"OK, then." He didn't slow down.

Show off.

"You reckon that ten individuals have been murdered in plane crashes because they knew too much about energy generation and supplies." Sam started.

Wolfgang interrupted. "That's nine men and one woman. All of them were involved in their time with nonfossil-fuel power generation. I've got all the details on the Lattice spreadsheet. Hang on!" He braked heavily, forcing Sam to jolt forward against her seat belt, which held her firm. Wolfgang grimaced—she thought probably because of the strain on his arm.

"Sorry. Let me continue. Starting with the solar furnace, through tidal power, hydrogen and methanol fuel cells, ground-source heat pumps, and, latterly, nuclear fusion—they're all there."

"But haven't most of these methods gone on to be developed in any case?" Sam asked.

"Yes. But with what delay and cost to the industry involved? Hydrogen fuel cells were running parallel with electric batteries for car propulsion, until Dr. Vincent Pope died in the Flash Airlines Flight 604 crash. The aircraft crashed into the Red Sea. Hydrogen is the most commonplace atom in the world, and fuel cells are very efficient. The technology behind the key exchange membrane was being spearheaded by Pope. His death meant the industry was put back long enough for batteries to take the lead. Bring on the Toyota Prius, all manner of other hybrid cars, and, latterly, the Tesla Saloon."

Sam shut her eyes as Wolfgang dropped a gear and sped past a dawdling tractor.

"But who wins—and why? In that example, batteries were the winners." Sam was trying to establish a motive.

"I don't know. But the reason why I'm pretty sure that this is the right track is that our dead man in New York—Ned Donoghue, by the way—was looking over all of these emerging technologies. Concurrently, he kept a close handle on oil, gas, and nuclear. And, what is interesting, his split was oil and gas versus renewable and nuclear."

"You got all of this from your hacking?"

"Yes—with my magic fingers."

The Quattro's four-wheel drive system worked *its* magic as the car negotiated a sharp left-hand bend, at a speed that Sam struggled to comprehend. She momentarily closed her eyes.

"And what about nuclear?"

"Well, if you include the Pennsylvanian nuclear incident in the Lattice, which as far as I can see doesn't involve someone murdered in an air crash, that accident alone put the whole nuclear industry back years. Gas and coal power stations were the winners there."

Sam slid right then left in her seat as Wolfgang overtook a BMW.

"And, I guess, if the Koreans were that close to containing nuclear fusion, it would only be a couple of decades before new fusion power stations replaced every other kind," Sam suggested.

"I think it's wider than that. If they get nuclear fusion right, you and I could be driving a fusion-powered car."

"What, like Doc Brown and Marty McFly?"

"Why not?"

Sam shook her head.

"Your dad didn't have a DeLorean?" Sam smiled.

"Sadly not."

Wolfgang looked down at the gauges. For the first time, Sam thought that he was driving using the instruments, rather than by feel. "We need to get some fuel."

Sam continued. "But how does Donoghue's death fit into this? Maybe he was doing what you were doing and, like almost happened to you, they decided to put a stop to it? And they hung him from the rafters?"

"Possibly, although what I have been able to glean from the documents I hacked is that he was just monitoring stocks, shares, futures, that sort of thing. I could find nothing about aircraft. My work has a different dimension. It associates setbacks to renewables and the nuclear industry with dead people and nasty accidents."

Sam thought some more. She spotted an OMV sign. "Look, up ahead. There's a service station."

Keeping them on track, she added, "We have to focus on who the winners are. Why would they be doing this? And why is it so important to them that people like you don't find out?"

The Quattro braked late. Wolfgang pulled in with a flourish of squealing tyres just as Sam's phone rang. She looked at the screen. It was Jane.

"I've got to take this. It's my boss." Sam pointed at the phone as she got out of the Quattro. "I'll give you some money for the fuel when you start driving responsibly."

Wolfgang smiled and nodded.

"Hi, Jane. Can we go secure?"

Sam had already decided to tell Jane everything. This morning's incident had given the whole affair a dimension that she knew was bigger than her.

"Sure, Sam."

Sam pressed the appropriate red icon on her phone and the bleeping noise stopped, although immediately there was a delay, as the security algorithms encrypted their speech.

She looked up at Wolfgang who, with one arm functioning properly, was managing the fuel pump without too much bother. Her eyes trained across to the kiosk. There was only the attendant in the building. He was looking at the Quattro as he picked up the phone.

"I do need to talk to you about something, and it may take a while. But you phoned me?" There was a slight delay before Jane replied.

"I was wondering if you've had chance to look over the latest satellite images. The US team has sent through the third hamlet. They're being quicker than I thought they would be."

Bugger. I must have missed the ping against the noise of the wild animal under the bonnet.

"Sorry, Jane, not yet. We've stopped to refuel. I will look at them now."

"We? Sounds fun."

God, she must be bored.

"That's what I need to tell you about. Have you got ten minutes?"

"Go ahead."

Sam walked further away from the car and sat on a bench that was outside the kiosk. The language on the posters was in the diacritic alphabet. They were well into the Czech Republic. She'd have difficulty buying something here without pointing.

By the time she'd been through the key parts of the history and got as far as this morning's shooting incident, Wolfgang had joined her and presented her with a coffee in a Styrofoam cup. Sam acknowledged the drink by lifting it up.

"Can you get me the photos of the two men?"

"Sure. And later today, if Wolfgang's happy, we can share his database with you."

There was a longer-than-usual delay. Jane was obviously thinking things through.

"Just now that might be too much information for me to cope with. Look, Sam, whilst this is all very interesting, other than your involvement, it's not really SIS business." There was a further pause. "I assume that you've told the police . . ."

"No, not yet. And hang on, Jane. I've been holding back, something key. Something that might make you change your mind about whether this is or isn't SIS business."

"Go on, Sam."

"One of the photos I found of Herr Bischoff was at an antimigration riot in Hoyerswerda, that's in Eastern Germany near the Polish border. The image was taken eighteen months ago. The picture included a friend of ours."

Sam let it hang. She wasn't sure if Jane was trying to work it out or the line had gone dead.

"Go on, Sam."

"Ralph Bell."

Silence. Sam looked up across at the forecourt as a battered old blue Mercedes trundled up to the pumps.

"Are you sure?"

"One hundred per cent. I'll send you the photos."

There was silence again.

"I need to think about this and come back to you. On one level it makes perfect sense. On so many other levels it jars. Let me call you back in, say, half an hour. We need to think about involving the BfV. And I will talk to the CIA now. They need to know."

Sam took a sip of her coffee. She felt relieved that she was no longer completely responsible for the direction of where this was travelling. She trusted Jane with her life, but she wasn't convinced about the BfV. Whom *do* you trust?

"Jane."

"Yes?"

"Do you know anyone in the BfV you can trust?"

"I don't know anyone in the BfV. Period."

"Then can we keep this at arm's length at the moment? Until someone in the building has a contact in Berlin that he or she trusts implicitly?"

"Sure. That makes sense. Look, I'll call you back."

Then Sam remembered that she hadn't mentioned the Church of the White Cross.

"Hang on, Jane. Just for completeness, but I'm not convinced it's important, Bischoff has an affiliation with *die Kirche des weißen Kreuz*."

The line was silent again. This was becoming a bit of a habit.

Jane hesitantly said, "Translated, that means the Church of the White Cross."

"Correct answer." Sam tried to lighten the tone a touch.

A car sped by, a silver four-door Skoda. Probably an Octavia.

The prolonged silence from Jane prompted Sam to ask, "Is everything OK, Jane?"

"Sure, yes, fine. Look, I need to think about this, quickly." There was an alertness in her voice now; it was sharp—any previous hesitancy had gone.

What's changed? Is it something I said?

"Look, Sam. You may have hit on something. Something big." Another pause. "I can't tell you about it. Not yet, anyway. But I do need to make it clear that you're both in danger. My advice is to head home as soon as possible. Bring Wolfgang with you if you must, but I would abandon any further investigation. If you don't mind me saying, neither of you are trained for the sort of situation you could be in."

Well OK, Jane. But we were shot at this morning and survived without too many perforations.

"I need to think about that advice as well, Jane." Sam's mind was whirring. Wolfgang, who had listened to everything Sam had said since he'd delivered the coffee, had a frown on his face.

"Do we have any agents in Germany? Berlin?"

"What do you mean, Sam?" The question had thrown Jane. "I don't think so. The Wall came down almost twenty years ago. Germany is an ally."

Sam was looking back the kiosk. The attendant was on his mobile having an animated conversation. He was looking their way again. Something instinctively told Sam that they had outstayed their welcome.

She pulled the phone away from her face and put her hand over the mouthpiece.

"Get the car moving." It was a hiss at Wolfgang. He jumped up, looked over at the kiosk, and jogged over to the car.

"Jane. I've got to go. But before I do, if the firm doesn't have an agent in Germany and the problem is as big as something you're not prepared to tell me, then you need someone in country who's up to speed on the issues. That's me. Phone me in a bit."

Sam didn't wait for an answer. She was on her feet and met the gold Quattro as Wolfgang skidded the car to a halt. He was leaning over and had already opened the passenger door. Sam launched herself into her seat. As soon as her bum was down, and before she had chance to close the door, Wolfgang had pressed the "go" pedal.

Chapter Fifteen

Western Czech Republic, Heading Northwest

It took Wolfgang just a split second to also realise that the service station attendant was showing more interest in them than was necessary. They left the forecourt at speed, accompanied by a hail of gravel. Not long afterward he was back in the groove, driving what must be one of the best cars ever made.

As the Czech countryside flashed past, Wolfgang held fleeting thoughts about the last couple of days. It was all something else. The whole thing. His life had been turned upside down by a combination of factors, the major one being Sam Green. He had no problem following her instructions, doing as she asked—actually it was more like "ordered." That surprised him, as he wasn't a natural follower. He'd much rather be in charge, but she had a sixth sense that he didn't have—a sort of frequency dial that immediately tuned in to danger. And her reactions were razor sharp, both intellectually and physically. She was like no one else he had ever come across. A sort of female version of Jack Reacher. Only shorter and slightly more edgy.

"How did they know we were at the petrol station?" Sam interrupted his chain of thought. It was another one of her rhetorical questions. "It doesn't make any sense."

Wolfgang was too busy snaking the Quattro around the sublime Czech roads, all curves and dips, to add anything sensible to her questions.

"Do you trust Tomas?"

Whoa! That was too much. He nearly hit the brake pedal and threw Sam out of the car at that point. She might live in a world where you only trusted yourself and maybe one other person but, for him, family was family.

272

"Explicitly." He couldn't stop himself from spitting out the word. "The Javiers have provided staff for my family for as long as anyone can remember. Tomas has been at my side since the day I was born. I will not have a word said against him." He stared directly ahead, currently not wanting to engage Sam any more than he needed to.

"OK, sorry, Wolfgang. What about, what's her name? Gertrude?"

Wolfgang drummed his fingers on the steering wheel. *That's a completely different question.*

"She's been at the schloss for a couple of years. She's a local girl from the village. She works terrifically hard, but I can't say that I know her well."

It was Sam's turn to remain quiet for a while. Wolfgang noticed that she gripped her seatbelt as he dropped a gear to overtake a large, slow-moving farm lorry that was stacked high with straw.

"Is your phone off?"

That wasn't a rhetorical question. He nodded and said, *"Ja."*

"My phone is untraceable. Or, as I understand it, puts out multiple traces. Only my firm knows which one is kosher." She raised her hands as if she were about to juggle. "So, the only answer is Gertrude?" Her hands quickly returned to her seatbelt as Wolfgang bent the Quattro around another sharp corner.

Wolfgang thought it through. It made some sense. Not only did whoever was chasing them know that they had left the house, that person also knew which way they were heading. Did they need to change their plans?

"If Gertrude had been eavesdropping, then she would have heard that we're heading to the central library in Leipzig," Wolfgang surmised.

"My thoughts entirely."

Wolfgang expected Sam to come up with an immediate change of plan, but her facial expression had changed from nervous passenger to one of real concern. She appeared to be looking in the wing mirror.

"Behind us!" Sam shouted, as she turned her shoulders around to look through the car's slanting rear window.

Wolfgang checked the rear-view mirror. It was a black or dark grey car, travelling at least as quickly as they were.

"BMW. Tricky to say at this distance. Possibly an M3." Sam was difficult to hear over the engine noise, especially now that she was facing backward.

"Come off at the next junction . . ."

Sam hardly had time to finish the sentence before Wolfgang slammed on the brakes and, with a quick pull of the handbrake, slid the back end of the Quattro around to join the front, which was now accelerating down a farm track pursued by a cloud of impenetrable dust. In the distance, Wolfgang noticed, was a ribbon of forest.

"Slow down! We need to be able to see if they're following us. And I can't see a thing," Sam was shouting to be heard.

Wolfgang dropped the revs; with that, the dust started to settle to something less opaque. He checked the speedo: sixty clicks; fifty clicks; forty clicks . . .

"Step on it!" Sam yelled.

The lowering cloud of dust had dramatically changed colour. The billowing sand was cleaved in two by the bulbous bonnet of the black BMW. It was travelling so quickly that it took a combination of the Quattro's acceleration and hard braking by the driver of the Beemer for the two cars not to shunt each other.

Wolfgang used the near miss to accelerate away.

After no more than a minute of frantic driving, they were in the forest, thick trees on either side, the track just wide enough for one car. The BMW was still on their tail.

"Can we outrun it?" Sam was back in her chair now, still shouting to be heard above the noise of the tyres, the flying dirt, and the engine.

"If it's a new M3, not on the flat. But on these tracks . . ." Wolfgang stopped speaking as the Audi took off, having been launched from a rise and then slamming back down on the ground, its racing shocks easily soaking up the impact. "On these tracks we should be able to get ahead of it." It was his turn to shout now.

The car slid from side to side. Sam was hanging on. At one point, when the bank on the right-hand side of the car scraped along the door and took off the wing mirror, Wolfgang noticed that she'd closed her eyes. *It's not like her to be frightened.*

He checked the dials. All was well with the Audi. *Shame about the mirror, though.*

They broke out of the forest, back into a sea of flat, arable farmland—ploughed fields after ploughed fields, with the odd barn and tree breaking up the pattern.

Crack! Thump. Crack, thump! Ping!

"Bastards!" Sam screamed. "They're shooting at us." She immediately got on her haunches, facing backward, trying to work out where the other car was. After a sharp turn, which slammed Sam against her door, Wolfgang looked over his left shoulder—they were fifty metres ahead of the Beemer, but now side-on, a broader target.

Crack! Smash! The side window behind him burst into a thousand pieces. He looked immediately to his right. Sam was still very much alive. *Thank God!* He floored it again.

"Can I get into the boot from here?" Sam was at screaming pitch.

Wolfgang's mind was racing. "Probably. The backseats come down. I think there's a lever on the . . ." He shut up as he negotiated another ninety-degree bend. In the far distance was a village. He scanned left and right. It looked like the track zigzagged all the way there.

"Scheiße!" Sam hit his arm with one of her feet as she scrambled up over her chair to get into the backseat. Wolfgang felt momentarily faint as a wave of pain swept through his shoulder and torso. He regained control.

"Sorry!" was the muffled apology from the backseat.

Crack! Crack! Thump! Thump! There was no additional

sound. Wolfgang assumed the shots had gone wide or high. But he checked in his rear-view mirror and saw Sam's bum bouncing around. She seemed OK.

As Sam cursed and swore in the back, Wolfgang expertly negotiated the tracks. Left, then right. Accelerating, braking, sharp right, accelerate away. He checked in his one remaining wing mirror. They had a hundred metres on the Beemer now. They might make it. But what about when they got back on tarmac?

Sam unceremoniously clambered back into the passenger seat, expertly missing Wolfgang's arm this time round. She had one of the Browning rifles in her hand.

"Stop! Now! Past that old trailer!" Sam was pointing to just ahead of them.

Wolfgang threw on the brakes and, thinking that he knew what Sam was going to do, slid the Quattro to a halt behind the trailer in a billowing cloud of dust. As best he could, he had got the Quattro out of sight of the BMW.

Sam was already out on her feet when he heard her shout, "Keep the engine running."

Wolfgang bent forward, and by the time he had twisted his head, Sam had the rifle in her hand, had cocked it, and, with her eye on the scope, had fired off a shot. *Toward a tree off to their left. What?* That was nowhere near the BMW! . . . which he could now hear approaching, gravel spitting everywhere. Its engine screaming at high revs.

Sam, having turned to face the noise, raised the scope to her eye, took a breath, and, as calm as a sniper, let off two rounds—one directly after the other.

Clump! Clump!

Wolfgang couldn't see what he heard; he was behind the trailer. The ensuing noise mirrored every staged car crash he'd ever seen in an action movie. A massive clunk!, a smash!, then nothing, as he imagined the car spinning through the air. Another clunk and smash. Some scraping, grating, and then, at the end of it all, the noise of a wheels spinning.

Wolfgang tried to get a view of the broken car by straining his head around behind him.

"Let's go." Sam was already back in the passenger seat. She was wearing a faint smile. The rifle between her legs.

"Are they dead?'

"I don't know. Don't care! I didn't kill them! I put a couple of rounds into the engine compartment. I think one must have caused the car to crash. Come on, let's get going!" All at a gabble. Sam was using her hands to gesticulate forward movement.

Wolfgang wasn't going anywhere. "Shouldn't we check?"

Crack! Ping!

That sounded like a bullet ricocheting off the trailer. *Scheiße!*

He didn't need any further instructions. Within a split second they were off down the farm track, spewing grit everywhere, accompanied by another couple of shots that Wolfgang recognised as flying overhead. A few seconds later they were out of harm's way.

Neither of them spoke until they got to the village, at which point Wolfgang slowed the Quattro right down, almost to a crawl.

Everything was covered in dust. Them, their clothes, the dashboard. Sam was staring straight ahead. Under a sand-coloured film, flecks sticking to her eyelashes, she appeared dazed, but somehow in control.

"Where to now?" He needed new instructions.

"Anywhere where we can access computers in a public place—that isn't Leipzig. Although, as you do the geography, we will need to visit Leipzig tonight. To Bischoff's place."

Sam's tone was already softening. Wolfgang thought that her adrenaline levels were probably dropping. He'd seen the same thing in the forest. Fight, then flight. During the fighting, some button on Sam was pressed; a switch flicked. She changed from being a very quirky, slightly odd, reasonably adorable but recognisable human being to an automaton. Now that facade was slowly fading.

"And we need to lose the car. Sorry, but we do. And sorry to your dad."

Wolfgang was working through the first instruction when he took in the second. Where to? Computers, public place, and hire car. Close to Leipzig. *And then get Tomas to recover the Audi and get it sorted!*

"OK. I know where we should go. Dresden."

SIS Headquarters, Vauxhall, London

Jane was waiting for the chief to say something. He looked fraught, distracted. After her telephone conversation with Sam, she'd very quickly pinged him an e-mail. He was out for lunch with his wife in town, a liaison he dropped like a heavy rock to come straight into the office.

"So what we're saying is—and I'm going to leave the source, Green, out of this. You trust her completely?"

"Yes, sir. Completely."

He shook his head, bewilderment now an accompanying look. "We have images showing Ralph Bell very likely supporting and possibly manipulating an antimigration riot, in some far-eastern provincial town in Germany?"

"Yes, sir."

"In terms of time, that bridges the gap between when we last saw him in West Africa three years ago and very recently in Yemen. In between which, we thought he was dead."

"Yes, sir, that's correct."

"And the rally was attended by an ex-Stasi thug who has links with an ultra-Orthodox Christian religious cult called the Church of the White Cross. To be exact, the German wing of the church called *die Kirche des weißen Kreuz*. The US version of which we know is likely to have been involved in recent firebombings of mosques in California and Vancouver—when was that?"

The chief was pacing, up to the window and then back to his desk.

"Three months ago now, sir."

"To which Miles Johnson, the ex-DD of the CIA, is one of only six known church leaders."

"So far, you're spot on, sir."

"Thanks, Jane. I'm known for my retentive memory."

Jane wasn't sure if the chief was sharing a joke or scolding her. She decided to abandon any further quips. This obviously wasn't a time to be jocular.

"And we know this because a German, a Herr Bischoff, ransacked and subsequently set fire to the apartment of a German count, whom one of my staff is currently dating?"

"Well, we don't know if they're an item, sir." *That wasn't necessary.* "But what we do know is that, on the basis that her bloke had been hacking into US and other computer systems, they were shot at this morning. The count caught it in the arm. He seemed to have been following a wild hunch that air disasters are a way to murder prominent renewable and nuclear energy experts without getting noticed."

The chief had both hands on the back of his chair. Jane thought he looked odd not wearing his usual Savile Row suit.

"That's where you lose me, I'm afraid."

"Me too. But it is likely that, for some reason, somebody is trying to stop the count from . . ."

Jane's phone rang.

"Excuse me, sir."

She looked at the caller. It was Sam.

"I need to take this."

"Is it Green?"

"Yes, sir."

"Put her on speaker."

Jane made the connection, and they went "secure."

"You're on speaker, Sam. I'm in the chief's office."

There was no reply to begin with, other than what

appeared to be background mechanical noise of an engine revving and the odd squeal of rubber.

"Hi, Jane. Hi, sir." Sam's voice dropped a bit and they heard, "Slow down, Wolfgang—I can't hear myself think!"

"We have another situation here in the Czech Republic. We were pursued by a Black BMW. I'll SMS the registration to you once we've finished. We went off-road to lose them, and they shot at us a number of times. High-velocity rounds. The car took a couple of hits—we're both OK."

Jane looked across at the chief, whose face was scrunched up in concentration. He was mouthing, "What a bloody mess."

"I took the car out. When we left the schloss this morning . . ."

Schloss? Where the hell has she been, thought Jane.

"We took a couple of hunting rifles with us just in case. Anyhow, the Beemer crashed. I know at least one person got out alive, as they shot at us again. But we've lost them."

The chief exhaled noisily. Then he asked, "Where are you now?" His frustration was not well hidden.

Again, a quiet Sam. "Where are we, Wolfgang?"

They heard Wolfgang say "Odrava."

"Odrava."

"OK, Sam. We'll get the embassy in Prague to deal with this mess. Where are you heading to?" The chief was trying to piece the jigsaw together.

"Dresden, sir. We have the mobile from the guy who shot at us this morning. Wolfgang has the expertise to hack it. We have no idea who the man is, although I'm guessing the local police now know. We told Tomas to hand him over after we left."

Jane looked as confused as she felt. "Tomas?"

"Wolfgang's . . . the butler at the schloss. It sounds grander than it is."

In the background they heard Wolfgang say, "No, it *is* as grand as that! He *is* my butler!"

The chief looked at Jane. She knew this was probably the

weirdest SIS telephone conversation he'd ever had. But she didn't see incredulity; she saw deep frustration, bordering on anger.

"I have the shooter's photo, so I might be able to find him on the Interpol database, if he has a record. And we're also going to Bischoff's house later, to get a feel for the lie of the land in Leipzig."

The chief was shaking his head. "I'm going to put you on mute just for a second, Sam."

Jane obliged.

The chief ran his hand through his hair.

"Are we seriously going to let Green play Ethan Hunt in the backyard of one of our closest allies?" the chief demanded of Jane.

I'm not sure why you're asking me; it's your call.

Jane composed herself. Yes, the situation was difficult. Complicated. Sam Green was just an analyst. One who, only ten days previously, had had a breakdown for which she probably should have lost her job—she guessed David hadn't told the chief about that. Now they had an even more complicated situation, and Green was in the thick of it. They were a man down in Yemen; finding him would be such a fillip for everyone involved—*especially Tony James!* They had two ex-CIA operatives on the loose, with absolutely no idea what their role was in anything—and they were popping up everywhere. Op Greyshoe was now being taken very seriously by the Americans. And David had been spiked with Stasi poison. All of which could be linked.

And Sam Green, for all her inadequacies, was demonstrating an impressive resilience that might just help piece this together. However, looking at how effectively she was now being pursued, Jane didn't think the window would be open for very long.

"Let her run, sir. Just for another twenty-four hours. We have no one in the Berlin embassy we can task. And none within a day's travel that could get up to speed and with the operation to start poking around."

The chief still wore a face of consternation. He smacked his hand on the back of his chair.

"Whatever I decide, we need to let the BfV know now." The chief was emphatic, although, strangely, Jane thought she could talk him out of it if she wanted.

"Do you know anyone in the BfV whom you can trust with this? The right-wing camp across the whole of Germany has stretch—do we know how far? Or how deep? Sir." Jane added the last word a little too late to be completely sure she was showing due deference.

"Yes, of course." It wasn't the chief's strongest commitment.

He blew out hard.

"Put her back on." His tone was now one of resignation.

Jane pressed an icon on the phone.

"Sam?" the chief led.

"Yes, sir."

"You understand that currently everything you are doing is way beyond any boundaries we would ordinarily set for an operation like this. And I don't have to tell you that you are acting outside the law in two countries we currently consider to be allies."

"Yes, sir. I understand that." Sam carried straight on, obviously keen to make a point. "But, sir, if we go cold now and come in, any momentum we have with this will be lost. I feel we're just ahead of the game at the moment."

The chief put his hand up just in case Jane was going to say something.

"You have to understand that we can't protect you."

There was a pause.

"Of course, sir."

"OK. Much against my better judgement, here's what we're going to do. I'm giving you exactly twenty-four hours to pursue your leads. At that point, I am going to brief my opposite number in the BfV—you know who they are?"

"Yes, sir."

"And then you come in. No questions."

"Yes, sir."

"Jane will brief the embassy in Berlin now, so they're not surprised if the pair of you are arrested for whatever it is you're going to do next."

"Yes, sir."

"And I want every piece of intelligence you get passed directly back here as soon as you get it, so that we are fully briefed. And we will both have our phones with us. You must do the same. Got it?"

"Yes, sir."

The chief, who had been leaning forward with his hands on the back of his chair, stood up.

"Good luck, Sam. And that count friend of yours. Any questions?"

There was a short pause—all Jane got from the phone was the revving of an engine.

"No, sir. Thank you."

The chief nodded, and Jane hung up the phone. He walked to the window and didn't say anything for a few seconds.

"I'm not happy about this, Jane. It's a mess. I want a full, written brief on everything by five o'clock this afternoon. It needs to be penned in a way that we can share it with Greyshoe. I will speak to their director tonight. This is going to send some pretty big hares running over the Pond. Find someone in the building who knows someone in the BfV at their level whom they trust. And get one of your staff in now to be your wingman on this. I'd go for an analyst who can look over images. But it's your choice."

That'll be Frank, then.

"Yes, sir. Thank you."

They had made the briefest of stops at an old pal of Wolfgang's in a suburb of Dresden. Sam hadn't got involved, but she let Wolfgang talk his friend into lending them his car. Money and man-hugs were shared. It all seemed very convivial.

As they drove away in a twenty-year-old, pale yellow Opel Kadett, Sam had asked, "Do you trust him?" To which Wolfgang had replied, "Whom can you trust?" But they had both agreed that borrowing a car from a friend was less likely to get them noticed than using either of their bankcards to hire one.

The Kadett worked. That's all you could say for it. Sam hoped they didn't get into another car chase, otherwise the yellow peril might have a heart attack and blow a gasket.

They had found a free computer in the library, which was slightly out of the way. Sam had created a bit of cover by standing nonchalantly in front of the desk, while Wolfgang got on his hands and knees and attached some wires to the back of the tower. He was now working on a screen that Sam didn't recognise and doing things she didn't understand. The screen was all dark grey, and, as Wolfgang typed, the letters emitted a light green hue. It was like watching someone attempting to get into the Matrix.

Using her tablet, Sam flipped through the Interpol images, trying to find a match with their assailant from this morning. She remembered that it took her a couple of hours to have success with Bischoff, so she needed some luck. Or, she hoped that Wolfgang could find something on their assailant's phone that might help.

Her phone pinged. It was an e-mail from Jane.

The BMW was registered to a Michael Maus. Unless the Germans are completely humourless, that's a dead lead.

Frank has come in. He can act as a remote analyst if you need him. He's going to try to get the embassy to see if they can establish the name of the man who shot at you this morning by going straight to the local police.

Note also, new images are in from Yemen. I realise you have your hands full, but you chose the targets, so if you get the chance, look over those.

And finally, be careful. I have some unshareable intel on the Church of the White Cross. This could be the key ingredient to what's going on. Look out for it.

Keep in touch.

Jane xxx

What is it with that church?

Sam chastised herself for forgetting her day job and made a promise to Tony James that she would look over all of the images before close of play. They would have to find time. She went back to the Interpol images.

"Sehr gut," Wolfgang retorted.

Sam, who was sitting next to him on an uncomfortable plastic chair, looked across at his screen.

"What do you have?"

"Look, here." Wolfgang pointed to a long list of initials and what looked like telephone numbers. "These two are Berlin landlines, this is Leipzig . . ."

Sam pointed at one near the bottom. The letters were HL. The number started with 001.

"That's a US number," she said.

"Correct. A US landline number." He stared at them some more. "But no names. Just numbers and initials. But . . . look. Here's HB. Which could be Bischoff's mobile number."

Sam drew her seat closer to Wolfgang's. Their legs touched. It was a good feeling.

"Can you cut and paste them into an e-mail?"

"Yes, of course."

"Do it now."

Wolfgang swiftly did as he was told.

"That's not your e-mail address." Sam was confused.

"I have a number of them. This is the least likely one anyone can associate with me." Wolfgang looked pleased with himself.

"Don't be so confident."

"To whom do I send the list?"

Sam gently pushed him aside and took hold of the keyboard. In the "To:" box she typed in Frank's insecure work address. She topped and tailed it, asking him to get whatever he could from GCHQ. If they could tap the HB one, that would be a bonus.

"Who's Frank?"

"A colleague of mine. He knows some people who should be able to put faces to a few of these initials. And, do we know the number of the mobile?" Sam pointed to the smartphone on the desk that they'd taken from the man in the forest.

"Yes. Can I?" He gestured to the keyboard and typed it in.

Sam pressed "Send."

Wolfgang's mailbox got a response from Frank immediately. It was three words:

"Roger. Be safe."

"Have you been able to find out who the phone belongs to?" Sam pressed Wolfgang.

"Not yet. I'm now going to look at any SMS history and then see if we can access the e-mail account and any Internet search history." He was already typing.

Sam was just about to add something when she stopped herself. She looked at him, tapping away. *What were they up to? What forces had they taken on?* Once before, in West

Africa, she had led a man into a situation that had almost cost him his life. Was she doing the same now? Looking at Wolfgang, could she afford to lose him?

Four years ago, in Afghanistan, she had loved and lost a wonderful man. It had broken her, and, even now, any thought of the event that took him made her want to lie down and curl up into a ball. After Chris's death, she didn't think she could ever love again.

But Wolfgang was different from anyone she'd ever met. And, while she had absolutely no idea what her true feelings for him were, or if her fledgling feelings might be reciprocated, she knew she wouldn't cope if she lost him.

He turned to her, that rakish smile spreading warmth.

"What?"

"Nothing, you idiot. Get hacking."

Kaltstrasse, Leipzig, Germany

It was getting dark as Wolfgang drew the Kadett to a stop on the side of the road. They were maybe two hundred metres from where Sam reckoned Bischoff lived.

"Drive past," Sam instructed.

Wolfgang did as he was told.

The road was a normal German suburban *strasse*. Most of the buildings were sturdy three- and four-storey blocks, purposely built as apartments. Wolfgang was always amazed at how the British needed their independence and, where possible, lived in detached houses. In Germany, particularly in the old East, most people were happy to live in a block of flats.

Cars were parked on both sides of the road. Behind the buildings there were other areas for parking and some garages. Each block had a narrow front garden, and most seemed to have access to cellars—a very German necessity. The street was well lit and, at first glance, reasonably affluent. Most of the cars seemed new. Looking through the odd window that didn't have its shutters down, the rooms appeared tidy and well looked after. Large flat-screen TVs lit up the rooms in ever-changing colours, and through one window, Wolfgang spotted a couple decorating a Christmas tree. *In November?*

Sam spotted Bischoff's apartment block and pointed it out. It was no different from the others.

"Pull over," Sam said quietly.

Wolfgang slid the Opel in behind a Mercedes and turned off the engine.

"OK, as we discussed, I'll go and check on the entrance and exits to the house and clock all of the cars. You see if you can find a telephone junction box." She smiled and touched his arm below the wound.

"How is it?"

"Throbbing. But OK." Actually it hurt more than that, but as is always the case with an injury, Wolfgang only really noticed it when he sat still long enough. And that didn't happen much with Sam Green around.

"I'll re-dress it later." She stopped herself from getting out of the car, just for a moment. "If anything happens and we get split up, I'll meet you at the *hauptbahnhof* as we agreed. And put your phone on every hour for ten minutes."

Wolfgang nodded. He looked over his shoulder to check the Browning was still on the backseat. They had loosely covered it with a blanket his friend had left in the car. Seeing the rifle jogged something that had been playing on his mind.

"Why did you shoot at the tree?" he asked.

Sam turned around and stuck her head back in through the passenger door. She initially looked confused, and then a light seemed to go on when she understood what he was after.

"I zeroed the rifle. Picked a spot on the tree, fired at it, and checked the fall of shot. As a result, I was able to aim off when I shot at the BMW."

"And if you hadn't done that?"

"I'd have hit a crow and we'd now be tied up in someone's cellar."

"Oh . . ." *That makes sense.*

Then she was gone. Wolfgang got out too, but he didn't lock the car. He had his laptop and some wires with him.

He took in the scene. Sam was already across the road, skipping up the steps that led to the main door of the apartment block. He looked up and down the front of the flats, hoping to spot a telephone junction box. If he could find one, and the computers in the street were still fed Internet over copper wire, he might be able to clip in and hack into the systems. If they were fibre optic, he'd be stuck.

He crossed over the road, stopped, and looked toward the apartment block. There was nothing on the front of the building, or in the street. He moved on, turning left to walk down a side-alley that led to some garages. *Nothing here.*

Wait. In a garden, to the right of the last garage, was a small box, raised from the ground on a concrete plinth. He made his way over to it. The grey plastic box had the inscription *DT* on it—*Deutsche Telekom.* It was partially covered by a bush affording some cover. The rest of the garage area was lit, but not so brightly that he couldn't find a shadow or two if needed.

The box was locked with a normal Yale-type lock. But between the door and the housing there was enough room to force a screwdriver. He looked around and up to the windows that were not shuttered. All seemed clear.

Wolfgang took his screwdriver out of his jacket pocket and, after a bit of effort, the lock burst and the door flew open with a *chhewang*! The noise made him cower—his heart was pumping so loudly that his ears reverberated and his arm throbbed. In the dim light, he glanced down at the wound and saw some red coming through his jumper.

Blood.

Calm down, Wolfgang.

He looked around again. Nothing. Still quiet.

He opened his laptop and let the light from the screen

illuminate the switches, connectors, and wires in the darkness. There were four sets of the six wires coming out of a central connection box. Four separate apartments. He recognised the six different coloured wires—they were standard *Deutsche Telekom*. He had the same in his flat. Out of the bottom of the box was a central black rubber sheath heading into the plinth and then, probably, trunked underground and away.

He should choose one apartment. Which one? Or, he could open the sheath with his pocketknife and see if there were an obvious couple of wires that might provide the Internet tracking for all of the apartments. He discounted the latter option. When cutting the sheath, his knife might slice through a wire.

Bischoff lived at Number 3. That would be on the bottom floor. The four sets of six wires were laid out vertically. Which one? Two from the top? Or two from the bottom? He chose the bottom.

The next bit was relatively straightforward. Using a pair of tiny crocodile connectors, he gripped onto the red/white and yellow wires making electrical connections through the coloured rubber. On the end of his wires he had already made up a modem junction box. He plugged his computer into that and—*hey, presto*—he had Internet. Except he wanted to track backward to the apartment, and not just piggyback on the free connection. Now he needed to engage his coding expertise.

He typed some code against the DOS prompt and pressed "Enter."

Then he was spooked.

Somebody had come out of the back of one of the houses into the garden. Although his computer was partially shielded by the bush, Wolfgang was out in the open. The person in the garden paused, lit up a cigarette, and coughed. He then turned to walk on his way. After a split second of indecision, he gently closed the lid on his laptop, leaving it ajar enough to keep working. It still gave out a sheath of blue light, but that was a risk he'd have to take. On tiptoes, Wolfgang shuffled quietly away from the man into the shadow of a tree by one of the garages.

He stood perfectly still. And waited. He forced himself as close to the tree as he could. In shadow.

The person turned out to be an old man, but no one he recognised. The man walked toward him, puffing away at his fag. He sang to himself. Wolfgang thought he recognised the tune? *Was it: "Eins, Zwei, G'suffa"?*

The old man got so close to Wolfgang's laptop he almost stood on it. He shuffled for a second, looking directly at Wolfgang.

Wolfgang stopped breathing. How could the man not see him?

The man took a couple more puffs of his cigarette and then threw it on the ground.

Turning, he stopped abruptly and blurted, *"Guten Abend."*

Wolfgang recognised the *"Guten Abend"* reply straight away. It was Sam.

The man shuffled off, back into his house, humming away. Sam walked forward a couple of paces and stood over Wolfgang's laptop.

"I can see you. You can come out now," she quietly teased.

"That was close! How come he didn't see me?" Wolfgang's whisper was hissed at Sam.

"You hid well."

"How come you saw me?"

"Because I'm good at this."

Wolfgang ignored Sam's playful conceit and got down on his knees and checked his laptop.

"I have the e-mail address and computer details of someone here . . . hang on." He tapped away on his keyboard. "The e-mail is a *familiebischoff* Gmail address. I know the port details. Good!" He was talking to himself. He looked up at Sam. "I now know how to find him and hack

291

his machine from a distance. I can do that later." He started to pack up.

As he rose with his laptop under his arm, he said, "Did you get anything?"

"Not a great deal. Let's talk about it in the car."

"Where now?" He realised they hadn't discussed "what next."

"I don't know about you, but I'm ready for food. And I need some sleep. In that order."

Hotel Hiemann, Leipzig, Germany

Sam was full. And exhausted. They'd booked into the hotel as Mr. and Mrs. Schultz—taking a twin-bedder—eaten *Wiener schnitzels* in the hotel dining room, and showered. With Wolfgang sitting on his bed, his laptop on his legs, and Sam on the end of her bed with her Nexus open, they went back to work.

"Can you connect my tablet to the TV so I can look at the pictures on a bigger screen?"

"Sure," replied Wolfgang. He put his laptop down, jumped off his bed, and walked around to where she was. He sat next to her, playfully pushing her along with his hips.

"Oi!" she said, laughing.

He smelled clean. He was wearing one of the three Thomas Pink shirts he'd brought with him, doubling it up as a nightshirt. She hadn't meant to peek, but he also had on a pair of blue-striped boxers. She wore a clean version of the same nightie she'd sported the other night. For modesty's sake, she put one of Wolfgang's cashmere sweaters on top. They were like an old couple, sharing clothes.

Where had they got to?

Frank had been in touch by e-mail. The assailant was a Herr Gert Mauning from Berlin. The embassy, without too much trouble, had spoken to the local police. He had been released after questioning. Without testimony from

Wolfgang, there was no evidence that he'd committed a crime other than trespassing. The local police said the man had no criminal record.

GCHQ was still working on the telephone numbers from Mauning's phone. They'd have something in the morning. The US number was a landline in Abilene, Texas. Frank had found that out himself. He had added that, when he had told Jane, she had almost fallen off her chair. He had no idea why.

Finally, Frank had looked over the SMS and e-mails that Wolfgang had sent through that had been taken off Mauning's phone. So far he'd picked out nothing significant, unless e-mails about family members and Amazon orders were some form of code. *Probably not, Frank.*

So nothing of significance from Gert Mauning's phone — or what is it that Jane isn't telling me?

"There. It's up on the screen." Wolfgang pointed. His arm seemed freer, now that she had cleaned and re-dressed the wound.

"Thanks, Wolfgang. How's it going with getting onto Bischoff's machine?"

He was on his feet, heading back to his laptop.

"I'm not there yet. On the face of it, the security looks low key. But it's much more complicated than that. It's clever. Overly so. I'm linked to my servers in Munich. I'm going to use them to attack with some high-level coding. Probably overnight."

"Sounds very dull, if you ask me." Sam smiled across at him.

"Like looking at photos of the desert isn't dull?"

She stuck her tongue out at him.

Sam knew that what she was doing broke a zillion SIS rules. She was accessing secret images in the presence of someone who was not security cleared, who wasn't even British! And she assumed that projecting the Yemeni satellite images onto a TV screen in a hotel, where all TVs are linked together to feed movies, broke many more rules.

She couldn't care less. She knew she had about an hour before her brain shut down, and she needed to look over these images now, with the best resolution possible.

There were forty-five keyhole photos, covering four of the seven targets she had identified. The cloud also had another sixteen "closed" source images and another thirty or so public, "open" source shots—all from Yemen. She had to work smartly.

For each of the keyhole images, she was looking for vehicles. They were all plan photos, taken from above. Unless a person were sunbathing, there was no way she could make out a face. It was pretty much vehicles or nothing.

After about forty minutes, she popped to the loo, came back, and opened another image. She swiped gently, up and down. The quality was outstanding. The granularity very fine. *Nothing.* Hang on. *No. Nothing.*

Sam had got to maybe the thirty-eighth image, the northeast sector of a hamlet named Shabwah, which consisted of around fifty buildings, and she checked herself. *Stop. Look again.* She swiped gently back and then zoomed in. She was staring so hard her eyes had started to dry out. She blinked a couple of times.

There's something here.

The hotel room was quiet. It was close to midnight, and there was very little noise outside. Sam hadn't noticed before, but Wolfgang had stopped typing. All she could hear was her own breathing. She swiped gently left and then enlarged again. Without the image-sharpening software back in Babylon, the picture pixelated, so she zoomed slowly back out again.

"What have you got?" It was Wolfgang.

His question interrupted her thinking.

"Sshhh!"

She moved the image about a bit and then stopped again.

"It's a black pickup. A relatively new one. In a compound."

Silence won the battle for the room. For a second.

"Aren't there scores of black pickups in the desert?"

Sam wasn't listening. She moved the image to its right a touch. The black pickup stayed in the frame. To its right was the roof of a building. It could have been the same as any of the other roofs that formed a hollow square around the courtyard where the black pickup was parked. But this roof was different. It wasn't a roof over a dwelling. It was a roof over an open space. Sam knew that because, sticking out from under the eaves, was no more than fifty centimetres of white metal frame. She checked again. It was the back end of a second pickup. It was *definitely* the back end of a pickup. A white one. She couldn't make out what the truck was, other than the back frame was thin—an older vehicle. But the paint was good. It was well looked after.

She knew she was looking at a black Nissan Terrano in the centre of the courtyard. She'd recognise the vehicle from any angle. Wolfgang was right, though. There were many black pickups in the desert. But not that many *new* black Terranos. And, if you added the coincidence of finding an old white pickup in the same location, albeit almost hidden from view, you might just have something special.

"It's this, look." Sam was on her feet, pointing to the roof.

"It's a roof."

"No, it's not! It's the back end of a white pickup." She sat down again, grabbing hold of her Nexus. "Hold on, Wolfgang, I need to send this home."

Sam cropped the photo and, with accompanying notes, pinged it to Frank. He needed to check the original black pickup from the terrorist camp for bangs and dents against this one. And see if there were any connections. Then, he would need to check if he could get a nonpixelated view of the back end of the white pickup.

Sam was 75 per cent sure these were the two vehicles she knew: Manning and Bell's black Terrano and the old white Toyota Hilux with the chrome wing mirror. If she had been at work, she'd be 90 per cent sure by now—or would have discounted the work. Frank would add that extra 15 per cent in her absence. She pressed "Send," and the e-mail disappeared into the ether.

"Do you have anything?" Sam asked Wolfgang.

"Maybe. My servers will run overnight, and they might be able dig deeper through the security wall. In the meantime, it seems our man Bischoff is interested in someone's itinerary. There are maps of Köln, with some markings on them. I've no idea what they're about."

Sam was sitting beside him now, looking over his laptop, which he had turned so she could see the screen.

She pressed the "Up" and "Down" arrows to move the image.

"I don't get it."

"Me neither," said Wolfgang.

"Before we close up, can you Google 'the Church of the White Cross'?"

Wolfgang did that. There were a number of entries, including a local Californian report about possible linkages with a recent spate of mosque bombings in the United States and Canada.

"Open up their main website. Please." She realised that she was being a little officious and belatedly smiled at him. A soft smile.

And there it was. The Church of the White Cross. Location: Abilene, Texas.

Abilene? Mauning had the number of someone in Abilene on his phone. *Result.* That made two of them: Bischoff *and* Mauning. The two men they were pursuing had links with the German wing of the Church of the White Cross: *die Kirche des weißen Kreuz.* An organisation that threw bricks at police, burned apartments, and shot at people. Its sister church in the United States had bombed mosques, killing several people.

And what had Jane said in her e-mail? *Look out for it?*

Sam sighed. And then yawned. She realised that she'd

not told Wolfgang about Ralph Bell. That was definitely a secret that he might not need to know. The whole thing made her brain hurt.

"We need to get some sleep, Wolfgang. I think we're dealing with something that is much bigger than we might have originally thought."

Chapter Sixteen

SIS Headquarters, Vauxhall, London

Jane drew the meeting to a close. Even though it was a Sunday, she'd called in all her staff. Key to her decision was Sam's report from last night concerning the new compound in Shabwah. They really needed to get eyes and ears on. And they desperately needed to find Captain Tony James.

Tim, who at the beginning of the meeting had made some quip about his Sunday dinner getting cold, had perked up when Jane had told him that the Yemeni team had been allocated another hundred thousand pounds to get someone close to, or preferably in, the compound. Tim reckoned that after the executions of Groves and Jarman, the Sana'a team might chance an arm and get up there themselves—maybe come in from the desert, get close enough to the compound to secure some decent images.

Jane had made it clear that any such action would need her and probably the chief's nod. Nobody wanted to lose SIS agents in Yemen. It was bad enough having four SRR soldiers down.

Mike had confirmed that he'd already tasked the Doughnut to search for mobile signals; should Tim's men get within reach, they would try to tap the landline—if there was one. Sue explained that she'd been in touch with her SF colleagues. They were looking over plans to assault the compound should more reliable intelligence become available.

It was all go, and the team had a real buzz about it. Thanks in no small part to Sam—and Frank. With Sam's initial information, Frank had worked late into the night and had finally assigned a 90 per cent certainty to the two vehicles—which was as close to perfection as you could get with intelligence gathering at this level.

The only outstanding question was whether or not Tony James was in the same compound as the vehicles. Her team had just dashed off to try to establish whether that was the case.

Jane asked Frank to stay behind, just the two of them. Jane didn't want Sam's exploits in Germany to become common knowledge—although there was definitely a Ralph Bell connection between Yemen and Germany, bringing that detail to the team at this point would muddy the waters. When what they needed was a single focus.

"Anything more from Sam overnight?" Jane asked.

"Just some maps of Köln from a couple of loose Bischoff e-mails that Wolfgang was able to hack. What we all think is significant is that Bischoff's machine is encrypted with 256-bit technology. That's pretty impenetrable. I'm no expert, but what I do know is that Sam's friend is very good at what he does. His machines, which are based in Munich and accessed remotely, are among the best you can buy. If he says Bischoff's machine is tricky to get into, then I believe him. But, with Sam's permission, I've given the e-mail and web addresses to Defence Intelligence. They may be able to do something that Wolfgang hasn't been able to do. But I doubt it."

Jane was impatient to move on.

"Anything from the stuff taken from Mauning's phone?"

"As well as the Abilene number, which we now know for certain is a landline into the Church of the White Cross, we have thirteen German mobiles with names assigned. One belongs to Heinrich Bischoff, which is good, as it links the two men. None of the others have Interpol records; without going to the BfV, it's impossible to check if any of the names have local history."

"Yes, well, we've given Sam our word that we won't approach the BfV until after lunch." Jane looked at her watch. It was 10.45. In terms of "lunch," they hadn't agreed which time zone.

"If you don't mind me asking, Jane, why are we loath to

299

involve the BfV at this point?"

That's a good question, Frank. She briefly thought back to West Africa, where David had been adamant not to involve their contacts in the CIA because he'd assumed there was a loose connection there. And he had been right. Here, now, there was absolutely no intelligence to suggest the same with the BfV, but . . .

"Good question, Frank. I think the chief feels that the current German right-wing, anti-immigration lobby could well have one or two police sympathisers. Which might be true. He wants to give Sam time to get ahead of the game before we alert the BfV."

"Do we have someone in the BfV we know we can trust?"

"I spoke with Tim this morning. He's still got good contacts there and knows a couple of old pals he could have a frank conversation with. We're going to do that after lunch. Sam's aware. Now, let's have a look at these Köln maps." Jane pointed to Frank's iPad.

He opened it up and double-clicked on one of the attachments that Sam had sent through. It was a map of Köln's city centre, with the tourist attractions penned in 3D. She recognised the dark, twin towers of the city's cathedral. Overlaid on the map was a blue line, which looked like a route. At one end was the main railway station. The line snaked around the town and ended up at the university. She reckoned the route, which wasn't direct, was about two or three miles long.

Why would Bischoff have this? What does it mean—if anything?

She pulled her head back as if to take in the whole screen. It was a puzzle.

"What's wrong, Jane?" Frank asked.

"What are these marks?" Jane pointed loosely at the screen.

"Which ones?"

"These ones on the top and bottom of the map. It looks

300

like something has been expurgated, just leaving a white splodge."

Frank looked closely at them, leaning forward. He used his fingers to zoom in. Jane guessed he hadn't noticed them before.

"I don't know. It looks like it might be part of the original diagram. Or, maybe something has been taken out? A heading, or even a security clearance?"

"I don't know either." She frowned. "Over to you, Frank. Let's see if these blank bits can throw some light on what this is about."

"OK. I'll do that now."

Frank nodded his head, closed his iPad, and looked to leave, when Jane interrupted him by gently holding his arm.

"Well done, Frank. Thanks for coming in." Jane smiled.

Frank looked a bit embarrassed. "It's no problem at all, Jane. Pleasure." And, with that, he scurried away.

Jane leaned back on the chair and took a deep breath. She looked at her watch. It was a few minutes later than the last time she had checked. She had a call arranged with the deputy director at 11:00 a.m. to talk about the note she had sent through last night on Greyshoe. It was going to be a very interesting conversation.

She collected her things. Before she left the conference room for her office, she walked over to the window. Another good view of the Thames.

I wonder what Sam Green is up to now?

Outskirts of Berlin, Germany

They both seemed to be enjoying the silence. Over breakfast Sam had reviewed where they were. Wolfgang thought that, apart from being in mortal danger at least twice in the last twenty-four hours, they weren't any further forward. His servers had been unable to access Bischoff's machine, they'd got very little from Mauning's phone, and even Sam's friends in the UK hadn't come up with much from the stuff they'd sent through last night. The one big, but not surprising, thing was that Bischoff's mobile number was on Mauning's phone. They were obviously pals, possibly connected through *die Kirche des weißen Kreuz*.

None of it had shed any additional light on the Lattice, nor were they any further forward on that British chap, Ned Donoghue. Had Sam mentioned it to her boss?

"Sam?"

"Mmmm?"

"Did you mention Ned Donoghue to your boss? You know, the chap in New York?"

Sam scratched her chin.

"I did, didn't I?"

"I don't remember you doing so. It's just that we've been necessarily focusing on Bischoff and Mauning, or, should I say, they've been focusing on us. I wonder if we're missing the bigger picture? Should we be in New York, not Berlin?"

Sam looked across at him, wearing a gentle smile. One that was so much more preferable than the look she sported when she was in *action girl* mode.

"New York. Now there's a nice thought." It was a whimsical comment.

"Why not?" Wolfgang slowed the Kadett down as they approached a roundabout.

"Other than that I should really be back at work tomorrow?"

"But I thought you were now your firm's girl in Germany? You can't be in two places at once." He pulled her leg.

Sam didn't say anything. She was too busy taking her phone out of her pocket and pressing buttons. Wolfgang remained silent.

"Hi, Frank. How's it going?"

Wolfgang couldn't pick up any of the return conversation over the noise of the traffic. He just saw Sam nodding and heard her acknowledge with an, "OK."

"Look. Could you do some digging for me? There's a British guy, probably murdered in New York, about a week ago. His name is Ned Donoghue." Sam seemed to wait to let her friend Frank write this down. "D-O-N-O-G-H-U-E. Yes, that's right. We think he might be part of the whole play. Wolfgang hacked his machine in New York, only to find that Donoghue was looking at exactly the same sort of thing that Wolfgang was. Energy companies and the like."

Sam stopped talking for a second and replied to Frank with an, "Uh-huh," nodding as she did.

"He might be the link as to why Wolfgang was originally targeted. OK?"

There was a further response from Frank, then Sam hung up.

She sighed. She was obviously still in thought.

"Look, Wolfgang. I know you think it's a waste of time, but let's do the BStU now and get it over with. We might find something."

Wolfgang pulled away from a set of traffic lights. Berlin was getting busy, even for a Sunday morning.

"I think you'll find that Federal Commission for the Stasi Records prefers to be known the name of its current head." Wolfgang smiled knowingly across at Sam. *One up for the German.* "I Googled it last night! Whatever, I'm not sure 'the Jan Behorde' is going to have any details of actual Stasi members. All it does is hold the old Cold War records the Stasi put together on East German suspects. It's a working museum, designed to allow any German to see if the Stasi had a file on them. I doubt Bischoff kept a file on himself."

"You're probably right, but let's do this. By then it'll be lunchtime and, as they say in the films, this whole thing will be 'handed over to the proper authorities.' That's when my boss will get in touch with the BfV. You and I will then have to decide what we do next." She looked out of the Kadett's window and, almost to herself, said, "Although I did promise to go straight home."

Wolfgang let out an "harrumph." He hated to admit it,

but the last thing he wanted at the moment was this thing to end. He pulled up for another set of traffic lights.

"And, if you go back to work tomorrow and nobody else tries to kill us, will you come to New York with me next weekend?"

Sam looked across at him, displaying the biggest smile she had in her armoury. She also, very softly, tapped his leg.

"I'll take that as a yes, then."

Wolfgang stopped the car in the traffic. They were a few blocks from Karl-Liebknecht-Strasse, where the BStU was based. Ahead of them was a group of people with banners and flags.

"What do they say, Wolfgang?"

"It's . . . a march against the current chancellor. The banners say 'Chancellor Go to Syria,' and similar. It's probably a reaction to her stance on letting in refugees from the East. Fuelled by, I guess, the appalling bombings in Paris a couple of months ago. Feelings are running high."

Sam craned her neck to get a better view. Wolfgang noticed that many of the protesters had their faces covered. There was a mingling of police on either side of the group, but, so far, it all looked peaceful enough.

"Not all Muslims are extremists. And not all extremists resort to violence," Sam said.

"True," replied Wolfgang. "But the more there's terror, the more xenophobic people will become. And soon, all those people will want appropriate action."

"And what action is that?" Sam's tone was harsh. It caught Wolfgang by surprise.

"Bombing Syrian targets. Boots on the ground. That sort of thing."

"Don't you think that's what the extremists want? The more we bomb places like Syria, or invade countries like Iraq, the more everyday Muslims are going to hate us. And, as a result, the more they're going to support hard-line groups. For every terrorist you kill, you spawn two more. It's a hopeless strategy."

Wolfgang was about to say something, but Sam continued. She was obviously on her high horse.

"Name one terrorist organisation since the Second World War that we have actually beaten into submission with bombs and bullets."

Wolfgang was in unfamiliar territory now. He threw some names out there.

"The IRA?"

"We improved the lot of the Catholic population in Northern Ireland by giving them what they deserved—civil rights equal to those of the Protestants. And then we sat down and had a conversation with the IRA. And, by the way, there were as many active members of the IRA at the beginning of the conflict as there were when we all signed the Good Friday Agreement. We didn't beat them by fighting and killing them. Actually, our 'boots on the ground' just extended the war."

"The Red Army Faction?"

"The German government agreed to release some members of the RAF if they deescalated their violence. The RAF, which operated in what was then West Germany, was supported, and probably funded, by the Stasi."

While Sam had been talking at him, Wolfgang had negotiated the crowd—he looked to see if Bischoff was in the group, but he couldn't spot him. He noticed that as Sam was lecturing him on how to defeat terrorism, she was doing the same. As they pulled up into the BStU car park, he was pleased that eventually Sam had shut up. She looked intently across at the building. It was typical of the Soviet era, concrete, high rise. and very ugly.

They'd checked that the place was open the night before, and so headed straight for the front door and found the information desk. Sitting behind a long white counter was an elderly man. He had a name badge on: Hans Abbing. Open in front of him was what looked like a register; there was a telephone to one side and a single computer monitor and keyboard. Other than that, the entrance to the BStU was unremarkable. Sitting next to Hans was another elderly man. Wolfgang couldn't see a name tag on the second man. Both were having a convivial discussion about the latest Bundesliga football results—in German. He'd have to do some translation for Sam.

"Guten tag!" Wolfgang got their attention. They both stopped their conversation and returned Wolfgang's greeting.

Wolfgang then asked them about the latest football and if they knew anything of the protests they had just driven through.

"It's the chancellor! She's no good. We've let in far too many terrorists already. It's only a matter of time before we all get bombed out of our homes. We should build a wall between us and Poland to stop them all getting in!"

Wolfgang quickly translated for Sam, who frowned. He was equally frustrated with the elderly man's argument.

Wolfgang replied. "And we need a secret police to spy on our neighbours to find out if any of them are practicing Muslims!"

The man replied, *"Ja!"* and then stopped himself. He smiled at Wolfgang, shaking his head.

"Good point, well made, especially here. Please excuse an old man his right to moan."

"Of course. We live in difficult times." He turned to Sam as he translated. He faced the men again.

"Do you have a record of ex-Stasi staff here, or just files of those on whom they kept records?"

Hans spoke to his friend next door. No, they didn't. Sorry.

Wolfgang turned back to Sam and, having translated, raised his hands in resignation.

Sam nudged him. "Ask them about Bischoff." Then she shrugged as if to say "why not?"

Wolfgang did as he was told.

"My father remembers a young Stasi policeman named Bischoff. His first name was Heinrich. Do either of you have any recollection of such a man?"

Wolfgang thought it was the longest shot in history.

The man in front of him looked blank, but his friend took on a completely different appearance. His face seemed to drain of blood, and his mouth curled down at the edges.

Nobody said anything for what seemed like an age. Sam moved closer to the counter.

"Do you know of him?" Wolfgang pressed the friend. In front of the man was an unfinished Sudoku puzzle. He was holding a pencil in both hands. He bent his pencil so far it snapped. The action seemed to wake him from his trance.

"He is a bastard."

That's all he said. He didn't look at Wolfgang; he just stared straight ahead. The colour had not returned to his cheeks.

"Can you tell me more?" Wolfgang's gaze shifted quickly between the two men. "My father is dying of cancer, and I need to go back and tell him something."

Wolfgang was a lousy storyteller. He had no idea if what he had just said sounded believable or not.

The man without a name badge continued in German. "There were five of them. Heinrich Bischoff, Luis Schmidt, Lutz Gunther, Ramhart Haas, and Gert Mauning. A special group. We called them the 'Famous Five,' which wasn't without irony. They worked outside the law, what little law there was for the Stasi back in the 1970s and 1980s."

Wolfgang was quietly translating as the man spoke.

"They took away my brother. He was never seen again. We heard they were responsible for hundreds of disappearances. They used poison. They took people in the woods and shot them. There was a rumour they killed people with their bare hands, they enjoyed it so much."

"What poison?" Sam interrupted. Wolfgang translated her question.

"Ricin and some other drug. I can't remember which."

Wolfgang didn't need to translate *ricin*—it was the same in both languages. Sam appeared to step back when she heard the word.

"Who's we? You translated *we heard*. How does he know so much?" Sam asked.

Before Wolfgang could relay the question in German, the main attendant answered in nearly perfect English.

"My friend is ex-Stasi himself, but on the administration side. He despised everything they did. He works here for free to make amends for what his organisation did back then."

Sam quietly replied, *"Danke schön."*

"Do we know what these men are up to now?" Wolfgang asked.

The friend spoke again. Wolfgang translated for Sam.

"Schmidt and Gunther are gone. They escaped the country when the Wall came down. Possibly to South America. The other three were all jailed as a result of the inquest, but they were only imprisoned for a few years. They could be anywhere now."

"Thanks." Wolfgang looked at Sam. The question in his expression was "what now?"

She shook her head and quietly said, "We should go."

Wolfgang offered his hand to Hans and then to the badgeless man. They both shook it warmly.

He and Sam had turned to walk out when the second man, among other words, murmured in a whisper, *"Die Kirche des weißen Kreuz."*

Both Sam and Wolfgang stopped in their tracks.

Wolfgang turned sharply and interrogated the man. "What did you say?"

"He said 'the Church of the White Cross.' The three men are members of the church's congregation," Hans, the main attendant, replied.

"Do either of you know where the church is?" Sam stepped in.

Both of the men looked at each other. They knew something but seemed unwilling to say any more. It was as though they had already stepped over a line. They both shook their heads. All of a sudden, Wolfgang thought, both men looked very old indeed.

Sam was about to ask a supplementary, but Wolfgang knew it wasn't the right thing to do. Not now. Not to these two old men.

He put his hand up to stop her.

"We should go." He took Sam's arm and escorted her out of the building.

Somewhere on the Saudi Peninsula

They had beaten him again last night. Up until that point, Tony had thought that he was doing well. His stomach felt better, the swelling on his leg had calmed down, his breathing was no longer laboured, and even his ribs were less sore. However, last night after prayers, two men had laid into him with their feet. They had dragged him back to his cell, thrown him to the floor, and, in broken English, had screamed "Down! Lower! When pray!" Then they had beaten him.

He got the message. They really didn't need to kick him twenty times to reinforce the point. He was prepared to do whatever they said—anything. Wasn't he showing enough contrition? Could he do any more? Everything hurt so much when he knelt and bent forward. He was trying as hard as he could.

As he lay there afterward, unable to move, what surprised him was his own reflection on his punishment for not praying correctly. Perhaps they were right. He should try harder and show the correct deference to God. Maybe he'd have done the same if someone had been disrespectful about his religion. Didn't he deserve it?

As a result of the beating, this morning he couldn't even think about crawling over to get his food and medicine. They hadn't kicked him in the head, but anything below the neck had been fair game. Everything hurt. Everything was stiff. So he just lay on his mattress. Yes, a mattress. It was another welcome addition to his ever-growing list of luxuries: coffee instead of weak tea; a change of clothes; a toothbrush; and some dark chocolate, just a small cube, which he had been given with his goat stew and bread yesterday at lunchtime.

He couldn't move. So, instead, he lay and listened to the wind, which had picked up overnight. Whilst anything before the last couple of weeks was hazy, he seemed to remember that with the wind, came sand. Sand that stung like hail; sand that got into everything: in your ears; up your nose. Sand that forced you to close your eyes—seeing was impossible. When the wind got up, the sand came; so, you took cover and waited for it to abate.

His cell's window rattled in its casing. His door clunked and banged. At first, the sand that got in through the cracks just hung in the air like an early morning mist. Then it started to settle, the gentle swirling currents in the cell pushing it into a pile in a corner. Dirty sand. Sand that got into everything.

Tony felt very protective of his newly acquired possessions. *Sand was bad. It would mess with his stuff! I have to do something!*

Even with an abdomen and limbs that screamed in pain and were hopelessly ineffective after the beating, he forced himself off his mattress. Tears rolled down his cheeks as somehow he managed to drag his mattress into the far corner of the cell, away from the accumulating sand. Using his arms to pull himself along, he moved both of his buckets inch by inch, positioning them where he felt they were as far away from him and the growing pile of sand as they could be. Equidistant between him and the intruder. The smell of the slop bucket was sickening. He spilt some on the floor and over his hands. But it wouldn't do for it to be covered with filthy sand.

He even moved the cassette player and the cassettes, so they were least inconvenienced by the sandy onslaught. The tape had finished. He turned it over and pressed "Play."

As he flopped back on his mattress, his last act was to

place his lovely blue toothbrush under the corner of his mattress, so it was as protected as it could be. Only then, when all was as well as it could be with his world, he thought about resting.

As he lay there watching the dirty sand build in the far corner of his cell, self-loathing was the overriding emotion. He was furious with himself for getting into this position. Why did he choose a career that sent him spying on other people? Why did he even think that it was the right thing to do, to look into other people's worlds? What would he do if he thought people were spying on *him*? He'd be furious! It was diabolical. And why, now, couldn't he get it right? They were asking him to follow a simple set of rules. Pray correctly. And he wasn't even able to do that well. *What was wrong with him?*

He tried to stretch his legs, but they were far too stiff and they hurt too much to allow him to do so. He didn't deserve to be able to stretch. He didn't deserve to get better, to be able to walk again, or to lead a normal life.

It was at that point that an unfamiliar picture of a woman with a child came into his head. It was a glancing image, one that immediately wanted to take over, to force everything else into the mire. He tried to focus on it, but it was gone. Lost in the swirling sand.

Self-loathing was gone now. The image had jolted something in his head. Pity soon took complete control. And with pity, came tears.

Falkensee, Berlin, Germany

Sam checked her watch. It was four thirty. They were sitting some one hundred metres or so from where Gert Mauning lived. Frank had e-mailed them his address earlier in the afternoon. He'd pressed the embassy to chase up on Mauning's brush with the police the previous day at the schloss, and this had been the result.

Well done, Frank.

Until Sam had gotten Frank's e-mail confirming Mauning's address, she was at a real loss as to what to do next. She had briefed Jane about the "Famous Five," and she had also told her of the comment from the man at the BStU, that the five had previous expertise in the use of "ricin and another poison."

"My God! David!" Jane had said. "Surely, this is more than just a coincidence?"

"There are too many coincidences here, Jane."

Jane had added that she was just about to file a report to someone in the BfV "they trusted." She'd put this latest intel into the report. The chief had briefed his opposite number about an hour ago, and the report would fill in the gaps.

"It's time for you to come home now."

Had that been a question or a statement? Sam hadn't known. All she did know was that there was unfinished business here in Germany.

Thankfully Frank's e-mail answered the question for her. Herr Mauning lived just outside Berlin and, as it was Sunday and Christian congregations met on a Sunday, she and Wolfgang decided to go and pay Gert Mauning a visit. Her initial thoughts were that if the church met in the early evening, Mauning might lead them to its location.

They'd just arrived. Wolfgang expertly parked the yellow Kadett in the trees down a nearby lane. Sam had reminded him to back in "so they could make a quick escape if necessary." As always, he followed Sam's instructions without comment. *Bless him.*

They were looking at a medium-size farmhouse, set back from a main road. It was partially hidden by dark green pine trees and bushes. In typical German fashion the house and the main cattle barn, all red brick and wood, were an item. The pair were protected by a large roof, with its apex at the join between the house and the barn. The dwelling took up the right half of the building. Sam could see four windows and a front door. The barn was to the left; no windows, just a large arched wooden door. There were no signs of livestock in the fields, so Sam bet that the barn hadn't seen cattle for a long time.

As they lay on a damp mound under some trees looking across at Mauning's farmhouse, Sam realised that Mauning wasn't going to church this evening. It was coming to him. Cars were arriving, and the congregation was building.

Their mistake had been not bringing a decent camera. As a compromise, between them they used their phones to take long-distance pictures of the house, the surrounding area, and the cars.

"That's Bischoff!" Sam whispered incisively.

"What?"

"There. The silver-grey Audi that's just pulled up. Look, he's getting out of the car now. He's the one who's limping."

"I've got twenty-twenty vision and I can't make him out at this distance! How do you know?'

"The silver Audi. It's an A8—very uncommon. It was parked outside Bischoff's apartment last night. And the driver is dragging his leg!"

"Yes, well, we all know why that is. Uncle Ferdinand strikes again!" Wolfgang laughed quietly at his own joke.

"There's another car. How many are there now?" Wolfgang asked.

Sam counted. "Seven. No, an eighth is just pulling up."

They both lay still. Sam felt the cold creeping in through her clothes, and her toes were already starting to go numb. They couldn't stay here too long, not without a flask of hot tea, which they hadn't brought with them.

"What do we do now?" Wolfgang asked, looking at Sam. His face was close, their shoulders almost touching. In any other situation, at any other time, it might have been considered romantic.

"How's your arm?"

"It's OK, thanks. The cold isn't helping, but it doesn't seem to be getting any worse."

"Good." She thought for a second. "Let's see if we can

get closer to the farmhouse, take some photos of the cars, and find a telephone junction box so maybe later you could tap into their Internet? And whatever else we can find."

Wolfgang didn't require further encouragement. He was already pushing himself back off the mound in the direction of the lane, making sure he didn't ruffle any of the branches above him. Good military drills.

Well done, Wolfgang, you're picking this up quickly.

Just behind him, and now on her feet, Sam whispered, "Follow me and do as I do."

They walked down the lane for about thirty metres, until trees obscured the farmhouse completely. It was getting dark now, and soon, with the heavy cloud cover, they'd be able to walk around the fields without fear of being seen—*unless someone had a nightscope?*

She stopped by a barbed-wire fence. Instinctively she ran her hands up and down between the wires. Nothing. Good. If this place were *die Kirche des weißen Kreuz* and she were in charge of security, she'd have the area wired and watched.

She straddled the fence; Wolfgang did the same. Quietly, they headed off in the direction of the farmhouse, keeping low and placing their feet carefully.

As they approached the trees, Sam could make out the lights of the farmhouse on the other side. Apart from the wind whistling through the branches, there was no noise. The ground was becoming moist, but it hadn't seeped into her boots—yet.

Another fence. Another check. Nothing. They were both over, and, again as quietly as they could, they made their way through the trees. Beyond them was a gravel car park and then the farm. It was, maybe, twenty metres away. Sam put up her hand. Wolfgang stopped and dropped down on one knee. *Another good drill. Well done, fella.* Sam slowly picked her way to the tree line and came upon another fence, this time a wooden one. She stopped and knelt down. She scanned left and right, judging distances, looking for security devices, anything that might catch them out. She checked the fence for wires. Nothing.

There! There was a security camera on the left eave of the barn, looking out over the car park. It had low-light capability—she could tell by the size of the front lens. There was a single light on in the house, the bottom left window. Other than that, it was quiet. The barn, however, seemed busier. Whilst the main wooden doors looked well and truly closed, above them was a small cross-shaped ornamental window. It was illuminated by light from within, which, if you stared at it long enough, appeared to flicker.

Someone's having a party in there.

Sam turned back to Wolfgang and whispered, "Stay here. I'm going into the car park to take a photo of every car and its number plate." She put her hand up to reinforce "stay here." Again, Wolfgang did as she told him.

She shuffled down through the tree line until she was as close as she could get to the cars. From this distance she could take a photo of two of them, a red Mercedes C220 and a black Ford Focus. Making sure she couldn't be seen by the camera, she slid under the bottom rung of the fence, scraping her jacket on the gravel. On her hands and knees crunching as quietly as she could, she made her way among the cars, taking photos as she did. The silver Audi A8 was definitely the one parked outside Bischoff's house. *Result.*

She froze. The front door of the farmhouse opened, letting out a sheath of light. A man exited, saying something in German to someone inside. He walked over in her direction.

Sam very gently slid around the back of a blue Toyota Rav4 and tensed herself for a confrontation. She looked for a weapon, but she couldn't find one. Just gravel. The car beeped and its indicators flashed. The driver's door, which was opposite to where Sam was hiding, opened and the interior light came on. She held her breath as the man shuffled about inside, opening what she thought was probably the glove compartment. There was a clunk as the door closed. The Toyota beeped again, and the orange lights flashed. The man's crunching feet indicated that he was heading back to the farmhouse.

Sam exhaled. *That was close.*

She was on all fours again, quickly making her way to the end of the row of cars. She snapped her final photo and slid back along the gravel to the fence, where she was surprised to meet Wolfgang crouched by a post.

"I thought I told you to stay where you were!" she whispered angrily.

"The man took out a handgun from his car!" he whispered back.

"Oh." She was caught between thanking and scolding him. "Thanks." She opted for the former.

She crawled back under the fence.

"Do you think we should get the rifles before we go any further?" Wolfgang obviously had a liking for guns and having seen the enemy with a pistol, felt safer with something in his hands that shot people.

"No!" Sam didn't need to think about the answer. "They're no good at short range, and if we have to make a dash for the car, they'll get in the way."

It was Wolfgang's turn to say, "Oh."

"Let's go around the side and see if there is some way we can get a look at what's going on in the barn."

She didn't wait for a reply.

Sam led the way, following the fence line around to the left. If they stayed this side of the fence they would remain in the trees. After about fifteen metres they had to negotiate another fence; as she put her foot down, she broke a large, but old, branch, which she hadn't seen in the dark. Snap!

They both stayed perfectly still, waiting to see if anyone was outside the barn who may have heard the snap. Nothing. There was a quiet reverberation coming from inside the barn. *Just the congregation talking?*

The side of the barn was very dark, the overhang from the roof so low it almost touched the ground. About halfway down was a wooden side door. Where the door met the barn wall there was a pencil-thin sheath of light. The door obviously didn't close cleanly.

Sam stopped Wolfgang with a raised hand and then pointed to the door. She then pointed at herself and back to the doors. Wolfgang nodded. She would go and have a look; he would stay where he was.

She was under the fence in no time, and with the ground more concrete than gravel, she quietly tiptoed across to the door. As she approached, the voices inside the barn got louder.

Bugger. It's all in German. D'oh! She'd have to get Wolfgang.

Sam turned and immediately almost fell over as she discovered Wolfgang directly behind her. *Idiot!* If someone were watching this, it would look like a scene from a Laurel and Hardy film. In the very dim light, Sam could see that he was smiling. She shook her head to indicate her displeasure.

They both crept forward; at the sheath of light, Wolfgang stayed standing, peeking in through the gap. Sam knelt down to do the same.

She couldn't see much. There was a glimpse of what might be a makeshift altar, and a man in a white cloak standing behind it was addressing the crowd. Most of them had their backs to her. On the man's cloak she spotted an emblem: the church's white cross on a black background and accompanying thistle. *Definitely the right place, then.*

The crowd was made up of about fifteen people—no, she checked again, not just people—they were all men. The group was standing around, listening to the preacher. Each had a chair to sit on, but the chairs weren't laid out in a regular fashion. The men just had them by their sides. It all seemed pretty ordinary. That is, if you consider a group of men in a barn receiving some form of religious homily, ordinary. *What was she expecting? A horrendous ritual, maybe the slaughtering of a braying sheep and cauldrons of boiling liquid?* To reaffirm her view that it was just odd, rather than extraordinary, they started to sing a hymn. She recognised the tune, but couldn't understand the words.

Wolfgang tapped her on her head.

Sam looked up.

He mouthed at her, "Not the same words."

She didn't get it. The men were making enough noise for her whispering not to be heard.

"What?"

"The words. They're not the usual Christian words. And they're not singing in German." He shrugged his shoulders.

She went back to her observation position and listened intently, trying to pick out a word or two. The dialect was strong; it was almost lyrical. Then she got it.

She half stood; Wolfgang dropped down so she could whisper in his ear.

"Ancient Hebrew?"

He nodded and shrugged his shoulders at the same time.

The singing stopped. The men then sat down. As they did, looking above the line of the men's heads, Sam spotted an easel with a flipchart on it. The preacher left the altar and walked across to the chart. He spoke to his small congregation in German. Sam recognised the language, but picked out very little.

But she did hear the word *Köln. That's familiar.* Then the man turned over the top layer of the chart to reveal something Sam also recognised—the map of Köln that Wolfgang had picked off Bischoff's e-mail. The preacher spoke some more, none of which she understood. There was discussion among the group, and there appeared to be agreement. A couple of the men nodded, and two or three of them stood up and shook hands. Sam was desperately looking for either Bischoff or Mauning, but she couldn't pick them out—just a sea of backs. They must be deeper into the crowd, blocked by the three or four men she could see in front of her.

Oh, hang on. The preacher said something, and a man got up and came to the front. *It was Mauning.* He had his shoulder in a sling. *That'll teach him.*

He started speaking. Again, Sam only made out the odd word. One was *Neuenburg*, and a short while later, she picked up *Fraulein Green*.

How the hell do they know who I am?

There was some discussion at that point; one of the crowd seemed to shout abuse at Mauning, who immediately came back at him with a splurge of German. He was red-faced and angry. She looked up to see what Wolfgang was up to, but she was met by his chin, as his head was pressed firmly against the crack between the doors.

Mauning continued. He seemed to call for someone to come forward, and a man, holding a handgun, made his way to the front. In what now became a ritualistic affair and certainly off the "odd" scale, the preacher took the gun to the altar and seemed to bless it. He then handed it back to Mauning, who continued to brief the small crowd, using his free hand to gesticulate.

Just then, Sam knew something was wrong. Wolfgang tensed dramatically and pushed the door so hard it clanked against whatever was restraining it. He let out an audible *"Grrr."* Sam stood up immediately and tried to restrain him. *Calm down, Wolfgang!* His reaction and the banging of the door would have definitely alerted the men inside the barn.

"What the hell's wrong?" Sam spat out the words as quietly as she could. She was holding his shoulders, still careful of his wounded arm.

Wolfgang had his eye back against the crack, but almost immediately he flinched as the doors took on a life of their own. Somebody was pushing them from the other side.

"They've got my mother," he said, his eyes wide with anger. "I'm going to get the bastards." He pressed against her restraint, but immediately she felt that common sense was returning to him. His push was now more for show; it lacked real intent. He knew, as she did, they *had* to get away.

"Let's go! You can't help her here." Sam started to move across the car park and pulled at Wolfgang's good arm. Any initial reluctance disappeared, and he quickly followed her.

As she ran toward the fence, with Wolfgang's hand in hers, from behind she heard locks being unbolted. As they vaulted the wooden fence their immediate route was lit by the light that poured out of the barn.

They had a head start, and they knew where the fences were. Beyond the trees was darkness.

"Same route. Follow the same route," she rasped.

Behind them she heard shouting, and when they were halfway across the field, a car started up. Then another.

Wolfgang was keeping up with her. As they got to the final barbed wire fence, in a single motion Sam placed one hand on a wooden upright and threw her legs over the top wire. Wolfgang tried to do the same, but caught his boot and went down on the far side of the fence. He let out a groan.

"Scheiße!"

He wasn't down long and was up on his feet as quickly as he had fallen.

Sam offered him her hand, but he was too engrossed in reaching into his pocket for the car keys.

Crack! Thump!

Not again. When will these people stop shooting at us? Sam instinctively ducked as Wolfgang threw open the driver's door. She was already on the other side of the car and launched herself into the passenger seat, immediately turning and reaching for a rifle.

Crack! Ping! The yellow peril had taken a hit. Hopefully it wasn't serious.

"No lights!" she shouted at Wolfgang.

She needn't have bothered with instructions. Wolfgang instinctively knew what to do. With no lights he had expertly set the car in motion, off down the track toward the main road. As they sped away, Sam, rifle in hand and looking back through the rear window, saw the first of the men reach the track. He was unarmed.

At the junction, Wolfgang didn't wait to see if there was any traffic coming. He pulled out onto the main road, screeching tyres holding the Kadett on the road as they swerved left in the direction of the farmhouse entrance.

What is he playing at? We should be driving away from these lunatics!

"What are you . . . ?" She didn't finish her sentence when she realised what Wolfgang was up to.

Wolfgang threw on the car's lights as two cars and then a third sped past them in the opposite direction.

Genius.

They drove at a sensible speed until they came across a side road off to the right. Wolfgang took it. And, a little while later, he took the next left. Within ten minutes Sam sensed that they were out of danger. The Kadett slowed further.

"What did they say?"

His hands were gripping the steering wheel as if it were Mauning's throat. His eyes were fixed on the road ahead of him, and his mouth was tightly shut.

"What did they say, Wolfgang?" Sam tried to be as kind but as forceful as possible. She touched his shoulder.

That did the trick. He pulled the car over onto the side of the road and turned to face Sam. She could see now that he had tears in his eyes.

"They have my mother—not here—they said at the 'warehouse.' And . . ."

"What, Wolfgang?"

"They were blessing the gun that was going to be used to kill her. Tomorrow night."

Conflagration

Chapter Seventeen

Farmland Near Falkensee, Berlin, Germany

"Well? What do you think we should do now? You're always full of ideas." Wolfgang knew he sounded unreasonable. He *felt* utterly unreasonable. He was staring ahead into the dark of the German night. "Dark" was an apposite description. Dark was how he felt. No, *dark* wasn't a strong enough descriptor. *Black* would probably be better.

Was he being fair on Sam? Without her in his life, would his mother still be facing execution? Possibly. Probably? Would it not have come to this anyhow if he'd continued to pursue the stupid Lattice? Was it *his* fault? They had warned him, *richtig*? They told him to stay away. But he hadn't. He'd dug deeper. He and Sam Green had dug deeper.

What am I going to do?

He turned to face Sam, who had a sympathetic look about her. *It's a bit late for that.*

"I need to tell my people. They've been in contact with the BfV. You never know, the BfV might be onto the church. They could be ahead of us." Her voice was calm.

He disregarded Sam's answer. He'd just thought of something else he needed to do.

"Wait!" he hissed, in a tone close to contempt.

He knew he was wrong. He knew Sam didn't deserve to be treated like this. But, right now, he needed an escape valve. Something to press while he ruminated. While he fumed. He reached for his phone and turned it on. The bastards knew that he and Sam had just looked in on their gathering and heard much of what was going on in the barn. They might just want to get in touch.

Sam remained quiet.

He looked at his phone as the screen went through its start-up routine. It was too slow. Far too slow. He jammed

323

his jaw together. He wanted to scream; to open the Kadett's door and hurl the useless contraption into the field. *Why don't these things work when you want them to?*

As he was about to launch the phone out of the window, it finished its start-up routine. A tiny LED in its top corner flashed white, telling him he had new mail. It was from another indecipherable Hotmail address.

We told you to drop it. Your mother will die as planned. And you and your friend Green will be next. Too late for apologies.

Wolfgang smashed the phone on the steering wheel. He wanted to scream. To yell out to the world against the injustice of it all. But he didn't do that. Instead something inside him burst. He did the only other thing he could do— he broke down.

"Why have we ended up here? Why, Sam, why?" His words were interspersed with sobbing. He stared at her, wide-eyed, tears streaming down his cheeks.

She looked out of sorts. Unclear as to what to do next. Clumsily, she held out her arms, and he, uncomfortable with the gear lever and handbrake in the way, fell into them.

He felt no embarrassment that he'd lost control. He had not cried when his father had died. Now, he was going to lose his wonderful mother because of something he had done. *It's my fault.* That, surely, was too much for anyone to bear.

Sam stroked his head and held him as close as the confines of the Kadett allowed. She took his phone from his hand, looked at it, and placed it gently back in his hands.

"We have to move, Wolfgang. Your mother is not dead yet."

What? He pulled away from her. Confused, angry again.

"Who are you to say that my mother isn't dead yet? How do you know? *Who are you?*" The strength of his last sentence was accompanied by tears that sprayed onto her face, caught in the force of his words.

Sam didn't flinch. She stared at him impassively.

"I understand why you're angry, Wolfgang. You can blame me if you like. Go ahead. In the meantime, I need to phone my people and see what they've got. But before I do that, I want you to answer a couple of questions. Are you ready?"

Wolfgang wiped his eyes and mouth on the sleeve of his thick merino wool jumper. It would make a mess of the weave, but he couldn't have cared less.

He nodded for Sam to continue, sniffling back the mucus that had started to drip from his nose.

"In the barn. Was it clear who was going to kill your mother?"

Wolfgang thought for a second, the angry fog of the last half an hour being forced to one side. "Mauning. He took the gun. It was definitely him who was being tasked to kill Mother."

"And did they say anything other than 'the warehouse'?"

He thought through the scene again. He ignored the first bit about Köln. That was a distraction. He almost lost it again when he visualised the handgun, but then he pulled it together.

"No. All they said was the word *warehouse*."

"Is there anything else they said about your mother that might help us?"

He thought some more.

"No. I don't think so."

Sam took an audible breath.

"What about the stuff at the beginning, about Köln?"

Wolfgang didn't answer to begin with. He just faced the front. His mind was a blank. All he could think about was the plight of his mother. *That's all that's important right now.*

"Nothing. It was nothing. Just some stuff about a forthcoming visit. That's all."

"Are you sure?" Sam was pressing.

"Yes! Of course I'm sure." He smacked both his hands on the steering wheel. His phone took another hit. He looked at it. The screen was cracked. Other than that, it seemed to be working.

There was silence for a few seconds. Then Sam spoke, quietly but firmly.

"We're going back in the direction of the farmhouse. I will talk to my people and see if the BfV have got anything. They may know where the warehouse is, and this could all be over tonight. They might have something more on Mauning. Who knows? We'll see if the farmhouse is still occupied." Sam paused for a second, in thought. "If it is, and we don't get anything from my people, we'll try to follow Mauning and see if he leads us to the warehouse."

Wolfgang computed all that. It seemed logical. Then he had his own minor revelation. *Perhaps it made more sense to storm the farmhouse? Now!* They had weapons, didn't they? All of a sudden his mood had lifted. He could do something. Take action!

"Why don't we go and attack the farmhouse? Take Mauning and force him to show us where the warehouse is? We've got the two rifles."

Sam seemed to think for a bit and then, much to Wolfgang's frustration, came back to the original plan and added afterward, "The thing is, Wolfgang, more than anything else, we need to find the warehouse. Mauning is ex-Stasi. He's not going to take us to the warehouse under guard; he's too well trained for that. And who knows what weaponry they have in the farmhouse. We might not make it through the front door. Let Mauning lead us to the warehouse. And then my colleagues and the BfV can do the rest. We're not the people to storm a building and take our own hostages."

He thought about it for a couple of seconds. Then, without answering Sam, he started up the Kadett and spun her around.

"Where shall we stop?" His tone was distant and

resentful. He knew his actions and words were childlike, but he didn't care.

"I don't know. We need to get close to the farmhouse so we can follow Mauning, but far enough away so the car can't be seen. You choose."

Wolfgang was soon on the main road. It was very dark, a confusion of forest and field devoid of light. A two-dimensional, two-colour scene: black and dark greenish-grey; no moon. And with the cloud cover, no stars. He spotted the farmhouse and had to grip the steering wheel tightly to prevent himself from turning into the drive. *That would be such a good feeling.*

Just beyond the entrance, he pulled up and backed into a small track that was closer to the farmhouse than they had parked in before. After a few metres of reversing, the Kadett was tucked away and couldn't be seen from the road.

Sam hopped out and, without explanation, jogged down the road about ten metres, constantly looking across to the farmhouse. After a prolonged stare, she turned around and jogged back. Wolfgang was out of the car waiting for her, keeping in the shadow of the trees.

"What have you been up to?" He spat it out. He couldn't stop himself.

Sam was calm. "The two original cars that were parked in front of the farmhouse before the congregation arrived are still there. There's a black Mercedes E Class saloon and a red Toyota Rav4. His and hers, I reckon. Can we see the road entrance to the farmhouse from inside the car? It's there, where that sign is." Sam was pointing.

He didn't know. He got back in the Kadett and strained to look for the signpost. Yes, he could see it. He got out to acknowledge to Sam that they could, when he realised she was on the phone.

"Jane. OK we have a situation here . . ."

Sam told her boss the story of the farmhouse. She mentioned the map of Köln. She then asked a question.

"Are the BfV involved?"

Wolfgang couldn't pick up all the details, as the response from her boss on the phone was too quiet.

"So they're sending a rep to you tomorrow morning?"

A muffled response from Jane. Wolfgang moved closer to Sam, who pulled the phone away from her ear so he could hear the responses.

"Are they aware of the church and the Famous Five?" Sam asked.

Wolfgang could hear Jane now. It was high pitched, but he could make it out.

"Yes. They've been investigating the church for some time but have never found anything to stick. They're also aware of the Five. Two, Luis Schmidt and Lutz Gunther, as you found out, are thought to have disappeared. Probably to South America. They have records on Bischoff and Mauning and seemed pleased that I was able to provide some additional intelligence. Ramhart Haas lives in Berlin. He's a lawyer and an academic. They have nothing on him, other than he's a member of the church's congregation."

"Do we have anything else from any of the stuff that we sent across from Mauning's phone and Bischoff's computer?'

"No, nothing. Bischoff's computer is more secure than Fort Knox, according to DI, which is interesting intelligence in itself."

"OK, Jane, thanks. In a second I'll send through the details of the cars that were parked outside the farmhouse. And Wolfgang"—she touched his arm—"is understandably keen to do something. We are back outside the farmhouse. If Mauning leaves, we'll follow him. Hopefully to the warehouse. I'll let you know if and when that happens."

"That's a mistake, Sam. I've assured the BfV that you will come in by this evening. They can't operate freely if you're out on the ground. Blue-on-blue and all that."

Sam stopped herself at that point and looked directly at Wolfgang. He shook his head violently and pointed to himself and then to the ground. *I'm staying here!*

"OK, Jane. That's not going to happen. We're still one step ahead of the BfV at the moment. Give them my number. If they can replace us on stakeout here, I think I might be able to persuade Wolfgang that they can take over. Until then, we're going to remain with Mauning and follow any journey he takes."

Wolfgang noticed that it was the other end of the phone that went silent for a while.

Then Sam's boss said, "I'll tell them that Wolfgang is staying where he is. As a German citizen he can do whatever he wants, I guess. I'll also tell them that you're coming in—I just won't put a time on it."

"Thanks, Jane. I'll call in first thing tomorrow, unless something happens between now and then."

Sam closed the call. She seemed to be getting cold, she was hopping from one foot to another, her hands buried in her armpits. One part of Wolfgang wanted to hold her, to make her warm. But another part disregarded her feelings as an irrelevance. He was really struggling with all this.

Then Sam said, "I'll take the first two hours and you take the next two. We both need to get some sleep. Everyone's reactions lose their edge with lack of sleep. I think we're going to need every ounce of our wits in the coming twenty-four hours."

Wolfgang nodded.

This might just work . . . Follow Mauning. Get to the warehouse. Save Mother. This might just work.

He touched Sam's arm.

"Thanks, Sam. Thank you."

Sam smiled, nodded, and made her way to the car.

Kevin checked the GPS. They were five hundred metres short of the compound that London had marked as the latest possible location for Captain Tony James. The pair of them had dropped the battered old Land Rover County at the base of the small range of hills that lay just north of Shabwah. The best they could do was hide the vehicle in a shallow hollow, half sticking out behind a large sandy rock. He and Martin had then laid a desert poncho over the top and tied it down with brown bungees, in the vain hope that it would be difficult to be spot from a distance. On reflection. it wasn't such a bad job.

They weren't soldiers. They weren't trained in vehicle camouflage, nor did they have the right equipment to hide big, white boxes, like their trusty Land Rover, in a landscape of sand and rock. They were spies. Their job was to run agents and informants. Mix with politicians and senior military officers, elicit state secrets, and, on the odd occasion, go undercover in urban areas—not work on the top of an exposed hill, in the middle of the Yemeni highlands.

But, as the senior SIS officer in Yemen, Kevin had made the decision that they needed to do something. The execution of the two SRR soldiers had hit them all hard. His team's inability to find a reliable source close to Sahef had meant that there was little they could have done to prevent their deaths. They had tried—pushed their known informants and, in the process, had lost one of their most valuable assets. He had failed to turn up for a drop a couple of days ago, and subsequent efforts to track him down had proved fruitless. Kevin assumed that his body would come to light at some point in the future.

When London identified a new target for Tony James's location, he really had no choice. He'd asked Martin, accompanied by a smile, if he had anything else better to do over the next couple of days. Then they'd packed up and, after dark last night, had driven the six hours from Sana'a to

330

Shabwah. He'd pinged London with their intentions after they had left. An e-mail reply had come back immediately from his desk officer Tim: *Stop! Reconsider.* He had ignored it and kept driving.

Between them they had two Canon Eos5 still cameras, a FLIR infrared camera, a couple of small tripods, two pairs of binos, their usual communication paraphernalia, and an additional small rucksack holding water and some basic provisions. Kevin planned on spending no more than twelve hours in the OP. If they hadn't seen signs of James by then, they would have done their best.

They both carried their SIS-issue Glock 17 9-mm pistols. These were great personal self-defence weapons and were accurate out to about fifty metres. But they weren't long-range rifles. The enemy would doubtless have at least a couple of Kalashnikovs, which were accurate up to 250 metres. If they spotted the pair of them first, they'd have a real struggle extracting. If you looked at it like that, what they were doing was reckless. Hence the recall from London, which he had ignored.

They had to do something.

Martin, who was also breathing heavily when they reached the ridgeline, motioned for Kevin to stop. It was still dark. Looking over his left shoulder, an orange hue was just beginning to make itself known on the horizon. He reckoned dawn was about forty minutes away. They both took off their rucksacks, and Kevin dropped the additional holdall he was carrying. Martin, who was now flat on his stomach on top of the ridge, beckoned him forward.

Once beside Martin, he took in the scene below. It was far too dark to pick out any of the details, but he orientated the satellite photo he had in his mind to the scene below him. There was a single road that ran away into the distance. The hamlet straddled the road. There were five dwellings to the left of the road, three on the street, and two behind. On the right were two farm-like compounds. Closest to them was a small mosque, a single minaret proclaiming the centre of religious worship. The target was the farm/compound furthest away on the right.

He remembered what it should look like, but he couldn't make out any of the details. It was still too dark.

Piercing the silence of the early desert morning came the call to prayer. It caught them both by surprise. The melodic wailing resonated from the hamlet below. *It must be almost dawn.* The call was the Fajr, or predawn, call, the first one of five that broke up the day. As is often the case, it was prerecorded, but it was easily loud enough to wake everyone in the hamlet. Kevin knew the early morning call, wherever it was played, often frustrated non-Muslims living within earshot. He admired the tenacity of those who responded to the call and prayed. And it never bothered him that he often woke with the lark because the local mullah had proclaimed it essential that he did.

A new day was just beginning in the hamlet of Shabwah.

I wonder if it will be our *day?*

Martin slid back off the hill and returned with the infrared camera. He set it up. It took him a couple of minutes.

"Anything?" Kevin asked quietly.

"No. There's the odd warm body in the farm, but nothing to suggest that it's James."

"Are there any vehicles?"

"Possibly. But if they've been cold all night, they'll be difficult to make out from the surrounding ground and buildings. Especially after the night we've had. Hang on."

Martin spent a few more seconds looking through the sight, twisting the focus as he did. Kevin waited for Martin to come back to him.

"There's nothing in the central area, so either the black pickup has moved away, or it's in a garage somewhere." He stared some more. "No, we're going to have to wait until it's light to get a decent view."

Kevin motioned for Martin to move to one side. He looked into the eyepiece. It was, as he expected, a pretty indistinguishable mass of irregular shapes in various shades of green. He could just make out the far farmhouse. They had a good, clear view from here—which was a stroke of luck. But, the heat differentials weren't strong enough to help with the detail. What they needed to do now was set up their daytime cameras, wait for dawn. In the meantime, have some of that hot coffee that they had brought in the flask.

Farmland Near Falkensee, Berlin, Germany

"Sam! We're off!"

Sam felt her shoulder being shaken, and then the Kadett's engine started. She came to about a second later. She'd been flat out and had woken abruptly to the very uncomfortable feeling of being perishingly cold. It was beyond dawn, but they were in that in-between time when it's so damp, grey, and bitter, that you'd prefer if it were still night. There was no range of colours, just greys and greens.

"Are you sure it's him?" she said, rubbing her hands together to try to warm them up.

"Hang on!"

A black Mercedes sped past their nose. It was impossible to say if the car was being driven by a woman or a man. Last night they'd both agreed that Mauning would be driving the Merc. His wife, if he had one, would drive the Toyota. They'd follow the Merc.

They'd struggle to keep up if the Merc carried on at that speed!

Wolfgang was a superb driver. The Kadett screamed out for mercy as he forced the car through the gears—but there was none coming. Wolfgang pressed the poor car harder. As a result, they were soon a sensible distance behind the Merc and maintaining the same speed; the engine noise from the poor old Kadett was tiresome. It had probably never been worked as hard in its life.

While keeping one eye on the car in front, Sam checked her phone. Nothing. She opened up her messages and

SMSed Jane and Frank: *"On the move now, following Mauning—we think. Heading into Berlin."*

"What time is it?" Sam knew the answer, but wanted to engage Wolfgang. They'd hardly exchanged words the three times they'd handed over lookout during the night. Sam hadn't been able to test Wolfgang's mood; she was trying now. She really felt for him. Who wouldn't? She couldn't expect any less than his initial reaction. Sam was more than happy to be the scapegoat for as long as it took—unless he put their lives in danger. *That wouldn't do.*

"Seven thirty." He steered the Kadett onto a *schnellweg*. Sam hoped that the dual carriageway wouldn't encourage the Merc to take off into the distance. Thankfully there was already a buildup of traffic into Berlin, and the target car settled down to a sensible pace. Wolfgang pulled the Kadett into the slow lane, three cars back.

With Wolfgang still uncommunicative and not a great deal else to do other than wait for the Kadett's very poor heating to warm her joints, Sam decided to check both the rifles. She reached into the back and took the top weapon, careful to keep it below window height.

"What are you doing?" Wolfgang demanded; his histrionics hadn't dulled overnight. *Oh dear.*

"Just checking. That's all."

With cold fingers that still ached, Sam took off the magazine, pulled back the breech, and unloaded the seated round. She blew into the body of the weapon, wiping it clean with a tissue, and reassembled it. With another tissue, she cleared the front and rear lenses of the scope, which were covered in condensation. She checked the magazine housing, pressing down on the rounds to make sure the spring was working. She did the same with the second rifle, putting them both back onto the bench seat when she'd finished, and then covered them with the blanket.

She turned to Wolfgang and smiled at him. It was a forced smile, but the point was to try to produce a reaction.

Nothing.

This is dull.

The heating in the Kadett was working its hardest against the cold central European autumn morning. Sam was warming up—a bit. Seemingly unaffected by the chill, Wolfgang followed the Merc through the traffic until it pulled over in a suburban street, opposite a row of shops. He was caught out by the move, but he rolled the Kadett past the Merc and stopped further along. Neither of them looked into the car as they sailed past.

Checking his wing mirror, Wolfgang looked at what the occupant of the Merc was up to whilst Sam played with the rear-view mirror so she could get a better view. Thankfully, they both saw it was Gert Mauning who got out of the car, his arm still in a sling. He crossed the road and headed into an O2 phone shop.

"He's getting a new phone!" Sam exclaimed.

She was already on hers. Tapping away.

"Where are we, Wolfgang?"

Wolfgang looked around and found the nearest signpost.

"Wilmersdorf Strasse."

"Thanks." Sam replied quietly as she focused on her screen. "Is he out yet?"

"No."

"When he is, see if you can work out what make of mobile he's bought."

They waited for ten minutes. Then Gert Mauning, oblivious to the yellow Kadett, came out with a mobile in his good hand. In his slung hand he was holding a Sony bag.

"It's a Sony. And he's off."

Without responding to Wolfgang, Sam finished typing and pressed "Send" to the e-mail she had been composing.

Hi Frank,

We're following Mauning. He's just bought a Sony handset from an O2 mobile shop in Wilmersdorf Strasse, Berlin.

Get the number and, if nothing else, triangulate it.
Assumption is he's heading to the warehouse
sometime today. Let BfV know of his movements.

Thanks.
Sam xx

The Kadett followed the blue Merc into the depths of Berlin.
It eventually stopped in a car park outside of an office block
not far from, Sam noted, Altglienicke Strasse. Mauning got
out and, with a briefcase in his slung hand, locked the Merc
and disappeared into the entrance of the offices. They had
pulled up on a road that ran alongside the car park.

"Work?" Wolfgang barked.

"Presumably." Sam replied. A one-word question
deserved a one-word reply. "Look, Wolfgang, we might be
here for some time. Let's find a better parking spot and I'll
pop out and get some coffee and food. We can then rotate
again, like we did last night, and try to get some more sleep."

Wolfgang just nodded, still no words. *I'm not getting
through to him.*

He drove the Kadett a couple of spaces down and parked
up. He turned his back on Sam. She assumed it was so he
didn't have to crane his neck to get a clear view of the
entrance to the offices and of the Merc, but she wasn't so
sure.

This is tough. I'd rather be on my own at this moment.

Sam's frustration at Wolfgang's lack of communication
almost broke through. She very nearly said something along
the lines of, "You have to help me, Wolfgang. I am on your
side," but thought better of it. Instead she sat still for a
couple of seconds with her eyes closed, finding what little
humour she had. After about a minute, she got out of the car
and jogged back down the street in the direction of where,
previously, she had spotted a Starbucks. *Decent, strong
coffee. That's what we need.*

Claire popped her head around Jane's door.

"You've got a call from the deputy director." She winked at Jane.

Jane moved some things around her desk to make it look tidy—*that was completely unnecessary.* She picked up the phone.

"Hello, sir, Jane here."

"Hi, Jane. Thanks for the briefing note on Greyshoe. I'm sorry I didn't get chance to call you yesterday. We've been busy with the Israeli thing. You know how it is."

"I understand, sir. Good luck with that." The DD was referring to the latest spate of tit-for-tat bombings and missile strikes between Israel and Lebanon, which had resulted in the deaths of two American tourists.

"Since your note, my team here has looked for equivalent churches in all of the main European countries, using our liaison officers who are based with the national security services. They've been trying to establish if this is wider than just us and the Germans. Both the Italian SISMI and the Spanish CNI have come up trumps. It seems that there are equivalent organisations in Italy, *Chiesa della Croce Bianca,* and Spain, *Iglesia de la Cruz Blanca.* Between us, we're now looking into these sister organisations." The DD's accents were poor.

"Wow," Jane said. "This thing has some stretch. Where's the hub?"

"We're pretty confident that the main organisation is in Abilene, although it's going to take some time to piece the whole thing together. Whilst its gestation might have been in, say, Germany, we're pretty clear that the church in Texas is the major player. After some digging, the FBI reported that just this year the Church of the White Cross has distributed over $10 million overseas; $3 million went into a Berlin bank account, $1.5 million into an account in Riyadh, $1 million to Milan, and a further $1 million to a bank in

Madrid. In addition, a large number of individual payments were transferred into unmarked accounts in Geneva and Luxembourg." The DD paused to take a breath.

"Where do they get the money from?" Jane asked.

"That's a good question, and that's why I phoned."

"Go on, sir."

"I'm letting you know that we've got a warrant to search the main church and its grounds this afternoon. That's no small task—the site is over thirty-five acres. The search is planned for three o'clock Texas time; that's ten in the evening your time. It's a federal event, so the FBI is leading. They're going in with support from state and local law enforcement. I'm telling you because you probably want to alert your team on the ground in Germany. And I was wondering whether or not you want to brief the BfV. We're talking with the CNI and the SISMI."

Jane took stock just for a second.

"I've got a BfV liaison officer coming here in about"— Jane looked at her watch—"any moment now, actually. I'll brief him. I'm guessing they'll be wanting to keep a close eye on the congregation in Berlin to watch for any reaction."

"Precisely."

"What are you expecting to find?" Jane asked.

"We're not sure. Thanks to your team's work and the German linkage, at least now there's enough evidence for a judge in Dallas to issue a search warrant. We could have given it a couple of days, but the problem with waiting is that, whilst additional investigations might throw some more light on the workings of the church, the longer we leave it, the more likely we are to have spooked them. Then who knows what they will hide, if they haven't hidden things already."

"I can see that, sir. Any further news on Johnson, Manning, or Bell?"

"Johnson's coming in next Wednesday to the Hoover Building. He'll have his testimony concerning the five hundred thousand taken under oath. That's another good reason to search the church now, before he thinks we're really onto him. My team's casual review of online records has shown that both Manning and Bell are noted as congregational members of the Church of the White Cross, which is a significant piece of intel. Also, what about this interesting snippet..." The DD didn't finish the sentence.

"Go on, sir."

"Manning is only second-generation American. What do you think of that?"

Think of what? Jane didn't think anything of it. But, to humour the DD, she ran through likely originating countries. And then, the penny dropped.

"His grandfather came to the States from Germany"— Jane did some maths—"eh, at the beginning of the Second World War?"

"Spot on."

"So the gestation of this organisation might well be German based?"

"That's what we're looking at, Jane, yes."

"OK, sir. That makes sense. Will someone back-brief me on how the search of the church goes?"

"I'll do that first thing tomorrow. Unless, of course, it makes the news first."

What are you expecting to find, deputy director?

The call ended, and through the glass panelled wall, Jane spotted Frank waiting in the corridor. She motioned for him to come in.

"Hi, Frank. How can I help?"

"Hi, Jane. We're out of favours with GCHQ, I'm afraid. I have used them all up. As you know, they're doing their best to tap landlines and mobiles around Shabwah and are making real progress there. I'll let Mike brief you when we meet after lunch, but the Doughnut's SIGINT indicates that the compound/farmhouse definitely belongs to Sahef. They even reckon he might be at that location as we speak."

"That's great news, Frank. Don't worry—I'll sound and

look genuinely surprised when Mike mentions it this afternoon. And?"

"We're onto Mauning's new phone, the one Sam spotted this morning. The Doughnut is not prepared to access the mobile without the chief's say-so. Apparently, there's an issue about tapping within an ally's boundaries. They can triangulate without that level of authority, although they'd rather not. But I know some people." Frank tapped his nose and looked very pleased with himself. "So, assuming it's turned on, we can now see where the phone is."

"Good work, Frank. Does Sam know? Oh, and whereabouts is she at the moment?" Jane had lost touch with exactly where Sam was over the past couple of hours.

"I've told her. And they're both still parked outside the offices. And, because I have the GCHQ feed on my machine, I've been able to corroborate Mauning's location. Sam and Mauning's phone are all at the same place." He playfully stuck his thumb up.

Claire stuck her head around the door. "It's Oberwachtmeister Klaus Homberg to see you, Jane."

A slim, middle-aged man wearing a fawn ankle-length coat waited behind Claire.

Frank mouthed, "BfV?"

Jane nodded.

"Come in. My colleague here was just leaving."

As Oberwachtmeister Klaus Homberg came in, Frank left, giving Jane a cheeky little wave as he did.

Jane and the Oberwachtmeister exchanged pleasantries and, via Claire, she ordered some coffee. The Oberwachtmeister insisted that Jane call him by his first name. As Jane was at least an equivalent civilian rank, if not higher, she irreverently thought—*and you can call me Jane.* She really needed to get some sleep; otherwise, she didn't know how long she could keep these flippancies to herself.

"It's good of you to make the effort to come to the UK, Klaus." They both sat on the only two comfy chairs Jane had in her office. There was a small coffee table between them.

He was medium height, medium build. He had short, dark, glossy hair—*which could be gelled?*—and sported small, steel-rimmed glasses and a goatee beard. Jane thought he'd just come off a modern-day *'Allo 'Allo* set.

"It's no problem. Clearly SIS has a healthy interest in *die Kirche des weißen Kreuz*, and we have to thank you for alerting us to its US connections. We were aware, as you know, of the poorly entitled 'Famous Five' and had made the link between Heinrich Bischoff, Ramhart Haas, and Gert Mauning and *die Kirche*." Jane was grateful that Klaus spoke good English, even if his *th*'s were pronounced *z*'s and his *w*'s as *v*'s. More *'Allo 'Allo*. It was a scream.

I must concentrate.

"Unfortunately, we have little evidence that any of the three men have committed a crime that we can pursue in a court of law."

Jane sipped some coffee. Looking over her cup, she said, "But we have video evidence I shared with you of Bischoff breaking into an apartment rented by Wolfgang Neuenburg, an apartment that was later set on fire . . ."

Klaus stopped Jane sharply, politely raising his finger.

"Count Neuenburg is also of interest to us. We have immutable evidence that the Count has hacked many business's computers, both in Germany and abroad."

Jane wasn't so happy with being stopped midsentence, so she continued as soon as Klaus took a breath.

"And one of my agents reports that Mauning shot at her and Neuenburg on the grounds of the count's schloss two days ago. The count was wounded in the arm. That's attempted murder."

"Once the good count reports the crime formally to the police." Klaus smiled, a smile that was very gently laced with arrogance. "Please don't misunderstand me, Jane. We are clear that some of *die Kirche des weißen Kreuz*'s activities are illegal. Certainly, one or two of the church's congregation have stepped outside the law. For example, we know that Bischoff has attended a number of antimigration rallies, and we were very close to putting him behind bars for arson just over a year ago."

Tell me something I don't know.

"But not close enough."

Jane wasn't convinced that the BfV had really understood the size or gravity of the situation. *Surely they had thought through the US connection? She'd made that clear in the briefing note.*

"Have you seen my note from last night? My agent and Count Neuenburg were shot at again at a farmhouse, just outside Berlin late last night, having been fired on earlier in a car chase in the Czech Republic. The previous morning, Count Neuenburg had been shot and injured in the south of *your* country. And we believe the church has kidnapped his mother, the countess." Jane was on her feet now, turning away and stopping the Oberwachtmeister from replying directly to her. She needed to effect some form of power play over the German. To get him to understand that this was bigger than just a touch of reckless rioting and casual arson. And she loved the fact that she could call Sam "her agent." It was pretty much the truth, as things stood at the moment. *Agent* sounded so much better than *analyst.*

She walked over to the window—the old "David trick." Klaus the German remained quiet. She looked out across the Thames and let things hang for a second.

He started speaking as soon as she turned to face him.

"We need the count to come in and make a statement. We understand that he is working alongside a member of the British Secret Intelligence Service. An agent, you have to understand, who is not registered to work in Germany and who has no BfV-level clearance to operate independently. They both need to make themselves known."

As the German spoke, Jane had put her desk between herself and Klaus. Another power-play trick. She wore her sternest face.

"My agent is following a lead that she cannot afford to lose. Currently, she is sitting outside offices in Altglienicke

342

Strasse, Berlin, waiting—hopefully—for Gert Mauning to lead her to a warehouse where members of *die Kirche des weißen Kreuz* are holding a member of your royal family." She paused for effect. "With the clear intent of murdering a German countess. *If* they haven't done so already. Has the local Munich *polizei* been in touch yet to say she is missing?" It wasn't a question that Jane waited to be answered. "My staff passed my agent's phone details to your team this morning. Both she and I would be delighted if someone from the BfV would get in touch with her and there could be some form of handover. In the meantime, she is not going to lose Mauning by sloping off to a police station in Berlin." She softened her tone. "You must understand that?"

Klaus had turned his whole body to face Jane, moving his chair as he did. He was nodding.

"I'm sorry. I was unaware that your agent had passed her phone number through this morning. One of my team will get in touch. And Jane, you have to understand that our constitution and laws make it difficult to pursue individuals, to intercept *handys*, sorry, mobiles, to search premises, and similar. Our covert forces are very closely regulated."

Jane headed back across to the small table.

"My agent's view is that Mauning will kill the countess in the next twenty-four hours. If you know where *die Kirche*'s warehouse is, I strongly suggest you pursue legal authority to get eyes on. If you don't know where it is, then my agent will lead you there. Isn't that fair?"

Oberwachtmeister Klaus Homberg nodded.

"I need to make a phone call to Berlin. Is the room secure?"

I give up.

"Yes, of course. I'll get us some more coffee."

Chapter Eighteen

One Kilometre North of Shabwah, Yemen

Click, click, click. Kevin's Canon camera worked hard to keep up with the demand for his shots.

"He's moving from right to left, across the courtyard now," Martin said. He was watching through his binos while Kevin operated the camera.

"Do you think it's Sahef?" Kevin asked. He couldn't make out the man, as the image blurred as he swung the camera slowly left to keep the target in the centre of the small screen.

"Too far from here to say. But your shots should do him much better justice," replied Martin.

The camera was at maximum optical zoom, currently at times-thirty. Kevin knew that subsequent digital enlargement, even on the camera's small screen, should enable a very clear view of the man in the shot.

"Hang on," Kevin said under his breath. "He's unlocked a door and gone into a room on the bottom right of the courtyard. Have you got him?"

"Yup. He's left the door open."

Both their gazes were fixed on the developing scene that was just under a kilometre away. Kevin knew that catching sight of Tony James was always going to be a long shot. He was incarcerated, and unless his captors needed to move him from his cell, he would stay put—if he was even in one of the farm buildings. But having Sahef on film was as good as halfway to saying that James was in the same location. Somewhere.

"You keep eyes on; I'll go and have a look at what I've got."

Kevin dragged himself and his camera off the ridge. Putting his torso between the intense sun and the small screen, he flipped through the images he had just taken. The best one was where the Arab-looking man was halfway across the compound and had glanced in the camera's direction. It was in perfect focus. He expanded it so just the man's face was visible. It was a good, clear shot.

He had brought with him a green A5 Nyrex folder in his holdall, which was among a pile of rucksacks and equipment stuck beside a rock at his feet. He reached for the holdall and took out the folder. In it, slid between multiple plastic inserts, he had paper photographs of the main Daesh players and a couple of Tony James. He leafed through the three images he had of Sahef and compared them with the face on his Canon's screen.

It was remarkable. The man on the camera was definitely the man in his folder. The likeness was uncannily sharp. He was even wearing the same-colour thawb and keffiyeh. Kevin really couldn't tell them apart. *Fantastic.*

He turned to face up the hill. Martin's boots were a few feet from him.

"Martin?" Quiet, but forceful.

"Yup?"

"It's definitely him. One hundred per cent certain. I'm going to get my Iridium out and send the details to London." He was already playing with the secure satellite phone. His camera was set up to Bluetooth the images to the Iridium. A few lines of text and the images would be on their way.

"No you're not! Up here now with your camera! Quickly!" Martin was insistent.

Kevin dropped everything and scrambled to the top of the hill, immediately placing the camera down, its small, bendy-legged tripod lifting it just off the dirt.

"It's James. Sahef is leading him from the room into the centre of the compound. I'm sure it's him." Martin was talking at a rapid pace, his binos pushed hard against his face.

Click, click, click. Kevin focused the camera. Click, click, click, click.

"Where's he taking him?" Kevin asked, knowing that there was no way Martin would know the answer.

"He's not. He's leading him very slowly around the compound. Like a horse in a manège. He's exercising him." Martin's last sentence was laced with incredulity. "I don't get it. It's like he's keeping him fit."

They both watched the Arab and the white man. The Arab leading, and the white man, a hesitant follower, parading around the compound. Another Arab had come out into the courtyard with a video camera. He started taking clips of the activity.

Kevin got plenty of snapshots of the bearded Captain Tony James as he staggered around the square. He was dragging one leg, his shoulders were hunched, and at one point he tripped and almost fell. What was extraordinary, but difficult to be sure of from this distance, was that it appeared Sahef was being gentle with James. He led him by a rope that was tied round James's hands, but he didn't drag him. He shepherded him, much like a proud Crufts competitor would lead a prize dog. It was shameful, but in some obtuse way, touching.

"It's as London said in the report of a couple of days ago—Sahef is showboating James. A monkey on an organ. And I could think of a number of other sickening metaphors." Martin's voice trailed off at the end. Kevin kept his opinion of how he felt Sahef was treating James to himself.

Click, click, click.

"OK, Martin. I'm going to get these to London. The remaining question is, what should we do next?"

Kevin didn't expect an answer. He left his colleague with his binos pressed against his face. He was sure he heard Martin mumble, "I can't believe they're doing this. The fuckers."

Within a minute all of the photos had been transferred to the Iridium phone, and Kevin penned the following accompanying text: *"Sahef and James. Looks like James is*

being exercised. Another Arab also there taking video clips.
Are very exposed here. Send instructions. K + M."

He pressed "Send" and crawled back up to the ridgeline.

FBI Briefing Room, Abilene, Texas

Albin was sitting toward the back of the room. He reckoned there must be close to fifty folks at the briefing. Up front was Special Agent Nick Rafferty, his boss. This was his show, and Albin was the boss's driver. He was very proud of that. Albin wasn't an agent, nor was he on the firearms or technical side. He just drove the fantastic black Ford Bronco pickup. Got the boss to the right place at the right time and he drove well, even if he was relatively new to the job. "It's my anniversary coming up, Mamma," he had said to his mother at breakfast this morning. "One year next week. I get a pay raise, you know!"

He spat his baccy pinch into a tissue he carried in his pocket and looked again round the room. At the beginning of the briefing, his boss had said that this was the largest joint operation in Texas for over ten years. You don't say! There were six FBI agents. Two local—one was his boss. And four had come down from Washington to help out. There were two firearms teams who, his boss had said, would stay "tooled up, but out of sight" unless required. Earlier, Albin had asked to look in the back of their white Dodge van just before they'd started the briefing. He'd never seen so much hardware! He lost count of the number of M48s and MP5s. He spotted an M72LAN and a couple of Uzi 9 mms. He was pleased that they were on his side.

There was a media team from the FBI technical wing. Their job was to record the operation—he was glad he was wearing a clean checked shirt. Media were also "standing by to corral reporters like steers!"; he loved that joke from his boss. There were a couple of national TV channels; they would be held some distance back and only called forward should there be a story.

His boss had then introduced the three members of the IRS—geeks and boffins in Albin's eyes. That's when he had struggled to stay focused. They and an FBI lawyer were responsible for the document and computer search across the whole premises. He wasn't great with computers and always admired anyone who could get them to work properly—he should have studied harder in high school. Important, but plain dull. That was his view. And finally, at the back of the room with him, wearing big hats and chewing just as much baccy, were a couple of teams of state troopers, four members of the local sheriff's department, and a first-aid section from the city hospital. He couldn't count them all, but with drivers 'n' all, it was close to forty. Maybe fifty. The parking lot had more cars, jeeps, and pickups than the local mall. All that was missing was the National Guard! *Were they on call?*

It was going to be one helluva show.

"OK then, folks, to summarise." His boss was still talking. He was *so* good at that. Albin was always impressed when his boss spoke in front of people.

"You've all been issued maps and diagrams. At fifteen hundred hours, Samantha, the media rep, Jim, and I"—he was pointing at the tall special agent from Washington—"will leave the holding area at the parking lot at Abilene. Unless you get a call to stay firm, I want the second Bureau car, one state trooper vehicle, and the local law to follow at 15.10 hours. Sort that out among yourselves. Your job is backup, with a little bit of menace—flashing lights, but no sirens."

Albin's boss pressed a button on a laptop. The projected image, which until then had been the FBI logo, changed to an aerial view of the church's real estate.

"You've all seen this and have copies. If we get no trouble, and I'm not expecting any, I'll call the rest of you forward and we'll break into the teams we agreed: blue, green, red, yellow, and black. Your allocated search areas are shown by the boundaries displayed on the map. We search everything; leave no stone unturned. And with sunset estimated for 20.45 hours, we don't have that much time. I do not, repeat, *do not* want to come back and have to do this again. Are we clear?"

Albin joined the room with a resounding, "Yessir!"

"Any questions?"

"Special Agent Rafferty?" It was one of the state troopers from the back.

"Yes, sir," was Rafferty's response.

"What do we do if one of the perps decides to make a run for it?"

Albin noticed his boss give out an audible sigh.

"First, they're not all 'perps.' We understand that one or two members of the church might be undertaking some criminal activity. Our job today is to search, *only*." He reinforced *only*. "It is possible that, in light of all of us turning up, one or two folk on site might decide to flee the premises. Unless you get a direct order from a Bureau agent, or firearms have already been used, then you are to let anyone who wants to leave, leave. Is that clear?"

"Yessir." There was some murmuring at the back of the room following the clarification.

"OK. Time check. I make it 11 . . . 38 precisely. Meet you all back here at 14.30. And I don't need to remind you that this is a closed operation!"

SIS Headquarters, Vauxhall, London

Jane was quickly penning an e-mail to the JIC covering four of the photos they had just got through from Kevin and Martin. It was the best possible news. If the SF could get to the farm buildings, they could rescue Tony James *and* take out Sahef. *All in one shot.* But there was a torrent of water to flow under that bridge between now and then.

The chief had reluctantly ordered Kevin and Martin to

remain in position for the time being. It was the only call. If the SF were to launch, they would need to have up-to-the-minute confirmation that James was "still in the building." To make that happen, either the two SIS men would have to stay put for as long as it took, or the SF might be able to fly in an early recce party to relieve Kevin and Martin in situ. It would be on the JIC's recommendation, assuming that Brigadier Alasdair's team was able to get some men there quick enough. The chief could veto any decision to delay the SIS men's extraction, but she thought it was unlikely that he would.

Her scant knowledge of SF operations led her to think that the earliest they would attempt a rescue would be tomorrow night. Tonight, just hours away, was too tight a call, but tomorrow night could well be too late for the SIS men. It was a dilemma.

Every second counts. She rushed to finish her work. The e-mail was straightforward:

Dear JIC members,

See attached four photos. They were taken today at 12.15 Zulu, 16.15 Local. They are all of the farm buildings at Shabwah. Photo 1 is Sahef. Photos 2, 3, and 4 are of Sahef "exercising" Captain James. The second Arab in photo 3 is a man taking video footage of the exercising.

As you know, we have two agents in overwatch position in Shabwah. They are currently still in location, but they are very exposed. The chief would like them relieved in place as soon as possible. His view is that they must leave overnight tonight.

Advise please.

Jane Baker.

Jane knew she had overplayed the final sentence and those weren't the chief's words. But she had to do what she could to expedite Kevin and Martin's extraction. She pressed "Send" and then looked at her watch: it was 4.10 p.m.

She had her team meeting in twenty minutes. In an ideal world, Mike, somehow or other, would have got the Doughnut to get ears on the Shabwah farm buildings. With phone taps in place, it might allow Kevin and Martin to get the hell out of there without the need for the SF to take over. But her guess was that there was no way the JIC would sanction an SF attack of the farm buildings without *guaranteed* intelligence that James was in the building. Covering a mobile phone, or landline or two, probably wasn't going to be good enough. She had real sympathy with that view. But that didn't help the very exposed Kevin Boswell and Martin Crane.

Altglienicke Strasse, Berlin, Germany

It was almost dark. They hadn't seen Mauning come out of the building, nor had the Merc moved from its parking place. Sam's friend Frank had kept in touch, and his view was that Mauning's phone was still in the office block. That all seemed to indicate that Mauning had remained at work. But, as Sam had said, "He's an ex-Stasi agent. I wouldn't bet on anything." That hadn't helped Wolfgang's disposition. Nor had Sam's further interrogation on the Köln affair. He'd pushed back any additional questions, and she'd finally given up.

It had been a tense day. They had been given one or two odd looks from passers-by, but nobody seemed overly concerned. Sam had kept them supplied with rubbish food—he'd never drunk so much coffee. Thankfully he'd been able to sprint to Starbucks, relieve himself in the men's room, and get back without incident. And they'd both managed to get some sleep.

It was now getting cold, and, in a late light-bulb moment, he had checked the Kadett's fuel gauge. He reckoned they had no more than seventy kilometres left in the tank. That would have to do.

When they had both been awake, they hadn't spoken of much. There wasn't a great deal to say. The atmosphere in the car was so different from that of just twenty-four hours ago. Then, they couldn't have been closer. But now . . . ? Sam had to appreciate that things had changed.

Anyhow, he preferred the silence to needless talking. Sam seemed to understand that.

They had one moment of boredom relief when Sam's phone received a text from someone in the BfV. Sam's boss had told her to expect them to contact her. The text was noncommittal. She had read it out.

"It says: *'We are currently obtaining legal authority to pursue Herr Mauning. We expect to have this in the next four hours, at which point we would aim to meet up and take responsibility for the operation. Herr Vintner.'*"

Sam had been derisory at that point until she realised that she was having a go at a well-respected arm of the government to a nonplussed German citizen. Then she had shut up.

These British. They always think they know best.

Wolfgang checked his watch. It was five thirty. Sam had received the text just after two. What if Mauning appeared now? They'd follow him, of course. Where would that leave the BfV?

Maybe she was right about them. Maybe they were slow and bureaucratic. Mind you, the way he felt at the moment, nobody got a fair hearing.

He hadn't been able to get his mother out of his mind, no matter how hard he tried. He had thought through all the possible scenarios, but the only one that took hold was the one where she was dead. What would he do then? She was only fifty-eight! He needed her for at least another twenty years. His father had been his rock. His inspiration. His mentor. But his mother was his safety blanket, his comfort. He felt that she never judged him. He could have done pretty much anything, and she would have approved. More importantly, she was always there for him. A soft cushion on parquet flooring. *There was no other woman like her.*

Since last night, if nothing else, *that* had become clear to him.

As a result, he couldn't stop himself from ruminating over the events of the last ten days. Trying to establish fault. Apportion blame. Had Sam Green taken him here? Or was it all down to him? Was he constantly looking for approval from his dead father? And had that led him to this madness? Was that it?

His thought process was interrupted.

"He's coming out!" Sam whispered. "Look!"

Wolfgang shook himself and saw what Sam had just seen. He didn't start the car. Fuel was precious, so he would wait until the last moment.

Mauning got into the Merc—it was dark so they couldn't see what he was carrying. It took him a few minutes to sort himself out. Then the car switched on its lights, backed out of the parking slot, and drove around the car park. Seconds later it pulled out into the road ahead of them.

Wolfgang started the Kadett and followed on. What was immediately apparent was that they were heading east, not back toward Mauning's farm—that was in the west. Mauning was going somewhere else. *To the warehouse?* Thankfully, the Mercedes kept a steady speed, and the Kadett was easily able to match its pace. Tailing in the near dark was trickier than it had been this morning when it was light. He tried to keep at least one car between him and the Merc. But when a car in front turned off and the Merc stopped at some lights, they got within a few feet of its rear bumper. At that point, Wolfgang thought he saw Mauning check his rear-view mirror. *Did our eyes meet?* Surely it was too dark. He let the Merc get ahead and worked harder at keeping his distance.

Sam was tapping away on her phone.

"Letting work know what's happening?" Wolfgang asked without taking his eyes off the road.

"Yep. Still nothing from the BfV. Oh well." She pressed her screen and put her phone back in her pocket. "Just as a reminder, Wolfgang. When we get to the warehouse, my rifle is the top one—that's the one I used the other day. Happy?"

He didn't need to be reminded. He nodded his answer to Sam's question.

The Merc drove on. The Kadett followed. In the dark and one car back, it was difficult to see clearly what Mauning was doing. Wolfgang was pretty sure that he saw him making a phone call.

"Can you see that?" Wolfgang asked.

"What?"

"Isn't he making a phone call?"

Sam leant forward and looked hard.

"Sorry. Can't see from here."

"I'm sure he was on the phone."

Maybe not.

How long before we run out of fuel? He checked the fuel gauge. The yellow warning light had come on.

"Scheiße!"

"What?" Sam asked.

"We have about forty kilometres of fuel left. Let's hope he stops soon."

Sam didn't reply. She was too focused on the Merc.

They were out of central Berlin now, driving down a road with old, communist-style, high-rise flats on both sides. Thousands of apartments were built in the 1950s to house postwar East Germans who had come in from the countryside looking for work. They were depressing and, with the darkening skies, added to his feeling of foreboding. For the first time he felt his initial drive and excitement knocked by a touch of fear.

In the distance Wolfgang made out an industrial complex.

There were huge gas cylinders and what looked like a petrochemical plant. Flames shot out of the top of a tall, thin metallic chimney, burning off unwanted gas.

"He's turning right." Sam noted.

Wolfgang gave the Merc a few seconds and then followed it. He could make out the taillights about a hundred yards ahead. The minor road led on and on, dissecting factory complexes and large brick-style warehouses. *We're getting close.*

"Warehouses," Wolfgang said under his breath, stating the obvious. As he did, Sam quickly turned around and brought one of the Brownings forward. She rested it on her legs like she was sitting on the porch of an American ranch. *She's good.* Cool as a cucumber. *I'm so glad I'm with you, Sam Green.* With his stomach turning amid growing anxiety, he meant it. He also knew he was a fickle so-and-so.

The Mercedes indicated left and turned off the road into one of the industrial complexes. Wolfgang gave it some room. Craning forward and looking left where the Merc had turned, he made out a couple of brick-style four-storey warehouses that were immersed in darkness and shadows. Behind them, more brightly lit, were stacks and stacks of shipping containers, piled eight to ten high.

"Turn off your lights." Sam said.

He did as he was told.

"Poke your nose around the corner—we have to keep eyes on."

Wolfgang pulled halfway across the road and looked for the Merc's taillights. The vehicle was still driving further into the complex, now maybe fifty metres away. It was dark around the buildings, the light from the container park shielded by the warehouses. *Once I'm in the shadow of the warehouses, the Kadett will be hidden.*

He accelerated around the corner and into the lee of the first warehouse. Looking ahead, the Merc's lights were further away now. *How far down does this place reach?*

He drove on slowly. Sam had wound down her window.

The cold air caught their breath, turning it to mist. The Mercedes kept driving on.

Just ahead was a gap between two of the towering redbrick warehouses. A shaft of dull light turned blackness into brown. It wasn't like a spotlight, but neither was it shadow. *Is it bright enough that we'll be spotted crossing the gap?* Should they make a dash for it? Then, ahead of them, the Merc's lights turned right, moving out of sight.

"Go for it!" Sam shouted through her teeth.

Wolfgang put his foot down. The Kadett responded, accelerating forward. But progress didn't last long. As they reached the middle of the gap, someone unleashed the dogs of war.

The crunching sound of metal on metal was so shocking, he couldn't stop himself from flinching; his left hand involuntarily released the steering wheel. The momentum of the spin forced him against the driver's door. The immediate excruciating pain in his wounded arm made him yelp. Sam, who was wearing a seatbelt, still managed to smash into him—her rifle flew in front of his face and exited through his side window, which broke into a thousand pieces. How it missed his head was a mystery.

They spun through three hundred and sixty degrees, maybe more—all the time he felt consciousness draining from him. Something was digging into his leg, something sharp and uncomfortable. As he spun the pain in his leg grew, and as his world reeled out of control, it was difficult to say which of his limbs hurt more. Both his leg and his arm screamed out for attention.

The turning movement subsided, but it was replaced by a dawning sensation of terror. *This was no accident.* Above all of this, the crash, the spin, and the now intolerable pain, he heard Sam shout, "Get out, Wolfgang!"

He tried to respond. But then, all was peace.

Church of the White Cross, Abilene, Texas, USA

As Albin drove the Ford at a very sedate pace up the gravel drive, they arrived atop a rise, and there, in front of them, was the main church about three hundred metres away. It had been built on a small mound, a white clapboard building with a single tower and red-tiled steeple. It was pretty. The church was surrounded by a group of buildings. The biggest and most impressive was new-looking, concrete, brick and glass, and single-storey. It was where the gravel track led them. A brand new billboard made it clear they were approaching a serious Christian establishment: *"The Church of the White Cross. God welcomes those who repent!"*

If that was the entrance test, Albin wasn't sure he would be welcome among the congregation.

His boss Jim, the Washington agent, and Samantha, the FBI media rep, had all remained quiet on the drive from Abilene. By the time they approached the main entrance to the offices, Albin would have described the atmosphere in the Ford as "tense."

He stopped the black pickup directly in front of the entrance. His boss had made it clear that he wasn't to park in a designated car space, but "leave it right out front." That's what he did. He *always* did as he was instructed. He *always* did it right.

Without any discussion, the team of three got out and made their way to the main door of the administration building—Albin had just noticed a sign by the door, which gave the place a title. There was a single, tiled step leading to a double glass door, which the three of them entered. Albin stayed in the Ford with the engine running. The engine's cooling fan hummed into life—the dash was reading eighty-five degrees in the sunshine. Albin was comfortable, though. The aircon worked beautifully, and it was certainly a good deal less than eighty-five in the cab.

The minutes ticked along. He couldn't see into the building, even though he bent his head forward. The glass doors appeared to lead into a small lobby, but he wasn't sure. The bottom halves of the doors weren't see-through, and above the smoked glass, all he could make out was a ceiling fan. There was certainly no sign of his team who had just gone in.

Albin drummed his fingers on the dashboard, chewing away at a new piece of baccy. The main radio clicked, and he expected some words to follow. But there was nothing. It was all eerily quiet. *That's good, isn't it?* If his boss needed support, he would be calling for it. He was sure of that.

He checked the dashboard clock: 14.37. Three minutes and the main team would be here. Red and blues flashing away. Just like in the films.

Wait. What's that? Albin spotted a window to the left of the glass doors being opened. He couldn't be sure . . .

But now he was. The barrel of a rifle emerged from the gap. *Holy shit!* His eyes darted around, matching the speed of his rising heart rate. Then, on top of the admin building, he made out a man crawling on the roof. The man wore green fatigues and appeared to be carrying a weapon of some sort.

Holy shit! And now there was a second man on the roof. And a third? *This is all going belly-up. Shit! Shit!*

What should he do? *What should I do?* Albin was instantaneously caught between getting the hell out of there and, well, what exactly? He was unarmed, so couldn't storm the building. But running away—that was the wrong thing to do. Wasn't it?

Impulse didn't wait for any further discussion.

Albin reached for the radio handset at the same time as knocking the Ford into drive. He flattened the pedal to the floor, turning the wheel sharply with one hand, whilst pulling the handset to his mouth with his free hand. As gravel spewed from all four tyres he screamed into the mike, "AMBUSH! AMBUSH!"

As the Ford slung its back end around to align itself with the front wheels, which were heading back down the drive, sounds and noises like he had only ever heard in a war movie burst into his brain. A hail of bullets sprayed the Ford, the rear window shattered, the front windscreen splintered into see-through crazy-paving—he had to smash a hole so he could see where he was going. The padding on the passenger seat split open, as if it had a will of its own. *Shit! That's a bullet.* Albin involuntarily brought his knees together to protect what was important to him.

Other pieces of the Bronco took hits with accompanying pings. He twisted and turned the Ford, snaking it down the drive, trying to save his life, which he knew was never more than an inch from ending. Steam was now billowing out from under the bonnet of the Ford, and the driver's side window was no longer there.

Ping, ping, ping! *Where did those bullets go?*

As he launched the Ford up the rise, he was met by the lead vehicle of the second tranche of the search. It was a state trooper patrol car.

Except soon it wasn't. As it hit the brow and showed the underside of its radiator grill to Albin, an almighty whoosh flew past his left ear. The whoosh was followed by a trail of dark smoke, that was pursuing instant death to its target. The patrol car appeared to stop and then lift, as if it had been hit by the club of a giant. The car, its blue and red lights announcing the second wave, took off like an aeroplane at the end of a runway. Albin saw a firework of spinning, black undercarriage and blue and red flashing lights as the patrol car twisted in the air accompanied by sparks and shrapnel. He was at the scene a second later, rounds still hitting the Ford. Somehow the bullets miraculously missed him. He turned the steering wheel violently left to avoid the airborne patrol car—which was on its way back down to earth. At that point, the Ford hit a large rock or something similar. It was now Albin's turn to cartwheel in four tons of pickup. Airbags blew and pinging noises ricocheted around him as the Ford continued to take incoming fire as it rolled. He was in his mamma's washing machine. But the smell wasn't detergent. It was chaos and death.

And then it stopped, as abruptly as it started. Just a gently rocking movement, the dust from the airbags, and no gunfire. The Ford was on its tyres, but it was no longer the vehicle that he knew. He shook his head—he was all right, wasn't he? There seemed to be a lull in the battle. *Am I out of view?*

In front of him was a convoy of static vehicles, patrol lights flashing: the second tranche. He snapped his head backward to look behind through the open gap where there was once a rear window. All he could see was a mound of grass and beyond that, only sky. The Ford had travelled far enough to be out of sight of the admin building. *Am I safe?*

Albin closed his eyes, exhaled, and shook his head.

"Hey, son, are you all right?"

Albin opened his eyes. It was one of the local police officers.

"Yeah. Yeah. Think so. Shaken a bit. What's happening?"

The policeman had now been joined by a Fed. They were both wearing Kevlar vests. He should really get one of those if they did this again. As he looked around, everyone was out of their vehicles. Men were crawling up to the skyline; others were on their radios. The lead state trooper vehicle was at the very top of the ridge, upside down, flames and smoke lapping at its black and white paintwork. Albin saw a man in police uniform crawling to reach the vehicle.

Shit! Is this really happening?

"What went on back there?" the Fed asked.

Albin was brought back to the here and now.

He dithered.

"The team went in as planned. Err, you know—my boss, the Washington Fed, and media. And they didn't come out. And then . . ." All of a sudden he felt very emotional. *Hold it together, Albin. Come on!* "Then I saw a gun at the window and two or three men on the roof. I just tried to get away."

He drifted again, looking around, trying to take it all in. He looked away from the two men who were standing there, questioning him, by his nonexistent window. Around him, others were barking orders at men wearing helmets and flak jackets. Further away to his right, the crawling man in uniform had just about made it to the upturned state trooper car on the brow of the hill. Albin noticed that the engine compartment, which was facing away from the direction of the church, was burning hard, licks of flames coming out from where the front left wheel used to be. *That could go up any minute.*

Crack! A single shot. The crawling man's body lifted and fell; then it was motionless. Everyone else ducked. Albin flinched involuntarily. *Shit!* It was like something from *Armageddon*. He was playing an extra's role to Bruce Willis. It was unreal. He stared at the man who was no longer crawling up the hill, and his stomach gave an involuntary lurch. He couldn't stop himself. He threw up all over the steering wheel and onto his pants. He felt the two men by his window reel, as if to avoid the vomit. Thankfully it had all stayed in the car. They needn't have worried.

He was shivering now. Uncontrollably. Something was happening to him.

To add to his embarrassment, a woman in a green uniform had just turned up. She must have been a medic. The woman pushed the two men out of the way. She was elderly. Perhaps his mamma's age? She had a nice smile.

"Come on, son. It's time we got you out of here. Any pain? Can you move your legs and your arms?"

Albin tried. Yes, they all worked.

"I'm OK. Just mighty cold."

"That'll be the shock. You'll be fine."

She tried to open the door, but it was so badly dented it stuck. Between her and the Fed they managed to open it— the creaking sound hurt Albin's ears. The woman in green reached for the seatbelt buckle and undid it. He tried to stop himself from falling out of the Ford, but he couldn't. His body had turned to a sort of jelly. She held him as he fell.

"There, there, son. Everything's going to be OK now."

"What have we got, Frank?" Jane was standing by Frank's shoulder looking at a fairly detailed map of eastern Berlin on his main screen. Oberwachtmeister Klaus was standing by Frank's other shoulder. *At least he's taken his raincoat off.*

"Both phones, Mauning's and Sam's, came to a halt here."

Frank was pointing to what looked like an industrial complex. Jane reckoned that it was twenty kilometres outside central Berlin. There was no electronic indication on Frank's screen to say that the phones were still bleeping where he had his finger, although she did spot a red dot moving westward, back through the centre of Berlin.

"And?"

"Well, that's the strange thing. Sam's phone stopped communicating with us, at"—Frank looked down at a notebook—"17.45; that's 18.45 central European time."

"Why?" Jane was impatient. Sam's phone not working wasn't good news. She didn't have a great feeling about this.

"Turned off, out of batteries, broken, or smashed?" Frank gave a list of options from which to pick.

The last one is my bet.

"Go on, Frank."

"Mauning's phone remained at the spot, which is an old industrial complex next to a container depot—I've Googled it to be sure—for another forty-five minutes." Frank twisted his head to speak directly to the Oberwachtmeister. "I've relayed all of this to your team in Berlin, sir. They're up to speed." He turned to face Jane again. "Then Mauning's phone left, just ten minutes ago. As you can see, it's now here." Frank was pointing at the red dot, which had travelled another centimetre to its left.

Jane was about to ask a supplementary when Karl started talking in German into his mobile phone. Her French was adequate and her Arabic pretty sharp, but her German wasn't great. She picked out very little. She focused back in on

Frank's screen.

Where are you, Sam Green?

Karl finished his conversation and closed down the phone.

"We have a team at the gates of the industrial complex now. They will move in ten minutes. I hope they're not too late."

I think they probably are.

Chapter Nineteen

*Disused Warehouse Complex, Altglienicke Industrial Estate,
Berlin*

Sam's teeth were chattering uncontrollably. Her whole body
was a spasm of shivers. She was bitterly cold. The metal of
the shipping container was acting as a heat sink for any
warmth she and Wolfgang generated. She had suffered from
hypothermia before and had survived. She recognised the
tell-tale signs: the lethargy; the lack of focus; the clamminess
of her skin. She knew that at some point in the future, unless
their situation changed dramatically, she would become
delirious. All the heat her body could generate would be
directed to keep her vital organs warm. Her brain wasn't as
important as her heart and lungs; it was a minor organ in the
fight for survival over debilitating cold. Starved of warmth,
the brain would shut down. And then her organs would give
up one by one, as her involuntary muscle spasms failed to
generate the heat needed to overcome what she was giving
away. It was only a matter of time.

She had done her best for Wolfgang. He was out of it. It
was a combination of the Kadett taking an almighty
sideswipe that, from what she had seen and latterly felt in the
blackness of the container, had punctured a hole in his leg.
The horror of what happened next had finished him off.

Once they had been thrown in the container he had
slumped to the floor, spent. Sam knew immediately that if
Mauning and his merry men didn't come back soon and
finish them off, the seeping cold and their leaching metal cell
would beat them to it. At the back of the container,
surrounded by suffocating darkness, she had fumbled around
and found some old wooden pallets. She counted nine. There
was nothing else. She lay three in a row next to Wolfgang
and, with a Herculean effort, had lifted him onto the

makeshift bed so that at least his body was off the metal floor. He had groaned as she moved him, but hadn't uttered a sound since.

She had touched his new wound. It felt as though the gear lever had ruptured his thigh. It didn't seem as bad as the wound in his arm had been, but it was bleeding; her fingers were wet and sticky. She had pulled back his jumper and ripped the arm off his shirt, using her teeth to start the tear. At first, she thought she might need to apply a tourniquet to the upper reaches of his leg. That would stop the flow of blood in its tracks. But it would also eventually kill the foot and the rest of thc leg as the blood failed to carry out its normal duties. So she decided to opt for a simple pressure dressing. She used her bra, which at least was reasonably clean, and placed it on top of the wound. She then wrapped the ripped sleeve around the leg and tied it tightly.

She'd checked her watch and every half an hour had felt the dressing for blood. The last time she had touched it there was a little dampness, but she seemed to have stemmed the flow. Wolfgang was unlikely to die from loss of blood. He might, however, just perish from a combination of freezing temperatures and a broken heart.

The horror that followed the car crash was unspeakable. It was the most malicious act Sam had ever witnessed.

She had tried to get away from the Kadett after it had been impaled by a forklift truck. It had smacked into them as they had attempted to cross the gap between the warehouses. The moment she had stepped out of the car, a man had knocked her down. She had no idea what had happened, except she now had a huge bruise on the back of her head. The next half hour or so had been hazy. A blur. She remembered someone searching her; her mobile and wallet were taken out of the pockets in her trousers. They had manhandled her into the second warehouse; she wasn't sure if they had dragged her or if she had been carried. The next thing she remembered was being thrown onto a concrete floor in a large open space. They hadn't climbed any stairs, so she assumed they were still on the bottom floor. It was a large open area, maybe as big as a school gymnasium, but segregated by square brick columns rising up to the ceiling. Two opposing walls had windows—she had tried to check to see if they were locked, but she couldn't make anything out. And the other two walls were wholly brick, with a couple of wooden doors breaking up the monotony of red.

A minute or so later, Wolfgang was flung down next to her, and the man who had thrown him stood watch over both of them. Wolfgang was unconscious. Sam had spotted the leg wound, which looked like a puncture—blood oozing from it like ketchup from an upturned bottle. She had tried to say something to Wolfgang, but she had been slapped across the face by the man. *Bastard.* The slap was hard enough to ensure that she wouldn't do that again.

Sam looked out for an escape, but she saw no possibilities. As far as she could see, there were four men in the large room, one of whom was Mauning. She recognised a second from the church's congregation, but not the other two. All of them had rifles slung, except the man looking over them. His rifle was pointing in Sam's general direction.

What caught her attention, but for all the wrong reasons, was that to the edge of the room was a crate—the only furniture in the huge space. The crate was partially covered with a decorative piece of purple cloth. And on the cloth was a handgun, just like the one that had been blessed in the barn. That didn't bode well for either of them.

Over the next minute or so, two of the men had laid out a large green tarpaulin, maybe twenty metres square. It was so big that they had to turn the corners up to get it to fit between the brick stacks. In another universe, it would have been a fairly humorous moment. But not now. Not with the ritual gun in the room. And then they laid out three chairs on top of the tarpaulin, the vertices of a triangle. Facing each other. Mauning stood in the centre of the tarpaulin and appeared to undertake some form of religious ceremony, as if he was blessing the space. It was, she guessed, in Hebrew. It was weird. And it scared the hell out of her.

Sam knew then that she was facing her death. She got that two of the chairs were for her and Wolfgang—but she had no idea who the third was for. Maybe Mauning would sit in one and take pot shots at them from a distance? Anything was possible.

Soon enough, Sam found out that she was right about the first part. After a babble of German from Mauning, two of the men lifted Wolfgang onto one of the chairs. He gave no resistance as he slumped into the seat, his head lolled back, barely staying upright. Then they lifted her by her arms and carried her across to the second chair.

She had thought that she might want to resist, to make a dash for it, at least die trying to escape what appeared to be her impending, cold-blooded killing. But some strange dignity came over her. She knew escape was completely futile. An unarmed woman against four men, carrying rifles and at least one handgun. This wasn't a film set; she wasn't Uma Thurman. So, rather than give these savages the pleasure of watching her squirm, she knew straight away that she would face her death like Anne Boleyn. She would be unflinching. Stoic.

But then the setup changed. Two new men—*shit, that makes six*—brought out someone who she immediately knew was Wolfgang's mother. Her legs and hands were tied and she was gagged. As soon as she saw Wolfgang, she turned hysterical. It took the two men all of their effort to drag her across the floor.

Sam's resolve snapped.

She saw a chance, or, more honestly, she just lost it and launched herself from her chair toward the two men, determined to make some gesture—to intervene in some way.

What she hadn't realised was that there was a stalker behind her. He'd obviously spotted her starting to move, and the next thing she knew she was on the floor, her legs having been taken out from under her by something, possibly a rifle.

As she raised herself to launch for a second time, a boot caught her in the stomach, and all the wind was forced out of her. Debilitating pain spread from side to side. At that point she was a rag doll. Good for nothing.

Back on her chair with "her man" holding her shoulder, she watched Wolfgang's mother being tied to the third chair. She jumped and pushed, so they hit her. First it was a slap across the face. But she had more spunk than that. She thrashed her head from side to side, trying to bite through her gag, her eyes out on stalks looking across at Wolfgang. The noises coming from her were those of a mother faced with the worst possible fate for her and her son, muffled by an inconveniently placed cloth. So this time, they hit her straight in the face with a rifle butt. As Wolfgang's mother's head snapped backward, Sam heard a crack. A bone had been broken, maybe a couple. Her head rolled about, blood pouring from her nose, her remonstrations stopped by a single blow. She was conscious and making a pathetic sobbing noise, but the will to fight had been smashed out of her.

Next their attention turned to Wolfgang. They had the simple treat of a bucket of water, which they threw over him. The slosh took away some of his delirium, and he slowly lifted his head. His eyes were glazed and his face etched with pain and tiredness. Sam couldn't tell if he recognised his mother, where they were, or what was happening.

Except . . .

. . . when Mauning took the pistol from the top of the crate and walked over to the countess. He aimed the gun at the back of her head, released the safety catch, and, with no hesitation and no further ceremony, blew her face off.

Walk, aim, shoot. Bang!

Death.

Wolfgang's whole body lurched as though the bullet had hit him. It might have been the ear-shattering noise of a pistol being fired in an enclosed space, the sound reverberating around the room for seconds afterward. Or, he had indeed recognised the despicable spectacle of his mother being slaughtered like a farm animal before his eyes. Whatever the case, immediately afterward, his head dropped again. He was gone.

As if in harmony with the horror, Sam couldn't stop herself from throwing up all over the tarpaulin-covered floor. She spat out bile and vomit, and then she retched some more. Next it would be the lining of her stomach.

Mauning walked toward Sam.

She knew it was her time. She was ready. She had cheated death twice before. First in Camp Bastion, Afghanistan, where she had held her insides in her hands through an opening in her stomach that shouldn't have been there. The second, having been drugged and then being left to die in an inferno in Kenema, Sierra Leone. Third time lucky. She didn't care. Not now. She might have a few days ago. That was before Wolfgang's demeanour had altered from knight in shining armour to, perhaps understandably, self-obsessed mummy's boy. It was a cruel comparison, but she was in no mood to be generous.

Now they could take her. Just as someone had taken Mum, Dad, Uncle Pete, and Chris. *My Chris*—how she missed him. How she now longed to join him.

Sam closed her eyes and waited for Nirvana.

Her waiting was shattered by a piercing, but daftly incongruous, polyphonic ringtone. *Was it "Super Trouper" by Abba?*

"Scheiße!"

Sam opened her eyes. Mauning had stopped midstride, pistol in hand. He reached into his pocket for his phone. He looked at the number, consternation spreading across his face.

"Halten sie fest," he shouted. Her stalker held her tightly by the shoulder.

Sam was lost, angry, and very tearful. *What's so important that it stops my execution? Come on, you bastards. Get it over with!*

369

The only words she picked up from Mauning's German conversation with his phone were *Ja!* and *Kurt*. It all meant nothing to her.

Mauning put his phone away and barked orders at the men in the warehouse. Sam was surprised to be manhandled from her chair and dragged toward the door they had come in through. As she was unceremoniously pulled away, she glanced behind to see Wolfgang slung over a man's shoulders a few steps behind her. And, most pitiful of all, his mother being wrapped up in the tarpaulin. *No mess. No evidence. Clever.*

And now she and Wolfgang were here in the container. It had taken the thugs a couple of minutes to find the right one. It was an old and rusty-orange one, set back four or five rows from the front line. They were well and truly hidden. No one would hear her calling from this cell.

Sam checked her watch. It was one thirty in the morning. It was time to look over Wolfgang's wound. She had to find a routine. If she could survive another four hours it would start to get warmer, and then there might be some respite from this biting chill. She had been given a stay of execution. Again. For the third time. She needed to find the inner strength to make it through to another day.

She stood up, her legs wobbly.

I'll walk. Up and down. Down and up. Until I drop. Keep warm. Exercise. That's what I'll do. First though, I'll check on Wolfgang.

One Kilometre North of Shabwah, Yemen

It was dark on the hill and getting cold. It had been a long, nervous day. Kevin felt his phone vibrate. Keeping the glare of the screen within the confines of his jacket, he checked the SMS he'd just received: *"Charleston. We're at the Land Rover."*

Thank God, the cavalry has arrived. *OK, let's go.*

Over the past twelve hours there had been a slow stream of e-mail and SMS traffic between Kevin's Iridium and London. Early this morning the first order, "to stay put," was understandable—but worrying. He reckoned they had already outstayed their welcome.

If he thought their location on top of the hill was fragile, he was even more concerned about the Land Rover. It was well off any main road or even a track, but was visible from a wide angle if you looked hard enough. The Bedouin nomads were inquisitive people and attuned to things not being "just so" on their land. A white truck, thinly disguised as an extension to a piece of rock, wouldn't fool them. With the Bedouin kicking about, staying put into a further day was a real worry.

But that's what they'd been asked to do. The plan had developed throughout the day. Eventually, London had sent through a short set of instructions, a military Op Order, which included some code words. He didn't see the point in code words, as all of their communication devices were encrypted up the yin yang, but the army had its ways.

The long and the short of it was that an eight-man SAS recce party would be dropped in after dark that evening and rendezvous with them at the lookout. The SAS would then take responsibility for keeping eyes on and hold the position until the following night. Assuming James remained in the compound, a larger group of SAS would be helicoptered in and attack the farm buildings the next evening. That was about twenty-four hours from now.

As Kevin had read the Op Order, he'd asked himself the question, *Where does this leave us?*

And then he reached the bottom of the instruction:

7.b. Coord. SIS team to remain under command of C21B. They are to extract with C21B by hel. Veh to be left in situ. All sy eqpt to be either destroyed or taken with team.

That made sense, then? Kevin had assumed that once the SAS were in place, they'd make a dash for it back to Sana'a. But that didn't appear to be the plan. They would hang about for a further day and fly out with the army. Anything for a free helicopter ride.

Kevin tapped in a reply to the SMS: *"Am coming down now. Be with you in two minutes."*

"Martin!" A quiet call through a clenched jaw.

"Yes." A hushed reply from the OP on top of the hill.

"The SAS are here. I'm heading off the hill."

"OK. Mine's a beer."

Bloody hilarious.

Picking his way carefully off the hill, almost tripping over twice in the dark, Kevin made his way down to the Land Rover. There, with his weapon initially pointing at Kevin, he was met by a soldier.

"Charleston!"

OK. If I must.

"Quickstep!"

The soldier lowered his weapon.

"Hi. I'm Sergeant Barry Fawcett." In the dark, Kevin noticed that he was holding out his hand. He shook it.

"We have some provisions for you, and a couple of my boys will head up the hill and take over the OP, if you can lead the way. And . . ." The soldier seemed to be hesitant. "We're going to move the vehicle. Maybe a couple of clicks down the ridgeline. So if anyone sees it they won't necessarily link it to the OP. Can you empty it?"

Kevin thought for a second.

"It's got nothing in it that we need. By the way, I'm Kevin Boswell."

"Thanks, Kevin. Anything incriminating in the vehicle?"

Kevin wasn't very happy with being treated like a complete idiot.

"No. Everything with our metaphoric name on it is up on the hill."

"That's good. If you could get the keys out and give to

them to Jack over there." Kevin looked at an area of blackness, out of which appeared another soldier. *How do they do that?* "And then lead me up to the OP. That'll be great."

Kevin dug out the keys from his pocket and handed them to Jack the magician. He then turned to head up the hill.

SIS Headquarters, Vauxhall, London

Jane knew David wouldn't mind her using the pulldown in his office. The bed was comfortable, and with the bombproof glass in the outside windows, the room was quiet. But she couldn't sleep.

It had been a night of mixed emotions. By the time they had got confirmation that the SAS had linked up with Kevin and Martin, it was past two in the morning. With still no idea what had happened to Sam, she couldn't think about going home.

It was odd. She had deep professional interest in how the Op in Yemen went. She knew Martin Crane well and had met Kevin Boswell on a number of occasions. They were both outstanding field agents, and their work in Yemen was highly regarded. *And bloody dangerous.* So she was delighted and relieved that the small isolated team had met up with the Special Forces. Between them they should be able to handle themselves, and wouldn't it be wonderful if they came back with Captain Tony James?

Sam Green was a different story. She, or more fairly SIS, hadn't *used* Sam—well, not exactly. She was pretty sure of that. Sam was her own woman. Completely and utterly independent. Sam did what Sam wanted to do, and the SIS were lucky that, most of the time, it was in tune with what they had in mind. She had, with the help of her friend, the German noble, pieced together the top left-hand corner of a complex and significant jigsaw that was enabling the CIA to finish the bottom right. The Church of the White Cross, in

Jane's mind, was definitely central to some anti-Muslim, antimigration, anti–almost everything but religious adherence to some ancient script, worldwide conspiracy. And Sam, in a matter of days, had helped to bring that conspiracy into sharp relief.

Unfortunately, she had most likely paid for it with her life. In fact, no matter which way you looked at it, there was little hope that Sam was alive. After their late-night discussions with Klaus the German, she and Frank had war-gamed all the possible scenarios. None of the versions closed with Sam Green being alive.

That hurt Jane—so much. So much it ached.

At least now the BfV was up with the game. Klaus had said that they had raided the industrial area where the pings from Sam and Mauning's phones had come from. The Op went ahead at 8.10 the previous night. They had found nothing. Not a thing. Essentially, there were two large disused warehouses, one of which they assumed was "the warehouse" Sam had reported. They had searched them thoroughly, spending four hours on site, and they had found absolutely no evidence of foul play. With accompanying arc lights, they had searched the whole compound, including the adjacent container park. And had still found nothing.

Whilst the search was ongoing, they had picked up Mauning before he had gotten home. He was still in the BfV's custody, but he had given nothing away. Mauning's line was that he was a qualified quantity surveyor. He had visited the warehouse complex at the request of a client—with a view to renting the buildings. Karl had said that a friend of his had conducted the interview and wasn't happy with Mauning's testimony—there was something odd about the man—so they had decided to keep him in their cells for a further day while they did some more analysis.

Jane had pressed Karl for the BfV to go back to the warehouses in daylight. But Karl had refused to put the question to his team in Berlin. Searches of that magnitude were costly and manpower intensive. In any case, he assured

Jane that if there had been some evidence, they would have found it in the first place.

They had, however, left a small covert overwatch team on the warehouse complex that would stay in place for seventy-two hours.

At least that was something.

At that point, and with nothing else to hold Karl at Babylon, he had gone back to his hotel. He had left Jane his mobile number and had said she could call him at any time. If no new intelligence came through, he would leave for Berlin in the morning.

The chief had popped into her office late on. They had discussed Sam Green and had spoken about informing her next-of-kin, but decided better of it. Jane had dug out Sam's next-of-kin from the system after the chief had left her office. Sam had only designated one—and that was her uncle, Peter Green. Jane had held back tears at that point. There was no family to tell. *God that hurt.*

She looked for her watch, which was on a small table next to the bed. It was four thirty. She turned on the bedside light and reached for the TV remote. She'd catch the news.

The BBC was replaying the latest House of Commons vote to send a UK brigade to Syria. This was part of a growing list of coalition nations that were signing up to putting boots on the ground under the auspices of an emerging UN mandate. The sporadic and often uncoordinated air campaign had destroyed a good deal of Syrian territory and doubtless killed hundreds of so-called IS soldiers, along with countless civilians. But the terror campaign across Europe and the Far East hadn't abated. In many ways the threat of attack on UK soil had increased, making the intelligence agencies' job increasingly difficult. Syria was much more of a mess than before the air campaign had started. Various ceasefires had come and gone. In the end, it had been one bomb forward and two bombs back; and that was almost a literal interpretation.

Jane's firmly held view was that you could never kill

enough terrorists to get the job done. One dead martyr inevitably spawned two more. Any military campaign against Daesh needed a parallel line of action to deal with the underlying causes of why there were terrorists in the first place. And that always, in her mind, came back to Israel's role and position in the Middle East, exacerbated by well-intentioned, but ultimately failed, Western intervention in Iraq and Afghanistan. This thing was going to be with them for some time.

Jane switched to CNN. There was breaking news from Texas.

Oh my God!

The reporter was standing in the dark. Her backdrop was a large white sign, with the words "Church of the White Cross" on it. Jane turned the volume up.

"So, Michael, what we have from the local sheriff's office is that three officers have been killed and that there are an additional three suspected hostages in the church buildings which are"—the reporter turned so she could point in a general direction—*"about a mile in that direction. There must be a hundred or so law enforcement officers on the ground—you can see some behind me. We haven't got much more than the initial statement from the police chief. He reported that they went in to conduct a legal search of the premises, and three team members were taken hostage. After that, the state trooper vehicle was shot at by a bazooka of some kind. And that's when the two officers unfortunately lost their lives. A further officer died trying to reach the two troopers."*

"Hang on, Susan, we have some overhead shots now."

The screen switched to a helicopter view of the area. Much of the central picture was in darkness. A huge circle of vehicles with their lights on, further illuminated by red and blue flashing lights, surrounded a vast blackness. It was like a two-mile-wide, luminous daisy chain. Underneath the video footage was the banner "Another Waco?"

"What are the police saying is going to happen next?"

"Well, it's still relatively early days here, Michael. I've just seen another six vehicles arrive—big black trucks—I guess full of reinforcements, weaponry, and other equipment. At our last briefing, forty minutes ago, the police chief said that their priority was for the three law enforcement officers in the building. And, if this were a siege situation, for any civilians in the building who didn't want to be there of their own free will."

"And do we know how many civilians are in the buildings?"

"No, Michael, we don't. We've been told that, as well as a church, there are eight other buildings on the site, including some residential buildings. But there is no estimate as to the number of civilians who might be holed up behind me."

Jane pressed the "Mute" button.

Blimey.

She needed to phone the deputy director. But that would have to wait until he had had some chance to get some sleep. And she did need to check with Klaus the German, to see if there was any new intelligence on Sam Green from Germany.

Disused Warehouse Complex, Altglienicke Industrial Estate, Berlin

Sam felt the shower coming before she heard the tapping of raindrops on the side of the container. It had got warmer in the last couple of hours. She imagined cloud cover holding in the heat and a change of wind direction bringing in moist air, carrying with it a small, but discernible, rise in temperature. It was still bitterly cold, but as she trudged up and down the container, she no longer felt what was left of her body heat draining away.

At the front end of the container, their entrance point, was the smallest sliver of light where the doors at the top didn't quite meet. Anyone who wasn't awash with time probably wouldn't have noticed it. But she had plenty of time. Time to walk up and down the container one thousand five hundred and sixty-seven times.

"Sixty-eight!" she said as she hammered on the door where the tiny shaft of light had proclaimed daybreak.

She had done what she had set out to do. Walk until she dropped; she just hadn't dropped, yet. After the first ten or twelve laps of the container she added a twist to her regime. She would bang on the door every time she got to it, shouting the lap number at the top of her voice. If anyone was around, every twenty seconds or so they would hear her cry.

The fact that it was daylight—actually, it was seven fifteen, according to her watch—added impetus to her exercise. It gave her a reason to bang and shout louder at each turn, hoping beyond hope that someone might be at work among the containers and hear her.

But how long could she go on? She'd been on her feet for almost six hours. Six hours of, at times, staggering in the dark. She was exhausted to the point of falling over. And so, so hungry.

I have to keep going!

She had to keep going. To keep believing that someone would come. Someone would hear. She had to.

Among the staggering, Sam had religiously taken a two-minute break every half hour to check on Wolfgang. He was alive; that's all she could say. His breathing was shallow and his skin so cold to touch. But there didn't seem to be any new blood on his dressing, which was a positive. Whether he would still be breathing in another thirty minutes was anyone's guess. He seemed to be wistfully hanging on to life. She couldn't think of anything else she could do to help him, apart from keeping herself alive. And keep banging and shouting.

The noise of the rain turned from a patter to a ferocious knocking, as the shower became a deluge. *Oh, come on!* The noise would drown out her shouting. *Never mind—it can't rain for ever.*

"FIFTEEN HUNDRED AND SEVENTY-TWO!" Sam slapped the door and screamed at the top of her voice, aiming to be heard over the watery percussion. Then she turned and started walking to the back end of the container for her next lap.

Chapter 20

SIS Headquarters, Vauxhall, London

Jane was tapping away on her keyboard. She had two documents open that needed constant updating: Op Glasshouse, which, after tonight's forthcoming rescue attempt, she would hope to close in the next day or so, and Op Greyshoe—they had decided to use the same operational name as the Americans—which, with nothing further materialising from the BfV, looked like it could also be closed pretty soon. Op Greyshoe had subsumed Op Umbrella—David's poisoning. Jane agreed with Sam's original analysis—one was a subset of the other.

Both she and Frank had undertaken extensive research to see if they could find a sister organisation to the Church of the White Cross in the UK, but there didn't appear to be an equivalent on British soil. Both the Met and MI5 had dug around and found nothing. Nor were there records or links in the UK to the German "Famous Five," the ex-Stasi officers Sam had uncovered. And whilst SIS had history with Manning and Bell, Jane couldn't find any evidence to associate them with a Christian organisation in the UK. From a UK perspective it was a collection of dead ends. That was, in some ways, a good thing.

Assuming that Sam was dead, Op Greyshoe didn't seem worth the throwing in of further manpower or resources. She would follow German developments keenly and press the BfV and local German police, probably via the embassy, to recover Sam's body. Nothing would stop her from finding and bringing Sam home. Hopefully, at some point, they might uncover how and why David was poisoned. Logic indicated that it was at the hands of one of the Famous Five. But she couldn't see any reason to spend too much more time on it. They had so much else to do.

The city of Köln, the map, and the strange expurgated

markings, played on her mind. But not enough to press her into action. The BfV had all the detail—it was their problem.

Claire stuck her head around the door.

"I've got the deputy director on the phone, Jane. Don't worry—you look fabulous." Claire shot a cheeky smile.

Jane raised her hand and nodded. *What would I do without Claire?* When all this was over she would get her something by way of thanks.

What time is it in Washington? She checked her watch. It was 11.30 a.m. in London. It felt like the middle of tomorrow. Her brain was only working at 50 per cent efficiency. *Come on, girl.* Eleven thirty here; six thirty in the morning US East Coast. She almost had to use her fingers.

Jane picked up the phone.

"Hello, sir. How's it going?"

The deputy director let out a snort of a laugh, all the way from Washington.

"I've had better days."

"Did you get much sleep last night?" Jane asked.

"No. Did you?"

"Not really, sir. We've lost our agent, Sam Green, somewhere in Berlin, plus the German man she was working with. You may have picked up some of this detail in yesterday's report."

"I haven't had the chance to read much, I'm afraid. Lost as in *lost*?"

"Yes, sir. We're thinking the pair of them are down. Maybe untraceable."

The deputy director gave out a loud sigh.

"I'm sorry about your agent, Jane. I really am. Are you convinced she's down?"

"Well, she was hot on the heels of Gert Mauning, one of the Five. We lost both phone signals when they got to a warehouse complex in the east of Berlin, yesterday evening. If you remember from a previous report, the church people said they were going to murder the German's mother in a warehouse. It seems likely that they've met the same fate."

381

There was more than the usual delay on the phone. Jane imagined the DD with his hand on his forehead, shaking his head.

"We lost two troopers and a local sheriff yesterday. All three were married and had seven kids between them. We have two FBI agents and an FBI media rep being held hostage in the complex in Abilene. We currently have no idea how many shooters or what weapons they have in the church. Correction. We do know that they have an Airtronic Mark 777, a US Army rocket-propelled grenade—that's what blew the trooper vehicle to kingdom come. The only good news is that at least we now know that the Church of the White Cross *is* a terrorist organisation. And whilst we might lose a few more good men and women bringing it down, it's a fight we will win."

The deputy director sounded really tired. Jane guessed that the thought of planning a joint Op to take out the church, involving the FBI, state and local police, and maybe even the National Guard *and* the US military was draining everyone over the Pond. Mix in the long lenses and critical tongues of international media and you have an event nobody would want to go wrong.

"I'm sorry, sir. I really am. Are you going to let it soak?"

"Yes, Jane, that's the plan. We are ready to go in at a moment's notice if there is any indication that the three hostages' lives are at risk. But, for now, we're going to sit back and watch. We have a negotiator at the scene, but so far he's not been able to make contact. This could take weeks."

Jane wouldn't want to be the person to make the call to eventually go in. She guessed that might now be in the hands of the president. Everyone was making comparisons to the Waco siege of 1993. The name immediately rang a bell from her childhood, but it took the BBC news to remind her of the details. After a siege lasting fifty-one days, seventy-six members of a Christian cult, the Davidians, died after the complex burned down during an assault by the FBI and US military. What was also chilling was the similarity of how it

382

started: four FBI agents lost their lives trying to search the establishment. The religious cult was only being investigated for simple weapons violations. A straightforward search operation had turned into a bloodbath seven weeks later.

"Do we know if Johnson is at the church?" Jane asked.

"No. He is still in his office. We are keeping an eye on him."

That's a bugger.

Jane thought that now might be a good time to change the conversation.

"Do you know that we have an SAS operation ongoing in Yemen? We think we found Captain Tony James at a farm complex in a place called Shabwah. The complex appears to be owned by Ali Abdullah Sahef, Daesh's deputy in Yemen. We believe he's at the location as well. We have eyes on. H-Hour for the assault is planned for one o'clock in the morning, local." Jane tried to make her voice sound as positive as she could.

"That's great news, Jane. Really great." *That's cheered him up a bit.* "Well, best of British luck with that."

There was silence again for a short time. Both of them were taking a breather.

"You'll let me know how that goes?"

"Sure, sir. Of course—although if it's a success you'll hear about it in the press long before I have the chance to phone you." Jane had a playful tone. She knew that Number 10 would make the best possible hay whilst that particular sun was shining. And why not?

"Finally, Jane, and sorry I didn't ask at the beginning, how's David?"

"Stable, sir. He's off a ventilator as of last night, but still in isolation. The last we got from the doctors is that his body may well make a full recovery, but they're worried about the impact that his coma and the toxic shock might have had on his mind. They won't know that until he wakes up. And they're not sure when that's going to be."

The line was quiet again. Jane looked out of her window.

It was grey and dark. Another stormy day in Vauxhall.

"We need to get these bastards, Jane. We need to nail them. We have to take them down. They might just be an anti-Islam cult in the United States, with wings in a couple of European countries. Or they could be operating widely within the Middle East and Africa, bizarrely doing as you suggested—actively supporting Islamic extremists to fuel the fire of a pending religious war. To polarise us. To make us hate *all* Muslims. I don't know. But we have to bring this to an end. Now." The strength of conviction in the deputy director's voice left no room for doubt. The Church of the White Cross's days were numbered.

"Sure thing, sir." She wanted to add something weighty, but it didn't seem her place. So she kept it light. "Best of luck with the siege."

"And you with the Op tonight." He breathed out heavily. "By the way. Don't give up hope on that agent of yours. It's not over till it's over."

"Thanks, sir. I'll take that advice."

Incident Headquarters, Abilene, Texas, USA

It hadn't taken Albin long to persuade the medics that he was OK. He had a bruised rib, that was all. After a cup of coffee and six hours sleep on a camp cot in the makeshift headquarters in the Abilene Community Center, he felt right as rain. He looked for, and found, Federal Agent Ben Carmen, his boss's oppo. Agent Carmen was surrounded by a group of agents, policemen, and soldiers. They were poring over an aerial photograph that was pinned out on a table. He was obviously as busy as hell, especially now that they had US military liaison officers in the mix. When Albin had popped to the men's room earlier to freshen up, he had seen six armoured vehicles in the car lot. Who knew what else was on its way?

He wanted to be a part of it. As far as he could tell, his

boss was still being held in the church's administration building. And if his boss was still in danger, then he should be there to help in some way.

Federal Agent Ben Carmen looked up from the table and smiled as Albin approached. He straightened up and made excuses to those at the table, walking across to meet Albin.

"How you doing, son?"

"Good, sir, thanks. How's it going?"

"Complicated."

Albin knew that Agent Carmen was a man of few words.

"Sir, can I be of help? If my boss is in there"—he pointed in the general direction of where the action was—"then I'd like to help out, sir."

Agent Carmen smiled again and warmly patted Albin on his shoulder.

"Good, son, good. Go over and see my driver, Huck. He's with my vehicle in the lot. Tell him that I sent you. You can be my spare driver. Travel in the trunk if necessary."

The agent nodded in the direction of the door, making it clear that the conversation was over and he should get going.

"We're moving out in ten minutes, up to the Incident Control Point. So be quick."

Albin was already on his way, shouting, "Thank you, sir!" as he jogged off.

He had no trouble finding Huck. He recognised him immediately. He'd shared a mug of coffee with him a couple of months ago at a conference. Huck was standing beside a Ford Bronco identical to his own, which, earlier on, had been shipped off to forensics in Dallas. This was good news—should he be asked to drive.

"Hi, Huck," Albin offered his hand. Huck took it, almost squeezing it to death.

"Albin! How ya doing?" Huck was a monster of a man, big and square. Albin was unsure how he managed to get into the driver's seat.

Albin was about to talk through what Agent Carmen had

said, when a shout from behind stopped any further conversation.

"Let's go! Up to the ICP. Now!" It was Agent Carmen.

Huck was in the driver's seat much quicker than Albin thought possible for such a large man. He dithered.

"Get in, Albin! In the back!" Agent Carmen barked.

They were off. The Ford's five-litre V8 engine burst into life. Huck had the vehicle out of the lot and in the direction of the turn-off to the church in no time. Albin was impressed.

Agent Carson reached for his dash handset.

"ICP, this is Carson. I'll be with you in two. Send Sitrep. Copy."

The radio crackled.

"Good. It's Dennison here. We have their demands. Let's talk face to face. Copy."

"Copy. Out." Agent Carson put the handset back in the clip on the dash.

Huck drove the Bronco effortlessly. With lights flashing, but no siren, a couple of minutes later they pulled up into the newly fenced car park, just short of the ICP.

"Huck. Stay with the car. Albin, come with me. You can act as a runner if I need one."

Albin felt immediately elevated in rank. His boss had only ever asked him to drive from A to B. Now, in the heat of a major operation, his new boss might just ask him to run errands and pass important messages. He really wished he'd brought a notebook and pencil with him. As he strode after Agent Carson, he reached into his pocket and found a handkerchief. He tied a knot in one of its corners—he'd remember next time.

It took them no time to reach the white tent, next to which a massive generator was chugging away. There was a sign outside the entrance: "ICP." A state trooper guarded the canvas door.

"Stay outside, Albin." Agent Carson put his hand out to gesture Albin to stop.

Albin walked to the gable end of the tent, careful not to trip over the hundreds of wires that led to numerous poles with antennas on top. He took in the scene.

They were in a hollow. In front of him, rising up the ridge, was the gravel track that eventually led to the church. On top of the ridge, where the track crested, were the remains of the state trooper car. It was still on its back, blackened by fire. He wasn't sure, and his stomach didn't want him to think about it, but were the two officers still inside? The officer who had tried to reach the car, the one who was shot, was definitely not there anymore. Had they been able to retrieve the two other men? Probably not.

His eyes followed the ridge around. Every twenty metres or so there was a couple of officers, just off the crest line. Above every second pair there was what appeared to be a remote camera or some other sensing device. To his far left, maybe a hundred metres away, were a couple of armoured vehicles. One had a turret with a gun that looked big enough to blow a hole in the moon.

He stuck his head around the end of the tent and looked right. It was the same setup. There were men and munitions everywhere.

He'd been so busy focusing on the hardware that he didn't realise that he could hear what was going on in the tent.

"So, what is it they want, Dennison?" It was Agent Carson's voice.

"You're not going to believe it. They want the sale of the Koran banned across the whole of the United States. They know it will require legislation, and I have a fax here that looks like a load of lawyer-speak to me. But the bones of it are clear: no more Koran on US bookshelves."

Albin couldn't see the expression on Agent Carson's face and didn't really understand the enormity of what the two men were discussing.

"No shit. Are they kidding? Are there any other demands? Or a timeline?"

"No other demands. I asked the guy, who refused to be named, if there was anything else. He said that they have no need for money, nor did they indicate that they wished to escape."

"And the timeline?"

"The three hostages will be shot on Sunday, November fifth, at eleven in the morning."

"But that's over three weeks away!" Albin could hear the frustration in Agent Carson's voice. "Do they really expect us to sit around here and wait for them to execute three of our own?"

"I guess they expect the president, the House of Representatives, and the Senate to have passed a new bill by then."

"In three weeks? Are they out of their minds?"

"Apparently, the guy said that he already knew of fifty-eight Republican senators who would support such a bill. I don't know how many you need to get it through, but it might just be possible."

"Or three good people will die?"

There was quiet for a bit. Overhead, a recently arrived helicopter was more than making up for the break in the conversation.

"Keep this on close hold. I'll take the fax back down to the headquarters and pass the details to Washington. I'll make it clear to everyone down there that we're in for the long haul—with an almighty big punch-up at the end of it. We'll need to get a political and a legal rep here to help out with the dialogue. I'll make that happen as well."

"Thanks, Ben."

"Oh, and, Dennison . . ."

"Yup."

"*We* have a demand. Tell them we're going to remove the two dead troopers from the car. Tell them we're going to do it at . . ." There was a pause. Albin imagined Agent Carson looking at his watch. "Fifteen hundred hours. Tell them that, as Christians, they'll get this. And tell them that we won't take no for an answer."

"OK, Ben. And if they disagree?"

"Tell them we'll nuke the place before midnight. I'm off now."

Albin rushed around to the front of the tent and met Agent Carson on his way out.

"Come on, Albin. This thing has just got a whole lot tougher."

Disused Warehouse Complex, Altglienicke Industrial Estate, Berlin

Sam felt the temperature dropping well before it started to get dark. It was 4.35. She had been laid out on a couple of pallets for over an hour. She just couldn't go on. Everything ached, and she had blisters on her feet. Her left hand, where she had been hitting the metal doors, felt like it was twice as big as her right—a hand that had only recently started to look like it belonged on the end of her arm after the washroom incident. Her stomach groaned with hunger, and, above all, she was overwhelmingly tired. Now that the temperature was dropping, she reckoned that when hypothermia came, and it would very soon, she would be gone within an hour.

She had lost her resolve. At some point during the afternoon she thought she heard someone or something outside. The rain had stopped, and there was a clanking sound. It was a long way off, but it wasn't a sound she had heard before. She had screamed until she was hoarse, and she had banged on the door with her fists when her voice had given out.

But no one came.

The noise had given her the briefest of hope that someone might find them. However, within half an hour, this hope had turned to desperation. Half an hour after that, her desperation had slid into depression. She'd stopped walking,

389

and she'd stopped banging. She had resigned herself to not making it through the night. She would die here. In the cold.

Why had they left them to die in the container rather than shoot them when they had shot Wolfgang's mother? It jarred—it made her angry. Maybe Mauning had received an order that it was better that they were left to perish in this cell. That didn't make any sense. None of it did.

Who cares? Who gives a shit?

To her credit, even if she said so herself, she had continued to check on Wolfgang. It was possibly, she thought, her military training. *Never leave a man behind.* Or maybe the sense of duty that had been drilled into her by her parents. "Look after others—they will look after you."

Regardless, Wolfgang was, somehow or other, hanging in there. He had grunted a couple of times during the day; maybe it was a dream surfacing—not that she would want to be exposed to any of his dreams after the murder of his mother. During her half-hour checks she had often spoken to him, offering some solace. A couple of times she held his cold and clammy hand. Sam thought he had squeezed hers at one point, but as she had lost all sensation in her fingers since the debilitating cold of last night, she couldn't really tell.

She would look at him again, and no matter how rubbish she felt, she would continue to look at him until she couldn't make the short journey from her couple of pallets to his.

Voices.

Clunk. More voices. Clunk.

Sam's heart rate shot through the roof. She was on her feet, but was so short of energy she had to make two attempts to stay upright.

Clunk. And then that wonderful scraping sound of her prison door being opened.

What's happening? Who is it? What will they do?

The open doors allowed what little light there was outside to infiltrate into the container. She couldn't stop herself from looking around. It was as her mind described it in the dark.

Nine pallets and four metal walls. She'd missed nothing.

Three men came in. One lifted Wolfgang onto his shoulders. She was relieved that he gave out a groan as the man carried him off. *There's life still in him.*

Two men came for her. It was the same two men from yesterday. They spoke some German to each other and, without any ceremony, picked her up by putting a hand under each arm and dragged her out of the container. *Their hands are so warm!* The heat of their bodies was like two radiators. She pulled her elbows in tight and felt the warmth spread under her arms. *What a fabulous feeling.* She closed her eyes and willed the heat from their arms and shoulders to penetrate her fleece, bring back some energy to her cold and limp body.

They were back inside the warehouse within a minute. Any sense of elation that Sam had briefly felt was shattered when she saw the tarpaulin back out on the floor with two chairs placed in the middle of it. Both chairs faced away from the direction they entered. They were maybe six feet apart. Wolfgang was put on one chair, and she was dumped on the other.

She felt her mood shifting again. Depression had been replaced briefly with elation as she had been pulled from the container. Now she had a new feeling. It was an odd sensation, as if her body had taken on an electrical charge. She shivered, but in a way that she thought probably looked like a fit. Her head flicked left and then right, in a sharp motion. She looked at her hands. They both seemed to jump, independently of each other. Her head went again, jerking, a jagged movement as though she were plugged into the mains. Everything was involuntary. *I must look very odd.*

Even with her head moving uncontrollably, she tried to take in the scene. Recce a route out. Find a gap.

Unless it was behind her, there was no crate with a purple cloth. And no handgun. That was some relief. There were four, maybe five men. They were all standing around as if they were waiting for something. She tried to keep her head still, and when she thought she had it under control, she twisted to her right to see if she could work out what was happening behind her.

Smack! A flat hand to her face.

Shit! That hurt.

Someone was on her shoulder, keeping an eye. She wouldn't do that again.

She and Wolfgang sat there like dummies for what seemed like an age, but it was probably no more than five minutes.

"Hello, Sam Green." An American accent.

What? The words came from the direction of the entrance behind her. She wanted to look, but she didn't want another slap. *I recognise that voice.* Her head was full of cotton wool, and nothing was working as it should. She continued to fidget and jump without intending to. *Get a grip, Sam!*

Then she saw him. He gave her a wide berth and came into her peripheral vision about three metres away. He stopped in front of her just off the tarpaulin, and then, she thought possibly to get on her level, he crouched down, his hands on his knees. It was a patronising stance. Like talking to a child.

"We meet again, Sam Green."

It was Kurt Manning. *It's Kurt Manning!*

Her brain went into overdrive—all other sensations were lost. She stopped jerking; her limbs become her own again. A rush of heat seemed to percolate throughout her body. She was momentarily alive, the fog in her brain cleared, the red mist not far from taking control.

"Kurt Manning. You shit." It was meant to come out much stronger, but her voice was still raspy after her shouting match in the container earlier in the afternoon.

"Oh, don't be so hard on me." He stood up, smiling. "Are you not well?"

Sam didn't say anything. With her faculties back, even temporarily, she took in the scene with a greater sense of awareness. She couldn't see behind her, but there was at least one man on her shoulder and three men to her front. They all had rifles.

Manning gave a nod to the man behind her. He slapped her across the face.

"What the . . ." *That hurt!*

"Talk to me, Sam Green. Answer my questions. You know you're going to die. But I need to understand a few things first. Things you will tell me." He nodded again. This time the accompanying pain came from a punch to the back of her neck.

Shit! She fell to the floor, her hands preventing her head from hitting the concrete. Her head span. She had to stop herself from throwing up. Her breathing was short and erratic.

"Get back on the chair, Sam Green."

She was on all fours. She was down, but her mind was her own. This was her Daniel Craig moment.

"Fuck you, Manning." The swearing lost its impact with the rasping of her voice.

It was her torso this time. A kick from the man's boot. The pain was instantaneous and flooded her senses. She collapsed on the floor. She closed her eyes, but she couldn't stop the tears from dripping onto the concrete, turning patches from grey to black.

Sam was then manhandled back onto her chair. As her minder dragged her, she noticed that he was limping. She glanced up at his face. *It's Bischoff. What a surprise.* He roughly turned her head to face forward and held her in place. His hand on her shoulder.

Everything hurt.

"Where did you learn about the Church of the White Cross? Was it here in Germany?"

Sam stared across at the monster. If she told him everything, would she die sooner? If she didn't, the beating would continue. How long would she last? Would her body give in before her mind did? She hoped it would. Could she hold out? She would have been dead if she had stayed in the

393

container. Could she channel the pain to give her more resolve?

Above all, she wouldn't talk. At all. She would die first. She could get through the pain. *Somehow.*

Sam spat on the floor. Blood was mixed in with the sputum. It dribbled down her cheek.

"OK, Sam Green. Let's do it your way."

Manning nodded at Bischoff again. She was treated to an earful of fist. She couldn't stop herself from falling sideward off her chair again. Stars floated in front of her eyes, her head throbbed, and her ear felt like it had been poked at with a screwdriver. Everything went grey for a while, her eyesight briefly gone. Even with her eyes closed, her world span. She opened them and looked up at Manning. She saw two of him. He eventually coalesced into one. Colours returned. This time she spat because her mouth was full of saliva. Blood was ever present.

She didn't wait to get picked up and placed back on the chair. She didn't want to give Bischoff the satisfaction. She lifted herself off the concrete floor, and, as best she could, she crawled up the chair. And then something came to her. As she was climbing what felt like an alpine mountain just to sit herself back down, she looked across to Manning. She caught him side on. A penny dropped. A big penny. It might not have been the right penny, but she thought she was onto something.

Not that it mattered now.

Holding on to the chair with all her strength, she put her bum back on the seat, tentatively turning around, avoiding any movement that she thought might add to the pain. She settled down and breathed out through a closed mouth, rasping—her cheeks inflamed like a trumpet player.

"You and Gert Mauning are related." Sam spat some more red saliva on the floor. It was warm and silky. She took another breath. Her lungs felt like they'd just completed a marathon. "Your surnames are similar. There's a family connection?"

Manning looked confused, frustrated. And then angry.

He nodded at Bischoff again. As Sam imagined him winding himself up for a punch to the side of her head, she ducked, dropping her head between her knees. He missed her and the momentum of the man's punch, which was obviously designed to create as much damage as possible, spun him around. Out of the corner of her eye she saw him struggle to stay upright.

From somewhere inside, Sam found humour. She laughed, a suppressed childlike giggle that spread to her shoulders. She raised her fist to her mouth, a physical movement to stop the laughter. The whole thing was ludicrous. Ridiculous. For her, it was like watching *Reservoir Dogs* without the comfort of a sofa and a giant bag of popcorn. Her laughter, which teetered between hysteria and tears, took neither route. Eventually it died a natural death. She shook her head, smiling broadly. She coughed a final, embarrassed, laugh.

"Sorry. Couldn't resist that."

Manning's face had turned red. He displayed all the signs of a man on the edge. He barked at one of the men, off to Sam's left.

"Rifle!"

The man quickly jogged over, handing the rifle to Manning.

Manning inspected the rifle and cocked it.

"This one is expendable." To Sam's abject horror, Manning walked across to Wolfgang, raised the rifle to his shoulder, and took aim.

Crack!

Sam didn't know where to look. She flinched at the sound, but couldn't close her eyes. She couldn't stop watching the horror. To her complete amazement, rather than seeing Wolfgang pirouette over the top of his chair, it was Manning who span around. He released the rifle, which flew away. A bulge ballooned from the back of his coat as an exiting bullet took out a lot of Manning's insides that would have served him better if they had stayed where they were. He fell to the floor.

Sam's immediate reaction was to dive to the ground—to get out of harm's way. She did this, but she decided to take Wolfgang with her. As she threw herself in his direction, all manner of chaos broke out.

"Polizei—halt!"

But the words were lost in a hail of gunfire. Gunfire that seemed to last forever. Sam dragged Wolfgang to one side, glad that neither of them appeared to be targets. A couple of Manning's men went down. She thought Bischoff had run through one of the far doors. There was further gunfire outside, so he may well have copped it there. The noise was deafening, the cracks of the rounds accompanied by pings of ricochet. Glass smashed; in a corner, one of her captors screamed in pain—down, but not dead.

After a time she couldn't specify, the firing inside the warehouse stopped, but German voices continued. She listened to her breathing. It was erratic, but her senses were alive. She was feeling human, as though she had been injected with a new lease on life. As she lay on top of Wolfgang, one friend protecting another, she looked around. Both chairs were on the floor. Next to one was Kurt Manning's lifeless body.

One down.

A German policeman, dressed in khaki and dark green, but sporting the very latest black Kevlar vest, jogged up to her. He bent down, slinging his rifle as he did. The smell of burnt cordite, which hung in the air, was all the more powerful as his weapon came within a few feet of her nose.

"Are you OK?" The accent strong and clipped, but the English sound.

"Yes. Thank you. This man"—she motioned to Wolfgang—"he's injured in two places and very cold. Hypothermic. He has also suffered emotional trauma . . ." Sam continued talking, describing in unnecessary detail what they had been through. The policeman broke her diatribe.

"Mediziner!" The policeman shouted. An order that reverberated around the room. The command did the same outside the warehouse as others passed on the instruction.

Sam was on all fours now and was about to try to stand. Before she did, she wiped her mouth with her hand and inspected the outcome. More blood and spit.

"Sam." It was the quietest of calls.

What?

It was Wolfgang!

She looked down. He had one eye partially open.

"Don't talk, Wolfgang. You're safe now."

"Köln." It was barely audiblc.

Sam bent down further so her ear was by Wolfgang's mouth. She was about to ask him what he meant when a medic arrived, all bright green and white, with high-viz stripes. Sam pushed her hand out, stopping the medic from getting close to Wolfgang.

"What about Köln, Wolfgang?"

He coughed, and she saw the pain spread across his face.

"Chancellor. They're going to kill the chancellor. Thursday. University. Eleven." The words were raspy, quiet.

She racked her brain for times and dates. *That's tomorrow!*

"Are you sure, Wolfgang?" She was insistent, but gentle.

He just nodded and then passed out, his one slightly open eye closing slowly.

The medic was no longer prepared to let Sam keep him to herself. On her command, the policeman gently lifted Sam and allowed the medic to access Wolfgang. Within seconds, space blankets were the order of the day, and drips were being prepared.

Sam offered, "He's got a wound on his left arm, and he's got a puncture to his right leg. Above the knee." It was incidental chatter as her brain thought through the gravity of what she had just heard. Instinct took over again. She was upright and human. Exhausted, starving hungry, and still bitterly cold. But human.

"Can I borrow your phone?" she snapped at the policeman. "It's important. I work for the British Secret Service! Phone. *Handy.* Now. Come on! *Schnell!*" She'd picked up a few new words since she'd got off the plane in Munich.

The policeman shook his head in bewilderment and dug a mobile out of his pocket. After a couple of flicks of his finger, he handed it to Sam.

She dialled Jane's number. It took an age to connect. When it rang, Jane picked it up straight away.

"Jane Baker."

Sam took a breath.

"Hi, Jane, it's Sam." Sam's voice was still croaky.

The line went briefly quiet and then exploded.

"Sam! I don't believe it. Oh, Sam! Where are you? Are you OK?"

"I'm fine, Jane. There's a lot to tell you. But first you have to listen to some new intelligence."

"Where are you, Sam? At the warehouse?"

"Yes. We've just been rescued by the German police. Manning, that's *Manning*, not *Mauning*, was here. I don't know where *Mauning* is—he was here yesterday." She pronounced both surnames emphatically. She knew it sounded confusing, but she needed to press on. "He's dead— *Manning*, that is. And Bischoff was here. He ran out, but I think they got him outside." She realised at that point that any further explanation might well lead to confusion. And she had to move things along.

"Now listen!" Sam was losing it. They didn't have time for pleasantries. She took a deep breath at the same time as another green-clad medic put a space blanket over her shoulders.

Come on, Jane. Get this.

"They're going to kill the German chancellor. Tomorrow at Köln University. Eleven o'clock. You need to tell the BfV."

Sam sensed Jane taking it all in.

"Are you sure? How can you be sure?" Sam didn't know what to make of Jane's tone. Did she believe her? *Listen to me, Jane. Come on . . .*

"Wolfgang overheard it. And you've seen the map—the one with the blue route marked on it. It's her itinerary. Don't ask any more details. You need to pass it on. Now."

"Sure, sure. It might be difficult to sell. Is Wolfgang OK?"

"Yes, I think so. He took a hole in the leg and saw his mother executed in cold blood, but he's alive."

"Oh my God." The words trailed off as Jane said them.

"Listen, Jane. Please. I need a member of the embassy staff here *now*. I'm going to Köln. I can't drive, I can hardly stand. Even if I could find transport, I wouldn't make it—so they will need to drive me. Get someone here. Like, now. We are at the warehouse. You know where that is? And then phone me back on this number and I'll talk you through what's happened. OK?"

"I'm not sure I have that authority, Sam. I just can't order the embassy to provide a driver for you."

"Yes—you can, Jane." Sam's frustration was not far below the surface. "And you must. If you can't do it, get the chief to. I need to be there. I might be able to help. You have to make this happen."

Sam waited whilst Jane thought.

"OK, Sam. Of course. I'll do that straight away. I know where you are. I'm so pleased that you're still with us. And, Sam . . ."

"Yes, Jane?"

"Look after yourself."

"Sure, Jane."

The phone went dead just as the medic returned with a steaming cup of coffee.

Bliss.

Chapter Twenty-one

Farm Complex, Shabwah, Yemen

Tony felt his mood lifting. Just slightly. He had developed a routine. And he liked routine. He longed for it. It made him feel safe. He didn't like changes to his routine. He didn't like it when his food was delivered late, or when it came on a different plate.

So tonight he hadn't coped well when they had changed the prayer routine. But, looking back, it had been an unexpectedly special occasion. The first real joy in his life for what seemed like a very long time. Up until this evening, he had prayed in a room across the courtyard with the other men, on a red and white mat. It had upset him that the mat was dirty and dusty, but it was *his* mat. He liked his mat.

After dark, a few hours ago, they had come to collect him for prayers as usual. He looked forward to it. Not the religious side. That still made him feel uncomfortable. It was complicated. Even after the countless recitations of the Koran, he still didn't get it. He didn't understand it. Religion was a big thing, and his mind couldn't cope with big things. It wasn't just Islam; it was the whole of religion. Christians and Buddhists and . . . He couldn't think of any more religions. It was all far too deep. Something prevented him from having deep thoughts. He wasn't sure what was stopping him, but something inside told him not to think about it.

No, he enjoyed the prayers because he liked to be with the other men. To feel their warmth and friendship. They smiled at him, said the odd word or two that he understood, like, "OK, English?" They patted him on the back, and they prayed with him. He felt part of a family. A brotherhood of sorts.

Tonight, things changed. Not huge things. But change

nonetheless. They had come to collect him as usual, the nice man with his rope and big smile. But they hadn't taken him across the courtyard. This time they had led him through some gates onto a street. That is, they had tried to. But he didn't want to do that; he couldn't cope with it. It was different, and he struggled with different. He fought against the change. He knew he didn't have the energy to stop them from making him do something he didn't want to do, but he couldn't stop himself from pulling back and digging his heels in. He was frightened and confused.

He even said some words! *No* and *Please*. It was a revelation. Shocking. It had stopped the man with the rope in his tracks. Tony hadn't said anything out loud since Ted and Sandy. Words hadn't come, although he had practised and practised in the quiet of his cell. So it had surprised him that words had popped out. Not big words, not sentences. But words nonetheless. Words of disquiet and rebellion.

The man with the rope had slapped him across the face. The shock of being hit and the anger in the man's eyes were enough for him to overcome his fear. To quell his small rebellion against change. Reluctantly he had followed on, his eyes looking left and right, trying to cope with the difference. The unknown.

They had taken him out of the compound to a mosque. It was a short walk, although he was tired by the time they got there. His leg was still sore, and he dragged it behind him. His energy levels were low, and he was weak and feeble. He knew that. But that changed when he entered the building. He wiped his feet. With his head bowed, he walked into a big, angled room that was highly decorated with white walls and red, black, and gold ornaments and decorations. Candles lit up the space, and carpets adorned the floor—it was beautiful. Mesmerising. Enchanting. It was an island of colour and compassion, afloat on an ocean of sand, grit, rock and hurt.

He loved it. He wanted to get down on his knees and pray straight away. Pray to someone for the beauty of this space and for its majesty. For its colour and its calm. He was led to his space beside a blue and brown mat, next to the man with the rope. That mat was clean, and it was bright. He felt everyone looking at him with inquisitive eyes, but no one spoke above the silence of the mosque. He felt different, because he was. But he also felt just a little bit special. He was in a wonderful place, and people were looking at him because he was special. At that point, the sting left over from the slap across his face dissipated. With his head bowed, he found himself smiling. Just a half smile.

Prayers lasted for a while. He didn't do time well nowadays, so couldn't be specific as to how long, but it took longer than usual. Afterward, he shuffled out of the mosque into the semidarkness, following the man with the rope. Many men came up to touch him, to feel him. He liked the touching; he liked their warm hands. He nodded and smiled at the men. There was quiet discussion in Arabic. He knew some words, but the dialect was so strong most of it was unintelligible. The man with the rope had seemed proud— proud of him. That made him feel good too. He was worth something. Something to someone.

And then they were back in the courtyard, and he was back in his room. There was a coffee ready for him when he arrived and another small chunk of chocolate. New, small, pleasant additions to his routine. Good additions. Not bad ones.

He was content. He washed himself with a slab of soap the man had provided earlier, and, having sat on the slop bucket and wiped himself, he lay down on his mattress.

Sleep, which had been elusive for so long, came to him immediately.

Bang! Crash! Bang! Thud!

Tony's dreams, which were all purple, reds, and golds, were interrupted by the noises of the devil.

Crack, crack, crack, crack! Bang, bang, bang, bang! Shouting. Now screaming.

He was awake and immediately frightened. Still lying down, he pulled himself into a ball and pushed his hands against his ears. Like a young child escaping from a nightmare.

Please, make this go away. He was crying again now, his pillow already damp.

Crack, crack, crack! Bang!

"32 Alpha, room clear!" Some words that he recognised.

Bang! Thud! Crack, ping, crack, crack! More screaming. Shouts in a language he didn't understand, followed by some words he did.

"32 Alpha, room clear!"

Thud! Thud! It was his door. His own door.

"Captain James?" A bark from outside, just about distinguishable through his hand earmuffs, amid more loud bangs and shouts.

He curled up tighter. He wanted everything to be as it was. For all this noise to go away.

Crack, crack, ping, crack! A scream.

From a far distance, "32 Bravo, room clear. Two enemy dead!"

Thud! Crack, crack, ping!

"Captain James! We're going to blow the door off its hinges. Please get as far away from the door as possible. In ten seconds. I'm going to count."

Tony understood that. He was now feverish, panicky. What to do? He was close to the door, but not so close. He wanted for it all to go away. For these intruders to leave him alone.

"Ten! Nine! . . ." Then something small changed. Flight took control. He uncurled himself, and with all of his effort, he scrambled for the far corner of the room, knocking over the slop bucket as he did. The smell was repugnant.

Crack, crack, ping! Seemingly a huge distance away. The counting was closer.

"Five! Four! Three! Two! One!"

Bang! Thud! Whoosh!

He had his back to the door, curled in a ball. The orange light of the explosion came first, bouncing off the walls. Then a peppering of his back as if some bully had thrown stones at him, followed by shafts of white light. Lights that flickered left and right, up and down, among dust and sand.

He pulled himself tighter still, protecting himself from the onslaught. The change. The shattering of his routine.

"Captain James?" A man had his hand on his shoulder, gently pulling him around. He looked toward the light. There were three dark figures and two beams of bright light. The man closest didn't have his own light, or he had switched it off. He could just make out his face. It was blackened with dirt, but his teeth were white. He was smiling.

"Come with us, sir. We're taking you home now."

German Autobahn A2, Heading West toward the Ruhr and Then Köln

Sam had slept for a straight four hours. She was woken as they pulled into a *tankstelle* to get some fuel, the change of speed and the bumping on the uneven tarmac shaking her. She felt her face. There was bruising on her ear. Her side hurt like hell from where she had been kicked. But the cold was gone. And although her hands were useless, she could move all her fingers. She checked again. *Yes, they all work.*

"Ten minutes here?" Mandy said.

Sam shook the sleep from her head and nodded.

"Yes, please, Mandy."

She glanced across at the satnav. It showed a time to destination of 9.15. She checked her watch. It was 5.10. Dawn was moments away.

Mandy had been brilliant. She had arrived at the warehouse about half an hour after Sam's first conversation with Jane. While waiting, Sam had been treated to a full medical by the lady in bright green and white and had been wrapped in more space blankets than a space shuttle. And fed more hot coffee than her bladder could cope with. Thank goodness for the "peeing in a bush" training she'd not forgotten from her army days. Sandwiches and buns were also on the menu, but when they had asked her to go with them to the station, Sam had refused. She was waiting for "Mandy." Jane had passed on the name of the woman from the embassy.

She'd had time to give the briefest of statements to a particularly attractive German BfV officer. He was a true Aryan: tall, blond hair, blue eyes, and a charmingly efficient smile. Dressed in black coveralls, but having taken off his Kevlar jacket, all he lacked was a box of Milk Tray to complete the vision. The giddiness following the rescue had sent her libido into overdrive. She guessed it was her natural feminine instincts surging through: breed before you die. *And get on with it.* The caffeine probably wasn't helping. Unfortunately, due to the state she was in and with her hair all over the place, she couldn't see Herman the German obliging her. But it didn't stop her imagination from running riot.

Jane had phoned back to the policeman's phone that Sam had used originally. He had come and found Sam, showing her the *handy* and smiling. Sam had taken it, and she and Jane had had a long chat. It was emotional for both of them. Sam had cried when she recounted the death of Wolfgang's mother and had cried again when she described her captivity in the container. It was too raw, too new. Jane sounded like she was in tears for most of their conversation.

The revelation that Manning had flown from the Middle East just to question her was surprising to both of them. His decision to do so had saved Sam's life and had ended his. *That was no bad thing.* Sam had checked with the police, and they confirmed that five men had been killed in and around the warehouse. A further man had been injured and was on his way to the hospital, along with Wolfgang.

Sam had mentioned to Jane about Manning and Mauning being related. It was complete conjecture, but it seemed to make sense. Manning, a third-generation US citizen with links to the church in Abilene, but originally from Germany, and Mauning, a German citizen, a member of the equivalent church in his own country. It seemed like a very plausible and convenient link. Jane said they would look into it.

As to how and why the police arrived in the nick of time, Jane was able to throw some light on that. She told Sam that the BfV had staked out the warehouse, having originally searched the place and found nothing. Jane guessed that when Sam's captors had come back and she and Wolfgang had been taken out of the container, the BfV had muscled in—guns blazing.

They had cut their conversation short when Mandy arrived. Jane said she had Mandy's number and would phone back in a while.

Sam and Mandy had worked out timings. With a couple of hours spare to get to Köln, Mandy had insisted they drop by her place, where Sam could shower and get into some of her clothes. The shower had been a luxury that came with more tears. As for clean clothes, Mandy had obliged. They were a size different. Sam had to use a belt to hold up her borrowed jeans. She had always been into baggy jumpers, even if Mandy's bright-red woollen jumper was a little too "look at me" for her taste. Combined with a black, roll-necked top, the setup worked perfectly. A brief look in the mirror, and Sam thought she did a good impersonation of Velma from *Scooby-Do*!

They had set off with an hour and a half to spare. Mandy, so far, had driven like a demoness. Not that Sam had noticed—she was too busy sleeping.

Sam popped into the loo and was back with the car after just a couple of minutes. Mandy was hot on her heels. As Sam got into the car, Mandy's phone rang; it was Jane. She passed it to Sam.

"Hi, Sam. How are you feeling?"

"Warmer. And less hungry." Sam had asked Mandy to keep the heat on in the Golf. At one point Mandy had had to open her side window to cool down. Sam, however, couldn't get enough heat.

"Two bits of news."

"Go on." Sam encouraged.

"This is an insecure line, so bear with me while I talk in riddles. James has been rescued. He was in the location you found. It couldn't have gone more smoothly."

Relief engulfed Sam, and tears came again. They dribbled down her cheeks, and she batted them away with the sleeves of her borrowed jumper. She looked at the dampness and then across at Mandy and mouthed, "Sorry."

"That's such good news. Was anyone hurt?'

"Just Sahef and a couple of his men. Hurt is an understatement, I have to say."

"No! Two birds—one stone. That's even better news!" Sam was smiling now, almost giggling. God knew what Mandy thought of her.

They sped past another car. And another. Sam was thankful that German autobahns didn't have speed limits.

"You probably won't have seen the news, but the Americans lost three men when they tried to search Church of the White Cross in Texas. There's a siege situation ongoing, and three more FBI staff are being held hostage."

Sam thought for a second.

"Do we know what the demands are?"

"I do. But the public doesn't. I can't tell you over the phone, but maybe if you get to an embassy line we can discuss it. The demands cannot be met, so there's going to have to be a confrontation."

"Shit. That won't be pleasant."

"No." A single-word answer was all Jane needed.

"Sam?"

"Yes, Jane."

"Why are you going to Köln?" Jane didn't wait for an answer. "Look, I've informed the BfV. The chancellor won't stop her visit—she's attending the university's graduation ceremony as guest of honour. She's handing out the degree certificates and making a speech. The BfV people there have said that they're beefing up security, but they were reluctant to push the chancellor to call off her visit. Not without better intel. What difference are *you* going to make?"

Sam was looking out the window, watching. In the dull, early morning light, cars shot behind them as Mandy kept the Golf in the outside lane, eating up the kilometres.

"I don't know, Jane. I just don't know. But I need to be there until it's over. Then I can come home."

"OK, Sam. That's fine. As long as you're not keeping something from me."

"I wish I were, Jane. At least then I'd have a plan."

"Be careful."

"Sure, Jane. And speak soon."

Universität zu Köln, Köln, Germany

They made it to the university with an hour to spare. Mandy parked up and followed Sam to the front of the building. The large, red-blocked and multiple-windowed facade looked prewar—old, but not historic. The front entrance was closed off. Police tape warning people not to enter and a couple of businesslike policemen standing by, armed and ready. Signs directed guests around the side, and, sure enough, at the back, on a large paved square, there were tents, banners of welcome, and bunting. Rather incongruously, there was also more police tape and many more policemen. The only way in was via three door-shaped metal detectors, which, set in the middle of the square flanked by temporary metal fencing, looked unwelcoming.

"Can you get us in, Mandy?"

"I'll try."

Sam stood back as Mandy had a fluent conversation with a German policeman. A plainclothes man came over. More discussion ensued, including a couple of calls on a mobile by the man in a suit, during which he gave Sam the once-over. Sam checked her watch; they were running out of time. When the second call ended, there was shaking of hands and a smile. Mandy beckoned Sam over.

"It's OK. They have spoken to Berlin officials, who appeared to fill them in on the last couple of days. We can go in."

Sam followed Mandy into the building and down a corridor into a huge chamber. It was filled with seats that were slowly being taken by hundreds of students wearing black capes. One or two had multicoloured hoods that draped down their backs. Having never been to university, it was alien to Sam. At the end of the room was a very elaborate raised stage, equipped with a dais, a microphone, and six green velvet and gold-legged chairs. At the back of the stage there was a table festooned with silver cups, shields, and stacks of papers.

Sam checked her watch. It was 10.50. The chancellor would be here any moment now.

She needed a vantage point. She looked toward the stage, above the crowd, and up and around. Long, tall, multiple-hued stained windows filled the left wall—it was at least thirty metres long, and the windows were ten metres tall. The opposite long wall was just as tall, its space festooned with honour boards and portraits of past dignitaries. *No vantage points there.*

Behind her, and above, was a gallery. She walked forward and craned her head to get a better view. It was full of video cameras and, she assumed, the press.

"I'm going up there!" Sam pointed to gallery. "I need your phone."

Mandy dithered, unsure.

"What do you want me to do?"

"Stay here. Look out for something unusual. If you see anything, speak to"—Sam looked around—"that policeman there." She pointed at a young policeman a few metres away. He looked Sam's way and smiled. Sam smiled back. She stopped her still bubbling libido in its tracks by looking away and thrusting out her hand to Mandy, demanding, "Mobile!"

Mandy shook her head, reached into her handbag, and handed over her phone.

Sam was off. As she headed out of the main entrance doors and back into the corridor, she had to duck under the hands of another policeman who, with his back to her, was stopping movement. As Sam slid past, she knew why. Just in front of her, heading for the hall, was the chancellor's party.

The chancellor stopped herself as Sam emerged from under the arms of the policeman. Their eyes met. Sam immediately put up her hands to show she meant no harm and said, "Sorry, ma'am." It was the briefest of encounters, but a connection was made. Sam dashed past in search of the entrance to the balcony. No one pursued her.

Phew.

It took Sam a couple of minutes to find the stairs, and she climbed them two at a time. She got onto the balcony via a double door, which was already open. The platform was about a metre deep, stretching the whole length of the end wall. There were industrial-size video cameras, normal still cameras with long lenses, and about five operators. She was able to stand to the right of the first tripod, squeezing in between two men to get a decent view. No one said anything to her.

She looked around, searching for the absence of the normal. What was not there that should be there? Other thoughts ran through her mind. *If she were going to take the chancellor out, how would she do it?* Who would be able to do it? And get away?

It all drew a blank. She had no idea.

This is hopeless.

The stage party took to their seats. A man, who she assumed was in charge of the university, got up, walked across to a microphone, and started talking. Sam kept looking. She searched everywhere. Nothing. She spotted four policemen in uniform and maybe two in plain clothes, one on the dais with the chancellor. But nothing else.

The man talking went on and on, and Sam started to get bored. And restless. Tiredness was an ever-present threat, and the bruising to her face, torso, and hands throbbed away, sapping her energy further. *I have to stay awake. I have to.*

The students, Sam reckoned there must be at least three hundred of them, looked like they were getting bored as well. They became fidgety. She could see one or two of them talking surreptitiously to each other, whispering behind their programmes.

Programmes? *Programmes!*

How would I assassinate a member of the stage party? What expertise do I have? Do I want to die trying? No!

Wait. Yes! That's it. Come on, Sam!

Sam looked around for a programme just as the chancellor got to her feet to a rapturous round of applause. There was one in a bag on the floor. It looked like it belonged to the man to her right who was taking photographs. He had a big camera, sporting a large telephoto lens.

She bent down and picked out the programme. As she did so, the man glared at her. She smiled and waved the programme at him.

Sam opened it up, her bruised hands not working as quickly as her mind was. She was looking for a name. She scanned the first page. It was all in German, but seemingly introductory stuff. The second was blank, apart from a few words. Then the list of names started. A single title: *Doktor der Philosophie.* And then names, all followed by the initials PhD. There were about forty of them. He wasn't among them.

Sam stopped briefly and looked up. The PhD students were being called forward. There was clapping, the chancellor was handing out certificates, and, beside her, the camera lens was clicking away. *It's done in order. Next page.*

Come on!

411

Over the page the list of names was longer. Sam reckoned seventy. She made a guess at a translation of the title: *Master's Degrees.*

The clapping continued, and the train of students kept coming.

Come on!

Using her finger, as she couldn't trust herself to see with her usual clarity, she ran down the list. Halfway down she found him.

Ramhart Haas MSc BA.

Ramhart Haas MSc BA!

The only one of the Famous Five who had kept a low profile. Bischoff and Mauning she knew. And she thought she knew where they were. One was dead, or injured. Jane had told her the other was in BfV's custody. Two, Luis Schmidt and Lutz Gunther, were thought to be in South America. Ramhart Haas. *Ramhart Haas.* How had Jane described him? Living in Berlin. A lawyer and an academic. *An academic!* He was picking up another accolade.

And murdering Germany's chancellor at the same time.

Where was he?

She didn't think that all of the doctorates had been issued. Those coming forward all wore black gowns with bright hoods. *How long do I have?*

She took out Mandy's phone, and, still keeping an eye on the students coming onto and off the stage, she dialled Jane's number.

Thankfully, as always, Jane picked up straight away.

"Sam?"

"It's Ramhart Haas."

"Who? What . . . ?"

"Haas is the third of the Five living in Germany. Bischoff and Mauning are out of it. Haas is an academic." Her words were quiet, but given at a gallop. She slowed herself. "Today. He's being awarded an MSc from the chancellor. His name's on the list. It's here in front of me. We've got about ten minutes before he's shaking her hand. I'm not sure how he's going to do it, and I'm not sure if I can affect things here, but I'll do what I can. Do something!"

"I'll phone Karl now." The line went dead.

Sam tried to work out what was happening on the stage. She thought the doctors were getting their degrees. The master's degree bunch would be next. She couldn't really see how they lined up. They just came out of their chairs and made their way to the front. But . . . there must be a system. This was Germany. *Everything has a system.* The first up were in the front seats. The master's students would be in the next set.

What should I do? I have no idea what Haas looks like, but I might be able to pick him out by the order in which they're called.

Without further thought, she left the balcony still holding the programme, the photographer remonstrating as she did. Sam mouthed "sorry" again—*that's becoming a habit*—as she darted downstairs.

Bugger. The main doors to the hall were locked.

There must be a side door. She remembered seeing one at the front on the right. If she couldn't find it, she'd go back to the balcony and make a scene. *I must stop Haas somehow.* Muted clapping continued from within the hall.

Sam ran through the corridors with no real idea of where she was going. She came across a couple of dead ends and, at one point, turned a corner and nearly knocked over a middle-aged lady carrying a pile of books.

"Sorry!" *There I go again.*

She ran on, turning left and left. And there it was—a short corridor, at the end of which was a double door. The clapping had gotten louder—there was some cheering as well. She stopped and caught her breath. The corridor had no windows and was poorly lit. Focusing on the double doors, Sam realised that one was ajar. A man stood at the entrance, guarding it. Light from the Main Hall plastered the shadow of the man against the wall of the corridor. He and his shadow looked official—a policeman?

As she walked forward, Sam spotted a peaked hat and, at waist height, a pistol. Usual *polizei* accoutrements. The policeman turned as she approached.

"Halt!" He put out one hand. Sam edged forward. She was a couple of metres from him.

"Was willst du?"

Good question. Here goes.

"Sprechen sie Englisch?" Other than *kann ich bitte ein Bier haben*, she was out of joined-up German.

"Nein." He still kept his hand out. He looked nervous. Unsure. One hand hovering above his pistol.

Let's try speaking with conviction, without many verbs.

"Man." Sam opened up the programme and pointed. "Here. Ramhart Haas." The policeman stretched forward, looking at the programme, the pages lit by the light from the hall. Even with an outstretched hand it was too far away from him to read. "Kill. *Kaput!* Chancellor!" She drew her hand across her throat in a cutting motion. "Ramhart Haas. Here!" And then she pointed to the hall. "There! Halt! Ramhart Haas. Halt! Chancellor *kaput!*" As she spoke, her words got louder.

The policeman was at a complete loss. He'd obviously been briefed on an attempt on the German leader. But something was stopping him from thinking Sam was the threat. *Otherwise I'd have been shot by now.* Her loud English striking a note somewhere. He kept his hand out to prevent Sam from moving and lifted his spare hand from his pistol and reached for his radio. Clapping echoed around them.

Before he could use it, the radio burst into life. It was shrill. Orders seemed to rattle across the airwaves. It was incomprehensible to Sam, but she definitely heard Haas's name.

The policeman dropped his hand that was stopping Sam from moving forward and stuck his head around the door and into the hall. Sam gently took the door from him and pulled it open further, also sneaking a look. She was right on the policeman's shoulder, their bodies touching. She was sure she felt his racing heartbeat pounding away through their clothes.

They were in the far right corner of the hall, as she suspected. The side of the stage was in front of them, as was a set of stairs leading to the platform. A woman was about to climb the steps, and a man waited behind her. Sam could see him clearly. He was middle-aged, medium build. Significantly, he was red-faced, and she could see sweat dripping from the back of his short blond hair. *Was it him? Was it Hass?* Then she spotted the weapon. Not an AK-47. Or an explosive belt.

In his right hand he carried a pen. That was all. A pen. *A ricin-and-botulism-loaded pen?* Definitely mightier than the sword? She knew it was madness, the stuff of movies, but these people had history. David had been there. Haas could prick the chancellor and inject her with deadly poison. She would reel, but would it be seen as an attack? He would apologise and move on. Could he get away with it?

The tannoy continued with its announcements.

"Einen Master in Finance. Herr Ramhart Haas!" Another round of applause.

In a split second her policeman dithered. Sam pushed him forward, the double doors burst open, and she followed on. Haas was on the top step and about to reach the platform when the policeman launched himself at his legs. They connected, a bundle of two grown men, both of them falling left off the stage and onto the floor in front of the main crowd.

There was immediate uproar in the hall, but Sam tuned it all out. She was just behind the policeman as he and Haas struggled on the floor. In the octopus of arms and legs, Sam saw the pen jab the policeman through his sleeve—he immediately started to lose the fight. To her right on the stage, the chancellor and the other dignitaries were on their feet; one or two were screaming and pointing. The noise from the whole hall was deafening. Sam was focused on

Haas, but out of the corner of her eye she couldn't help noticing mass movement—a swish of black gowns and feathery coloured hoods as the crowd collectively flinched backward, toward the main doors.

In less than a second, Haas had thrown off the floundering policeman, and with a quick glance at Sam—all flared nostrils and wild eyes—he was on his feet. He shot a look to his left. Sam followed his eye line. The chancellor was still standing and still exposed. Haas placed one hand on the stage and started to vault the four-foot-high step.

Instinctively, Sam dropped to the policeman's side and fumbled for his pistol. *I have to stop Haas.* She had the pistol in her hand and was turning to take a shot when the blast of war reverberated around the hall.

Crack! The sound of a shot—immediately recognisable in a hall that was already a cacophony of screams and shouting.

Haas went down, his face scrunched on the carpet that covered the stage—eyes open, but lifeless. As he fell and in the gap left behind, Sam saw a man in a suit holding a smoking pistol. He had pushed the chancellor to the floor and was standing over his leader. Worryingly, the man was re-aiming. She was clearly his next target.

Time slowed.

As Sam dropped to avoid the bullet, she heard the crack of a second shot. The distinct, single sound overcame all the noise in the hall. It was louder than any person could shout, louder than all the screaming put together—all the noise.

But it didn't hit her. She crouched tighter, her back to the weapon. She waited for another shot—a double tap, like any professional hit. But there wasn't one. The sound in the hall took over again, swamping her senses: screams, shouts, and palpable fear. She couldn't hear herself think, but she needed to do something. She turned and stood up in one motion, releasing the pistol as she did. *What is happening?* In among darting and running bodies on the stage, two people were motionless. One was the shooter—Sam guessed a BfV special agent. And the other was the chancellor, who was now standing. The man's pistol arm was forced upward, smoke gently rising to the ceiling from the short barrel, like a Cuban cigar. It was held there by the hands of the chancellor, pushing the pistol toward the ceiling and away from the shooter's intended target: her.

The chancellor nodded at Sam, the earlier connection resonating between them. She mouthed, "Sorry."

Sam smiled and, without noise, mouthed back, "Thank you."

Epilogue

Three Weeks Later

Albert Ward, St. Thomas's Hospital, London

David sipped from his cup, sitting semi-upright in his hospital bed in a private room on Albert Ward. He was, he admitted thankfully, feeling a good deal better. He could make it to the bathroom without assistance and was now eating and drinking, although his appetite was not huge. "Little and often," his wife had continuously encouraged.

"So, what about the air crashes and the madcap theory that your German friend coined: kill many, murder one?" he asked.

He had Jane and Sam visiting. They had been in most days since he had been allowed visitors. Today was the first day that he'd felt strong enough to be back-briefed on Op Greyshoe. It had been an extraordinary sequence of events.

"We're still not completely sure. The deputy director reckons that the Church of the White Cross was funded by massive ownership in stocks of the big six oil companies—large enough to influence board-level decisions. As a result, any emerging energy industry, such as solar and nuclear fusion, that might negatively influence those stock prices needed to be contained—maybe even slowed. His view, which they haven't yet been able to corroborate, was that the oil giants would remain supreme no matter the cost." Jane was sitting on one side of David's bed—Sam on the other. Since the Köln incident, Jane had continued to oversee both Operation Greyshoe and Operation Glasshouse, as well as her usual portfolio. David thought she looked to be holding up well.

"And *did* they kill critical personnel in the emerging industries, hiding their murders among the deaths of many?"

"The Americans aren't sure. As you know, nobody in any authority survived the breaking of the siege at Abilene. So there was no one whom they could question as to how the money had been managed and whether the stock prices had been kept artificially high. Or if someone had sanctioned the bringing down of commercial aircraft to hide the death of an individual." Jane shrugged her shoulders in a "beats me" fashion. She glanced across at Sam who was helping herself to one of the chocolates they'd brought in for David.

"What about Miles Johnson?"

"Still at large. So far they've not been able to pin anything on him. There is an emerging dossier against him, as I understand it. The DD, along with his FBI oppo, is keen to get a bulletproof case before they try to take him down."

David breathed out heavily. His brain was working, that was for sure. He had blank sections, much of it from his earlier life, but he reckoned his powers of reasoning were still pretty sharp. The doctors had briefed him that he might not get all his faculties back after what he had been through. Although he wasn't sure he would need them all when he was pottering around the garden, attending his roses.

"The Church of the White Cross is now defunct in the United States . . ."

Jane interrupted him. "And in Germany, Italy, and Spain. Pretty much dismantled."

"But its assets are still live, and there are people like Miles Johnson at liberty to use those assets?"

David looked across at Sam. She was staring out of the window absently, now apparently bored with the whole thing. Her face was contorted—she was using her tongue to remove some toffee that was stuck in her teeth. She did make him laugh.

"The FBI people have frozen what assets they can find, but they can't be sure they have everything. And, yes, there are probably a number of Johnsons out there still pulling some strings."

David paused for a second.

"Ralph Bell? Do we know what's happened to him?"

Jane led again. "No idea. He's now top of the USA's wanted list."

David looked to Sam.

"What about you, Sam? When are you heading back over to Germany to collect your Cross of Honour?"

Sam stopped staring out the window and fidgeted a bit. She was clearly uncomfortable with the question.

"Sometime next month, I think." She nodded nonchalantly as she answered.

"And will the German chancellor present it to you personally?" David pressed.

"I don't know. It's all a bit of a fuss about nothing."

"Oh really . . ." David said with a touch of sarcasm. "I'm not sure that's how the German leader sees it, nor the chief. I believe he was pretty pleased with the way things went." David sipped some more of his tea.

"How's the spiked policeman?"

"He's OK, as I understand it. Because we had your history, the medic at the scene was able to take control of the situation really quickly. I think the policeman had a blood transfusion within an hour, which limited the damage of the poisons." Sam's reply was more engaging when she spoke about something other than herself, David thought.

"And Mauning?"

Jane led. "Waiting trial for numerous offences. The chances are he will go down for between five and ten years. I get the impression from the BfV that that is as much as they will be able to manage."

"And the Manning/Mauning linkage?"

"We're a hundred per cent confident they have the same bloodline. It didn't take my team long to establish that they were originally from the same Prussian family. *Manning* is a bastardisation of *Mauning*, which his family took on during the Second World War in the United States—trying to hide their previous nationality." Jane stopped for a second, as if taking a breather. "GCHQ has established a continuous comms link between the two over the past decade. It is clear that they were in this together."

David nodded, closing his eyes as he did. *God, I'm tired.* One last question.

"And Sam, what about your German friend?"

Sam smiled, a half smile, and gave out a little sigh.

"He's recovering, physically, that is. We've spoken on the phone a couple of times. He's still really struggling with the death of his mother."

"That's understandable."

David thought before asking a supplementary. "And you and him?"

Sam stopped smiling and looked over Jane's head, out of the window, across the river toward Big Ben. David couldn't tell how the question had gone down.

"We're not the same people who kicked this off together in the Alps. I think it's fair to say that we've both moved on." Sam was still wistfully staring out of the window. Quietly, as an afterthought, she added, "Which is a shame, because he lived in a very nice castle."

David and Jane laughed.

She's something else, this Sam Green. The woman who had, yet again, put her life on the line for a cause she didn't wholly comprehend. Regardless, she had battled on, persevered, and won.

She would make a fine agent. *Now there's a thought.*

Jane and Sam spent a further half an hour with David. By the end, he was obviously very tired. They said their good-byes and left the hospital to go back to the office.

"It's so good to see him recovering," Jane said absently.

"Mmm. Yes." Sam wasn't really tuned in to much. Since Köln, there wasn't a great deal that kept her attention. But, when she thought about it, it *was* good to see David making a speedy recovery.

She felt sharp enough behind her desk, staring at the latest images of migrants still flocking westward, toward what they considered to be their salvation. In the afternoons she was still picking out would-be terrorists heading west out of the Middle East. And in the mornings Russian soldiers on the wrong side of the Ukrainian border. But, other than that, she felt her life was flat. Dull. The dank, grey British winter wasn't helping.

They both weaved in and out of the late afternoon commuter traffic. Sometimes they were side by side; other times they were apart. At one point, walking down the Albert Embankment, they broke away from each other to pass a small group of young tourists who were standing in a huddle, staring at something in one of their hands. Sam glanced across at the group and realised it was an iPad they were looking at.

She didn't know why, but she was drawn to the crowd. The group's demeanour was a bond of shock and solidarity. Their expressions were laced with amazement, horror even—they certainly weren't poring over the latest comic YouTube clip. One of the girls in the group had tears rolling down her cheeks.

Sam stopped on the edge of the group, looking for a gap. Jane walked on for a few metres before she realised that Sam was standing with the small crowd. She checked herself and came back to see what was going on.

The people in the crowd were talking in hushed tones. Among the murmuring Sam heard, *"Mon Dieu!"*

"What's up, Sam?"

Sam didn't say anything. She was on tiptoes, looking over the shoulders of one of the shorter men. A girl in the middle of the group held the iPad flat so they could all see what was on the screen. Sam saw immediately that it was a live news feed from CNN.

"*Shit!* I don't believe it."

"What, Sam?" Jane's tone was immediate. She knew something wasn't right.

Sam came off her toes, turned from the group, and walked a few steps to the grey block parapet overlooking the

Thames. She put both hands on the wall as if recovering from a sprint. Her mind was a maelstrom of thoughts and questions—with no answers. She stared back toward the Houses of Parliament as if looking for some sense to it all.

"What is it, Sam? What's happened?"

Nothing.

"Sam!"

"There's been another one."

"Another what?"

Sam turned toward Jane. She couldn't stop the dampness building up around her eyes.

"Another plane. An Air France jet has come down in Spain on its way from Casablanca to Paris. Everyone on board is dead."

Also by Roland Ladley—the very first Sam Green novel

Unsuspecting Hero

Sam Green's life is in danger of imploding. Suffering from posttraumatic stress disorder after horrific injuries and personal tragedy in Afghanistan, she escapes to The Isle of Mull, hoping to convalesce. A chance find on the island's shores interrupts her rehabilitation and launches her on a journey to West Africa and on a collision course with forces and adversaries she cannot begin to comprehend.

Meanwhile, in London, MI6 is facing down a biological threat that could kill thousands and inflame an already smouldering religious war. Time is not on anyone's side, and Sam's determination to face her past and control her future, regardless of the risks, looks likely to end in disaster. Fate conspires to bring Sam into the centre of an international conspiracy where she alone has the power to influence world-changing events. Blind to her newfound role, is her military training and complete disregard for her own safety enough to prevent the imminent devastation?

18838778R00255

Printed in Great Britain
by Amazon